P9-CCZ-813

PRAISE FOR THE WARRIORS OF ATLANTIS

"The perfect blend of fabulous world-building and sexy romantic adventure."

—Jayne Castle, *New York Times* bestselling author

"A phenomenal new series." —*Fresh Fiction*

"Alyssa Day works her own brand of sexy sorcery in this fabulous new paranormal series. Warriors and witches have never been so hot!"

—Teresa Medeiros, *New York Times* bestselling author

VAMPIRE IN ATLANTIS

"The relationships between Day's cast of characters are layered and enduring and they make this series unforgettable. Day aces another one!" —*RT Book Reviews*

ATLANTIS BETRAYED

"Day serves up her best book to date with this exhilarating, funny adventure." —*RT Book Reviews*

"Action [and] hot sex . . . So hold on to your fan, you may need it." —*Bitten By Paranormal Romance*

ATLANTIS REDEEMED

"Day blends action, suspense, and fiery hot sensuality."

—*The Romance Dish*

"Day places her latest romantic pair in unique circumstances as they face both technological horror and an ancient curse . . . Day continues to deliver consistent quality and sizzling adventure!" —*RT Book Reviews*

continued . . .

ATLANTIS UNMASKED

"Action packed and hot and spicy." —*TwoLips Reviews*

"Day utilizes a nice blend of action, character building, and sexy sensuality in all her books. A terrific escape from reality."
—*RT Book Reviews*

"As always, I loved this book. Each time I settle down to read about one of the warriors, I know I'm going to want more."
—*Naughty Edition Reviews*

ATLANTIS UNLEASHED

"This character-driven tale will grab the reader's imagination from page one . . . An epic thrill ride that should not be missed." —*Romance Reviews Today*

"A terrific romantic fantasy thriller."
—*Midwest Book Review*

"Day is back and better than ever . . . She doesn't skimp on the action, but this story also delves into the psychological, giving the characters real depth. Power and passion unleashed make for outstanding reading!" —*RT Book Reviews*

"Action-packed adventure filled with magic and romance . . . Superb job of world-building that will leave you stunned with the richness of detail. The characters of Atlantis are sexy, intelligent, and fascinating. I absolutely loved it and cannot wait for more!" —*Romance Junkies*

ATLANTIS AWAKENING

"Fascinating, thrilling, and deeply romantic."
—Jayne Castle, *New York Times* bestselling author

"Alyssa Day's Atlantis is flat-out amazing—her sexy and heroic characters make me want to beg for more! I love the complex world she's created!"
—Alexis Morgan, national bestselling author

ATLANTIS RISING

"Atlantis Rising is romantic, sexy, and utterly compelling. I loved it!"
> —Christine Feehan, #1 *New York Times* bestselling author

"The Poseidon Warriors are HOT!! Can I have one?"
> —Kerrelyn Sparks, *New York Times* bestselling author

"Alyssa Day's characters grab you and take you on a whirlwind adventure. I haven't been so captivated by characters or story in a long time. Enjoy the ride!"
> —Susan Squires, *New York Times* bestselling author

"Alyssa Day has penned a white-hot winner!"
> —Gena Showalter, *New York Times* bestselling author

"Inventive and electrifying."   —*RT Book Reviews*

"Alyssa Day roars onto the paranormal scene with this tense and magnetic read."   —*Romance Junkies*

Titles by Alyssa Day

The Warriors of Poseidon

Specials

The League of the Black Swan

The Cursed

THE LEAGUE OF THE BLACK SWAN

ALYSSA DAY

BERKLEY SENSATION, NEW YORK

THE BERKLEY PUBLISHING GROUP
Published by the Penguin Group
Penguin Group (USA) Inc.
375 Hudson Street, New York, New York 10014, USA

USA | Canada | UK | Ireland | Australia | New Zealand | India | South Africa | China

Penguin Books Ltd., Registered Offices: 80 Strand, London WC2R 0RL, England
For more information about the Penguin Group, visit penguin.com

THE CURSED

A Berkley Sensation Book / published by arrangement with the author

Berkley Sensation Books are published by The Berkley Publishing Group.
BERKLEY SENSATION® is a registered trademark of Penguin Group (USA) Inc.
The "B" design is a trademark of Penguin Group (USA) Inc.

For information, address: The Berkley Publishing Group,
a division of Penguin Group (USA) Inc.,
375 Hudson Street, New York, New York 10014.

ISBN: 978-0-425-25577-3

PUBLISHING HISTORY
Berkley Sensation mass-market paperback edition / May 2013

PRINTED IN THE UNITED STATES OF AMERICA

10 9 8 7 6 5 4 3 2 1

Cover art by Craig White.
Cover design by George Long.
Interior text design by Kristin del Rosario.

This book is for Jim McCarthy,
my funny, brilliant, patient agent, who signed me when
I was in Sedona, encouraged me when I was in Japan,
laughed with me when I came back to Florida,
and gave me good news when he was in Germany.
Ours is a marvelous and international relationship.

And for the always delightful Cindy Hwang,
my editor, who said yes when I wanted
to take Luke and Rio on continuing adventures.

And, especially, for Mom, who always said,
"My daughter can do anything!"

And so I did.

ACKNOWLEDGMENTS

Thanks to everyone at Berkley who gets my books out to the world—and especially to George Long and Craig White for the amazing cover, which is exactly what I wanted!

Thanks to the always wonderful Sarah Wendell, who gave me the idea to use the High Line park for the border of Bordertown. The park, created from an abandoned railroad line, is a terrific example of how a community can come together to create beauty from ruin.

Thanks to the fabulous Morgan Doremus for her photographs and suggestions about places in the park for Luke, Rio, and my other characters to play.

Thanks to my Werearmadillos—Eileen Rendahl, Cindy Holby, Marianne Mancusi, Barb Ferrer, Serena Robar, and Michelle Cunnah—for nearly a decade of laughing with me about the insanity of the publishing business and sharing encouragement, support, and a kick in the pants when I need it.

Thanks to my new writers' group, the Fire-breathing Flamingos—Ava Milone, Lena Diaz, Madeline Martin, Sheila Athens, and Valerie Bowman—for monthly dinners, wine-fueled laughter, insightful feedback, and face-to-face writer time.

Thanks, always, to my children—Connor, for cho-
reographing fight scenes with his friends and for
researching supernatural creatures, and Lauren, for
character name inspiration and playlist song suggestions.
And to both of you for eating too much pizza when it's
deadline.

And, always, to Judd. You know why. (And the fact that
you're totally hot in your Navy dress blues doesn't hurt.)

CHAPTER 1

Getting stabbed is hell on the dry-cleaning bill.

Luke Oliver looked down at the silver blade stuck between his ribs and then up at the only person still alive who'd known him back when his name was Lucian Olivieri. "I'd kill anyone else for that, Maestro."

He pulled out the knife, wincing as it scraped a rib, wiped it on his jeans, and then put it in his pocket. "You didn't want it back, did you?"

The other man, his face hidden by the shadows cast by his fedora, laughed. His laugh sounded like rock being crushed beneath a giant's boots and was just as appealing. Luke suspected the maestro knew it, too, and used it as one of a lifetime's worth of weapons.

"Consider it a gift. And I was just checking," the maestro said. "When silver starts burning you like acid—"

"I know the terms of my own curse," Luke said, cutting off the reminder. Beating back the past. "What do you want? I have a job to get back to."

"Still doing those jobs? Trying to save the world from your hideaway in the dank, dingy corners of Bordertown?"

It was Luke's turn to laugh. "No hideaway. A crappy office. And I'm only trying to save one person. The world can go to hell for all I care, but right now I'm too busy to reminisce about old times."

"We didn't have any old times. We were on opposite sides. Your mother was a thug."

"Even enemies have old times. And my mother was an *aristocratic* thug. Never let it be said that Lucrezia Borgia didn't do her murdering with class," Luke countered, as he silently watched a trio of gangbangers, smelling of cheap booze and acrid smoke, saunter underneath the arch while trading raucous and profane insults. Secure in their mistaken belief that they were apex predators in the darkest hours of the night. He wondered briefly what they'd do if he dropped down among them and showed them the face and power of a true predator.

Wet their pants and run screaming for Mommy, no doubt.

"Do you still do it? Hunt the criminals?" The maestro's voice held only a calm curiosity, as if he were asking about the weather. "Do you feel the pull to stalk them as prey and crush them? Burn them to cinders?"

Yes.

Always.

No.

Never.

Never *again*, at least.

Luke settled on a nonanswer. "You have one minute to say something relevant."

The other man pulled an envelope out of his coat pocket and held it out to Luke, and then he said the two words Luke had never wanted to hear again.

"Black Swan."

Shock knocked Luke back like a crossbow aimed at his heart and he fell off the arch, but recovered in time to land with his characteristic grace on the path thirteen feet below.

The maestro laughed once more and tossed the envelope down through the night air before he disappeared. Luke caught the envelope as it fell, almost in spite of himself. The glossy black-and-red logo was embossed on one corner, as he'd expected—the sinuous arch of the black swan's neck stark against the Templar cross and mocking him with its elegance.

He needed to get back to Bordertown; back to his office. His client's missing niece was far more important than anything that could be inside this envelope. He'd burn it. Destroy any evidence that the League had ever reached out its slimy tentacles and move on with what was passing for his life these days. He told himself all of that, even as he tore open the envelope right there on the path and pulled out its entire contents: a single photograph.

The moonlight seemed to caress the woman in the photo, highlighting her perfect bone structure, the curve of her cheek, and her wary expression with vivid clarity. The world tilted on its axis, and the edges of Luke's fingers shimmered with blue flame, nearly incinerating the photo before he extinguished the fire. He stared at the picture— still perfect but for the charred edges—and another kind of fire flashed to an inferno inside him. He knew this woman. Her name was Rio Jones and she worked for the bike messenger service. He'd limited his contact with her when she'd dropped packages at his office. Admired her from afar, but made it a point never to speak more than a few words to her.

She was too beautiful. Too vibrant. Too dangerous to his limited amount of self-control. The last thing he needed was a complication like her in his life. But now the League of the Black Swan was back, and it wanted him to get involved with Rio Jones.

An immortal just couldn't catch a break.

CHAPTER 2

BORDERTOWN

Rio Jones knew she had maybe an hour, tops, before
somebody found her. She had that kind of luck: the kind
that trips over cracks in sidewalks, falls off her bike in the
middle of rush-hour traffic in the middle of Bordertown,
and sees a major supernatural heavyweight kidnapping a
kid in broad daylight.

A major *magical* heavyweight. She'd heard a flash of
something so wrong—so *other*—in his thoughts that she'd
nearly wrecked her bike when she'd turned to look at who
or what was making that horrible noise. The taxi hadn't
even clipped her that hard; she'd had far worse working as
a bike messenger for Siren Deliveries.

Not that most of the fancy companies she delivered to
would believe they'd hired a company owned by an actual
siren. They just knew they got their packages on time.
Ophelia liked to hire humans as messengers. She said they
were slower but harder to distract. More reliable. Gave her
the chance to focus on her budding opera career, instead
of dealing with Fae and demon hatreds, feuds, and failures
to deliver on time. Punctuality was king in the cutthroat

bike messenger wars, and Rio was human enough to pass muster.

Rio nearly growled at the thought of Ophelia and her damned rules. If Rio hadn't been so focused on making it to her next delivery on time, she wouldn't have taken that shortcut through the alley, and so she never would have rounded the corner in time to see the tall, dark-haired man step out of a limousine and snatch a small girl right off the street.

The girl had screamed, Rio had slammed on the brakes of her bike and gone over the handlebars, and the kidnapper had met her gaze with eyes that blazed a surge of dark power across the distance between them. Black eyes, almost all pupil, had tried to bore into Rio's mind until the struggling child had screamed again and the man had thrown the girl into the limo and slammed the door. He'd given Rio one last dismissive glance as she knelt, bleeding, on the filthy pavement, and then he'd angled his tall body into the front seat next to the driver. By the time he'd changed his mind and the brake lights had flashed on the limo, she'd seen them over her shoulder as she glanced back while racing away. She'd used her throwaway cell phone to call in an anonymous report to the sheriff's office, complete with license plate number, for all the good it would do.

Bordertown hadn't had any law of its own since the last demon uprising, when the rebels ate the sheriff. That very lawlessness was the draw for most of the people—human and, mostly, other—who lived, worked, and played in the five square miles of dimensional fold that lay hidden behind, beneath, and between the streets of Manhattan. Bordertown was the Wild West, but the cowboys and outlaws of the typical frontier town were demon and Fae here.

Dangerous and deadly, with or without six-shooters.

But she'd made the futile call, and a few minutes later, still shaking, she'd tossed her cell phone in the back of the first trash truck she saw, with some vague idea that the kidnapper might trace it back to her if she kept it.

It was all too little, too late, though. She knew it. She'd heard his thoughts—they'd shattered the everyday barrier she wore around her mind like an icy wind slicing through a flimsy scarf. Her mental shield was plenty to keep out human thoughts; if she heard everything that people thought around her all day long, she would have gone insane years ago.

But this man—the kidnapper—he wasn't human. Okay, she was used to that, working for a company in Bordertown and living there, too, but he wasn't a low-level demon or a Fae or an ogre or anything else she'd ever heard before. Fae and demon royalty never leaked their thoughts, so they were out, too. His thoughts had been *wrong*. Dark and raging and, yeah, demons were often the same to a degree, but this guy was something . . . *more*. Icy. Determined. Powerful.

She wasn't even sure how she'd known, but she'd somehow *felt* it. His thoughts had crawled with power and focus, and once he'd changed his mind about her being beneath his notice—*no loose ends; the king will destroy me* had been the exact words running through his jagged mind— he'd aimed that focus at her.

That had been eight hours ago, and she had no doubt that he'd been trying to find her every minute since. She'd heard the rumblings of a new force in town from Europe who played with the Old Magic; a man bent on taking over organized supernatural crime. It was too much to hope that this hadn't been him.

"And one little freak of a telepath isn't going to have a chance against that," she muttered to her tiny stuffed fox before tossing it in her backpack. She was already wearing her locket, as always, so there were the only two mementos of her childhood, safely retrieved. Other than that, she didn't know what to bother taking. A couple of changes of clothes, all available cash, and her laptop. Packing wasn't exactly difficult when you lived in a closet disguised as a studio apartment and owned next to nothing.

She was wasting time. She knew where she had to go.

The one person from whom she'd tried to stay away, because he scared the crap out of her. She knew he'd help—he was a private investigator. She had money to hire him. Problem solved.

Luke Oliver had power; she knew it and everybody, even the riffraff, in Bordertown knew it, too. He could help her figure out a way to find and help that child, and she was smart enough not to get caught up in the weird attraction she'd felt to the man whenever she'd made a delivery to him.

A knock on the door broke through her stupid mental rambling and scared her so badly she stumbled and nearly tripped over her milk-crate coffee table.

"Rio? Rio, it's me. Are you okay?"

Rio's heart slowly dropped out of warp speed, and she took a deep breath and opened the door. Mrs. Giamatto, her landlady, stood just outside the door in a pale pink robe that had to be older than Rio. The elderly woman gasped when she saw Rio, and the tips of her ever-so-slightly pointed ears turned a vivid pink where they peeked out of her fluffy white hair.

"Oh, honey, I'm so sorry to bother you at this time of night, but I had a very odd phone call just now, and I wanted to warn you—"

"I know. I'm leaving." Rio shouldered her backpack, picked up her bike, stepped into the hallway, pulled the door shut behind her, locked the door, and handed Mrs. Giamatto the keys. "Thank you so much. I might be in a little bit of trouble, so I'm going to go away for a while. I don't want to bring any problems here. Linda down the hall just had her baby, and of course I don't want—"

"No!" Mrs. Giamatto folded her arms across her frail chest and raised her chin. "I won't have it. I know you, Rio Green, and you're no troublemaker. Even if you did do something you shouldn't have—and the gods know that's easy enough to do in Bordertown—well, we stick together. Nobody is going to mess with my tenants."

For an instant—only a fraction of a moment—Rio saw

someone else underneath Mrs. G's little-old-lady surface. Someone ancient; far older even than the renovated Victorian home in which they stood, and maybe older than New York itself. Her landlady was more powerful than she appeared, it seemed, like so many in Bordertown. But the memory of the kidnapper flashed into Rio's mind, and she shuddered before shaking her head, too afraid to feel even her usual twinge of guilt for having given Mrs. G another of her many fake last names. She was Rio Green with Mrs. Giamatto, Rio Jones at work with Ophelia and clients, Rio Smith with strangers, and Rio To Be Determined when she got the hell out of town after this debacle.

Sometimes it was hard to keep all of her names straight, but a lifetime lived in the school of brutal knocks—and worse than knocks—had taught her caution. True names held power, and she knew better than to offer hers up— even if she'd known what it was. The names she used regularly were already beginning to take on a de facto sense of truth, at least enough for rudimentary spells to be cast. It was maybe time to become Jane Doe.

"I love you for it, too, but he's not an ordinary bad guy. This is more trouble than we can handle. I have to get help. There was a horrible man. Somebody with Old Magic. He . . . took a child. I think he plans to kill her. Or worse."

Mrs. G slowly nodded. "You're going to Luke?"

"I don't think I have a choice." Rio took a deep breath and hugged her landlady and dear friend, and then she held out her laptop. "Will you keep this for me? Just for now? I'll try to keep in touch. I'll try to come back."

They both knew neither might be possible. When trouble came to somebody in Bordertown, it was often of the permanent kind.

Mrs. Giamatto took the computer and nodded, a hint of tears shining in her eyes. She put her other hand in her pocket and held out an envelope.

"Take this. It should help."

Rio glanced in the envelope, which was stuffed with hundred-dollar bills.

"I can't take this. I'm fine. I have money; I just need to get to the bank in the morning—"

"You'll take it," Mrs. G said firmly, closing Rio's fingers over the envelope. "I never paid you for planting those flowers."

Rio heard the edge of panic in her own laughter and knew it was time to go. "The going rate for landscapers is not a thousand dollars an hour, but I'll take it as a *loan* for now. I have to go. If they called you, they know where I live."

"Go. The back stairs." Mrs. G hugged her again, the laptop caught between them, and then gave her a little push toward the dimly lit stairwell. Rio grabbed her bike and ran lightly down the stairs and opened the always-locked door a couple of inches. What she could see of the garden from her vantage point was empty of anybody or anything other than the marble statue of a very plump Pan eternally playing his lute in the fountain. She slipped out and made sure the door clicked shut behind her, not that a door would hold out anybody who really wanted to get in, and headed for the garden gate, only to skid to a stop when the gate crashed open and three enormous, oddly misshapen men pushed their way into the yard.

"Is that her?" one of them said, in a broken, growly voice, like only part of him was human and the other part was something ugly. Nothing unusual for Bordertown, but this guy was big. World Wrestling Federation big. Half a *mountain* big.

Rio dropped the bike and backed up, step by slow, cautious step, wishing for the millionth time that if she had to have a superpower it was something useful. Like flying. Or invisibility. What was the use, really, of reading other people's thoughts at a time like this? She wouldn't even be in this mess without her sorry excuse for a magical ability.

"I don't know, she has a long braid, the boss said she had a long braid," another one said in an unexpectedly high, squeaky voice that nearly surprised a laugh out of Rio. Things that ugly and that big shouldn't sound like Mickey Mouse.

"Look, if you're Rio Green, the boss just wants to talk to you," the first one said, his hands out at his sides in what was clearly meant to be a nonthreatening position.

Ha.

"I don't know anybody named Rio Green," she said evenly, eyeing the distance between herself and the fence. "You have the wrong person."

"See, that sounds like a lie," Mountain Man rumbled, taking a step forward.

The other two moved to flank her, and she pushed her fear aside and dropped her mental barrier, listening frantically for whatever they were thinking that might help her figure out how to escape.

Mountain Man's thoughts were so unsurprising that she wouldn't have had to be a telepath to figure them out. *Too bad the boss said not to kill her. Wonder if he'd mind if I play with her a little first?*

Squeaky's mind wasn't quite on business. *Shouldn't have had that spaghetti Bolognese. I need some antacids in the worst way.*

And the third guy's thoughts were so oily and incoherent that Rio nearly gagged just from brushing up against them. *Rip, shred, tear, bloody, bloody, Tuesday, lovely cake, lovely cake, rip, shred, tear—*

She slammed her mental barrier back in place and, in desperation, tried something that only an idiot would fall for. She whipped her head to the side, stared at the gate behind them, and screamed. "Rio! Run! These guys are here for you!"

Unbelievably, all three of them turned to look, so she ran the other way toward the fence like she'd never run before. She put her hands on the flat surface of the wrought iron between two spikes and vaulted over like some kind of track star, marveling even as she flew through the air at what adrenaline could do for somebody in fear for her life. Her ankle twisted a little as she landed; not enough for a sprain, but enough that she knew she'd need to ice it soon or pay the price the next day.

If she lived to see the next day. She hit the ground running and raced through the streets faster than she'd ever moved before.

Seventeen blocks. Hit Tenth, turn left at the charms and potions shop just past the High Line park entrance at Fourteenth, and she'd be there. If only *he'd* be there. Luke practically lived at his office, she'd heard, and it wasn't all that late for Bordertown, where business and social life came alive at night. Rio's breath came in short, harsh pants as she tried desperately to pretend she didn't hear the footsteps pounding after her.

The thugs weren't all that far behind, and despair tasted like rusted metal in her mouth when she realized she probably couldn't outrun them. A quick glance back showed them, if not gaining, at least keeping pace. They were fast for such big guys; again with her sucky luck. Terror-fueled adrenaline gave her enough of a boost that her heart sped up, her feet sped up, and she headed straight for the nearest place she could think of where she might find help. The Roadhouse was only a block away. Three A.M. was still happy hour at the Roadhouse, but hopefully the nightly stabbings and bar fights would be over.

It wasn't like she had a choice. She wasn't going to make it four more blocks without getting caught. She put on a burst of speed that made her ankle burn like fire and nearly flew under the garish neon sign and through the door of the Roadhouse, slamming into a brick wall that stopped all forward motion. Arms like curved boulders wrapped around her to steady her, and she looked up to discover that the brick wall wasn't a wall at all.

It was Miro, the ogre head bouncer.

"It's a little late for a delivery, isn't it?" His bushy black brows drew together in a tangled frown as he released her. He was a solid wall of muscle, eight feet tall and a good five feet wide at the shoulders. The coarsely woven shirt he wore with his jeans made him look like a farmer on the way to his barn in a land of giants. His ruddy skin only had the faintest tinge of green—those kids' movies had gotten ogres all wrong.

"No delivery, Miro; I just picked up some unwanted traffic on my trail," she said, in between sucking in deep breaths. She hadn't run much since she'd started taking the bike everywhere. Out of practice, out of shape. She glanced at the door.

Out of time.

"Miro, can I duck out the back door, and you stall these guys? They're big, and I don't want to cause trouble, but—"

Miro laughed his big, booming laugh, and the floor underneath Rio's feet actually shook, but only a few of the sparsely scattered bar patrons bothered to look up.

"I will snack on their bones like pretzels if they try to cause trouble. You run along, little girl, and bring me some jelly beans the next time you deliver."

She rose up on her tiptoes, and he leaned down so she could kiss his cheek. "I promise. No black ones."

Miro's cheeks flushed a deep red. "You're a good girl. Now go. I hear somebody coming. Time to do my Fee Fie Fo Fum routine. You go."

She went.

By the time she heard Miro's rumbling growl thunder through the room in warning or threat, she was already halfway out the back door. Her ankle was throbbing, and the initial burst of adrenaline was wearing off. She didn't know how she was going to make it all the way to Luke's office.

"That was a hell of a lot easier than I expected. I'm good, but even I'm not that good," a deep, sexy voice said from behind and to the left of the door.

A voice she recognized instantly.

"Hello, Luke. I was actually just coming to visit you," she said evenly, trying not to look like somebody who needed rescuing—even if she did.

"There's a funny coincidence," he said slowly, sweeping his gaze from her head to her toes and back up again, assessing, measuring, and probably finding her wanting. After all, he'd never had more than five or six words to spare when she stopped by with a package.

Damn him, though, he was as gorgeous as ever. Silky black hair just a little too long, unshaven jawline as if he were a pirate come to plunder, and chiseled face like a woman's secret fantasy. He was nearly six and a half feet of hard muscle and lean, dangerous lines, and rumor had it that his steel trap of a brain was always calculating his next moves at least ten steps ahead. It was why he was so good at his investigation job—some called him the Dark Wizard of Bordertown, even though he'd always denied having any real magic.

Some called him the man who should be sheriff, and it was rarely a compliment.

She'd never called him anything but Mr. Oliver. And yet here they were.

A cacophony of shouting and crashes sounded from the bar, and she hurriedly shut the door behind her. Luke glanced from the closed door to her, raising one silken eyebrow.

"That anything to do with you?"

She lifted her chin. "Why do you ask?"

A corner of that seductive mouth quirked up, and he shook his head. "Stubborn, I see."

She clenched her teeth against the wave of hostility that crashed through her. It wouldn't help her case to punch the private eye.

"Can we go to your office? I need . . . to hire you," she said, unable to say the *other* H-word. Unable to ask for *help*. She had money. She'd get more out of her savings account in the morning and mail Mrs. G back her cash. All she needed was to find that little girl, rescue her, and then maybe get out of town without being killed.

No problem.

Her shoulders slumped. She didn't even know how to begin to explain all this to Luke. Luckily, he didn't ask.

"Let's go," he said.

Just like that. Like women always came crashing into him asking for help in the middle of the night. She almost laughed at herself. They probably did.

He stood waiting, silent and watchful, although he tilted his head when the sounds of what might be a full-scale battle inside the bar grew louder. Luckily, she'd never heard that he could read minds, and she'd never been able to penetrate his, either, on those few occasions she'd tried. He was a strange anomaly, but she'd never been bothered by it. Until now, when she *wanted* to know what he was thinking.

What he was thinking about *her*.

"Let's go," she echoed, nodding firmly and taking a step toward him. She landed on her injured ankle and cried out, then tumbled face-forward toward the sidewalk. Strong arms scooped her up, and she found herself cradled against Luke's hard chest, her nose pressed against his shirt, breathing in his scent of forest and spice.

"This is not how I expected this to go," he said softly, almost as if he didn't want her to hear him. "I think I'm in trouble."

The door behind them smashed open, and Mountain Man stormed out, carrying an axe.

"I think we're both in trouble," Rio said.

CHAPTER 3

Luke leapt onto the roof of the Roadhouse with Rio in his arms before the creature could raise its axe. He lowered her so she was sitting on the tiles, careful of her injured ankle, and barely refrained from kissing the top of her head or those tempting lips. The fresh, clean scent of her hair teased his senses, and his mind was reeling at how fast she'd destroyed his carefully laid plans to stay strong and resist temptation, like he'd told himself to do all the way across town.

Do the job and keep your hands to yourself, Oliver, he'd repeated over and over like a mantra, expecting it would take so long to find her that he'd have drummed it into his thick skull. Every encounter he'd had with Rio over the past year or so had found its own place in his memory and dug in, resisting all attempts to uproot. She was smart, funny, and sexy as hell, and he'd known better than to have anything to do with her. So he'd kept his distance in the past, and he'd been determined to do the same while he figured out what the League wanted with her.

Well, she'd fallen into his arms in the first place he'd

looked, so he'd screwed up his resolve in ninety seconds flat, and now—he glanced down at the big pile of ugly currently roaring threats at him—yep, this was going to be fun. He shook his head and stared down at Rio, deliberately *not* noticing how damn beautiful she was. How tired she looked. Too thin. Too pale.

Nope. Not noticing any of that.

"How the hell did you manage to run afoul of a Grendel?"

She blinked. "A Grendel? *A* Grendel? Wasn't there just the one, and it's long dead?"

He rolled his eyes. "Sure. And fairies are all little and sparkly like Tinkerbell. So how did you—"

"I'm not an idiot, Luke. And this? It's a long story." She grabbed the end of her dark braid and flipped it over her shoulder in a purely feminine *oh, we're gonna have this out, now* gesture, and he was perversely pleased to see it. She was tough.

If the League wanted her, she'd need to be.

The Grendel roared out another threat, something about eating Luke's testicles, maybe. Luke wasn't sure. Grendels weren't the brightest, even in their human forms. Just then moonlight glinted off a very large something in the creature's ham-sized fist, and Luke dove for Rio, pushing her flat against the roof just as the gun went off.

"He has a gun," she said. "An axe *and* a gun."

"I noticed that," he murmured, distracted by the feel of her body underneath him. He was going to hell a thousand times over for this, but he hadn't been this close to a woman in longer than he cared to admit, and he took a moment to simply enjoy the feel of her body against his.

"Luke, he has a *gun*," she repeated, her eyes enormous in her pale face. "We need to *do* something before he figures out a way to get up here."

"Grendels don't like heights," he said, breathing in her scent, touching his forehead to hers before rubbing his cheek against her silky skin. "I swore to stay away from you, you know? Swore to myself. And here we are."

She put her hands flat on his chest and pushed with all of her strength, so naturally he leaned in even closer.

"Here we *are* on a *rooftop* with something that wants to kill or capture me *right down there*," she said, biting off every word. "Also, what are you talking about? You've never had any problem staying away from me, as I seem to recall."

The Grendel picked that minute to get off another shot, and Luke briefly wondered what had happened to Miro, dismissed it as temporarily unimportant, and jumped to his feet.

"You. Stay there," he ordered Rio, who glared at him but didn't try to sit up.

"You. Shut up, I'm coming," he shouted down to the Grendel, trying to be heard over the creature's increasingly inhuman roars. The damn thing seemed to be trying to shift to its monster shape. Nobody needed that. Border-town had seen enough of nightmare creatures lately, with the chimera infestation last month.

Luke eyed the distance between them and leapt through the air, somersaulted over the approximate axe-reach of the Grendel, and landed lightly behind it. Superior fighting skills were one of the bonus powers that he'd gained over the centuries. No black magic involved in increased strength and agility. No danger he'd invoke the curse.

The Grendel roared again and wheeled around to face Luke, the axe in one meaty paw and the gun swallowed up in the other.

"I have no fight with you, wizard," it growled. "Give me the woman, and I leave you in one piece."

"You don't want her," Luke said, as his hands drew fire from the air until they burned with hot, blue flame. "She's puny. Why don't you go find yourself a nice Grendel female and settle down? Raise a few ugly babies?"

The creature made a convulsive twitching motion all over its body. Luke knew the change wasn't far off, and a full-on Grendel in its monster form was damn near inde-structible.

"This is your last chance, fool," he said, raising his hands so the flames were clearly visible. "Back off or die."

"The boss said bring Rio Green. I will bring Rio Green." The Grendel's words sounded like they were being forced out as it swallowed its tongue, but Luke still understood. Barely.

"Aha! Wrong Rio. This isn't Rio Green," Luke said, glancing up to make sure *his* Rio, Rio *Jones*, was still out of harm's way, and then gritting his teeth because, of course, she was neither his nor safe. She was leaning so far over the edge of the roof it was a wonder gravity hadn't pulled her down to land on his head.

"Rio, I told you to stay down and back," he shouted. "This is merely a case of mistaken identity."

She shook her head and shrugged.

Shit. He'd heard rumors about her penchant for aliases.

"Kill you now," the Grendel growled. Its head was nearly completely transformed into something that would make Godzilla scream and run, and it slashed out at him with hands that were now tipped by six-inch-long, deadly sharp claws.

"I don't think so," Luke said, pulling one hand back to blast the thing.

"Find out who it works for," Rio called down.

"I don't think it's feeling all that helpful right now," he pointed out, as the creature's body shuddered all over and expanded until the Grendel resembled a pile of boulders with fangs. "I'll be killing it now."

"We need to know, Luke. His boss kidnapped a little girl. A little *human* girl."

He froze and looked up at her, and the Grendel took the opportunity to slash at him again, this time swiping his ribs even as he leapt back and away from the full brunt of its powerful arm.

"Damn, that hurts, you big pile of nasty—"

The Grendel lumbered forward and slashed at him again, but Luke managed to avoid this one.

"Rio, I don't think it's in the mood for talking anymore."

"Fine. Just . . . be careful," she called down, sounding furious. With him, with the Grendel, with the situation, who knew?

He gritted his teeth but then had to laugh. Rio'd been in his custody for only five minutes, and she was already driving him nuts. He didn't even try to fight the grin spreading over his face. Instead, he raised both hands and shook his head at the Grendel as it lowered its head and charged.

"Too bad for you, buddy. I tried to give you a chance. *Ignatio.*" The fire coalesced in his hands and poured outward in twin streams of blue flame, arrowing in on the snarling monster and punching straight into its chest. The force of the fire drove the Grendel backward through the air a dozen feet until it smashed into the wall and fell, dead, into a burning heap.

Luke leapt up onto the roof and pulled Rio into his arms again, in spite of her protests, and then jumped down, careful to channel air currents to cushion their landing so as not to jar her injured ankle.

"You're bleeding," she said. "Did it hurt you?"

He stared at her, briefly wondering why she had sparkly stuff flashing around her eyes, before he decided the reason really didn't matter. He hugged her closer to his chest and inhaled her scent.

"Pretty," he said, smiling down at her.

Rio's eyes narrowed. "Why do you suddenly look and sound drunk? Luke?"

The back door slammed open, and Miro trudged out, a rag wrapped around his head and one eye swollen shut. He stopped and looked down at the burning body of the Grendel, took a deep sniff, and then smiled at them with a whole hell of a lot of teeth.

"Yum. Barbecue."

"I think I'm going to be sick," Rio said. "Put me down. Now."

Luke tightened his arms around her and nuzzled her neck. "No. Mine."

"Miro, do you know anything about Grendels?" she asked, sounding a little breathless.

Good. Luke liked it when she was breathless. Naked and breathless and—oh, wait. He'd never gotten her naked yet, except in his dreams. Why was that again?

"Need you naked," he mumbled, lurching forward a little. "Whoa. Who moved the ground?"

Miro ambled closer and stared down at Luke. "Yep. Grendels have poisonous claws. Wouldn't kill this one, but probably leave him drunk and stupid for a while."

"'M already stupid," Luke volunteered happily. "Stupid for you, Rio Jones Green. Or is it Rio Green Jones? Heh. Green Jones Green Jones Green Jones."

He wobbled again and almost dropped Rio.

"Put me down, Luke," she said again, this time with a sweet smile that turned his brain to mush. Or made it mushier. Or something. Wow, that venom felt like a three-day whiskey bender.

He carefully lowered Rio to her feet and then leaned against her when the world kept spinning, nearly knocking her over. She winced and lifted her injured ankle off the ground but got a tighter grip around his waist.

"I think I'm going to need help, Miro," she said, just before her face got all swirly and the sky turned dark. Very dark. Almost fall-on-his-face dark.

Luke blinked rapidly to clear his vision and realized an ogre was moving in on his woman. Every protective instinct in his body went apeshit, and he pushed Rio behind him. Something familiar about the ogre . . . He shook his head, trying to shake off the effects of the venom, but everything in his line of sight started to collapse in on itself like a kaleidoscoping tunnel.

"Must protect you now," he said, whirling around and scooping Rio up again. He glared a warning at the ogre, called the Shadows, and stepped into them, carrying his precious bundle tightly against his chest.

"*Traversa*," he whispered, and the Shadows carried them to his office, where the wards on the door and walls recognized his magic. He made it through the door and fell back against it, putting Rio down before the venom overtook his immune system. The walls started melting, and his desk turned into a giant dandelion. He swayed on his feet and took a step with some vague idea of making it to the couch or to Rio.

"They could bottle this stuff," he told her. "Whoa."

"You are in very bad shape," she said, half a smile teasing the edges of her lips. She caught him when he stumbled into her, which brought her lovely face too close to him to resist.

"You are in very bad trouble," he murmured, as he bent his head down to kiss her. At the first taste of her lips, the world went black around him to the sound of her sweet, sweet voice.

"You idiot."

When Luke collapsed, Rio dropped her small backpack on the floor and guided him down to the ancient couch, which was the same dark-green-and-brown plaid it had been when she'd last delivered a package there. In fact, not much of anything had changed. Not even Luke. Not really.

She brushed a strand of his silky black hair out of his eyes and took the opportunity to look her fill of him, since he was out cold. He looked exactly the same as the first time she'd met him—but not. A little harder; the lines and angles of his face were more pronounced. A little older, maybe; but then again, no. He never aged, or so she'd heard. Mrs. G once had let slip that she'd known him for more than sixty years.

His shirt was ripped and bloody over his ribs, and sticky smears of his blood were drying on her shirt. She took a deep breath and forced herself to quit staring at him like an idiot and do something useful. She hobbled over to the small bathroom, washed her hands, and found the first-aid kit under the sink. With that and a clean wet towel, she limped back to the couch to clean him up and see if he needed a doctor. Not that he'd agree to go to a hospital, probably, but she knew a friend of a friend who might be willing to come out and help.

She pulled the ottoman over to sit on and unbuttoned his shirt with fingers that barely shook at all, pulling the edges apart over his muscled chest and abdomen. She caught her breath at the wave of heat that swept through her at the sight of all that masculine beauty but shoved her reaction aside to focus on his injury. The gashes from the Grendel's claws were an angry, puffy red, but they seemed to be closing already, courtesy of Luke's superior healing powers. She'd heard that he could heal from a gunshot wound overnight. Of course, that was the kind of rumor that made some want to elect him sheriff and made others want to shoot him on sight.

She'd gathered up all of her courage and asked him out for coffee once, wondering if the sparks that flew between them were only in her imagination. He'd shot her down, telling her he didn't have time for "meaningless flings."

The sting had dulled over the course of the year, so the memory didn't slice through her as sharply as it had before. She hadn't even tried to be social much since then, afraid to risk rejection all over again.

Not good enough. Not wanted.

"Not *now*," she told herself, impatient with her own stupidity.

Time enough for useless bouts of wounded pride when their lives weren't in danger. She concentrated on his wounds and cleaned the gashes out as best she could and then liberally smeared antibiotic ointment on them before bandaging them. The stark white of the bandages over his side contrasted sharply with the bronze of his skin and the silky arrow of dark hair that disappeared into the top of his jeans. Rio caught her breath at the sight and couldn't resist touching his hot, smooth skin. The last thing she'd expected when she'd planned to hire Luke was that she'd have her hands on him within thirty minutes of finding him.

She glanced up and found him watching her, the brilliant blue of his eyes focused all too clearly on her face. She blushed and yanked her hands away, clasping them in her lap.

"I was just cleaning your injury," she said, trying not to sound defensive.

He glanced down at the bandages, wincing a little when he moved his head. "Thanks. How long was I out?"

"Not even ten minutes. That venom hit you kind of hard, though, maybe you should rest—"

But he was already swinging his legs to the side of the couch and sitting up, the movement causing the muscles in his abdomen to pull tight, and her mind went blank before wondering how long it had been since she'd had sex. Way too long, if her reaction to Luke's taut abs were anything to go by. Damn. She was all but drooling on the poor man.

"What happened after the venom started working on me?" His voice was grim, and the narrow-eyed look he aimed at her was empty of any emotion or humor, so clearly he couldn't read her mind. "I remember going fuzzy—oh, shit. Did I really threaten Miro?"

"No, you just growled at him and then grabbed me and did something weird where we seemed to walk through a whirlpool without water, if that makes any sense, and then we were here and you collapsed." She jumped up off the ottoman and took the used cloths and first-aid kit to the bathroom, more to get away from him than out of any need to clean up.

She reached out mentally, tentative at first and then with a stronger push, but she couldn't read anything of his thoughts. She'd never been able to do it before, but she'd wondered if the venom would interfere with his shields. Apparently not.

"I'll have to get him a present. Ogres are touchy," Luke said. He stood up and pulled off the shredded remains of his shirt and tossed the whole mess in a corner.

"He likes candy," Rio offered, as she tried not to stare at his back and failed miserably. The broad, muscled expanse was scarred and bruised with old, healed marks and newer, raw-looking ones, and she wondered how much truth there was in the legends about his healing capacity.

"Is that a fresh bullet scar?"

He whirled around and scowled. "Nothing that needs to worry you. I protected you, didn't I? Did something happen that you're not telling me?"

He crossed the room in two quick strides and lifted her chin with his fingers, staring down at her with eyes that had gone glacial. "Did they hurt you before I found you? Did they get their filthy hands on you?"

"You're the only one with his hands on me," she began hotly, but then she realized what was going on and exhaled slowly. "Luke. I'm fine. Nobody hurt me. Even with the poison in your system, you protected me."

It was the way he was built. Mrs. G had once gotten a little tipsy on New Zealand wine and told her that Luke was like a warrior of old. She'd touched Rio's hand and then looked off into the distance, as if seeing a scene from long ago, and spoken so softly that she might have been talking to herself.

"He's the best version of a warrior. Or maybe a cowboy gunslinger. He has to protect others or it damages something deep in his soul."

When Rio had asked a question, Mrs. G had shaken her head and changed the subject, but Rio had always wondered about that conversation. Now she was apparently seeing the gunslinger in action.

He backed away, raking a hand through his hair. "I'm sorry. I needed to know—why are you here?"

"I'm here because you brought me here," she said slowly, wondering if the venom had completely worn off.

He shot her a look. "I know that. Why were you looking for me? Was it the Grendel?"

"Actually, it was Grendels, plural, but no, not exactly," she said. "It was their boss, or at least I guess it was their boss. It must have been the same man. No way would I have two major evil villains after me at once, right?"

"Rio," he said, leaning back against his desk and crossing his arms over his chest. "Maybe start at the beginning?"

She stared at him, helpless to stop herself. He didn't even realize how gorgeous he was. Right now, when any other man would be posing and showing off those corded muscles on his arms and his delicious chest, Luke was just impatient for her to get on with it. Tell her story, so he could get rid of her, probably.

Too bad for him. He was stuck with her, at least until they found that child.

"From the beginning? Okay, fine. Today I saw a very evil man, except he wasn't human, kidnap a human child in broad daylight. She was maybe ten or eleven, and she was terrified, and he was planning to do very horrible things to her. Some kind of demonic ritual, maybe, except he wasn't a demon. He was Old Magic. Now I need your help to find him and save her—*the end.*"

Luke didn't ask how she knew what the kidnapper had been planning. He'd let it slip on one of her first deliveries to his office that he was aware of her telepathy. He just watched her for a long moment, until she thought she might scream, but she refused to speak again until he said something.

Anything.

"What kind of big bad keeps a Grendel or two—"

"Three," she interrupted.

He raised an eyebrow but nodded. "Three Grendels on staff as enforcers? I can't believe I wouldn't have heard about him if he'd been around long. There are no secrets in Bordertown."

"None that people can keep from you, maybe. It seems like everybody has secrets from where I'm standing," she said. "Also, do you have a shirt? Or maybe two?"

"What?"

"You need a new shirt, and I would like to get out of this one, so I was just thinking, well, do you have a couple of shirts?" By the time she finished, her face felt like it was on fire, and he was grinning.

"I'd be happy to help you out of that shirt," he said, pushing away from the desk and stalking across the room toward her like he was the predator and she was his prey, and he wanted to eat—*oh.*

Oh, no, we're so not going there.

She backed up until she hit the wall and couldn't go any farther, but he kept on coming. Her breath caught in her throat at the determined gleam in his eyes, but she found her backbone and held out her hands in the universal "stop" position.

"No, Luke. No, no, no. You don't get to act all sexy and flirty after you so rudely refused to even have coffee with me. I need your help now. That's all. There is a little girl who needs us out there, so snap out of it and let's figure this out."

He stopped dead in the middle of the room and scrubbed at his eyes with his fists. "I'm sorry. I think that damn venom is still working on me. Most venoms and poisons have zero effect on my system, so I wasn't careful enough about staying out of range of its claws."

Rio shook her head, suddenly shaking with exhaustion. "It's okay. I understand, but we need to figure out what we're going to do. I just want to try to help that girl, if it's not too late."

"If the guy who kidnapped her hasn't already hauled her into one of the demonic realms," he pointed out.

"No, I don't think so. I got the impression he was here in Bordertown—permanently. Just fragments of thoughts; I didn't really put it together at the time, but . . . I don't know," she said, sighing heavily and sinking into his leather chair. "Maybe I'm just crazy. How could I get all that from a few minutes' contact with his bizarre thought patterns?"

Luke crouched down beside her and put his hand over hers where it rested on the arm of the chair. "You're not crazy. We'll figure this out, I promise you."

She smiled a little, even as she carefully pulled her hand away. "I knew I could count on you. Help me find her, and then I'll be out of your hair forever."

Luke's expression went from warm to wary in half a

heartbeat, and his fingers tightened until he held her hand in a firm, unbreakable grip. "Oh, no, Rio. You're not going anywhere. At least not until we figure out what the League of the Black Swan wants with you."

Luke wondered how he was still relatively upright when the inside of his skull was on fire. He hadn't let anger like that escape his tightly leashed control in more years than he could remember. The mere idea that Rio would leave him had set long-buried primal instincts raging.

Want.

Need.

"Hulk smash," he muttered, disgusted, as he shoved a hand through his hair.

Rio edged back in the chair, her beautiful dark eyes so wide he could see tiny flecks of gold and green shimmering in their dark amber depths.

"Luke, are you—and I ask this in the nicest way possible—are you nuts?"

She fidgeted with the end of her braid, and he was suddenly entranced with the delicate skin on the inside of her wrist. In the golden light from the lamps, he could just make out the faint blue tracings of her veins, beautifully curved as if drawn with gentle strokes by a master calligrapher.

Or maybe he *was* fucking nuts.

He stood up so fast that the room swirled around him in a spiraling haze of gilt-edged shadow, and it all clicked as he remembered. Again.

"The venom," he said. "It must be messing with my short-term memory, too, because I keep forgetting it's affecting me."

Her shoulders relaxed a little. "Oh. Of course. You should probably rest, but I need to tell you something first. Why I'm here."

She shifted her legs and then winced, raising her foot, and he remembered that she was injured.

"First, I'll get you some ice for that ankle and make coffee," he said, heading for the tiny kitchen off the back of the office space.

He walked straight to the sink, ducked his head under the faucet, and ran icy water on his head and face for a half minute or so, until the almost drunken disorientation from the venom faded a little. He toweled off, started the coffee, and then put ice in a clean towel and returned to face the woman who'd danced through his dreams on more than one occasion.

He could do this. He'd faced down a Grendel.

But when he walked back into the office, Rio looked up at him and smiled, and the entire world shifted underneath his feet.

Worse—he didn't think he could blame it on the venom this time.

"Luke? Ah, is that for me?" She bit her lip and he stared, fascinated, at her mouth.

Her wicked, sensual mouth.

"I want to kiss you," he blurted out.

She blinked and froze, like a startled woodland creature, and he did the only thing possible.

He smacked himself in the forehead with the towel full of ice.

"Stupid, stupid, stupid," he gritted out. "I don't know why this damn venom is having such an effect on me. Poisons usually race out of my system in seconds. The longest I've ever been affected is a few minutes, and I . . . Oh."

He shoved the ice at Rio, spun around and went for the silver dagger he kept in plain sight out on his desk. His clients thought it was a letter opener.

Only Luke knew it was a crucible.

With barely the slightest trace of hesitation, he forced himself to reach out and take it, closing his fingers rapidly around the sleek surface of the silver handle.

Which didn't burn him.

Not even a little.

He exhaled a long, slow breath, and Rio cleared her throat.

"Do you want to tell me what's going on?"

He shook his head. "No. Not now. Later, maybe. Your turn to talk. Tell me more about the child."

He shook his head to clear it and then turned to face her. She was still holding the ice in her hand, her brows drawn together as she stared at him. He dragged the beat-up red leather ottoman over to her chair and sat on it, gently lifting her injured leg into his lap.

As he took the bundle of ice out of her hands, he tried a smile, since she was looking at him like he was a deranged and possibly dangerous criminal.

"This works better if you actually put it on the hurting part."

She flinched a little when he moved her pants leg up and put the ice next to the swollen side of her ankle, trying not to let his fingers linger on the silken smoothness of her skin. Since she was in pain, he forced himself to ignore the fact that his pants suddenly felt too tight, just from her calf resting on his thigh.

He was pathetic. Pathetic and aroused. Bad combination.

And still a little woozy, probably, because he leaned forward and tucked a loose strand of her hair behind her ear. She caught her breath when his hand touched her cheek, and he almost thought she trembled, but when his gaze flew to hers, she looked away.

"Ankle hurts," she whispered. "I'm not very tough, I guess."

"You managed to get away from three Grendels. That's pretty tough."

A smile curved her lips. "Maybe two Grendels and one of something uglier. Miro must have taken care of the other two."

He whistled. "It's a good thing they didn't catch you. You'd be dinner by now."

"They didn't want me for dinner," she said, her smile

fading. "They wanted me for their boss. 'The boss only wants to *talk* to you,' they said, or something like that."

"Did you pick up who the boss was? He must be the kidnapper, right?"

"I don't know. Their thoughts were too one-dimensional for that. One of them wanted cake, one had indigestion, and the third—" She stopped and took a deep, shaky breath. "The third wanted to play with me."

Luke's hands stilled on the ice that he'd been rearranging around her ankle, and he had to close his eyes and count to three before he could fight back the searing rage burning through him at her words.

"You're safe now," he finally said. "They'll never get their hands on you."

A cold wet sensation tingled on his thigh, and Rio's eyes widened as she pointed.

"Luke! Your hands—you melted the ice."

He looked down and, sure enough, his hands were glowing with blue flame. The towel was charred, and the water spread across his jeans and ran down his leg.

She was safe. But maybe he wasn't safe—from her. He could tell the League to go stuff their mission; he'd gone into this knowing it. How could he tell Rio that he couldn't—wouldn't—help her?

He stood up, too quickly, and the room whirled around him in a carousel of spinning lights. Rio pushed her way up off the chair, balancing on one foot, and awkwardly put an arm around his waist. Her lips were pressed in a firm line, like she'd rather be doing anything rather than helping him, and he could see the pain etched in her face.

"This isn't helping anyone," he said carefully, feeling around for words that wouldn't make her want to leave. The certainty that if she left, she'd never come back pressed in on him, magnified by whatever the venom was doing to his mind. "Not that little girl, not you, and not me. We need to get some rest; it's the middle of the night and I've been up since dawn. Even if I didn't have Grendel poison floating around in my bloodstream, I'm not sure I'd be making much sense."

She glanced around the room, anywhere but up at him. "I don't—where? I can get you to the couch, and I guess I can curl up on the chair for a while. I'm not going to be able to sleep, but you're right. You're no good to me now."

He winced, but she was right. "No, I live behind the office. We can go through that door just past the kitchen to my place, and you can bunk in one of the guest rooms."

Rio finally looked up at him, her eyebrows raised. "One of the guest rooms? Luke, that venom must be worse than you thought. There's only room for a storage room behind your office. I've been in Helga's Tea Room just a few doors down, and she only has room for a week's worth of supplies in her storage room. Let's just get you to the couch."

He felt the unfamiliar grin stretch across his face. "It's okay. My house is bigger on the inside."

Rio just shook her head, clearly not a *Doctor Who* fan, but she turned toward the door he'd indicated and they started forward. The room had quit spinning, so he supported her slight form against him so she wouldn't have to put any weight on her wounded ankle. He wanted to lift her up and carry her, but he had a feeling that wouldn't fly—and might actually push her out of his door.

When he touched the door to release the wards and it swung open, Rio stopped short on the threshold and whistled.

"What in the world?"

"I don't exactly have the brainpower right now to explain the physics of interdimensional magic, not that I really understand it all that well in the first place," he admitted, as she stood there staring at the spacious expanse of the first floor of his house, which took up a good thirty times the square footage of Helga's storage room.

"I kind of have more house than most people expect," he said, and then the stabbing pain started in his gut, and he fell on his face.

CHAPTER 4

Rio crashed to the floor, too, because Luke was well over two hundred pounds of long, lean muscle, and he'd had one arm firmly wrapped around her waist when he toppled. Somehow, in a burst of creative chivalry or pure dumb luck—for her—he'd managed to twist so that he didn't fall on top of her. Considering the noise the back of his head had made when it hit the floor, she was pretty grateful. On the other hand, she was the only person conscious in a wizard's apartment, and there was no way that could be good. Not to mention that her traitorous body was entertaining thoughts of how delicious his long, hard body felt against hers.

She pushed away the idea and slowly sat up, hoping there were no wards primed to burn her to cinders or turn her into a toad, and spoke somewhat hesitantly to the empty room.

"I know that intent is important in magic, so I want to state clearly that I have no intention of harming Luke. I only want to help him."

She bit her lip and looked around, feeling like a fool, but nothing moved or changed. No magical, sparkly lights spelled out ENTER, but they didn't show up and spell out GO AWAY, either, so she decided to take her chances.

"Luke," she said, touching his muscular shoulder. "Luke!"

But his lashes didn't even flutter. He was out cold on the surprisingly beautiful hardwood floor of his house that was bigger on the inside. It must have been the venom.

"I hope it doesn't kill you," she whispered, suddenly feeling more alone than she ever had.

His eyes opened, and he stared up at her, blinking, and then his forehead smoothed as he seemed to remember where he was and what had happened.

"Need water," he said hoarsely. "The powder—pale yellow powder in glass vial over the sink. Please."

She pulled herself up and limped across the open space to the kitchen area, which was part of the entire living, dining, and relaxing space. Luke's home was restful, at least what she could see of it from here. Vibrant autumn colors that reminded her of the forest mixed with splashes of dark green and warm red. Nothing too new or flashy, but the entire effect was one of good taste and money. Old money.

She glanced back at the open doorway, briefly wondering why his office looked like it belonged to a man desperate to pay the rent, before deciding to worry about more important things.

She examined the several cut-glass vials standing in a neat row on a narrow shelf above the sink and quickly selected the only one with light yellow powder in it. She carried it and a glass of water back to where Luke waited, still flat out on the floor, and sank down next to him, trying not to cry out when her injured ankle twisted a little underneath her.

"I'm so sorry," he rasped, leveraging up onto his elbows and then into a sitting position before taking the vial from her. "I should be taking care of you, and I'm useless."

"You can owe me one," she said, trying to smile and failing miserably.

Luke poured about half of the yellow powder into the glass of water, where it dissolved into an unexpected bluish-purple shade, and then he tilted his head back and drank the entire glassful without stopping.

She watched his throat, oddly fascinated by the movement as he swallowed, and then she forced herself to look away as she took a long, deep breath. Her muscles, which had been tensed and ready to fight or flee all day, relaxed bit by bit until she wanted to curl up in a ball next to Luke and fall asleep.

He finished the water, inhaled a long breath of his own, and then put the glass down on the floor next to him. She could almost see the color returning to his face and awareness to his eyes.

"That's better," he said. "I think I'm okay now. Let's get you something for your ankle."

She laughed a little bit and shook her head.

"Come on," he said, a half grin quirking up one side of his sensual mouth. "You've pretty much seen me at my worst. Fair's fair."

"I was feeling a little like Alice after she fell down that rabbit hole," she admitted. "And then you downed the Drink Me potion . . ."

She laughed again. She was sitting on the floor, watching an injured wizard drink a magical potion, but for the first time since she'd witnessed the kidnapping, she no longer felt afraid. Something loosened in her chest at the realization, and she caught her breath at the warmth in his eyes. This man—this gorgeous, seductively handsome man—could be a real danger to her self-control.

"How about we get some rest and find the White Rabbit tomorrow morning?" He stood up in one smooth motion, pulling her up with him. "I really do have something that can help your ankle, too."

"I—I don't want to take any magic potions," she said quickly. "I don't mean to offend you, but—"

"Advil," he said dryly.

She nodded and let him help her to one of the tall, leather-padded, wooden-backed stools on the living space side of the kitchen counter. Her ankle was throbbing miserably, and now that she was standing up, she realized that she was exhausted to the point of nausea.

"This wasn't how I expected today to go when I woke up this morning," she offered, by way of apology for jumping to conclusions.

"Days never go how I expect them to go, so I quit having any expectations at all," he said, taking a green-and-white pill bottle out of a cupboard and then reaching into the gleaming stainless steel refrigerator for a bottle of water. "Smarter that way. Less prone to disappointment."

Rio knew more about disappointment than most, but she said nothing. Her life wasn't an anecdote to be traded in casual chatter. She downed the pills and drank the water while he retrieved his glass from the floor near the doorway and closed the door.

Luke put his cup in the sink and looked at her. "Now let's find . . . Wait. *Child*. You said child. I'm an idiot."

"What?"

"Child. You saw a child being kidnapped. Just today a client hired me to find her missing niece. I'm only now putting it together." He clenched his hands into fists. "Damn that venom. Rio, what did that girl look like?"

A deep gong, like that of a very old church bell, sounded before Rio could reply, and she shivered. This gong carried tones of menace rather than reassurance; foreboding wrapped up in a musical tone.

"Luke? What—"

"It's the doorbell. Sort of." He shoved a hand through his hair and sighed. "And it's not one I can ignore."

He waved a hand and muttered a few words under his breath that Rio didn't catch, and an unobtrusive door past the edge of the kitchen area glowed silver around the edges of its frame. The door slammed open, and the most beautiful woman Rio had ever seen glided into the room, moving so smoothly that it seemed as if her feet never touched the ground.

"Hello, Merelith," Luke said wearily. "I told you I'd call you when I had news."

Merelith, who was clearly Fae, glared at Luke, and Rio wondered how he had the strength to keep from falling on the floor under the power of the woman's gaze. Icy silver hair trailed down from Merelith's perfect head to the top of her rounded, feminine hips. She had deep red lips and eyes that glittered with an opalescent green fire. She should have been wearing a fairy gown, not simple black pants and a white shirt, Rio thought numbly.

Merelith had to be High Court Fae, maybe even on the royal council, and suddenly Rio wanted nothing more than to crawl under the kitchen counter and hide until the woman left. Naturally, this made her lift her chin and plant her butt more firmly on the seat of the chair.

"You have word of my niece?"

Luke stared at the Fae. "How do you *do* that?"

Merelith stalked toward them and then stopped about six paces away from Rio. She lifted her head and actually sniffed the air, and then her perfectly shaped head abruptly turned, and she locked that searing gaze on Rio.

"You? You!" Merelith flashed across the room so fast that Rio couldn't even think about running before the Fae was standing in front of her, invading the hell out of her personal space.

Merelith caught Rio's jaw in an unbreakable grip and turned her face one way and then the other. "It *is* you," she whispered. "How is it possible—but you must be nearly twenty-five years old now, then."

The Fae's perfume—or her natural scent—made Rio think of crushed ice over salted raspberries, and then immediately wonder why. The rich aroma deepened when Merelith leaned even closer and touched Rio's locket with one long, slender finger.

"So, you haven't lost this? How . . . deliciously surprising."

Rio jerked away from the woman's touch, her hand rising to cover her locket. "What do you know about my necklace?"

Luke made a deep snarling sound, low in his throat. "You can't trust anything the Fae tell you, Rio. Ever."

"But they can't lie," Rio protested. "Even I know that."

Luke never took his eyes off the Fae. "Get away from her. Now. Or you will have made an enemy that even you don't want to make."

Merelith smiled mockingly, but she stepped back.

"Fear not, little wizard. I won't hurt your companion. But if you think to make her your bedmate, be advised that your chances of living past the dawn are slim."

Rio's face got hot. "Maybe you should back off, Merelith. You may be from the High Court, but that gives you no right to make rude comments about me and my, ah, my—"

Luke moved around the kitchen counter and put himself between Rio and the Fae. His fingers were glowing with blue flame again, and his voice had gone hard and icy.

"Back away from her, Merelith, or you'll be sitting on your ass in the alley before you can say another word."

Rio's mouth fell open as she stared at Luke's taut, muscular back. He was protecting her from a High Court Fae. An overwhelming urge to touch him—in support or plea, she didn't know which—had her reaching out with one hand until common sense caught up with longing, and she yanked her hand back.

Merelith laughed, the sound like ice cubes falling into a crystal glass. "I don't want to hurt her, Lucian Olivieri. I am merely interested in the dynamic of why she would turn up now, in light of current circumstances. The Fates are amusing, are they not?"

Rio pushed Luke out of the way as she awkwardly stepped down off the stool. "I'm a little tired of being talked about like I'm not right here. What are you talking about, and how did you know how old I am?" She looked into the Fae's glowing eyes and swallowed. Hard.

"Please?"

Merelith swept a scathing glance over Rio from head to toe and back up again before she answered. "I expected you'd be taller," said the nearly six-foot-tall Fae.

"Why did you expect anything about Rio at all?" Luke sounded mystified, but he was still holding flames at his fingertips.

"Rio? Is that what you're calling yourself?" Merelith tilted her head, considering. "It's actually rather fitting, since you almost drowned in that river, I suppose."

Dread rushed through Rio, starting in the back of her head and pushing heat through nerves and muscles. The river . . . the Fae's words turned a switch in Rio's mind that almost—*almost*—unlocked a tantalizing clue about a memory from her childhood. Something—anything— from the lost years before the nuns had taken her into their sanctuary.

Curiosity raced to the forefront; caution pushed it back. "Your niece?" Rio finally said, choosing the path of the least terrifying unknown.

The child. They needed to find the child. Mysteries about Rio's past could wait.

Merelith paused and then inclined her head, a regal gesture of agreement. Rio didn't want to know what it looked like when Merelith disagreed with someone, but she had the feeling it involved pain. Lots of pain.

Luke leaned back against the counter, still between Rio and the Fae, and he finally allowed the flames at his fingertips to disappear. Then he casually put a hand on Rio's shoulder, while not taking his eyes off Merelith.

"You should sit back down and take weight off that ankle," he said quietly.

Merelith made an impatient sound and held up one slim, white hand. "Is that what's making her grimace like a stuck pig? Why didn't you say so?"

Rio narrowed her eyes. "I do not look like a pig, you—"

The band of icy cold that wrapped around her ankle caught her off guard, and she fell back onto the chair, staring at her foot. Within seconds, the icy feeling vanished, and so did the pain. Rio cautiously twisted her foot from side to side, and then she stood up.

"It's healed," she said softly. "You—thank you, Lady Merelith."

"Apparently cessation of pain helps you remember your manners, if not your good sense, Halfling," Merelith said dryly. "Now sit and stop annoying me while Luke and I discuss how to find my niece. You are not the imminent problem."

Luke frowned at Rio. "How long have you lived in Bordertown that you don't know better than to thank a Fae?"

Rio's mouth fell open, and for a moment she was too stunned to decide which one of them was ticking her off more. She decided to deal with Luke later, since Merelith was the clearer threat. She was pretty sure Luke would never hurt her; she had no such illusions about any one of the Fae.

"Halfling? No, never mind. You're right, the little girl is more important," Rio said. "Does your missing niece look almost exactly like you, or at least like you if you were ten years old and human?"

Luke and Merelith's eyes widened simultaneously.

"Did Luke tell you that or did you see her?" The Fae pushed forward again, as if to grab Rio, but Luke's arm dropped down like a barrier barring the way.

"Back off, and we may find out what she knows," he warned Merelith.

"She will tell me, or she will die screaming," the Fae countered, her eyes glittering.

"There's no need for all this drama," Rio said. "I came to Luke for help finding this little girl. If she's your niece, I'm more than happy to help you in any way I can."

She quickly described the events of the day to Merelith, who grew more and more agitated.

"That's her. It must be her. If this monster who stole her is Dalriata, I will tear his bones from their sockets and snack on their marrow," the Fae shouted, her lovely face twisting into something inhumanly dark and dreadful.

Rio's stomach shriveled up into a cold, hard ball as Merelith's rage and magic washed over her in an icy wave.

"Dalriata?" Luke shook his head. "The name doesn't ring a bell."

"He recently arrived from Europe," Merelith said, as she began to pace back and forth in the space between the heavy wooden dining table and the kitchen counters where Rio and Luke stood. "Rumor has it that he's a Pictish king. He has failed to present himself at court to announce his intent, thus we believe it is foul."

"Why would he want your niece? And aren't the Picts a small race? The man I saw was nearly as tall as Luke." Rio thought about it for a minute. "He probably wasn't your guy, though. The evil villains usually have minions."

Luke laughed, and even his laugh was sexy. It was decidedly unfair to Rio's equilibrium.

Merelith's gaze suddenly snapped to Rio as if she were a pet dog who'd performed an interesting trick, and Rio blushed, wondering if Merelith had read her thoughts on her face.

"Picts have intermarried so often since the old days that their height is no longer a defining characteristic," Luke said, apparently unaware of the entire interplay between the women in the room.

Merelith pinned Rio with a sharp stare. "Ah. Smarter than you look. *Why* would he want Elisabeth is the pertinent question. She is half human and will never have claim to the Winter's Edge throne. She has little if any discernible magic and plays no part in politics. The abduction makes no sense."

Rio tried not to show how appalled she was at the cold assessment of a child's possible value as a kidnapper's victim. The Fae were not an outwardly emotional bunch, though; the fact that Merelith was willing to hire Luke to find Elisabeth probably said more about her true feelings for the girl than anything else.

"He wanted her for some kind of ritual," Rio said. "Something dark—Old Magic. Are you sure she doesn't have any magical abilities that would make her a target for this?"

Merelith rounded on her and all but pounced. "How would you know what he wanted her for?"

"She heard his thoughts," Luke said, before Rio could think of a response.

"Or she heard what he intended for her to hear," Merelith said bitingly. "It is no small matter to deceive a person with a trifling talent for mind reading."

Rio clamped her jaw shut. Yelling at Luke that he had no business telling the Fae any of *hers* wouldn't help, and Merelith would only be ruder if she knew her barbs were affecting Rio in any way.

Merelith's expression changed subtly. Her eyes widened just the tiniest bit, but the emotion fell away from the rest of her face. "And can you read my thoughts?"

Rio held up her hands, shaking her head. "No. I can't read High Court Fae thoughts, or those of most demons, or Luke's, for that matter. It is, as you pointed out, a *trifling* talent. And I only got glimpses of what the kidnapper was thinking, but he has bad plans for the girl and, whether she's your niece or not, we need to find her. He was thinking moonrise, so she's safe for a while now, but we don't have time to spare."

Luke suddenly yanked one of the bar stools closer to him and collapsed onto it. "I'm glad we have a little time because our plans may need to wait until I get some rest. That venom isn't completely out of my system."

Merelith raised an eyebrow, and Rio explained.

"I cannot help you with the aftereffects of Grendel venom. You may rest for five hours, and then I expect you to continue to pursue your contacts and *find my niece*," the Fae said, turning to leave. "I have ordered every member of my court over whom I have any influence at all to search. Between us, we will find her."

"We'll find her," Rio said, as much to convince herself as to reassure Merelith.

The icy blonde whirled around, her hair floating as if

she stood in the middle of a gale-force wind. "But I have already found *you*, so that is an interesting development, is it not?"

Before Rio could reply, Merelith had gone, the door slamming shut behind her.

Rio shook her head. "She's not really the delicate flower that you expect of a High Court lady, is she?"

Luke laughed, but the sound was brief and underscored with pain and exhaustion. "Definitely not. Rio, I think I'm going to need your help to make it to bed."

She glanced at him. "From anybody else, I'd think that was a line. You know that, right?"

Luke's eyes flashed hot. "Give me a chance, later. You might be surprised."

Choosing not to examine that too closely, Rio put her arm around his waist and together they slowly made their way down the hall to the first room on the right. She told herself that he probably didn't even notice taking her hand, or the electric charge that jumped from his skin to hers.

She noticed enough for both of them.

"At least you're not limping," he said from between clenched teeth. "Who says the Fae are inbred, good-for-nothing pains in the ass?"

Rio laughed a little. "She healed my ankle completely."

"Better that you hadn't said thank you, though," Luke muttered. "Who knows what she'll feel entitled to now?"

"I've done my fair share of tough negotiations in my life, Luke. I was raised by nuns," Rio said grimly.

Luke grinned, probably thinking she was kidding. Ha. If he only knew. Nuns could be scary. Especially in Bordertown.

Rio had an impression of rich colors and clean lines in the shadowed darkness of Luke's bedroom, and then he was pitching forward onto his pillows, still clasping her hand tightly in his.

"Luke?" Rio tried to extricate her fingers, but he had her in an iron grip.

"Stay with me? Please?" he whispered. "We're going

to find Elisabeth. I promise you. But now I need to keep you safe. Need—"

She waited, but the end of the sentence never came. Whatever else he needed would have to wait until he woke up. His hold on her hand loosened a little, but not by much. It didn't take long for Rio to consider her options and decide on the only one that made any sense.

She climbed up on the bed and curled up next to Luke, wondering at the direction her life had taken. Not quite twenty-four hours earlier, she'd woken up alone in her apartment, ready for another mundane day of delivering other people's news. In that short space of time, she'd witnessed an abduction, staved off an attack by Grendels, demanded help from the Dark Wizard of Bordertown, and confronted a High Court Fae.

No matter what happened to her next, she could never again claim that she spent her life standing on the outside of other people's lives and adventures. Now she just had to decide whether that was a good thing.

Luke stretched in his sleep, still holding her hand, and then rolled onto his side, pulling her against him. Every nerve ending in her body lit up like the blue flames that had danced along his fingertips earlier, and it took several minutes of listening to Luke's slow, even breaths for her to relax. As her own exhaustion pulled her down into sleep, Rio smiled a little. Good, bad, who cared? At least this time it was *her* life that was interesting.

"Eat, drink, and be merry, for tomorrow we confront a Pict king over a Fae child," she murmured. "Oh, Rio, what have you gotten yourself into?"

Luke, wrapped around her in a soundly sleeping embrace of heat and muscle, didn't answer, so Rio let go of all her worries for just a little while and fell asleep in the arms of the most dangerous man in Bordertown.

Funny, how it felt so very right.

CHAPTER 5

Luke woke up like he usually did—all at once, gasping for air like a drowning man breaking the surface of the ocean after going under twice. But this time, something was different. The terror was muted, and it quickly receded to a manageable thrum just under the surface of his skin. As if whatever horror had haunted his sleep for hundreds of years was confused . . . or had been defeated.

Defeated by the almost-human woman sleeping in his arms.

He resisted the urge to touch Rio's silken hair, knowing that the slightest movement might wake her, and she'd probably jump away from him the second her eyes opened. So, instead, he stole the moment from her, luxuriating in the feel of her softness against his body and pretending she belonged there.

Next to him.

He'd followed her for a while, back when she'd invited him for coffee. After he'd instinctively recoiled from the certainty that here, finally, was a woman who would breach his defenses. He'd built those defenses carefully, damn it. Brick by brick, decade by decade—all spent avoiding entanglement with anyone he might care enough about to risk activating the curse. Killing someone in a jealousy-driven rage would certainly do it, and he'd wondered exactly what he would do to protect a woman like Rio.

Or, more to the point, what *wouldn't* he do?

He'd learned on the third evening of stalking her nights just how bad it could have become. A man had accosted Rio at the Roadhouse, and if Miro hadn't intervened when he had, Luke might have burned down the entire building and everyone in it. He owed the big ogre for more than Miro knew. But now—now Luke had Rio in his arms, exactly where he'd sworn she'd never be, and he knew, deep, *deep* in his soul, that he had no intention of ever letting her go. It didn't make sense, but after centuries of living under the threat of a curse, he'd learned that nothing that mattered ever seemed to make sense at first. It just *was*.

Her courage in the face of everything she'd had to face the night before, her sense of humor—oh, yeah. Life was about to get very interesting.

"You're smiling again," Rio said, startling him.

"Hey. I was just about to wake you—" he began, but he let the lie fade away when she flashed an amused grin.

"No, you weren't. You've been—" Rio's amber-flecked eyes widened, and she abruptly moved away from him and sat up. "We—you—I was exhausted, and you wouldn't let go of my hand, so I—"

He fought his instincts and won, letting her go. "Yeah. Sorry about that. Exhaustion and Grendel venom is a bad mix. I'm back to normal now."

She stepped lightly off the bed, looking around almost frantically. "Um—"

"Through there," he said, pointing to the bathroom door and then watching while she fled.

She could face down Grendels and a Fae princess, but pillow talk scared her. Even as it made him grin, he had to admit to himself that he was pretty much the same. Flirting, romance, and tenderness—what did he know of any of those? Not enough to attract Rio, certainly.

Not enough to attract a woman who'd been living on a deserted island for five years, either, probably.

He threw off both his self-imposed melancholy and the blanket she must have draped over him and stood up and stretched. His balance was restored, and he didn't feel any aftereffects from the venom, thankfully. So now it was time to go find that little girl.

His bedside phone rang, and he stared at it for a beat before answering. Two rings. Three. Nobody ever called him on that line with good news. He listened to the sound of water splashing in his bathroom sink for a moment, and then he sighed and reached for the phone.

"Oliver."

"This is Brock Dalriata. One of my associates mistakenly acquired a child yesterday, and I understand that you're the man to help out with situations like this." The man's voice was low and gravelly, hinting of murky swamps and murderous intent.

Or maybe Luke just needed some damn coffee.

"Is 'acquired a child' code for *kidnapped* where you come from, Dalriata?" Luke snarled. "I don't have much use for people who hurt children. Ask around Bordertown, and you'll find out what happens to people when I don't have much use for them."

Dalriata laughed. "Oh, I know who you are. I also know you've been approached on multiple occasions about becoming the sheriff, and you've consistently declined, so other people's welfare isn't exactly the most important thing on your mind, is it? Perhaps you could spare me the righteous indignation, and let's arrange a meeting. I don't care to have this child in my custody a single moment longer than necessary."

"She's Fae," Luke said flatly. "Call the High Court." Silence.

"She's not. She's human, or maybe a Halfling bastard, but she's not a purebred Fae," Dalriata said finally, the slightest hint of unease lacing his tone.

Luke closed his eyes and imagined reaching through the phone to rip the asshole's throat out, which calmed him down enough to speak. Before he could say anything, though, the door to the bathroom opened and Rio hesitantly walked out.

"It's the man who has Elisabeth," he told her. "He wants to meet."

She immediately sat on the floor and started putting on her shoes. "When and where?"

Luke repeated her question into the phone.

"My offices. Eighty-three West Hyde. Thirty minutes."

"Let me talk to the girl," Luke said. "Now."

"She's fine. I believe she's eating breakfast. Either come now, or I'll put her in a taxi to the Silver Palace and they can deal with her."

Dalriata hung up, and Luke slammed the phone down.

"We're leaving now?" Rio jumped up and pushed her hair back from her face. "Where is she?"

"No, *we're* not leaving now," Luke snapped. "*I'm* leaving now. I have no idea what kind of muscle this Dalriata has, but the kind of person who has Grendels *on staff* is not somebody I'm willing to let get anywhere near you."

Rio's eyes narrowed and she planted her fists on her hips. "Did you just say—wait. Dalriata? He's really taking this Pictish king thing seriously, isn't he?"

Luke shook his head, baffled.

"Dalriata? Dal Riata? Irish colony in Scotland way back when?"

He raised an eyebrow. "You're a Gaelic scholar, too?"

"Hey, I read, all right? Just because I'm a bike messenger who never made it through college doesn't mean I'm stupid," she said, flushing a hot red. "It was too hard to be in classrooms with all of those minds shouting at me."

"I never accused you of being stupid," he protested,

wondering how and when the conversation had gone to hell in a hand-carved basket. "I'm not good at talking to women when they're awake."

She raised her eyebrows, and he mentally replayed what he'd just said.

Oh, shit.

"That's not what I meant. We need to—I'm not—oh, hell. I need coffee, and we need to go." He threw up his hands and stalked out of the room. This was why he was better off alone, no matter how good Rio looked in his shirt.

Luke was a wizard and a warrior. Not—*ever*—a ladies' man, and he was pretty sure that if Rio hadn't figured that out a long time ago, he was cluing her in really well right now. His mood tanked in a split second, and he pushed everything out of his mind but the mission at hand.

Dalriata had picked the wrong child, the wrong town, and the wrong wizard.

✳

Rio waited at least five seconds after Luke stormed out before she let the laugh she'd been holding in escape. He wasn't good at talking to women when they were awake. Oh, boy. Luke might be scary and powerful and dangerous, but *smooth* he was not. Oddly enough, the realization lifted her spirits in spite of the fact she was on her way to confront the man who'd sent mythological monsters after her only the night before.

She took a deep breath and thought brave thoughts. After all, she had a thing or two to say to Mr. Dalriata that would blister his ears. Pictish king or not, he was in trouble. There were *laws*.

She involuntarily glanced after Luke. There were laws, yes, but without a sheriff, the outlaws ran Bordertown.

"I'll just have to find a cowboy hat," she told the empty room.

"Do you want coffee or not?" Luke called out, sounding surly.

She smiled, almost in spite of herself. Yeah. He was smooth.

"Yes, if you have a to-go cup. Let's go get that little girl," she said, heading down the hallway toward him.

When she reached the kitchen, he was standing by the door to his office, holding two travel mugs.

"Way ahead of you," he said grimly.

"If he has hurt one hair on that child's head—"

"If he took any hair, he plans to use it for a spell or ritual," Luke interrupted, a feral cast to his stark features. "I've never killed a wannabe king before, but I'm willing to try new things."

Out on the street, the cold autumn morning threatened rain. Luke gestured to a ratty old Jeep that was parked on the street next to a RESERVED sign that leaned drunkenly to the left, as if ashamed of the graffiti that adorned it. Every time she'd delivered a package on Pendulum Street, she'd amused herself by reading the new graffiti on Luke's parking sign. Apparently the taggers weren't afraid of getting turned into toads.

" '*Wizards do it with their wands*'?" Rio drawled. "Really, they can't come up with anything more original?"

"It's better than '*wizard pendulums hang low*,' which is what they wrote the last time," he muttered, heading to the driver's-side door.

The Jeep wasn't locked, which surprised her until she considered its ancient state and who owned it. Probably not many who would dare to steal Luke's car.

"To get to West Hyde, it's faster if you turn right on Poe and then take a left on Rivendell."

He shot her a look, and her face warmed up.

"Sorry. Curse of the bike messenger."

He put his cup in the holder and pulled out, his windshield wipers making a dragging sound as they worked. Rio took a long sip of her own coffee.

"It's just black. I don't even have cream or sugar, I don't think," Luke offered, sounding slightly apologetic.

"It's fine. Thanks for making it."

After that, they drove in silence to Brock's address, while Rio's thoughts spiraled further and further downward. What kind of man hired Grendels to kidnap bike messengers? Grendels with poisonous claws? In order to keep them in line, what kind of monster must Dalriata be? She figured there was no way he was the man she'd seen take the child because kingpins never did their own dirty work. So who was that guy? And yet, in spite of all the unanswered and unanswerable questions, here she was, driving to meet him, with an unpredictable wizard at her side.

"Watch out for that tree," she whispered, grinning, as Luke pulled into the office building parking lot.

"What?" Luke turned to face her, raising one dark eyebrow.

"Nothing. I do movie lines when I get nervous," she said, feeling her face heat up again, which annoyed the crap out of her. She was perpetually blushing around this man. "It's a long story."

"I'd like to hear it some time."

She stared at him, caught in his gaze for just a beat longer than she should have been, then nodded grimly and opened her car door. "If I'm still alive to tell it after this."

The doorman was a block of a man. His head was oddly formed, making him look like a goat had gotten confused and tried to turn into a donkey. He was shaped like a thick barrel, easily six feet tall, not counting the silver tufts on the top of his deep brown, furred ears.

"Leave," Donkey Man said.

Luke laughed. "Really? Are you going to be an ass about this?"

Rio rolled her eyes. "You had to go there? Like he hasn't heard that before?"

"Heard what?" Donkey Man rumbled, looking confused, if that was what the bushy eyebrows drawn low over too-large eyes meant.

"I'd be happy to teach you a lesson in manners, if you

don't get the hell out of my way," Luke said, smiling almost happily, as if he'd been hoping for a fight.

Testosterone. Stupid men and testosterone.

"We don't have time for this," Rio said, fighting hard to ignore her pounding heartbeat and the part of her that wanted to run like a scared human caught in a demon brawl.

She stepped closer to Donkey Man and held out her hand. "Hello. I'm Rio Stephanopoulos, and I'm pleased to meet you. Mr. Dalriata, whom I'm guessing is your boss, invited us here. Will you please check with him?"

The doorman gaped at her like she'd grown an extra body part. Which, she supposed, she kind of had. A backbone. Or at least more of one than she'd thought she possessed when she'd woken up yesterday morning.

Luke started to snarl something next to her, but the doorman carefully held out one huge, gnarled hand to Rio and gently touched her fingers.

"I am Abernathy," he rumbled. "I am pleased to meet you. Wait here."

He moved away from them and motioned to someone inside the glass revolving doors, and Rio saw the shadowy figure lift a hand, presumably carrying a phone, to its head.

Rio turned to Luke, proud that her knees weren't shaking. "You see? Sometimes it just takes a little bit of politeness."

Luke shook his head, looking stunned. "I'd never have believed it. A mountain troll. You just exchanged pleasantries with a mountain troll. Also, Stephanopoulos?"

She shrugged. "I like *Good Morning America.*"

"You do realize that Bordertown is a small place, right? Relatively speaking? You're not fooling anybody with all of these aliases." He folded his arms across his chest and rocked back on his heels, just an ordinary wizard casually standing around on the sidewalk.

"You do realize you're not fooling anybody when you try to act harmless, right?" she shot back at him.

Luke laughed, and she had the feeling she'd surprised it out of him. She also had the feeling that he wasn't surprised by much, so she was oddly pleased with the small victory.

Abernathy inclined his head with some dignity. "Mr. Dalriata will see you now."

"Here we go," Luke said, taking her hand as if he did it every day of the week.

She determinedly ignored the spark that shot between them. Static electricity; that must be it. She couldn't possibly be feeling a spark of attraction to the *wizard*, in front of the *mountain troll*, on the way to meet the *Pict king*, in order to rescue the niece of a *High Court Fae*.

Watch out for that tree.

CHAPTER 6

Luke led the way to the elevator, and they silently listened to Muzak all the way to the top floor. He'd let go of her hand, and she found herself missing his touch. Her fingers tingled where they'd been in contact with his.

She had to think about something else. *Anything* else.

"Seems wrong, doesn't it?" Rio asked, shoving her hands in her jeans pockets and affecting a nonchalant pose, when she felt anything but.

"What?"

"Listening to Barry Manilow on the way to the evil villain's lair. Seems like it should be AC/DC or a soundtrack of evil cackling, maybe." She started humming "Copacabana" and watched Luke try not to grin.

"I think lairs are underground, right? Can there even be penthouse lairs?" He shot her a speculative look and then shook his head. "Doesn't anything scare you?"

She caught her breath, wondering at, and then giving in to, the impulse to tell him the truth. Only him. "Are you kidding? *Everything* scares me. I'm a human with a single, not very useful talent living in a world where even the lesser of the predators could take me out with one bite. But sometimes they don't notice that if my attitude is bigger than I am."

His blue eyes glowed a hot blue for a moment, and then he reached out his hand as if to touch her arm, but the elevator slowed to a stop and the doors opened. Luke's hand dropped to his side, and he stepped out first and scanned the area before moving forward so Rio could enter the lobby.

It was huge, was her first thought. Rio's entire apartment could have fit into the lobby, with room to spare. A gleaming silver reception desk dominated the space, and the words DALRIATA INDUSTRIES were carved out of the front of the desk in a three-dimensional effect. The same words shouted at them in three-foot-tall letters from the wall behind the desk.

Luke snorted. "Maybe he's afraid he'll forget the name of his company?"

"Strange there are no guards here," Rio murmured.

"Don't underestimate Blondie," Luke said. "Who knows what she's packing?"

The blonde at the reception desk was as icy as her surroundings. Platinum-blond hair, pale white skin, gray eyes, and a white business suit with a white silk blouse beneath it turned the woman into a wraith. She looked unreal, as if some denizen of the underworld had conjured a colorless imitation of what a real employee might look like. The thick silver links twisted into a necklace that was digging into her slender neck hinted at something darker than *employee*. Possession, maybe.

Rio lightly scanned the woman's thoughts and fought the roil of nausea that swarmed up from her empty stomach. Obsession. Submission. A fawning, quivering desire to please someone.

Three guesses who that someone was.

"He's expecting you," the woman said to Luke.

She never once even glanced at Rio, which made sense.

It was always wiser to keep your eyes on the biggest predator in the room.

The door to the office behind and to the right of the reception desk swung silently open, and an airy office space that dwarfed the reception lobby came into view. Rio fought the urge to clutch Luke's arm for support.

"Here we go," she said.

The wall of windows offered a spectacular view of Bordertown that stunned Rio into silence, even though the overcast day diminished the effect. She never made it past reception areas when she delivered packages, and she certainly hadn't had any other reasons to visit top-floor offices before. She could see all the way to the shimmer of silver at the entrance to Winter's Edge to the north, and the dark, pulsating cloud that guarded the gate to Demon Rift on the east. The Summerlands border to the south couldn't be seen from Dalriata's office, and Rio found that fact oddly fitting, especially since the entire office suite smelled of stinky armpit and rotten fish.

But the view, the smell, and the tall, dark man sitting behind an enormous desk, with his back to the view of Demon's Rift, could only distract her for a second or two from the small girl waiting, very still and upright, in the middle of a slate-gray bench that ran the length of the left wall of the office. It was the girl from the alley, still wearing her sky-blue dress and clutching her pink backpack. Rio ran over to her before anybody could tell her not to do it.

Not that she would have listened.

She stopped in front of the silent, unmoving child and knelt down so as not to loom over her.

"Elisabeth? Are you okay?"

The girl slowly raised her head and aimed a silvery-green gaze at Rio. There were no tear tracks on her cheeks and no signs of fear on her face. Rather, the child looked dazed, and her eyes didn't seem to focus exactly right.

Rio put a protective hand on the girl's arm and half-turned to glare at Luke. "I think they've drugged her."

The man on the other side of the room stood and cleared his throat. "I must disagree. We have not harmed the child in any way, beyond the unfortunate trauma of her abduction, for which I apologize."

Rio glared at him, but she'd been right. This man wasn't the man who'd grabbed the girl in the alley. This man was pure, leashed power, and even though she couldn't read anything from his thoughts, his posture and presence fairly screamed menace and command.

Still, next to Luke? The man was a poser. There was nothing leashed about Luke's power. His fingertips were glowing with blue flames as he stared down the man who must be Dalriata.

"You Dalriata?" Luke asked, more quietly than she would have expected.

The man inclined his head. "I am he. Your fingers seem to be leaking, Mr. Oliver. Problems controlling your magic?"

Luke laughed. "The better to fry your ass if you annoy me. You want to try explaining how somebody *accidentally* kidnaps a little girl?"

Elisabeth shivered, and Rio sat on the bench beside her and drew the unresisting little girl into her arms, never taking her eyes off the wizard and the self-proclaimed Pictish king. When she bent to kiss the top of the child's head, an unpleasant *snap* of electricity smacked Rio in the lips and jolted her back.

Elisabeth raised her head and stared up at Rio. "You're not only human, either? You hide it really well, ma'am," she whispered.

Rio blinked. "I'm human. That was just . . . static electricity. Call me Rio."

She automatically scanned Elisabeth's thoughts with the gentlest touch and realized that, although Elisabeth was obviously Merelith's niece—the girl looked like a tiny copy of the Fae—she was also human.

"Clearly, it was a gross misunderstanding combined

with unacceptable stupidity," Dalriata said calmly, as if he weren't facing down the Dark Wizard of Bordertown.

On the other hand, he was new. Maybe he didn't know.

"My daddy is human," Elisabeth said wistfully, distracting Rio from the budding confrontation. "He lets me eat hot dogs at the baseball games. My mommy went to France for a job, though, and he went along. They'll be home soon, I hope. Have you seen Auntie Merelith? She's going to be so angry I was late."

"She's going to be so happy you're safe that she'll probably let you eat all the hot dogs you want," Rio said, hugging the girl closer.

"No, she won't. There are *rules*," Elisabeth said, either consciously or unconsciously imitating Merelith's icy voice so perfectly that Rio nearly shivered.

"And what are you planning to do about your stupidity problem?" Luke mocked, as he sauntered closer to Dalriata, placing himself between the man and Rio.

Since she couldn't see him anymore, she sent out a feeler toward his thoughts and got back exactly zero. Dalriata's mind was closed up tighter than a bottle of whiskey at a meeting of the Bordertown Temperance Union.

"A gift for the child's family, as my offer of recompense," Dalriata said. "I would prefer if your lovely companion retrieves it from my desk. You will understand if I'd rather you keep your distance."

"Not a chance," Luke snarled. "You keep your eyes and your thoughts off her."

"But you are the one who invited my attention by bringing her with you, are you not?"

Rio was fed up with being talked about as if she weren't in the room. She stood, pulling the girl with her.

"I'm right here, gentlemen. You can talk *to* me, instead of *about* me."

She leaned down to whisper in Elisabeth's ear. "Go stand behind Luke, okay, sweetie? We'll be leaving and taking you to your aunt in just a few minutes."

The girl shuddered once, all over, like a tiny fawn caught in a blizzard, but then she nodded and obediently followed Rio to the center of the room and stopped directly behind Luke. Rio continued until she was even with Luke and then paused to take a better look at the man who could consider abducting a child to be nothing more than an unpleasantry.

Dalriata wore a suit that had probably cost more than Luke's Jeep. His bronze hair waved back over a strong face that looked only about a generation away from gracing a golden coin. His brown eyes assessed her coolly, as if measuring her worth and finding her slightly—and only slightly—interesting.

"Rio of the many and varying last names, I'm assuming?" He smiled at her, and thoughts of earth-burrowing predators with strong, shiny teeth flashed through Rio's mind. "I must apologize to you, as well. The Grendels and their former supervisor were, shall we say, overenthusiastic."

"Not very smart, either," she pointed out.

"One takes what one finds, I'm afraid. Good help, and all that."

"We're leaving," Luke said flatly. "Now. I'm sure that Elisabeth's family will have their own conversation with you, but this is no longer my business. Stay out of my way, and keep your hands off the innocent people in Bordertown, and we'll never have to see each other again."

"Now, what fun would that be?" Dalriata said mockingly. "After all, now the League owes me a favor."

Luke's head snapped up, but before he could respond, Dalriata held up a basket that had been sitting on his otherwise pristine desktop.

"Ms. *Stephanopoulos*? If you please?"

Rio dodged Luke's restraining hand and crossed the floor to accept the basket. "Since it's an apology, we should take it. It might help avert something really awful."

"Don't touch that basket, Rio," Luke commanded, as if he had the right to tell her what to do.

She ignored him and put a hand out for the basket, but a burst of gleeful thought from somewhere in the vicinity of the empty space in front of the bank of windows stopped her. Slowly, she stepped away from Dalriata's desk, putting her hands behind her back.

"Luke, there's someone in front of the window, behind some kind of magical camouflage," she said quietly, keeping her gaze trained on the man behind the desk. "That's probably where that faint scent of . . . *yuck* is coming from."

"I know," he said, reaching out to pull her next to him. "Dalriata knew enough about me to find out my private phone number. Do you really think he'd face me alone?"

The air shimmered and then suddenly the two Grendels from the night before stood between them and Dalriata. They looked pretty beat up, so Miro must have given as good as he'd gotten, but they were definitely both still alive and well. Behind Luke, Elisabeth whimpered once, a tiny, muffled sound that pierced Rio's heart like a spear.

"If you did anything to hurt that child, I will kill you. Slowly," Luke said, his voice still calm and even.

His body, though, told another story. He was leaning forward, perfectly balanced as if ready to charge, and blue flames snapped and crackled around both of his hands.

The thugs growled, but Dalriata waved a hand and they stepped back. "Since you refuse to carry my gift, perhaps you will report to Lady Merelith on its contents."

One of the Grendels, snarling horribly, shoved the lid off the large basket, knocking it to the floor, and the head of the man Rio had seen grab the girl fell out with a *thunk* on the carpet. Rio put an arm out to keep Elisabeth from moving forward to see what had happened, and then she pulled the girl against her, blocking her vision, and headed carefully and slowly toward the door.

"That was a horrible thing to do, with this child in the room," Rio said, her voice shaking so hard she could barely get the words out. "You may be a king wherever you come from, but we don't do things like that here."

"I think the residents of Bordertown do things exactly this way," Dalriata said, his voice lightly mocking. "And perhaps there is need for a king here as well."

Luke slashed one hand through the air, and a line of blue flame, easily nine feet tall, seared through the carpet in front of the Grendels, creating a wall of fire between them and the rest of the room.

"They are not afraid of a little fire," Dalriata said, his eyes narrowing.

"That is not a *little* fire," Luke said, in a voice that had gone dark and hollow. "You have reminded me what you did to my—to Rio last night. That was unwise."

"Luke, we need to go. Elisabeth is terrified," Rio said. "Please."

"Ah, but you have reminded me that I have another debt to pay," Dalriata said, arrowing his gaze in on Rio. "For the harm my employees dealt you. What would you have of me?"

He glanced at the thugs trapped behind the wall of flame. "Another head?"

Rio shook her head frantically. "No. No, let's just call it even, and we'll—"

But a small, quiet voice spoke up, throwing Rio completely off her train of thought when she realized it was coming from inside her mind.

You should ask for me, if you would. I would be very happy to be your guilt gift from the Pict lord.

"Who said that?"

"Said what?" Luke asked, looking as if he wanted to blast something or someone else.

"Shh." Rio jerked her head around, searching for the source of the voice, and just when she was about to give up and ask Luke to see if his magic could discover it for her, a small, tapered head peeked out from around the corner of Dalriata's desk, and then the rest of the body followed the head.

It was a dog. Or, maybe it was a dog. It was the dirtiest, saddest-looking dog she'd ever seen; gray and brown dirt covered it from nose to its bushy, matted tail, and it was limping, carrying its hind leg at an awkward angle. A silver collar that looked exactly like the receptionist's necklace tightly circled its neck, and a silver chain trailed off from the collar to somewhere behind the desk.

"Oh, baby," Rio said involuntarily, taking a step toward it.

Luke grabbed her arm and jerked her to a stop.

"What *is* that?" he demanded.

"Some creature my employees found living in the basement," Dalriata said. "It amused my receptionist to chain it to my desk this morning, apparently."

His eyes lifted to stare at his office wall, as if his gaze could burn through to see the woman in question. "She will be punished appropriately."

A wave of fawning glee snaked through the air from the direction of the lobby. The ugly emotion was so nauseatingly powerful it nearly knocked Rio on her butt as it rushed through the room. The dog stared up at Rio with its enormous green eyes, and somehow Rio knew that it was the one speaking to her telepathically.

The woman enjoys punishment. I do not. I am meant for you, Rio. Do not fail me.

"I'll take that," Rio blurted out, pointing at the dog. "You said you have a debt to pay to me, and I don't want there to be anything owing between us, so I'll take that. You don't want such a dirty creature messing up your office, anyway, and you can have the silver back, it's probably valuable, and I'll just buy a leash—"

"You're babbling," Luke interrupted, so quietly that she was sure nobody else in the room heard him. "Stop. We don't even know what that thing is, or if it's dangerous, or—"

"Done," Dalriata said, and Rio didn't like the hint of triumph he'd let escape from his carefully shielded thoughts as he said it.

But now wasn't the time to second-guess herself. At a touch of Dalriata's hand, the silver chain and collar fell from the dog's neck, and it limped toward Rio.

"Out. Now," Luke said from between gritted teeth. "Unless you want to start etiquette classes for the Grendels?"

Dalriata broke into the first laugh they'd heard from him, and goose bumps raced over Rio's skin.

"I think I am going to like it here very much. Give my regards to the Fae," the wannabe king said.

Luke shot a pitying smile at him. "You are already a dead man. You just don't know it. The Fae here are not sparkly little gentle beings, Pict. Merelith will crush you."

"Now. We need to leave now," Rio said. Her arms were full with Elisabeth, so the dog would just have to limp its way over to the door. Unless . . .

"Luke?" She made it a request without even uttering the question, and Luke scowled at Dalriata, the wall of fire that he still hadn't put out but didn't seem to be burning anything tangible, and even at her, but he knelt down and scooped up the dog in a single, fluid motion, and they left the room.

Nobody followed them.

"I'll put out the fire when we're on the street," Luke called out, and they didn't speak again until they were all settled in his Jeep. Rio sat in back with Elisabeth because the girl wouldn't let go of her, and the dog curled up on the passenger seat up front. Luke closed his eyes in concentration for a moment, probably to stop the fire, and then he stared at the dog.

"Why did you want to take this smelly animal with us?" He sounded honestly curious rather than annoyed. "She probably has rabies. Do foxes even get rabies?"

"It's a fox?" Rio said, blinking. "A girl fox?"

The fox lifted its head and regarded first Luke, then Rio, from those unblinking green eyes.

I am a fox. I am female. My name is Kitsune, and I belong with you, Rio.

"She's a fox," Rio confirmed out loud to Luke. "And her name is Kit-SOON-eh. She says she belongs with me."

It was Luke's turn to blink, but he just shoved the key into the ignition, started the Jeep, and pulled into traffic.

"Of course she does. Well, hey, we have to get the Halfling daughter of a Fae aristocrat back home before Auntie Merelith destroys the city looking for her, and then we're going to have a long conversation with a man about a horse."

"I like horses," Elisabeth ventured, her first words since they'd left Dalriata's offices.

"Horses are lovely," Rio agreed, stroking the child's hair and staring at the fox, who was now sleeping with her nose resting on her tail.

A talking fox. Why not? How much weirder could her day get, anyway?

Luke muttered something that sounded a lot like a few mildly bad words. "Um, Rio? Things are about to get weird."

She started laughing. "*About* to get weird? You have very high standards for what constitutes 'weird,' my friend."

He silently pointed out the front window, and Rio's mouth fell open. A duck the size of a city bus was squatting down in front of them, pushing an egg the size of a VW out of its hindquarters.

"I like ducks," Elisabeth said sleepily.

Luke glanced down at the girl's head, now resting on Rio's lap, and then up at Rio. Their eyes met in a moment of perfect understanding, and they both started laughing. Really, really hard.

"It's Bordertown," he finally said, shrugging. "Gotta love it."

Rio nodded, but she was starting to wonder if she'd be better off somewhere—anywhere—else.

CHAPTER 7

After the Bordertown Road Hazards Crew got the duck and her egg out of the middle of the road, hopefully shepherding them off to a nearby pond, Luke spent the drive to his place dividing his attention between watching Rio in the rearview mirror and waiting for the fox to either go rabid-crazy and bite him or shift into a human right there in the front seat. He'd never heard of fox shifters, but that didn't mean much.

He'd never heard of giant ducks, either.

The puzzle occupying his mind the most, though, centered on King Assfart's snide little comment. The League owed him a favor, he'd said. "The League" had to be the League of the Black Swan. Luke doubted that the Bordertown Brew Pub softball league cared a tinker's damn about Pict kings and their schemes. Also, he wasn't much of a believer in coincidences. The League had suddenly jumped back into Luke's life, focused in on Rio, and then Rio had gotten caught up in a scheme that had folded too quickly and without bloodshed.

No bloodshed if he didn't count the fried Grendel and the headless goon, who were both Dalriata's thugs—so he didn't. Count them.

He snorted, and the bedraggled fox opened one eye to glance at him and then fell back into an exhausted sleep. Luke didn't know why or how, but he had a feeling the fox was more than just a random stray that had happened to be in the building. Especially after Rio had mentioned that it was communicating with her. He scanned the little creature for magic, and only confusing impressions bounced back at him. Clearly, the fox had some magic of her own or someone had cast a spell on her, but he needed a little time to figure out exactly what was going on.

Also, deciphering magical puzzles while driving wasn't the smartest idea.

"We should call Merelith and tell her we found her niece," Rio said softly.

"She doesn't exactly carry a cell phone. I'll put out the word when we get back to my place, behind the wards," he told her, swerving to avoid a crazed taxi driver. The cab drivers in Manhattan and in Istanbul, Turkey, were the only ones Luke had ever known who could compete with Bordertown cabbies for sheer reckless determination.

"That's another thing that's bothering me," she said. "Why was it so hard to find this little girl? I know High Court Fae have some seriously scary powers. Wouldn't they be able to track their own blood relative pretty quickly?"

"They should have been," he admitted, impressed that she'd picked up on that problem so quickly. Brains *and* beauty. "Dalriata may have some major Old Magic going on, but against Merelith? He wouldn't stand a chance, on his own."

"On his own? Do you think he had help?"

He glanced in the rearview mirror and saw her amber eyes flash with anger. For an instant, he could have sworn he saw actual gold sparks in the irises, which reminded him that he knew very little about the lovely Miss Rio Green Jones Smith Stephanopoulos, or whatever her name was.

He knew she was brave as all hell when it came to protecting the defenseless, like the little girl for whom she'd put her own life in danger and the small, dirty fox sleeping next to him.

He knew she'd had a lonely childhood and didn't let many get close to her, because he'd watched her go home, alone, every night during his stupid interlude of stalking her.

He knew that he wanted to wrap her in his arms and never, ever let her face anything dangerous again.

Okay, turned out he knew quite a bit about her, and every bit of it was a threat to his self-imposed, centuries-old bachelor status, which meant he was going to put a stop to this idea of hers that she could just march into harm's way.

"We need to talk," he concluded, pulling to a jerky stop in front of his building.

Rio shook her head, sending all that lovely dark hair flying. "Oh, no, we don't. You heard him. He's sorry, he won't bother me again, he owed me a debt, blah blah."

"I didn't quite catch the blah, blah," he said dryly.

He carried the sleeping child inside his office, holding the door open for Rio and her new pet to enter. She looked like she wanted to bolt, but it would have been hard to escape down the street with her arms full of filthy fox. Especially since he had no intention of letting her get out of his sight so easily, at least until he figured out what the League wanted with her.

Right. Keep telling yourself that you've got noble intentions, he thought, as he watched the lovely sway of her hips while she crossed the room until she glanced back and caught him at it. He yanked his office door shut behind him and wondered why he was suddenly acting like a horny teenager. Another problem to think about later. For now, he reset his wards and led the way back to his apartment. He gently put Elisabeth down on his couch and gestured to Rio to do the same with her fox.

"No way. Kit needs a bath. Now. Who knows what she may have picked up from the Grendels? They probably have fleas," she said, scrunching up her nose in disgust.

For some stupid reason, he found the expression sexy as hell. He decided to blame it on the residual Grendel venom.

While Rio took Kit to the bathroom to clean her up, Luke called a guy who knew a guy, and Merelith was banging on his door inside three minutes.

She flew into the room, nearly knocking him over, when he opened the door.

"Where is she?"

He pointed to the couch, and the terrifying Fae lady transformed, for the briefest of moments, into an ecstatic aunt. Merelith shot across the room to Elisabeth in a cloud of silver sparkles, and Luke's nose started to itch. He'd always been slightly allergic to Fae magic, and whenever they were dealing with heightened emotion, it was worse.

The little girl, now safe in her aunt's arms, opened her eyes and peeked up at Merelith through her tangled hair. "Can we go home now? I'm sorry I was late, Auntie Merelith, but I'm so tired now."

Poor kid. She was totally exhausted. Dark smudges purpled the delicate skin under her eyes, and she looked a little worse than she had when they'd found her. A thought tickled Luke's mind, but Merelith's icy voice shattered it before it formed.

"Who?" she demanded, glaring at Luke. "Why? Does he or she lie dead and bleeding on the ground?"

"I think you stop bleeding when you're dead. No pressure to pump the blood out," Luke pointed out. "You want to explain to me why you couldn't find her yourself?"

A flash of something that, in anybody else, might have been bewilderment came and went in Merelith's eyes so fast that he almost didn't catch it.

"My methods are none of your concern, wizard. Payment

will be delivered." She turned to leave, but he stopped her with a touch to the shoulder.

"She was very brave, but worried that you would be angry with her," he said softly, glancing down at the sleeping child. "I'm really glad she's safe."

Merelith nodded, and then she glided out his door to the waiting silver limo. Her voice floated back to him as she climbed into the car while still holding her niece close to her chest.

"Do not think to distract me from the Halfling, Lucian Olivieri. We will meet again soon."

Luke slammed the door and glared at it. "Damn Fae always have to have the last word."

He turned at a noise, just in time to see Rio walking toward him carrying a fluffy towel wrapped around a wet fox.

"Merelith?"

Luke nodded. "She took her niece."

Rio shivered. "I'm just as glad not to have had to deal with her again. Maybe everything can go back to normal in my life now."

He doubted it, since the League was involved, but decided to keep that opinion to himself for the time being.

"Any chance you can light a fire in your fireplace, so Kit can warm up and dry off? I didn't see a hair dryer in your bathroom," she said.

"You wanted to use a blow dryer on a fox?"

She tapped her foot, ignoring the question, so he pulled the lever to open the flue and then flicked his fingers at the logs in his fireplace to start a fire crackling. Rio arranged the fox on the towel in front of the flames, and Luke could see that the creature wasn't gray and brown at all, but rather the more typical luxuriously deep red. The fox shook itself, throwing off a fine spray of water droplets, and then turned around clockwise three times and settled back down on the towel.

"Lot of dirt?"

She sighed. "You have no idea. I hope you don't mind,

but I used all of your shampoo. The forest-scented one under your sink. It seemed appropriate. I'll go back and clean out the tub now."

Rio looked as tired as the child had been, and Luke inexplicably wanted to take care of her. He wondered how she'd react if he lifted her into his arms like the Fae had done with Elisabeth. Run screaming, probably.

He'd feed her, instead.

"Forget the tub. Let me fix you some breakfast. There are some things I need to tell you."

"I don't like the sound of that," she said, but she gave the fox one last gentle pat on the top of its head and followed him over to the kitchen.

"What can I do to help?"

He shook his head. "It's okay. You've had a busy morning, and breakfast is the one meal I can actually make."

She didn't argue, just nodded and sank down onto one of the bar stools. He was overly pleased at the idea of cooking for her—caring for her. It felt *right* in some indefinable way.

"Coffee? I'll make some fresh." He set up the coffee maker and then pulled out eggs, cheese, and other important omelet ingredients, all the while wondering how to begin the discussion that he really did not want to have.

"So. The league. What league, and why does it owe Dalriata a favor?"

He cracked eggs into a bowl and then looked up at her. "You're really good at that. Cutting to the heart of the matter. Is it a side effect of your talent?"

Her face closed up, like a storm shutter being slammed down over a window in defiance of impending destruction.

"I'm not sure I understand what you mean," she finally said.

Luke poured the eggs into the pan he'd been warming, arranged the other ingredients, and washed his hands before he looked at her.

"You know exactly what I mean. I think maybe we're beyond the point of polite prevarication by now, don't you?"

She smiled a little. "Ooh, good word. Points for *prevarication*."

"Hey, I read. I know plenty of big words. Like *dilatory*," he said, and then he watched, fascinated, as those golden sparks appeared in her eyes again.

She toyed with the turtle-shaped salt and pepper shakers that a grateful client had once given him, and then she nodded.

"You're right. I'm delaying that conversation. But can we just let it go for now? We have more important things to talk about, and I still get flashbacks to being locked in the attic whenever I talk about my . . . *gift*."

If her face had been closed before, it was locked down and on high security alert now. He realized his hands had clenched into fists at her mention of being locked in an attic, and he forced his fingers to relax. She'd brought it up, but she'd also shut down the subject as a topic of conversation. He'd respect her wishes.

For now.

"What do you know about Bordertown?" He poured two mugs of coffee and pushed one across the counter to her.

"Pretty much what everyone does, I guess. Bordertown is made up of several square miles of territory that don't show up on any map."

She took a sip of her coffee, and Luke got distracted by watching the muscles in her lovely throat work, but the sizzle of frying eggs alerted him to a possible tragedy, and he flipped his omelet to save it from turning to charcoal.

"Right. Do you know the human New York?"

"A little. I try to avoid it," she confessed. "I always get a terrible migraine when I try to leave Bordertown, so I've never really crossed over."

"We're on the west side of Manhattan, bordered by the humans' High Line park. The magic here is native to the spot; the middle of B Town rests on the spot where the strongest ley lines in the northeast United States intersect. The place was a hub of dark forces and a haven for nonhumans long before the Dutch West India Company founded New Amsterdam."

"Were you around for that?" She glanced up at him from beneath her long lashes, and he almost thought she was flirting with him, or at least teasing him a little.

He liked the idea more than he wanted to admit.

"No, although I've been around longer than you might expect," he said wryly.

"How much longer?"

He plated the omelet, dividing it onto two plates, and gave her one of them, and then a fork and napkin.

"Too long. Back to my story. According to para-archaeologists and historians of magic, a violent tectonic shift that happened thousands of years ago caused reality to fold over on itself twice, making Bordertown the one place on earth where the human, Fae, and demon realm all collide."

She put her fork down on her plate, swallowed, and shot a skeptical glance at him. "There is no way anybody can know what happened to reality thousands of years ago, not to mention that a collision like that would almost certainly have caused a massive three-way war. By the way, this is delicious. Thank you."

"Thank you. And who says it didn't cause a war? From what I've heard and read, there *was* a massive war. The Fae and the demons slaughtered each other first and then went after the humans. That war lasted nearly a hundred years and almost decimated the continent."

Rio blinked. "Yeah, a century-long war between the Fae and the demons would do it. How do you know all this again?"

"I'm friends with some scholarly types, and Fae histories go back a very long way."

He took a break to dive into his omelet and made short work of it. Then he pulled four bottles of water out of his refrigerator, handed her one, and drank the other three in rapid succession. She watched, tilting her head to one side.

"Expecting a drought?"

He tossed the empty bottles into the recycling bin under his sink and laughed.

"No, but it would feel like my insides had fried if I didn't replenish after using fire magic like that."

He almost saw her ears perk up at that, but he shook his head. "Now it's *my* turn to tell you we'll talk about something later. For now, Bordertown. I've told you about the history, at least as far as I know it, and now we should talk about the kind of people who live in a place like this."

"People like me," she said bitterly. "People nobody else wants. People who have no place else to go."

Something in his chest twisted a little, both at her words and at the way her body had slumped when she said them. Somebody—or lots of somebodies—had hurt this woman.

Someday soon, Luke would see about tracking those people down.

He started to speak, wondering what in the hell he could say to that, when her eyes widened and her head lifted. Her head whipped to the side and she stared at the fox, who'd woken up and was watching them.

"Kit is really hungry. Starving, in fact. Would it be okay if I gave her the rest of my omelet? I seem to have lost my appetite." She made an apologetic face at her plate, which still held most of her breakfast. "It really is delicious, though, and I can't remember the last time anybody ever made breakfast for me. Thank you again."

Her wistful expression gutted him. How was it possible nobody cooked for this woman? And, hard on the heels of that thought, savage satisfaction that nobody else cooked for this woman.

He took the plate, cut the eggs into bite-sized pieces, and walked over to the fire. Anything to calm down from the conflicting, unexpected emotions that kept buffeting him where Rio was concerned.

Crouching in front of the fox, he set the plate down and nodded to the creature.

"You say her name is Kit? And you know this how?"

The fox tilted her head in an uncanny imitation of Rio's gesture, and stared at him, making no move to touch the food.

Rio shrugged and walked over to join them. "She told me. She asked me to accept her as my 'guilt gift' from Dalriata, and she said we were meant to be together."

"She told you this how, again?"

"Mentally. It was a kind of telepathic conversation, which shouldn't be all that surprising considering my . . . ability."

Rio nudged the plate closer to the fox. "Please eat. It will help you get your strength back, and then we can decide what to do. I think we need to find a veterinarian for your leg."

The fox daintily began to eat the eggs, ignoring Luke completely.

"Is she talking to you now? Commenting on the deliciousness of my eggs, for example?"

Rio smiled, and Luke thought he would be happy to talk about silly things like eggs for the rest of the day, if she would keep smiling.

"No. I don't think the communication is easy for her. I got the impression that she was extending an enormous amount of effort to talk to me in Dalriata's office."

The fox glanced up at Rio and then continued to eat.

"Kit? But you called her something else in the car." Luke continued to study the small animal, who probably had barely weighed forty pounds soaking wet. She was beautiful, in spite of being thin and starved-looking. Probably young. The magic, though—that was something he needed to figure out.

"She said her name was Kitsune, actually. Like *Kitsoon-eh*." Rio gently ran her hand down the fox's flank, apparently not worried at all that the animal would bite her.

Of course, she'd just given Kit a bath, so evidently the biting danger was over. Most wild animals appreciated baths about as much as your average teenage boy did.

Rio moved to the couch and curled up on one end, so Luke took his cue from her and sat down on the other end.

"You know *Kitsune* just means 'fox' in Japanese, right?"

She rolled her eyes. "Sorry. My Japanese is a little rusty."

Kit opened her mouth and let her tongue loll out to the side a little, as if she were laughing.

"Okay, fine," Luke said. "We have a long list of things to figure out before we get to your magical, sometimes-talking, Japanese fox."

"Like the origins of Bordertown, apparently," Rio said, pulling a pillow onto her lap and hugging it to her.

"No, now we're on to the people." Luke stretched his legs out toward the fire and thought about how to proceed. Here he was on his couch, in front of a fire, with a beautiful woman, and he was going to give her a history lesson instead of make love to her for six or seven hours.

Something about that was very wrong.

"Luke?"

He sighed. "Yeah, yeah. The people and creatures who live in and on the edges of Bordertown are generally those with a reason to avoid the mainstream—in any of their worlds. Here, disinherited Fae royalty mingle with mercenaries who were banished from the demonic realm and humans who either don't know any better or, as you said, have no place else to go."

"Which are you?" She aimed a long, measured stare at him, and it tickled the hell out of him that she didn't seem to share the fear of him that so many in town harbored.

He grinned. "I'm always the one who doesn't know better. Also, I needed to get out of Europe."

"Most people say they needed to get out of town. You say you needed to get out of *Europe*. It's an interesting difference," she said dryly.

"I have a greater propensity to piss people off than most," he admitted.

Kit finished her eggs and lightly jumped up on the couch next to Rio. She curled her tail around herself and stared intently at Luke, as if she were listening to the conversation, too.

"That's B Town. Now, the League," he continued. "Which reminds me."

He took his cell phone out of his pocket and dialed a number he'd added only the night before. "Call me. Now.

"The League of the Black Swan contacted me last night. I haven't heard from them in a very long time. Since 1745, to be precise."

Rio whistled, long and low. "1745? Exactly how old are you?"

He sighed. Here it went. The kiss of death. Sometimes honesty sucked, but for some weird reason he couldn't even figure out himself, he knew she deserved it from him.

"I was born in the year 1500. You may have heard of my mother. I'm the bastard son of Lucrezia Borgia."

Luke hunched down farther in the couch and waited for the horrified outburst. He'd never have a chance with her now that she knew about his evil bloodline and how freaking old he was.

But Rio surprised him again.

She started laughing.

CHAPTER 8

Rio tried to stop laughing. It was probably a really bad idea to laugh at a wizard in his own home, but she couldn't help it.

"So you're more than five hundred years old. That's what you're claiming?"

He wouldn't look at her but folded his arms across his chest and stared into the fire. She took a moment to admire the view. He was absolutely gorgeous. His face was all hard lines and angles, with a hint of sensuality in the curve of his lips. The muscles in his long legs were clearly defined under the blue jeans he wore, and she suddenly had a perfectly unreasonable desire to climb into his lap and kiss the hollow in the tanned perfection of his throat. Or, conversely, curl up next to him, knowing she'd always be safe near him, and take a nap.

Naturally, this made her want to run the other way. But she needed to know what he was getting at with this talk of origins and the League of the Black Swan, so she forced herself to stay put and keep her budding libido in firm check.

"Okay, old man," she joked. "Let's say you are who you

say you are, and you are as old as you say you are. It's no weirder than a giant duck, that's for sure. So let's skip over all of that for now, and move on to what you wanted to tell me about this mysterious League."

He turned his head and caught her in the full weight of that ocean-blue gaze, nearly making her gasp. Darn it, but he was beautiful. Dark-angel beautiful. Pardon-me-while-I-tear-off-my-clothes beautiful. She had an insane, nearly uncontrollable urge to run her fingers through all that wavy black hair and almost laughed when she imagined his re-action.

He raised an eyebrow at her grin, but she shook her head and motioned for him to continue.

"It's not that I want to talk about it. It's that I *need* to talk about it. Because when they contacted me? It was about you."

A goose walked over Rio's grave at that precise moment.

Or—more aptly, she supposed—a swan. A black swan. The urge to smile fled.

She rubbed her arms to keep from shivering, and Kit, as if understanding the terror that had overtaken Rio at Luke's words, turned and rested her sleek head on Rio's knee.

"Why? I'm a bike messenger. This doesn't make sense." She absently stroked the soft, slightly damp fur on the fox's back. "None of it makes sense. Merelith, the way she acted—I don't understand any of this."

Luke made a frustrated noise. "I don't understand it, either. All I know is that a very high-level operative in the League stopped by to give me a message last night, and the message was a picture of you."

"Did you ask why? Why are they coming to you, any-way? Are you in the League?" She flinched as a thought popped into her mind, and suddenly it was very hard to breathe. "Do they want you to kill me?"

"What? No! Nobody's killing anybody," Luke said firmly. "If that were what they wanted, they never would've come to me. The maestro knows better than that."

Rio's heart slowed down, but only a fraction. "If they wanted someone to kill me, they would have gone to someone else, is what you're saying by implication. In other words, the League of the Black Swan has a habit of hiring assassins."

Luke jumped up off the couch and started pacing back and forth from the fireplace to the kitchen.

"Yes. No. I don't know," he said, shoving a hand through his hair. "I don't know what they've been up to since I quit."

Rio stood up and moved so her back was to the wall next to the fireplace. Not that she had any idea how to defend herself against a wizard, but something about the position made the cornered animal inside her feel minutely better. That would be just her luck—the hottest man she'd ever seen in her life would be the one sent to murder her. She'd die an almost-virgin, since awkward fumblings in her younger, drunk experimentation stage surely didn't count.

"So you were part of the League," she said quietly. "And now?"

"I have no intention of becoming involved with the League again, but I need to know what their plans are, and why they're interested in you. I can't protect you if I don't know what's going on."

He took a step toward her, and she held her hands out to block him.

"I need to go home. Back to my apartment. Dalriata said he's not after me anymore. You just admitted you don't know what the League of the Black Swan wants with me. So, while you figure it out, I'm going back to my real life," she said, putting every ounce of defiance she could muster behind the statement.

Kit, still seated on the couch, yipped.

Right.

"And I'm taking my fox with me," she blurted out.

Of course, then Rio felt like an idiot, and the grin quirking at the corners of Luke's mouth didn't help.

"It's a bad idea," he said. "The League usually gets what

it wants, and it never stops when it's after something or someone. I know how they work. Let me protect you from them."

"What exactly is this damn League, anyway?"

"The League is supposed to function like a supernatural police force. Back in 1300, the Knights Templar joined forces with the Summer Court Fae to defeat a bunch of demons who were trying to break free from what everybody thought was the mythological underworld."

Rio nodded. "Okay, but now we know the demons have their own realm that has nothing to do with Hades, hell, or any of our human beliefs."

"Right. But it didn't matter at that point. The League's *stated* mission ever since has been to protect humanity from evil, help the various supernatural factions negotiate treaties and keep the peace, and generally work as a force for good in the world."

"You said *stated* mission," she said slowly. "What's their real mission?"

Luke threw his hands in the air. "I have no freaking idea. A megalomaniac took over the League back in the mid-1700s, and his goal was to conquer the world in a way that Alexander the Great never could have dreamed of, because this jerk had magic on his side. I left, came here, and never looked back. The last thing I ever expected to hear again was *Black Swan*."

Rio thought about it and realized that none of it mattered. She needed to get out, get back to her normal life, and stop playing games with wizards, kings, Fae, and supernatural justice leagues.

For some weird reason, Wonder Woman popped into her mind, and she almost laughed.

"I'm leaving. I'm taking my fox. You should have my cell phone number on file from the delivery service, so you can call me—well, if the phone company gives me a new phone with my same number—if something comes up I need to know, but right now I can't take any more of this. I hope you understand."

She scanned the room for her backpack before remembering that it was still out in the office.

"I understand, but I don't agree. I think you should stay here where I can protect you until we figure this out," he said.

"You're the Dark Wizard of Bordertown. You'll figure it all out, I hope."

"*Hope* is exactly the wrong word, Rio. This is Bordertown. Most of the people who live here don't hope—they never hope. That's a fragile and precious commodity in this town."

Rio couldn't accept that. If not hope, then what? A never-ending circle of drudgery and helplessness? Lives lived unnoticed, in the interstitial spaces between survival and despair?

No. It wasn't enough. It could never be enough. Not even for an orphan whose only clues to her parents were a tarnished silver locket and a tiny stuffed fox.

She lifted her chin and tried to stare down the most dangerous predator she'd ever met. The fact that he'd made her eggs helped a little. The fact that he was so damn sexy made it hurt.

"Are you refusing to let me go?"

"No, of course not. But I want to be very clear that you have a place here, anytime you need it. If anything the slightest bit weird or dangerous happens, call me or come back. I'll reset the wards so they let you in whether I'm here or not."

She tried not to notice the way he was clenching his jaw, probably against yelling at her. She got that a lot. She also tried not to notice the lines of strain that had appeared on his face, probably from worrying about her.

She never got that at all.

Eileen, the receptionist, office manager, veterinary assistant, and all-around general everything at Dr. Black's animal hospital, squeezed Kit in to an appointment between an elderly ocelot and a flatulent bulldog. Rio had delivered urgent test results to the office often enough that she knew how much of a favor it was. The practice was extremely busy because everyone said Dr. Black was the best veterinarian in town.

The rumor was that she and her husband, who was also now Dr. Black, could both speak to animals and understand their responses. But the original Dr. Black had a special gift; she could visualize what was wrong inside her patients' furry, scaly, and feathery bodies.

Dr. Black the original smiled at Rio across the metal table on which Kit was stretched.

"She's going to be just fine," the veterinarian said. "It was just a sprain, not a break, and a mild one at that. As you can see, I've wrapped the leg and given her something for the pain."

Kit had winced when the doctor inserted the needle, but she hadn't moved at all or growled even a little. Rio was absurdly proud of her for that.

The woman lightly rested her hand on Kit and closed her eyes briefly. When she opened them, she smiled again. "Yes, definitely. We'll give you a few pills, in case she has any residual pain, but she should be perfectly healthy in a day or two."

"Thank you so much, Dr. Black, for fitting us in, and for taking such good care of Kit. I was really worried," Rio said.

"You should be worried," the vet said sternly. "Do you want to explain to me exactly how you let this lovely girl get so thin? Have you been starving her?"

Dr. Black's eyes lightened to a pale, feral yellow, and Rio began to worry for her own health if she didn't do some explaining, fast.

"I only rescued her today from a very bad man who had her chained to a desk. I promise I'm on the way to buy food for her, and I already gave her my breakfast," she said quickly.

The vet looked to Kit, as if for confirmation, and Kit

must have vouched for Rio, because the vet's eyes darkened back to a more human color and the muscles in her shoulders relaxed.

"Good job on you, then." Dr. Black awkwardly patted Rio's arm, and Rio suddenly had the amusing thought that the vet didn't quite know how to interact with nonanimal creatures.

"I promise I'll take good care of her," Rio said.

As she said the words, she realized they were true. She had been worried about the little fox, and she was already far more attached to her than made any sense at all. Maybe it was because they had both escaped the unwanted and unsavory attentions of the Pict king.

"Yes, yes," Dr. Black murmured, waving Rio's thanks aside. "She's a beautiful creature—an absolutely superb specimen of her kind. I'd guess she's about two years old."

"Kit, how old are you?" Rio looked into the little fox's eyes, but Kit wasn't answering.

"She's not saying," Rio told Dr. Black. "I'm sorry."

Dr. Black raised one eyebrow, but it was Bordertown, so she didn't ask any questions.

"Bring her back if she has any further problems. Eileen will give you the pain pills and a list of recommended diet and the like, in case you've never dealt with foxes before."

With that, the vet was clearly done with the human portion of the appointment, and she bent down to coo in Kit's ear. Rio didn't catch all of it, but "my beautiful little girl" was in there, and Kit was obviously loving every moment of it. Rio grinned at the back of the doctor's white coat as the woman left the room to go treat her next patient.

"I like her," she told Kit.

The little fox sat up on the table and panted, almost giving the impression that she was agreeing.

Rio briefly enjoyed the feeling of a task completed as she paid Eileen for the visit and tucked the written materials and little envelope of pain pills into her backpack. Kit insisted on walking, or at least that seemed to be pretty clearly what all the squirming and wiggling to get down had been about, so the two of them headed out on their own six feet for the next part of Rio's plan: buying a new cell phone.

The phone was easy—B Town Cellular even gave her an upgrade and the same phone number. Unfortunately, part three of her plan didn't go nearly as well as expected.

"I can't believe she evicted me," Rio told Kit for about the twelfth time.

She figured it might take another twelve before it finally sank in. Her landlady—and, she'd thought, her friend—had looked Rio right in the eyes and lied like a banshee on a bender.

No room. I thought you'd moved out. Did we agree that you were coming back next year, maybe the year after, dear?

Oddly enough, Mrs. G hadn't given up on her lame excuses until Kit, who'd been lurking behind Rio's ankles, had yipped up at her. Mrs. G had inhaled sharply and backed away from the threshold of her doorway.

"Where did you get a Yokai? Is she Zenko or Yako?" she'd demanded.

"Her name is Kit, and other than that I have no idea what you're talking about."

After that, the conversation had deteriorated until Rio had finally shoved Mrs. G's envelope of cash back at her, nodded numbly when her landlady had mentioned storing Rio's things until she got settled, and then taken her bike and wandered almost blindly off down the street. Now they were sitting on a bench in front of the bike store while Jeff installed a basket on the handlebars that was deep enough for Kit to use, and Rio still wasn't sure what had just happened.

"She evicted me," Rio mumbled, feeling shell-shocked.

Kit nudged Rio's arm with her nose, then stared left

toward the end of the street. Rio started to shake her head, but then the realization hit her over the head like a thunder god's hammer. The end of the street.

The end of Tchaikovsky Street, where the Black Swan Fountain burbled merrily away. The centerpiece of the square where lovers gathered and children played in the water all year long. Black Swan Fountain, Black Swan League—somebody was racking up the poultry and they were all arrayed against her.

Do not forget the duck, Kit sent solemnly, and when Jeff came out with her bike, Rio was cracking up.

"You sound like a hyena shifter on nitrous oxide, and let me tell you, I *never* want to run into one of those again," Jeff said, grimacing. "I've been too traumatized to go back to the dentist ever since."

Naturally that image, or maybe the combined stress of the past couple of days, or both, made Rio laugh even harder.

Kit fit perfectly in the basket and seemed content to ride along watching everything, wrapped in Rio's spare jacket. The rain had blown over and the day was actually pretty gorgeous; a crisp fall day with sunbeams slanting across the street to fall in mud puddles as if illuminating jewels.

So Rio was in a pretty cheerful mood when she moved on to the final part of her day's plan, right up to the point where she walked in the door and waved to her boss.

"You're fired."

CHAPTER 9

Rio lifted Kit out of the basket, rolled her bike into the space tucked behind the front corner of the Roadhouse, and set her bike lock. Not that it mattered if anybody stole the bike at this point. She didn't have a job to need it for.

"Well, it's five o'clock somewhere," she told Kit, almost apologizing, before she realized that carrying on a conversation with a fox had to look a little bit nuts.

There weren't very many people inside the Roadhouse. Rio looked around, interested, to see what other kind of people hung out in a bar in the middle of the afternoon. It was pretty much what she expected. A few seedy-looking Winter Fae played pool in one corner, six or seven goblins huddled around a big-screen TV in the back watching the rugby game and offering loud, creative, and obscene suggestions as to how the players could do a better job, and Clarice was at the bar, undoubtedly doling out drinks and astonishingly bad advice to the lovelorn, as usual.

Miro was nowhere to be seen, which was probably for the best. She briefly wondered if he'd had indigestion from the barbecue of the night before, but then a wave of nausea pushed the random thought out of her mind.

"Hello, Clarice," she intoned in her best sepulchral, Hannibal Lecter tone.

Clarice, a short, curvy, sparkling-eyed ball of optimism, groaned. "I've never heard that one before. Like, for example, every single time you walk in here."

"I figured you'd hear it from everybody," Rio said. "Does anybody watch the greats anymore?"

"Nobody in Bordertown cares about watching horror movies, Rio, when half the time we are all living in one. Or, at least, in a freak show. Did you hear about the duck?"

Rio started laughing. "I *saw* the duck. What happened to the egg?"

Clarice pointed to the Jeggleston Ale tap, and Rio nodded. "Yes, and make it a tall one. You would not believe the day I had. May I also have a bowl of water for my pal here?"

Clarice stood on tiptoe and peeked over the bar until she could see Kit sitting on Rio's jacket. "Did you find a new friend? She's gorgeous."

Rio glanced down at Kit, whom she could swear was preening at the attention. "I think she's a little vain, too," she whispered.

Kit bared her teeth, and Rio grinned. At least one of them was having an okay day.

Clarice slid the tall glass of ale across the bar, and Rio took a long drink. By the time Clarice came back from the kitchen with a bowl of water, Rio had downed almost half of the beer. When she stepped off the bar stool to bend down and give Kit the water, the room wobbled a little bit.

"Whoa. I think I need food. How about a hamburger platter—wait."

Rio fumbled in her backpack for the paper Dr. Black had given her. It didn't say anything about hamburgers being forbidden, and Kit looked hungry, too. At least as far as Rio could read the facial expression of a fox she'd only known for a few hours.

"Make that two hamburger platters, but no bun on the second one. Probably no French fries either."

Kit growled a little, and Rio rolled her eyes. "Fine, already. She wants French fries, too."

Clarice's eyes widened, and it was at least three full beats before she responded. "Suddenly you're talking to a fox," she finally said.

Rio drained the rest of her glass and held it up for a refill.

"Let me tell you about my day," she said to her best friend. "I think you'll be surprised I'm not heading straight for the whiskey."

Nearly an hour later, Rio was dragging her final, lonely French fry through ketchup as she finished her story. Kit, her own hamburger and a few of her fries long gone, was sleeping curled up on Rio's jacket on the floor.

When Rio looked up, Clarice, who'd pulled up her own bar stool a good half hour previously and yelled at the busboy to cover the bar, was staring at Rio with her mouth hanging open.

"Say something already," Rio pleaded. "I can't figure out what I'm supposed to do."

Clarice's mouth opened and closed a few times, she bobbed her head, and her red curls bounced around as if even her hair were shocked at the story.

"You slept with Luke Oliver?"

Rio wildly scanned the immediate vicinity to see who'd heard, but nobody seemed to be paying any attention to them, and Bobby the busboy was at the other end of the bar, trying to flirt with a water demon who had huge breasts. Of course, when you could manipulate water, you could pretty much conjure your double Ds whenever you wanted them, but that was *so not the point*.

Crap.

"Really? I just spent an hour telling you my story—a story in which I nearly died, I might add—and *that's* where you want to go with it?"

Clarice blinked. "You slept with *Luke Oliver*?"

Rio reached over, grabbed her friend by the shoulders,

and gave her a little shake. "Snap out of it. I did not sleep with him the way you make it sound. There was no naked. There was no panting or moaning. There was only *sleeping*, and it's because we were both sort of injured at the time."

"You slept—" Clarice blinked again, and then she finally seemed to snap out of it. "Okay, okay. But don't blame me for being freaked out when you tell me you slept with one of the hottest guys in town—the same guy you had a full-blown crush on not too long ago, by the way."

Rio felt her cheeks heating up. "It wasn't a crush. You make it sound so junior high. It was more of an . . . attraction."

"Riiight. An attraction in which you lovingly described his utter hotness to me every single time you had a delivery to his office," Clarice retorted.

"I won't be doing that anymore." Rio slumped in her seat, folded her arms, and pillowed her head on them on the gleaming bar. "I don't have a job. Or a place to live, for that matter."

Clarice waved a hand. "You can bunk with me—you and your adorable furry friend, by the way—and you know it. And jobs in Bordertown are easy to come by, since nobody but a few fools like you and me want actual, legitimate work."

"That's not the point, although I appreciate the offer of a place to crash," Rio said glumly. "I've lost everything in less than forty-eight hours, and I think this League of the Black Swan that nobody admits to knowing about is to blame."

"I assure you, we had nothing to do with it," a deep male voice said from so close behind Rio that she jumped and spilled a little of the coffee she'd switched to after the second glass of ale.

Clarice's glare turned to a speculative smile when she turned around to see who had interrupted them, which made Rio almost afraid to look. But they'd picked the wrong bike messenger if they thought she was a coward. She pushed the thought of running screaming for the door out of her mind and slowly faced the man who claimed to be part of the very organization that was ruining Rio's life.

"They call me Maestro," he said, holding out a hand.

At Rio's feet, Kit growled, fierce and low.

"How nice for you. They call me Empress of the World, but that and five bucks will get me a cup of coffee," she shot back. "My fox doesn't like you. Please step back."

"We need to talk," he said calmly, but at least he did step back a pace. "And that is almost certainly not *your* fox. Interesting that she chooses to be with you, however."

"Oh, and nothing good ever came out of those four words," Clarice said. "*We need to talk.* I don't think so, Buster. Rio, do you want me to call Miro or get the shotgun?"

Maestro turned his gaze to Clarice, and his lips twitched in what might, by the longest possible stretch of the imagination, be considered a smile.

"Allow me," he said.

The bar shotgun floated up over the counter and hovered in front of Clarice, who narrowed her eyes and snatched it out of the air.

"I hope you don't think that's impressive," she said, as she whirled on her stool to point the gun at the floor in Maestro's direction. "This is Bordertown, not Vegas. I get six more impressive stunts than that in here every evening before midnight."

The man—or whatever he was—laughed, and Rio flinched. That was not a laugh she wanted to hear ever again, under any circumstances. The sound made her think of death by suffocation under a ton of heavy rock. He, like Luke, looked a little like a pirate, but whereas she could see Luke commanding the ship and standing, tall and elegant, in the bow, complete with silk shirt and sword, this man would be the thuggish second-in-command who was always plotting mutiny and betrayal.

Or maybe Rio needed to cut down on the pirate romance novels.

"May I at least have a moment of your time?" He gestured to a booth that was relatively secluded from the rest of the room. "I assure you I will not harm you in any way."

Kit's growling increased in volume, but Rio was desperate for answers. She was in a public place, after all. What could he do?

Clarice made a *tsk*ing sound with her teeth. "Don't do it. Don't even think about it. Remember the Kelpie invasion of 2010?"

"I have to find out why they're hijacking my life, Clarice. Watch Kit for me?"

Kit's growling instantly stopped, and she rose and stalked over to the booth and hopped up on one bench.

"I think your fox has other ideas," Clarice said dryly. "Let me know if you need me to shoot him."

Maestro laughed and waved a hand, and a spinning roulette wheel appeared on top of the table nearest to them.

"You mentioned Vegas, I believe?"

While Clarice gaped at the roulette wheel, and the goblins loped over to see what was going on, Rio slowly followed Maestro to the table, wondering if she was making yet another mistake in a life that had been filled with so many.

"It's only a few days until your birthday," he said abruptly, as he sat down.

She gaped at him. "How could you—why—"

"The League keeps track of important dates. You'll be turning twenty-five, and we have an offer for you. Join us." He leaned back against the leather bench and stared intently at her.

Kit almost fell out of her seat. In a million possible realities, she never would have seen that one coming. They didn't want to assassinate her. They wanted to recruit her.

Kit growled, baring her teeth, and Rio shushed her.

"Why?" Why was the League interested in her birthday, why had a High Court Fae been interested in her birthday, and why was her world turning upside down?

"I can't tell you that yet," he said bluntly. "I can, however, offer you incentives."

"Like what? Chocolate cake with sprinkles?"

"Sarcasm doesn't become you, young lady," he said. "But if you really want a cake . . ."

An enormous slice of chocolate cake, complete with sprinkles, appeared on a plate in front of her. Temptation had never smelled so good.

"And Eve got Adam with a mere apple," she said mockingly, pushing the cake aside.

Kit's tongue shot out, and she licked a swath through the icing.

"Kit! We don't know if that's poisoned," Rio hissed.

Maestro sighed. "First, why would I poison you when I'm trying to recruit you? Second, the *Yokai* would never ingest a poisoned substance. Finally, I have no wish to go to war with Lucian Olivieri, and if I harmed you in any way, he'd spend the rest of his immortality trying to kill me."

Immortality? Now that was interesting. Rio also silently filed *Lucian Olivieri* away in her memory to ask Luke about, since Merelith had used the name, too, and she resolved to hit the Internet to find out what in the heck a *Yokai* was, as soon as she had a chance. In the meantime, she needed to deal with this guy.

"Why is my birthday important? Is November ninth even my real birthday? Do you know my real name? Rio is just a name I picked for myself because the nuns called me Mary and I didn't like it. I wanted—"

"You wanted something unique," he said softly, watching her with something that looked almost like compassion. "I know quite a lot about you, Rio, but there are certain things I've sworn not to disclose outside the oath of secrecy the members of the League of the Black Swan swear at induction. You're nearly twenty-five, which means you can choose to join us now."

"Are you the one who got me evicted and fired?"

He shrugged. "You're better off at Luke's, and you definitely don't need that job."

The sheer high-handedness left her speechless for a minute. "What right do you have to decide any of that?

"Over by the bar, you said you didn't ruin my life," she reminded him. "Were you lying then or are you lying now?"

"I don't consider it ruining your life. I consider it presenting you with better opportunities."

She wanted to blast him with words so harsh he'd shake in his shoes, but she just didn't have it in her anymore. Instead, she shook her head, weary of all of it.

"I've spent the past two days caught up in the games of men who plot bad things and hire others to carry them out. I have no reason to trust you or your League. I can't tell if you're lying to me—"

But then it hit her. She could. Or at least she might be able to tell.

"Let me inside your head," she demanded. "You want me to believe any of this BS, then fine. Let me read your thoughts."

A slow smile spread across his face, and she had the terrible thought that she'd just fallen into the middle of the web he'd been spinning for her since he'd first walked in the bar. Or since way before that, considering what Luke and Dalriata had said.

"Go ahead," he invited.

She shook her head and started to scoot out of the booth. "On second thought, maybe I'll pass. I'm not much of a joiner, and—"

His hand flashed out and caught her arm. "I know who your parents are."

All the air vanished from Rio's lungs and she collapsed back onto the bench, trying desperately to inhale. "You son of a bitch."

"Yes."

"You could have led with that."

"I considered it more of a trump card."

They stared at each other across the table so hard and for so long that everyone else in the bar seemed to disappear.

"Are you still willing to let me look inside your mind?" She realized her fingers hurt and looked down to see that she'd been digging her nails into the tabletop so hard that they'd left scratches.

"Go ahead." He closed his eyes and made a come-ahead gesture with his fingers.

Rio kept her own eyes open, but she threw everything she had at him. The reality of the bar dissolved around her, and she found herself standing in an empty circular room surrounded by gray stone walls. An icy cold breeze shivered through the room, although there were no windows. Rio whirled around in a 360-degree circle and realized there weren't any doors, either.

"Cliché, much?" She put her hands on her hips. "This is your mind? Fairly empty for somebody who calls himself Maestro."

A banner unfurled and draped itself down a good half of the room. Scarlet letters painted on white silk mocked her:
I Know Who Your Parents Are.

She smacked herself, hard, in the forehead with the heel of her hand and instantly snapped out of the vision or fugue state into which he'd enticed her. The smell of beer, chocolate cake, and unwashed goblin swept over her in a nauseating mix, and she jumped up from the table and raced for the door.

Fresh air, she needed *fresh air*, now, now, *now*, or she was going to be sick all over the top bully of the League of the Black Swan. She made it to the door and shoved it open, but then her knees gave out and she toppled forward, face first, toward the sidewalk.

Strong hands caught her as she fell, and for the second time in two days she heard Luke's voice as she was escaping the Roadhouse.

"We've got to stop meeting like this."

CHAPTER 10

Luke frowned and wondered what or whom he needed to kill this time. Rio's face was whiter than the chalk he'd once used to set magical circles, before he'd learned to do it with a thought. The fierce desire to protect her ate at his insides. Why the hell had he ever let her out of his house? The dark predator leashed inside him howled savagely, and Luke clenched his jaw against letting it loose.

"You—how?"

"Clarice called me," he said, answering the question he thought she was trying to ask. "She said somebody was threatening you. And I'm glad she did, since you didn't show any signs of letting me know you needed help. I should buy that bartender a car."

Rio leaned her face against his chest, and his arms automatically came up to wrap around her soft, warm curves. His body reacted so fast and so hard to the sensation that he had to fight to keep from embarrassing himself with an erection. She surrendered to the embrace for the length of several heartbeats, but then she pulled away, leaving him with a sense of loss and a hollow pang in his chest.

"I'm fine. It was just bar smells; suddenly they got to me, and your pal Maestro was playing games with my head, which didn't help."

Primal, uncontainable rage seared through Luke, and he moved past Rio and slammed the Roadhouse door open, barely missing the fox, who yelped and leapt out of the way.

"Sorry, Kit," Luke growled, and damn if the little creature didn't incline her head, as if she understood and forgave him.

Rio rushed in and picked up Kit, apologizing to the fox. "I'm so sorry, oh my gosh, please forgive me. I thought I was going to be sick, and I'm not used to worrying about anybody but myself, and—"

The fox stopped the flow of words by the simple method of licking the side of Rio's face in one long slurp. It surprised Rio into a little burble of a laugh, which brought some color back to her face, so Luke felt a moment of affection for the fox lighten his fury.

Briefly.

Then he turned to face the bar, fire already glowing at his fingertips, and nodded to Clarice, who was pointing a shotgun at the shadowed booth near the back.

"He's over there, Mr. Wizard, er, Mr. Oliver," the little red-haired bartender called out. "Miro's on the way, too, if you need help."

Luke headed toward the booth, barely sparing a thought for the new roulette wheel, which he was almost sure hadn't been there before.

"Maestro, you may as well stand up, because you and I are going to have this out right now," he snarled as he strode across the room, his boot heels sounding like cracks of thunder on the wooden floor.

But Maestro was gone, and he'd left behind a gift. A giant seven-layered birthday cake that said *Happy Birthday, Rio* and *I Know* in pink letters on white frosting graced the top of the table.

Rio walked up behind him and blew out a huge breath. "He has a thing for cake."

Clarice walked up behind them, holding out a glass of Luke's favorite whiskey, and he nodded his thanks before draining it in one long gulp.

"Nice cake," the bartender remarked. "He gave me a roulette wheel."

"I'm buying you a car," Luke said.

"I don't drive, but tickets to the Bordertown Opera would be nice," Clarice said, grinning. She thought he'd been kidding. He hadn't.

He snapped his fingers, and an envelope appeared in his hand. He handed it to Clarice, whose mouth fell open.

"Thanks for calling me," Luke told Clarice. "If he shows up again, let me know right away, and I'll convince him that he'd rather be somewhere else."

She nodded, clutching the envelope. She thanked him, but he caught her staring at his hands, which were still glowing, and he released his hold on the magic. The bartender blew out a breath and headed back toward the bar, leaving him alone to face Rio.

"Are those really opera tickets?"

He shrugged. "I know a guy."

"I found out what he wanted, Maestro," she said, staring down at the cake. Kit hopped down from her arms onto the bench and delicately licked a pink icing rose.

"Icing is definitely not on the vet's list," Rio said reprovingly.

The fox immediately sat down and pretended to be occupied cleaning the fur on her front left paw.

"Bandages, not a cast. So it's not broken?" Luke pointed to Kit's leg.

"Just a sprain. Aren't you going to ask?"

"Do you want me to ask?" He wanted to demand she tell him everything, every word, every gesture, that the maestro had said and done. He wanted to whisk her back to his place and tie her up—preferably naked—for the next five or ten years.

He knew better, so he waited for her to tell him.

"He wants to recruit me. Into the League."

She finally looked up and stared into his eyes, and he immediately lost track of what they were talking about. The golden glow of her eyes trapped him like a dragonfly in amber, and he understood the futility of trying to struggle. He cast about for something relevant to say.

"You're still wearing my shirt," he said stupidly.

She glanced down. "Ah, yeah. This is what you want to talk about? My clothing choices?"

"I thought you were going back to your apartment," he said. "I figured you'd change your clothes. So now I'm wondering if something went wrong at your place."

"No, my place was great. Well, other than the part where I got evicted," she said bitterly. "It was almost as much fun as when I went to my job and got fired."

Luke wanted to blast something. Hard. "What happened?"

"Your *friend* happened," she said, and he could hear the accusation in her voice.

"He's not my friend. He said hello to me yesterday by stabbing me with a silver knife," he told her. "Do you want to stay here, or can we go to my place and sit down and talk about all this?"

"Why not? I don't have anywhere else to go," she said, throwing her hands in the air in defeat.

Defeat wasn't an emotion he wanted to see on her face or in the slumped line of her shoulders. Not now, and not ever again. He started thinking up ways he could protect her from everything bad in the universe and realized his mental inventory was starting to look a lot like a list of people he'd need to kill.

Not good.

It wouldn't help Rio if she wound up needing protection from *him*, after he turned dark because he was trying to take care of *her*.

Damned if he did and damned if he didn't had never sounded so true.

❋

They took his Jeep to his place, after Luke paid a kid ten bucks to ride her bicycle over. On the drive, she told him everything that Maestro had said to her. Luke caught himself slamming his fist against the steering wheel and forced himself to stop. There was no need to scare Rio into thinking he'd gone over the deep end.

"But what I don't know and don't understand is why the League would want me. I don't know why everyone is so interested in my birthday, either. I don't know what significance twenty-five years old has. I don't even know if he's lying about knowing who my parents are," she said, her hands clenched together on her lap. "Argh. That's a lot of 'don't know,' isn't it?"

"I don't know any of that either, except for the significance of twenty-five years," he said, leading the way into his office. "The quarter-century mark is important to several magical traditions. It's also a major birthday for the Fae, who consider a child finally grown to adult independence at that age."

Rio opened the door to his living quarters, and a warm feeling of contentment spread through him at the idea that she was comfortable enough with him to act so at home. Maybe he should just ask her to move in with him right now. She could start out in the guest room, until he had time to figure out how to be charming and romantic and whatever else women wanted.

"Okay, then we know why the birthday is important, but why, specifically, is *my* birthday important? Why did Merelith even know anything about it? Why did she call me a Halfling?" Rio scowled, yanking him out of his fantasies of waking up next to her for the next twenty or thirty or hundred years.

He decided to be useful while he thought about it. He poured a bowl of water for Kit and put it on the floor, and then he stood watching the little fox daintily drink about half of it while he considered Rio's questions.

"I have no idea. None of this makes sense to me. The only way any—wait. Is there any chance your parents were Fae?"

Rio's face drained of all color, and she sank down into the overstuffed chair next to his couch, as if she'd lost the ability to stand upright.

"I have no idea who my parents were. I have two things that the nuns claimed came with me to the orphanage. A necklace and a little stuffed animal." She glanced at Kit. "Oddly enough, the stuffed animal is a fox."

"I'm not a big fan of coincidence, especially as the explanation for any fact in a mystery, but even I have to admit that the stuffed animal thing sounds like one." Luke grabbed a couple of bottles of water and headed over to sit down on the couch next to her.

"The important question, I guess, is what am I going to do? Maestro didn't even try to deny that he was the one who got me fired. Fired and evicted, for that matter. I can't imagine that he'll let me find any other job without exerting this unbelievable influence he seems to have in order to keep me unemployed."

Rio stared at the floor and then suddenly, in spite of the topic, she smiled. "Is that a brand-new cushion for Kit?"

They both watched as the fox turned around three times and curled up in the little pet bed he'd found at the store when he'd bought the bowls for food and water, the brush, the shampoo, and the freezer box of recommended fox food. Luke shrugged and pretended he was only imagining feeling the tips of his ears heating up.

"It's no big deal. I happened to drive past the pet store, and they were having a sale, and I thought if you stopped back by, Kit might be more comfortable in that than on the floor."

He scratched the back of his neck and changed the subject. "What I don't get is why Maestro had you evicted. What could he possibly gain from that?"

"You tell me. He wanted me to move in with you. How

exactly does that work? Is the League of the Black Swan suddenly your tenant pimp?"

Luke almost laughed, but the look on her face warned him not to do it, and he realized that he cared—cared quite a lot—what she thought of him. He was sinking into quicksand with this woman; slowly going under. Defiant and in denial with one breath, and wishing it would happen faster with the next.

"Soon it will be all over but for the sucking noises," he told Kit mournfully.

He could have sworn that the little fox laughed up at him.

"I have no idea why he'd want you to move in with me, but for once, I have to agree with the man. For whatever reason, dangerous people are suddenly very interested in you. You'd be safer here than anywhere else, at least until we get this figured out."

Luke's cell phone rang before Rio could answer him, and he wisely kept from making any comments about being saved by the bell.

"Oliver."

The voice on the other end was frantic. "I've got demons fighting in my shop! Help! They're destroying half my merchandise."

"Who is this?"

"Connor Kinney, down at the potions shop. Oliver, I can't—"

A loud crash interrupted whatever Kinney had been about to say, and Luke pulled the phone away from his ear a little. Rio raised her eyebrow, and Luke held up one finger to ask her to wait a minute.

Kinney came back on the line. "Never mind," he said, panting heavily. "They left. No thanks to you. When the fuck are you going to just accept the sheriff's job and be done with it? Things are getting worse and worse around here."

Before Luke could answer, Kinney hung up.

Luke dropped his phone on the couch next to him and

tried to ignore the throbbing that had taken up residence in the middle of his forehead.

"What was that about?"

"People seem to have the mistaken impression that they should call me instead of the sheriff's office when they have problems," Luke growled. "I've turned down that job over and over again. They can't sneak me into it through the back door, either."

"Why?" She tilted her head to one side in what he was fast coming to recognize as her expression of frank curiosity. "Clearly, you're the best person for the job. Nobody would mess with you, and the ones who were stupid enough to try would learn their lesson. Don't you think you ought to do your civic duty?"

He barked out something that approached a laugh. "Civic duty, my ass. Look how well that worked out for Wyatt Earp."

Rio pulled her legs up onto the chair and wrapped her arms around her knees. Luke tried not to notice how nicely she filled out her jeans, but it was a losing proposition. She was in trouble, and he was turning into a horny lecher. He was going to the special hell.

"How about this? You stay here. In one of the guest rooms," he added, when she shot him a look. "You stay here until things calm down. It's almost your birthday, right? We get you past that, nothing happens, and you can go back to your normal life."

She started laughing. "Oh, sure, rich boy. Maybe you rack up a big pile of savings when you live for five hundred years, but some of us have to work for a living. I can't afford to wait a week before I get another job. I need to pay my cell phone bill and rent a new apartment, which means security deposits on rent and utilities, and I have about enough in the bank to cover maybe half that. Bike messengers are not exactly rolling in money."

Luke winced and felt like a complete ass. It had been a few centuries since he'd had to worry about money, it was true. He kept the front office looking dingy deliberately, so as not to scare off his typical clientele, who were people who didn't have a lot of money to offer him to help them solve their problems. But he could afford to have nice things in his home, and he looked around, trying to see his place through her eyes, and wondered what she thought of him.

The perfect solution popped into his brain, and he whooped triumphantly, making Kit open one eye for long enough to see that all was well before she went back to sleep.

"You can work for me."

Rio slowly lifted her head from her knees and hit him with a glare so hot he was surprised it didn't set his couch on fire.

"I'm not a whore," she snapped. "Is that the kind of work you had in mind?"

"What the hell led you straight to that?" He was honestly baffled, and a little bit pissed off, and he figured it showed on his face because she looked embarrassed.

"I'm sorry. You've been nothing but helpful to me, and I shouldn't think the worst of you. It's just that I've had offers before, to 'leave all this hard work behind,' and it was almost always so I could take up a position in somebody's bed."

He could read every bit of how much it had cost her in pride and shame to admit that, in the way her shoulders tightened and she held her head perfectly straight.

"Well, that's not me. But if you want to give me a list of names, I'd be glad to beat some sense into the ones who offended you like that," he told her.

Kit lifted her head from her new cushiony bed and growled, as if in agreement, and pieces suddenly clicked in Luke's brain. He leaned down to look closely at the animal.

"How many tails do you have?"

The fox tilted her head and looked at Luke as if he'd finally done something interesting. She stood up and waved her single tail in the air, quite deliberately, and then she lay back down.

"How many tails were you expecting?" Rio asked, smiling a little. "Also, thank you for changing the subject. I'm on to you and your secret chivalry, but I'm happy to let you pretend you're just a gruff guy."

Luke wanted to kiss her when she smiled at him. He also wanted to kiss her when she was sad, to cheer her up, and when she was angry, to calm her down. Basically, he was falling like an iron cauldron dropped off a cliff, and the whole idea of it freaked him completely the hell out, so he ignored it.

"I think she might be a *Yokai*, and from what I remember, they can have up to thirteen tails."

"You're the third person to say that to me, and I haven't had a chance to go online. What's a *Yokai*?" Rio slipped out of her chair to sit on the floor, and she reached out a hand to stroke Kit's long tail.

"A kind of supernatural entity with special powers. Kit has already proven she's no ordinary fox, and her name— Kitsune—seems to point us in the direction of her being a *Yokai*. Now we sit back and wait to see if she leans toward the helpful, benevolent kind or the willful, mischievous kind," he said, privately betting on the latter.

It was the way his luck had been running.

Rio stared at Kit for a minute or two, and then she shrugged. "Whichever it is, she's not saying. So I'm just going to go with *fox* for now, and worry about the rest later."

Luke watched Rio, sitting at his feet with the fox, and told himself all the reasons why pulling her onto his lap and kissing the breath out of her was a bad idea. The problem was, the predator inside the thin veneer of civilization he wore around him like an easily discarded coat didn't agree with him at all.

Luke Oliver knew that if anything were to happen with him and Rio at some point in the future, he needed to take it slow.

Lucian Olivieri wanted to lick every inch of her creamy pale skin and then take her right there on the couch, lying on the shreds of the clothes he'd ripped off her.

The Borgias take what they want; the phrase had been the lyrics to the lullabies of his childhood. And deep down where it counted, he was a true Borgia. The curse never let him forget it. His mother's enemy had cursed Lucrezia's unborn son with immortality, to be lived out under the threat of a horrific fate: If his actions ever veered from the path of goodness and justice—if he showed even a hint of the true Borgia nature, in other words—he would be cast into darkness forever.

It would be difficult for Rio to enjoy a future with a man who'd lost his soul.

He shoved up off the couch and walked away from her, before he could do something that they would both regret.

"Where are you going?" she asked.

"I'm heading out to grab some Chinese food for us, and then we're going to eat, and I'm going to tell you all about how to become a private investigator."

For once, she was speechless, and he managed to make his escape. It was going to be an interesting couple of weeks.

CHAPTER 11

The door next to the kitchen slammed open, and Charlize Theron walked in, dressed in black leather and carrying a black duffel bag and three cloth tote bags from Dragon's Eye Market.

Rio had been sitting on the couch dividing her time between wistful thoughts of how unbelievably sexy Luke was, even when he was ticked off, and anxious thoughts of what to do about the grenade the League had tossed into the middle of her life. An Academy Award–winning movie star showing up with groceries was just the slightest bit unexpected.

"Who the hell are you?" Charlize barked out, and Rio flinched. Kit jumped up on the back of the couch and stared at the newcomer, growling.

"I'm Rio. This is Kit. We're friends of Luke's, and you—you—"

"Well, are you going to help me with these groceries or just sit there with your thumb up your ass?" With that, Charlize slung her duffel across two bar stools, put the grocery bags on the kitchen counter, and headed back out the door. "I'll get the rest. You unpack."

Rio's mouth fell open as she watched the woman stalk back out the door. "Kit, I think I've just hit my quota of weird for, maybe, the rest of my lifetime. The giant duck was more normal than this."

Kit yipped, as if agreeing, but didn't seem overly concerned. Rio jumped up and headed for the kitchen before she could get yelled at again. The actress returned, carrying three more bags, dropped them on the counter, slammed the door shut, and headed down the hall. "I'm going for a shower. Tell Luke not to touch those filets or I'll kick his ass."

Rio, in the process of studying an odd-looking green leafy vegetable and wondering what in the heck it might be, felt like saluting.

"She seems much nicer in interviews," she confided to Kit.

It occurred to her that she didn't have to do anything simply because the woman had ordered her to, but putting away groceries was sane and normal, and Rio figured she could use a little bit of that.

Luke walked in with the promised bags of Chinese food just as she was putting away the final tin of olive-oil-packed sardines.

"Charlize Theron brought us groceries and is taking a shower," Rio blurted out. "She told me to warn you not to touch the filets."

Luke started laughing, which was not at all the response she'd expected.

"Alice is back early," he said.

"Who's Alice?"

"I'm Alice." The woman who walked back into the living room, wearing comfortably faded jeans and an old Ohio State sweatshirt while toweling her hair dry, was attractive in a strangely generic way. Her wet hair was a dull brown that would probably be lighter when dry, and her eyes were hazel. She was blandly pretty; medium height, medium build, and medium skin tone. Someone you might forget as soon as you met her.

"Um, hi, Alice, but what did you do with Charlize?"

Alice grinned and rubbed the towel over her face. When she removed it, the face looking back at Rio was Jennifer Lawrence. While Rio stared, Jennifer shook her head and became Alice again.

"Did you get enough for me?" Alice indicated the bags of Chinese food.

"I got enough for an army," Luke said. "I wasn't sure what Rio liked, so I bought a little of everything."

Kit's ears twitched wildly.

"I don't know if Chinese food is good for you, Kit," Rio said, worrying she was feeding a wild creature horrible food that would harm the little fox.

"She'll be fine so long as it's nothing spicy. Foxes live on berries, grasses, and other veggies in the wild, in addition to their carnivorous main courses, don't you, gorgeous?" Alice said, sitting down on the couch next to Kit.

Kit took one look at her and promptly flopped over to give Alice access to rub her silky white belly. If foxes purred, she'd be doing it.

"I bet that feels good, doesn't it, love?"

Rio heard the hint of a British accent in the woman's voice. "So, where are you from?"

Alice laughed, shooting a sly look at Luke. "Worried that I'm moving in on your man? Luke and I aren't like that. I just borrow a spare room when I'm in town. I don't do wizards. Or men."

Rio's face flamed hot. "No, I didn't—he's not—we don't—"

Luke looked up from where he was arranging cartons of food and plates on the small dining table and scowled at Alice. "I'm helping Rio out with a little pest problem."

"Ahhh." Alice nodded. "Rats? Bedbugs? Shape-shifting horseflies?"

"Black swans," Luke said.

Alice froze, one hand still resting on Kit's fur, and her

eyes narrowed. Her face transformed from blandly pretty to sharp and dangerous in a heartbeat.

"If you need help with that problem, I'm carrying a Glock equipped with a little something special," she said. "I owe the maestro one, and I warned him he'd never see it coming."

Rio shivered at the obvious menace in the woman's voice and decided to help Luke with the food. Unfortunately, he turned toward her just as she started toward him, and they bumped into each other at the end of the kitchen counter.

Something dangerous and hot flashed in his eyes and, instead of stepping away, he pushed forward, gently nudging her back, and caged her in by leaning forward and putting his hands on the counter on either side of her body. Not even an inch separated them, and she could feel the heat of his hard body all the way up the length of her own.

"Am I in your way?" She meant it to be sarcastic, but it came out breathless.

"You're exactly where I want you to be," he said, so quietly she almost didn't hear it, and then he leaned forward even farther and bent his head to whisper in her ear. "This is a conversation we're definitely going to have later."

The warmth of his breath in her ear sent a shivering wave of sensation zinging through her body, and she was a heartbeat away from throwing her arms around his neck and kissing him when he leaned back and held up a bottle of soy sauce.

"Hungry?" he asked, smiling at her so wickedly she was surprised her skin didn't spontaneously combust.

She decided to serve his little seduction tricks right back to him.

"Oh, you have no idea," she said huskily, licking her lips.

Luke groaned and started to lean into her again, but Alice's sharp voice interrupted.

"Really? If you're going to get all kissy-face, go do it

in your room. Some of us would prefer not to have our appetites ruined, if you please."

Kit yipped, and Rio slid away from Luke, her face heating up again. She'd never been someone who was prone to blushing, until she started hanging out with Luke. Now her face felt like it was permanently red.

Red. She worried at the thought like a dog with a bone while she set out chopsticks and forks. Red was a signal color, after all. Fire, blood, and danger were all red.

Maybe there was a warning in that.

Luke, who obviously trusted Alice completely, filled her in on what was going on while they ate, after looking to Rio for permission to tell all.

Alice listened silently, raising an eyebrow occasionally for clarification, and then finally pushed her plate away and placed her chopsticks carefully down on one side.

"Those bastards. You want my advice? Find out whatever it is they really want and do the exact opposite," she told Rio.

Rio rolled her eyes. "That's easy for you to say. They're not trying to recruit *you*."

Alice pointed at Luke. "They're not trying to recruit Rio, either; there is something deeper and darker going on here. Or if they are trying to recruit her, it's for some nefarious purpose. Tell her. You know these bastards from way back."

"It's true," Luke said, taking another helping of shrimp and snow peas.

"Maestro has never done anything straightforward in his life. And the claim that he knows who your parents are? That's every orphan's secret dream, Rio," he added, gently. "He couldn't have picked any better way to get to you, could he?"

"But Merelith said, 'It *is* you,' as if she knew who I am. Does that mean she knows who my parents are, too?"

Alice whistled. "Merelith na Kythelion?"

Luke nodded.

"You *are* traveling in some interesting circles, Rio. High Court Winter Fae, Dalriata, the League—I'm not sure even I'd want to be on those radars all at once. Has anybody heard from Demon Rift yet?"

Kit, who'd been eating her way through a bowl of beef and broccoli, looked up at Alice and growled.

Alice laughed and scratched the fox behind her ear. "I'm not threatening your charge, little one. And you'll want to pick your battles. You may be two or three times the size of a normal red fox, but you're still quite small. Stay out of Dalriata's way in the future, so he doesn't regret letting you go."

A shudder snaked its way through Rio at the thought of Dalriata chaining Kit again, and Luke reached over and took her hand. The warmth of his fingers clasping hers sent a wave of reassurance to counter the fear.

Rio stared at their joined hands, resting on the table, and wondered how long it had been since someone had held her hand. Just that simple, human bit of affection—so common and so ordinary—and she couldn't even remember the last time she'd experienced it. She suddenly felt a little pathetic, so she pulled her hand away and put it in her lap, out of his reach.

"What do you know about Dalriata?" Luke asked Alice.

"Nothing good," Alice said. "He's new in town, and yet suddenly the drug trade leadership is swirling around him and fawning all over him. He's somebody to be avoided, at least until we have a new sheriff in place who can deal with all of this."

"Luke won't do it. We just had this conversation," Rio said, in response to the mocking look Alice shot across the table at Luke.

"Somebody ought to kick his ass for him and *make* him do it," Alice told Rio. "Nobody else would do a better job, and none of the usual elements of corruption would stand a chance trying to influence him."

"I'm right here, ladies," Luke gritted out.

Rio and Alice both started laughing.

"Well, I'm off. I have a date with a beautiful brunette," Alice said, standing up. "She's been all alone and lonely while I was in France."

"France?" Rio looked at Luke. "Another coincidence. Elisabeth said her parents were in France. Her mom was there for work."

"The Fae Halfling? Probably no coincidence," Alice said. "There was a major treaty convention there this past week between the different European Fae groups, and Elisabeth's mother—who is Merelith's sister, much as neither one of them likes to admit it—was there. I was hired as security for an Italian Summerlands princess who had an overwhelming fondness for meatballs. I may need to let my holster out a notch."

"You're a bodyguard?" Rio looked at the woman with a new measure of respect.

"I'm whatever I need to be. And sometimes, *whoever* I need to be. I prefer to travel as Academy Award–winning, or at least nominated, actresses, because I get everything free at the best hotels and restaurants. Also, nobody would expect Helen Mirren to be packing heat."

"Unless they'd seen *Red*," Rio pointed out.

Alice laughed and stood up. "I guess that's true. She kicked ass in that movie. I was glad I'd taught her a few of my moves."

"You taught—never mind. I don't want to know," Rio said, shaking her head.

Alice sauntered down the hall, presumably to get ready for her date, and Rio, suddenly nervous, jumped up to clear off the table, careful not to meet Luke's gaze.

"I won't bite," he said.

"Even if I want you to?" She froze, not knowing exactly why or how *those* words had come out of *her* mouth.

Luke was out of his chair so fast he knocked it over. "What did you just say? And don't even think about taking it back."

Before she could answer, or think, or breathe, he was on her, his hands on her waist, his big, hard body way too close. She glanced up at him, desperate for balance—for caution—but lost any hope of either when she fell into the heat in his ocean-blue eyes.

"You said you didn't want me in your bed," she whispered.

He shouted out a laugh. "I would never lie to you like that. I said the only thing I wanted to *hire* you for was to help me with my business. Trust me, angel, this part of our relationship is strictly personal."

"But—"

His mouth came down on hers, silencing whatever she'd been about to say, and the world went up in flames around her. Blue flames, the color of his eyes and his magical fire, seared through her nerve endings until she trembled from pure, crystallized sensation. She forgot how to talk, or think, or breathe, and simply surrendered to the feeling, kissing him back until she grew light-headed from lack of oxygen and pulled back, gasping.

"What was *that*?" She managed to get the words out between deep breaths, but he didn't answer.

Instead, he touched her hair, then pushed a strand behind her ear and traced the edge of her ear with his finger, and she inhaled brokenly at the jagged edge of desire that dug into her. Heat pooled between her legs, and her nipples tightened and ached for his touch.

"I have to slow down now," he finally said, his voice rough, just when she was about to throw caution—and her clothes—to the wind. "I have to back away from you right now, or I'll lift your sexy little ass up onto my kitchen counter and take you right here."

Part of her thought that was a really wonderful idea. The other part of her, drummed into her brain for years, pictured the nuns' horrified reaction to her wanton behavior.

Rio liked the first part better.

"Maybe you can give me a PI lesson now?" She was proud of her steady voice.

"I can do one better than that," he said, flashing a

wicked grin. "Let's go solve your first case. I know I have a few new ones that have come in over the past couple of days. We can worry about someone else's problems, which I've found always takes my mind off my own."

"That's the best idea I've heard in days," Rio said fervently, which was a flat-out lie, because the image of him making love to her right there in the kitchen was burning a hole in her brain. "I just need a shower first.

"A cold shower," she added, muttering the words. "Very cold."

Luke stared at her as if his mind had shorted out at the word *shower*, and she wondered if he was picturing her wet and naked because suddenly she was on the verge of inviting him to join her.

"Your clothes," he began hoarsely, but then he cleared his throat and took a deep breath before continuing. "Someone delivered a box of your things from Mrs. Giamatto while you were out. There might be clothes in it."

"Already? She didn't lose any time," Rio said bitterly, her good mood immediately starting to dissipate. "She also assumed a lot, sending them here."

She scowled, but Luke was having none of that, apparently, because he kissed her again, fast and hard and dizzying, and then he pointed to the hallway.

"First door on your right past my room. You have a private bathroom."

Rio blinked, again struck by how ridiculously large his home was, when from the exterior it looked like it occupied the same space as the Tea Room's storage space. "How many guest rooms do you have?"

Luke shrugged. "It varies depending on how many I need, as far as I can figure it out."

"Of course it does." Rio checked on her now-sleeping fox, curled up in her new bed by the fireplace, and then headed off to find her magical guest room so she could shower and dress for her first case as a private investigator.

She hoped it didn't involve the giant duck.

CHAPTER 12

Luke looked up when the door from his home to his office opened and promptly almost swallowed his tongue when Rio sauntered toward him, wearing a snug little skirt and a sweater that hugged her curves in all the right places. Leather boots completed the outfit, and they even had a sensible low heel, so he didn't know why S&M fantasies were suddenly playing in his head.

"Is this okay? I wanted to look professional, but this is the only skirt I own. Skirts aren't really useful at my job. Well, my old job."

She bit her lip, and he wanted to stand up and kiss her nerves away. Or throw her on the couch in his office and kiss everything away. He forced himself to look away from temptation and focus back on the three slightly bedraggled pieces of paper he'd been studying.

"You look great, but skirts aren't necessary. I hardly ever wear them," he said, deadpan.

She laughed and relaxed.

"Pull up a chair next to me, and let's sort this out. We've got a man who claims aliens are sending him messages through the fillings in his teeth, another man who claims Dr. Black's office stole his chihuahua and fed it to the office cat, and a woman who says she thinks her ex-boyfriend kidnapped her puppy."

Rio's eyes widened. "I can see why they want you to be sheriff, when you regularly handle big, important cases like that."

He nodded solemnly. "The problem is, this is Bordertown. Any of these allegations could actually be true, except for the veterinarian thing. If Dr. Black had stolen this man's chihuahua, she'd never allow any harm to come to it. Besides, I know for a fact that her office cat only eats caviar and swamp rats. It's a Cheshire."

He pushed the three intake forms toward her and watched as she studied them. The curve of her neck as she bent over the task fascinated him; its delicate line and pale skin more beautiful than any work of art he'd seen in any museum in Florence. As he stared at her, he realized again that something was happening to him, and he didn't know how to cope with it. She was having far more effect on him than any woman had ever had—on his attention, his emotions, and even his balance.

The worst part was, he liked every bit of it.

"The puppy, I think," she said, pushing away two of the forms and selecting one. "Her story sounds the most reasonable, although it's hard for them to tell us very much in this little box you allow for Explanation."

She'd said *us. Us* was suddenly Luke's favorite word.

"Yeah, that form was just something I dashed off when I started the agency, and I've never updated it. I'd be glad if you take on that project. I'm sure we can make it more useful."

He grinned. *We* was a good word, too.

He picked up the silver letter opener on his desk and turned it over and over in his hands the way a businessman might squeeze a stress ball. Although a stress ball wouldn't burn the average businessman's hand clear off his body if he had evil thoughts.

She leaned back, which did absolutely spectacular things for the sweater she was wearing, but Luke's appreciation was dimmed by the pensive expression on her face. She clutched the form, and the piece of paper crumpled a little in her hand.

"Do you really think I could do this? And why would you even want to let me try? I don't mean to be suspicious, but why are you helping me out like this?"

"That's what I do, little lady," he drawled in his best John Wayne impression.

She looked at him blankly.

"That's the problem with this new generation. You don't recognize the classics. Nobody knows John Wayne, Clark Gable, or Gerardus Mercator."

"I was having a similar conversation with Clarice about Hannibal Lecter," she said dryly. "Also, Gerardus who?"

"He was a famous cartographer in the sixteenth century."

She rolled her eyes. "There I go, forgetting my obscure historical facts again. Sorry, boss."

Luke flinched a little. "Don't call me that."

He didn't want to be her boss. He wanted to be her friend, and so much more. But not her boss—it brought a degree of unfair leverage into the relationship that was unpleasant, unwanted, and wrong.

"Don't call you boss? But—"

"I'll make you a partner," he blurted out. Anything to get rid of the boss idea. "Fifty percent of that ugly couch is all yours."

She started laughing. "Well, I am fond of that couch. But partner is a little extreme. How about we start with associate or consultant, and go from there?"

"If you help me get this place organized, I'll make *you* the boss," he said fervently.

The door to the street, which he'd unlocked and unwarded before he sat down, burst open.

A short, balding man wearing a dark blue jumpsuit with BORDERTOWN ROAD CREW and YOUNG embroidered in white over his left front pocket ran into the room, skidded to a stop, put his hands on his knees, and started sucking in deep breaths.

"You've got to find it. They'll kill us. Not to mention the paperwork. Oliver, I know you're not officially the sheriff yet, but you've got to help me." The man's words tumbled over each other, coming faster and more frantically as he caught his breath.

Rio jumped up and poured a cup of water from the dispenser in the corner and handed it to the red-faced man.

"It's okay, Mr. Young. Please calm down and tell us what happened. We'll try our best to help you." She glanced at Luke, as if to ask if she were doing okay, and he gave her two thumbs up.

Hell, he couldn't remember the last time he himself had been so professional. He usually opened with a surly *What do you want?*

Young was staring at Rio, his eyes so wide that Luke could see white all the way around the pupils.

"Are you a wizard, too? How did you know my name?"

Rio tapped her chest in the approximate vicinity of where Young's name was embroidered on his own, and the man stared at her breasts for just a little too long. Either he didn't get what she was trying to tell him, or he, like most normal, healthy, heterosexual men, appreciated the way Rio filled out a sweater.

Luke didn't care which it was, but it was pissing him off.

"Your name is embroidered on your chest, Young. Can we move on from show-and-tell, and you tell me what you're talking about?" He put enough growl in his voice that the man immediately snapped his attention away from the beautiful woman and to the dangerous wizard in the room.

"That duck. That overgrown, sorry-ass excuse for poultry. First it ran away from the Golden Palace, although why a duck wouldn't be perfectly happy in the Summerlands I have no idea."

He paused to gulp down more water, and Rio shot a

look at Luke. He could almost see the invisible finger she was twirling next to her temple. Or maybe that was just Luke.

"I always thought the Golden Palace would be a good name for a Chinese restaurant," she said, while Young was noisily drinking.

"Or a really great Bruce Lee movie," Luke offered.

"Bruce Lee I've heard of. Although I like Jet Li better. Cooler moves and less weird yelling."

"Bruce Lee is a classic," he protested.

Rio yawned. "Are you getting ready to pull any more sixteenth-century cartographers out on me?"

Meanwhile, Young was staring at both of them as if they were inmates in the insane asylum. "They told me you would be the best person to help. Do you even understand? Somebody stole that duck egg. If I can't find it real quick, the Summer Court is going to wipe me and my team off the face of the planet."

Rio's smile disappeared. "I'm sorry. Please have a seat and tell us everything."

Young nodded, but he looked skeptical and remained standing. "That duck was a ceremonial gift from the European Fae to the Summer Palace to say thanks for participation in the treaty talks. You may have heard we had a little problem."

"You mean the problem where the duck laid an egg in the middle of the street?" Luke asked dryly.

Rio nodded. "Actually, we saw the whole thing. Well, when I say 'whole thing,' I don't mean the whole egg— anyway, just tell us the rest," she said, getting a little flustered.

The blush rising from the hint of cleavage revealed by her sweater distracted Luke, and so he missed the first part of what the man said next.

". . . and now the egg is gone."

Young started to unzip his jumpsuit, and Rio took a step away from him.

"Mr. Young, what are you doing?"

But it wasn't some weird kind of road crew striptease. Young was removing a piece of an enormous feather that he had tucked inside his jumpsuit, probably to protect it.

"Somebody said you can do a finding spell if you have something, like an article of clothing. Ducks don't wear clothes, and thank the gods I don't have a piece of eggshell, but I thought this might help." He proudly held it out to Luke.

"Actually, you did good. I should be able to do a simple locator spell with this, and I doubt there are that many places somebody can hide a giant egg and nobody notices," Luke said.

"This is Bordertown," Rio reminded him. "It could be anywhere."

Young moaned and collapsed onto the couch.

"Nice bedside manner," Luke said admiringly. "A few more weeks, and you'll be almost as surly as I am."

Rio frowned at him and went to get the poor man some more water. Luke took the feather and a few items from his drawer and did his magic thing. Then he stood and frowned at the results.

"This doesn't make any sense at all. I'm getting that the egg is in the middle of Black Swan Fountain Square. There is no way somebody wouldn't have noticed it there."

"Black Swan again," Rio said. "Do you think Maestro is playing games with us?"

"I'd love to blame him for everything bad that happens in Bordertown, but even I can't figure out what he would want with a giant duck egg. Especially if the damn thing hatches."

"Guess it's duck season," Rio said, grinning.

"Wabbit season," Luke corrected her.

Both she and Young looked completely bewildered, so Luke just sighed and shook his head as they left his office to go find a duck egg. It took a rare person to appreciate a good Elmer Fudd line.

✱

Rio picked herself back up off the ground, for the sixth or seventh time, and wiped duck poop off her face with her hands.

"We were bringing you back your baby," she shouted at the freaking duck. "Don't make me get the orange sauce."

"Good one," Luke said, grinning like a fool.

Or at least she thought he was grinning. It was hard to tell because he was also covered in muck. Between the two of them, Rio didn't think there was an inch of clean or dry skin or clothing. They'd found the egg exactly where Luke thought it would be, resting in the water in the fountain, and then brought it to the park to return it to its mother.

Easy job. No problem.

Except for the duck.

When she'd caught a glimpse of Rio, Luke, and Mr. Young trundling her egg in on a cart, she'd completely lost her feathery little mind. Mr. Young had yelled something about no way did Bordertown pay him enough for this, and he ran off as fast as his government-worker legs would carry him. Luke and Rio had stayed to make sure the egg got safely off the cart and onto the duck's enormous nest.

Big mistake. Huge.

The enraged duck waddled right at them and knocked them down as if she were playing a wild game of Bowling for Humans. Fortunately for Luke and Rio, they were mostly hit by feathers and she didn't manage to stomp on them, so they weren't hurt.

Unfortunately for Luke and Rio, ducks poop. A lot.

So ever since, the two of them had been playing keep-away with a giant duck and a huge but fragile egg in a field of nastiness that Rio would have preferred to imagine was only mud.

Sadly, her imagination wasn't anywhere near that good.

"I smell like duck poop. I am *covered* in duck poop,

and I have ruined my *only skirt*. If this is what your normal day as a PI is like, you're out of your mind if you think I want the job," she yelled, over the sound of the loudest quacking anybody had ever heard anywhere in the history of the world.

"Distract her," Luke yelled back.

The duck picked that moment to take another run at her. Rio turned and ran, or at least that was what she told her body to do. Her feet were stuck in the muck, though, so she managed one step before she fell flat in the crap again.

The actual, literal, crap.

"I'm going to kill you," she told Luke. "I'm going to kill you slowly, and I'm going to enjoy it. And then I'm going to stand in the middle of a car wash for an hour."

The duck headed for Luke with murder on her mind.

"I think she has fangs," Rio shouted.

"She doesn't have fangs. Ducks don't even have teeth. Do they?"

The duck slipped in its own mess and fell on its fat feathery butt, and Rio felt triumphantly vindicated.

"Ha! How do *you* like it?"

"You do realize you're asking questions of the duck, right?"

Rio sneered at him. "It's only crazy if I expect the duck to answer."

Luke hid behind the egg when the duck got to its feet again.

"Distract her," he shouted again.

"Distract her? *Distract* her? Are you out of your freaking mind? How am I going to distract a duck bigger than a house when you have her baby in your stupid wizard hands?"

"Try singing," Luke suggested, as he tried to maneuver the egg the last few feet up and over the edge of the nest.

Rio screamed and waved her arms frantically when the duck began to turn toward Luke again.

"Over here, you sorry excuse for a bird. Your mother

has webbed feet. Your father made Donald Duck look smart," she yelled at it, and then she turned to stare at Luke. "Sing? Sing what?"

Luke kept pushing the egg, but he started laughing uproariously. "How should I know? Sing something about ducks."

If she ever got out of this mess alive, she was going to kick a certain wizard's butt for him. She stood up as tall as she could, threw her arms into the air as if she were conducting an orchestra, and started singing at the top of her lungs.

"Be kind to your fine feathered friends, for a duck may be somebody's mother," she belted out, keeping an eye on Luke's progress.

He very nearly had the egg tipped into the nest.

"Living alone in Bordertown, where it's always weird and bizarre," she sang, still at the top of her lungs.

The duck suddenly spread her wings and squawked, blocking Rio's view of the nest. A horrible sound ratcheted up, almost loud enough to drown out the duck's quacking, and Rio wondered if the duck had killed Luke. She also wondered if she'd be all that sad about it, right at that exact moment.

She wiped more muck out of her face, still singing, and looked around. Luke had finally levered the egg into the nest, the duck sat happily on top of her progeny, and Luke was standing about a half-dozen feet away from Rio, watching her sing like a fool and laughing his ass off. She did the only thing a woman could do in a situation like that.

She walked up to him and knocked him down onto a particularly nasty, reeking pile of duck shit.

"Take that! And that was John Philip Sousa, baby!"

Then, with every ounce of dignity she could muster, she picked her way out of the park and headed for the nearest car wash, or Niagara Falls, whichever she reached first.

CHAPTER 13

After nearly an hour in the Bordertown Road Crew hazmat tent, Luke doubted Rio would ever speak to him again. When he was done being cleaned to within an inch of his immortal life, he found her sitting on a marble bench, looking at the Black Swan Fountain. She was wearing the same kind of dark blue road crew jumpsuit that he had on, donated by the grateful workers who fervently believed that Luke and Rio had saved their lives from vengeful Summer Court Fae.

The swan was one of the most beautiful pieces of public art in Bordertown. The fountain itself was fifty feet in diameter. In the center of the fountain, a gracefully elegant black marble statue of a young woman stood with one hand held out to a beautifully sculpted swan. He'd once heard that there was a curse associated with the fountain, but you could hear rumors of curses around every corner in Bordertown, so Luke didn't pay that much attention as a rule.

"Are you ever going to talk to me again?" He cautiously approached from the side, wary of what she might do to him this time. He'd be glad if she punched him or kicked him in the shin, or anything other than freeze him out. When he'd planned to get her involved in the business, he'd never anticipated anything like this.

She raised her head and flashed him a dazzling smile. "We kicked duck butt, my friend. It was you and me against a couple thousand pounds of poultry, and we freaking triumphed."

Luke almost fell over. She wasn't angry?

She was *smiling*.

"You're not mad at me? You don't have a concussion, do you?"

She laughed. "Let me just say that I never want to have an experience like that again, but three cheers for magical hazmat teams. I have never been this clean in my life. In fact, they even asked me if I wanted the hair removal option."

Luke eased down on the bench next to her and stared at the fountain, careful not to meet Rio's gaze in case he started laughing. He didn't want her to think he was laughing at her. He was amazed that she had this incredible sense of humor; she was cheerful about an experience that most people would scream and run from.

She was incredible.

"They didn't offer me that one."

She stretched out her legs, which managed to look good even encased in an ugly blue jumpsuit. "Apparently microscopic bits of dirt could possibly survive even their strenuous, magical cleaning. But the hair removal option removed *all* hair."

She paused, and he knew she was blushing again, even without looking at her. He wouldn't have been able to tell in the dark, anyway, but he just knew it. He reached out a hand and touched the end of her damp, curling braid.

"I would have missed your hair," he admitted. "I've made it a personal goal to see it out of this braid as often as possible."

For some reason, his voice had gone husky, so he cleared his throat. She slowly turned her head to look at

him, and then she raised one hand and pulled the ribbon
out of her hair and loosened her braid, shaking all that
glorious dark hair over her shoulders.

"You have beautiful hair, Rio." He was afraid to touch
her hair—to touch her at all—in case he might break the
moment.

"You make me feel beautiful, and it's not something
I'm accustomed to. Nobody has ever had that effect on me
before," she said, her own voice soft and trembling a little.
"I'm in the middle of an awful situation. Danger is coming
at me from all sides. Suddenly, after twenty-five years,
people seem to know who I am and who my parents may
have been, and I just spent the evening rolling around in
duck poop and singing."

He started laughing. "John Philip Sousa, baby."

The ghost of a smile crossed her face. "And yet, with all
of that going on, I've never felt so alive. I've never felt so
utterly and completely content to be exactly who I am, and
I think—no, I know—that a lot of that has to do with you."

He started to speak, and she shushed him.

"No. You don't have to say anything. I have no idea why
I'm admitting all this to you, anyway. Maybe it's because
my birthday is almost here, and I don't know if I'll live to
see it. All I know is that I want to thank you for trying to
help me."

The lump in his throat blocked him from speaking for
a few moments, and it actually took him a couple of tries
to get the words out. He felt like his world had turned
upside down; that gravity had quit functioning.

"Don't thank me. Please, don't thank me. You will never
know how selfish I've been in keeping you with me. Monsters never get the princess in real life, but I'm selfish
enough to want to keep you near me for as long as I can."

She leaned toward him and he held perfectly still, afraid
that if he moved she would flee. She kissed him gently on
the lips, and he didn't push for more. For once, his body
was content with the tenderness of her offering, instead of
wanting to explode into sexual need. The beast inside him

quieted, its rages and lusts subsiding, until it almost purred with the peace spreading through him from her touch.

"This is going to sound completely wrong after what we've just been through," she said, grinning up at him. "But I'm really starving."

"Your wish is my command. What are you hungry for?" He stood up, taking her hands and pulling her up with him.

"Honestly? Anything but duck."

Rio slowly woke up and stretched, feeling slightly sore in every inch of her body. The bedroom was filled with sunlight because she'd been too tired to bother closing the curtains when she'd collapsed into bed the night before. She'd plowed her ravenous way through a steak, salad, and baked potato and then fallen asleep in Luke's Jeep on the way back to his place. He'd picked her up and carried her into the house before she'd realized what was going on, and she hadn't bothered to try to get down. Instead, she'd snuggled up to him, knowing she was playing with fire but not caring.

The honesty she demanded, even of herself, made her admit to a somewhat different story. Maybe part of her had been hoping she would get burned. Burned with his heat, seduced by his fire, but with the out that the next morning she could claim she hadn't really known what she was doing.

"That's just a little bit cowardly, coming from a mighty duck slayer, don't you think, Kit?"

The fox, currently curled up next to her on the bed, twitched one ear but didn't open her eyes. Kit had been very interested in smelling both of them the night before, in spite of the thorough hazmat cleaning, so maybe the hair removal option would have been a good idea. She involuntarily glanced down at her underwear and shook her head. On second thought, no. There were just some places she did not want to be bare.

She showered and left her hair loose. Then she dressed in jeans, boots, and sweater, ran a mascara brush over her lashes and a little gloss over her lips, and called it done.

She had things to figure out today, and there was no time to waste trying to be glamorous.

Luke was already in the kitchen, drinking coffee and scowling at his phone. His face lightened up when he saw her. "Lunch?"

He was so mouthwateringly gorgeous that she wanted to just stop and stare at him. His hair was still damp, too, and pushed back from those incredible cheekbones. He wore a blue sweater that a woman must have given him, because the color matched his amazing dark blue eyes. Faded jeans and old boots completed the outfit, and the effect of the whole thing made her want to rush across the room and jump him.

"Lunch sounds good, although I don't know how I could be hungry again after everything I ate last night."

"Duck wrangling is hard work," he said, flashing her that wicked grin that melted her insides and made her nipples twinge.

He filled a mug of coffee and set it on the counter for her, then turned to the refrigerator and pulled out four different kinds of coffee creamer and proudly placed them in front of her.

"Now you don't have to drink it black."

She couldn't help it. She smiled. The Dark Wizard of Bordertown had been out buying her coffee creamer.

"Butterscotch. Wow, that sounds delicious. Thank you for this. Nobody ever—well, I just really appreciate it."

She busied herself pouring cream in her coffee so as to avoid having him see her face. Luke was extremely perceptive, and the last thing she wanted him to think about her was *poor little orphan girl*.

"Are you ready to get your private investigator on?"

She took a long sip of coffee before putting her cup down and looking up at Luke. "I think what I need to do today is try to find some answers about my past and about why everybody seems to be so interested in me all of a sudden. Would you be willing to go to the convent with me, so I can try to talk to any of the nuns who are still there?"

It was one of the bravest things she'd ever done, asking him that. She'd sworn, the day she left the convent, that she would never, ever return.

He put his own mug down, frowning at it, and then looked up, his face troubled.

"Rio, I'm sorry. I've just been on the phone with five different nuns, all the way up to the Mother Superior. None of them will talk to me, and they warned me to tell you they would never speak to you again," he said gently.

The words hit Rio like a sucker punch. Not that she hadn't expected it, or at least not that she wouldn't have expected it if she'd ever thought she'd want to go there and ask them anything again. She'd left under bad circumstances—in fact, she'd arrived under bad circumstances—so she should have had no reason to expect help from them.

But all that logic didn't stop it from hurting. The convent and the nuns had been home to the only years of her childhood she could remember, and the pain of their rejection quite literally took her breath away and left her bent double and gasping to try to breathe.

Luke was around the counter in a heartbeat, patting her back and holding her hair out of her face. "What can I do? Tell me what to do, Rio. I'm losing my mind here."

She forced herself to calm down when she heard the intensity of his distress. *In and out. In and out.* The breathing exercises that she'd once learned to cope with childhood panic attacks surfaced in her mind, and she took long, slow breaths in and then steadily pushed them out.

"I'm fine. I'm really fine. It was just unexpected. I have—I guess I had, somewhere inside me, the dream that someday we would reconcile, and I would have a home. I've never—I've never had anyone who didn't abandon me, and without that kind of foundation, I'm left feeling adrift sometimes." She tried to smile but was horrified to realize that tears were running down her face.

"I'm so sorry, Luke. I don't mean to be a pathetic, whiny little girl. I can't believe I keep telling you all this stuff.

I'm normally a very private person. Are you sure you didn't whammy me with a truth potion?"

Luke whirled around, then stalked across the room and out the kitchen door, slamming it behind him. Rio sat, frozen, miserably aware that she'd driven him away. Surely it wasn't her feeble joke about a truth potion?

Before she had a chance to even think about her next step, a thunderous explosion shook the house, and then the door burst open, and Luke stomped back in, slamming it behind him.

"I just blew up the Helga's Tea Room van," he announced. "Blew it to smithereens. There's not a scrap of metal bigger than a shoe box left of it."

Rio's mouth fell open and she realized she was completely speechless.

He advanced on her, swept her up off the stool into his arms, and kissed her until she was having trouble breathing again, and then he walked around the counter and started drinking coffee while she sat, half-dazed, tingling in every nerve ending she'd ever even thought of having. He wasn't even breathing hard, darn him.

"I know. Don't yell at me," he said, half sheepishly and half defiantly. "I'll buy her a new van. Hell, I'll buy her two new vans."

"But why—" She couldn't wrap her head around any of it.

He scowled, but somehow she knew it wasn't directed at her. "I don't know how to have all these feelings. I know how to blow stuff up. You were hurting, and I wanted to help, but I didn't know how, so I blew something up."

It was the most ridiculous and the most romantic thing she had ever heard. She started to tear up again and rubbed her eyes with her fists.

"You do realize that you can't blow something up every time I get emotional," she said cautiously. "This—whatever this is—can't work if I have to worry about the imminent destruction of all human life and property in Bordertown."

He scowled again, even more ferociously, and epiphany

struck. Rio's world tilted and then righted itself on a different axle. It wasn't charm, flirtation, or big romantic gestures that would catch her heart and steal her soul, then. It was a hint of brokenness, a flash of need and longing that let her hope there was a chance for her to soothe a kindred wounded spirit and that maybe, just maybe, he would be able to offer solace in return.

More and more, she was coming to realize that the hole in her heart was shaped like Luke. It terrified her that nobody else would ever be able to fill it.

"I can try harder," he promised, so earnestly that she had to fight a smile.

"I think you're doing just fine. Maybe we should go talk to Helga about her new van before we get lunch."

He cleared his throat and looked everywhere but at her. "You might want to go wash your face. You, ah, have some of that black stuff smeared around your eyes."

Mortified, she jumped up and ran back to the bathroom, but when she got there she started laughing so hard that she had to hold on to the counter so she didn't fall on the floor. Why in the world was she worried about him seeing her with a little smeared mascara, when he'd seen her covered from head to toe with filth the night before? She washed her face and started over with a little bit of makeup, feeling suddenly lighthearted.

So the nuns didn't want to talk to her, did they? She'd go another avenue. There was more than one way to skin a duck.

Kit had decided not to join them for lunch, if the way she blinked, stretched, and went back to sleep was any indication, so Rio left her with a bowl full of shredded chicken, a plate of spring greens, and a bowl of fresh water.

"I'm worried about her," she confessed to Luke. "I feel like there's more I should be doing for her. Maybe take her to a wildlife rescue? Should she be in the forest, instead of in the middle of the city, especially a city like this one?"

Luke glanced down at her as they walked, a gleam of amusement in his beautiful blue eyes. "I get the feeling that if Kit wanted to be in a forest, she'd be in a forest. She's a magical creature, Rio. She talked to you and said she's meant to be with you. If it were me, I'd go with the flow for a while."

"I guess so. But I really need to fatten her up a little bit. If Dr. Black catches me again while Kit is still this thin, I have a feeling that I'll be the one she feeds to her office cat."

"That woman is a little scary," Luke agreed. "I once needed her help with a shape-shifting armadillo who was stuck midshift, and I thought she was going to singe the skin right off my body with the scolding she gave me before she realized that I wasn't the one who'd caused it."

They managed to talk about little things while they had soup and sandwiches in a sidewalk café, taking advantage of the unusually warm day. Funny adventures he'd had on cases; weird things that had happened to her on her bike messenger runs. Small talk and lunch, almost like normal people. Rio wanted to knock wood even as she had the thought, to keep the meteorite from smashing down on them.

Luke made a few phone calls during lunch. In one, he profusely apologized to Madame Helga. In another, he arranged for a new van with all the bells and whistles to be delivered to her tea shop.

Rio put down her glass of water and clasped her hands on the table. "You really have too much money if you can order vans the way most people order pizza. Also, shouldn't you make another call and organize somebody for the cleanup?"

"No, the scavengers will have taken care of it by now. There won't be a shred of metal, plastic, or cloth anywhere in the alley."

She nodded. It was true that very little went to waste in Bordertown. The creatures who lived here were amazing recyclers. The uses they might put something to would possibly scare ten years off your life, but at least everything was reduced, reused, and recycled.

And often eaten.

They paid the bill and walked back to Luke's office.

"Maestro hasn't returned any of my calls, so that's a dead end for now," Luke said.

"What a shocker. You politely threaten to rip someone's bones apart while he's still alive and awake to feel it, and he doesn't call you back. Who could have predicted that?"

Luke made a growling noise but otherwise didn't answer her, and she decided to accept that as agreement. When they got to the office, a woman was standing in front of the door. She was maybe early thirties and serious looking, with short dark hair and wire-rimmed glasses. Her thin face was pale and drawn, and there were dark shadows under her eyes.

"Are you Mr. Oliver?"

Luke nodded and unlocked the office door, motioning her in.

"Hi. I'm Rio Holmes," Rio said, holding out her hand. "I'm Mr. Oliver's associate. How can we help you?"

Luke rolled his eyes. "Wouldn't Rio Watson have been better?"

The woman blinked and glanced back and forth between the two of them, wringing her delicate hands.

"I'm Janet Evans. I left a form? About my puppy? Nobody called me, and I just—I wonder if you'd had a chance to look into it," the woman said, her lower lip trembling. "I realized I forgot to leave a picture for you, and I've heard about the wizard thing, I mean the locator thing, so I brought Penelope's weekend collar."

Luke had started banging around in desk drawers, but he looked up at that. "The dog has a weekend collar? What the hell is a—"

"We were just getting ready to call you," Rio said, interrupting Luke's sparkling customer relations skills. "Tell us all about it."

CHAPTER 14

Three hours later

When the smoke cleared, Luke found Rio on the floor, one knee dug into the back of Janet's scumbag ex-boyfriend, cradling the stolen puppy in her arms. He looked around at the destruction of the auto repair shop and realized he might be in trouble.

"Wow. Really? How many times are we going to have to have this conversation?" Rio asked, glaring at Luke.

The man she was holding down started swearing, his voice muffled by the simple fact that it was pressed into the cement floor, and she reached down and smacked him in the side of the head.

"That's for locking this poor baby up in a closet and for the disgusting plans you had for her."

Luke grinned, and she shot him a forbidding look. "Don't even think we are done with this conversation. I told you I had it under control. I looked around the shop and found the puppy while he checked out the problem I claimed to be having with the brakes on your Jeep. It was a perfect plan."

Luke folded his arms across his chest to keep from

snatching her up and away from the asshole. "He touched you. He put his hands on you and started shaking you. He's lucky to be alive. I don't know why we're even talking about this."

The man's moans abruptly stopped.

"We are talking about it because you can't just blow something up every time you think I have a problem. What about that sedan that was in the next bay over from your Jeep? Look at what's left of it! It looks like a car that somebody's grandmother used to drive, and I say 'used to drive' on purpose because nobody will ever drive that car again."

Luke was honestly baffled. He didn't understand women at all. How could she possibly expect him to stand by and do nothing when that thug started manhandling her?

Suddenly, what she had said penetrated, and he exhaled in relief. "Oh, I get it. It's the car. The car and the grandma. Don't worry about it. I'll buy her a new car. It was probably a piece of shit anyway, or it wouldn't have been in this low-rent garage. Grandma will be happy to have a new one. It will be like the lottery, but with sedans."

Rio made a noise that sounded like a cross between a laugh and scream, but before he could pursue the topic Janet came running up.

"My baby," she shouted, and the little dog leapt out of Rio's arms and ran for her owner.

Janet rained kisses all over the pup's silken little head, alternately laughing and crying. "You found her. You found her. Oh, Mr. Oliver, Rio, I can never thank you enough."

When she finally looked up and realized Rio was still pinning the dognapper to the floor, Janet hissed.

"If I ever catch you anywhere near Penelope again, I will have you arrested. No, scratch that, I will have you shot. First, I will have you boiled in oil, and then I will have you shot," Janet told her jerk of an ex, but she didn't yell at all. Instead, it was the quiet menace in her voice that convinced Luke she really meant business.

"I'd believe her, if I were you," he advised.

"We should leave now," Rio said, standing up and

brushing off the knees of her jeans. "Mission accomplished."

"You'll send me a bill?" the grateful dog owner asked, following them out.

They all ignored the man who was now curled up in a ball, cursing.

Rio waved a hand grandly. "No charge. We're just happy you're reunited with Penelope."

Luke watched, dumbfounded, as Rio strode off down the street, head high and shoulders back. He was so entranced with watching her tight little ass as she walked that she almost made it around the corner half a block away before he thought to retrieve the Jeep and go after her.

He pulled up beside her and called out the window. "Get in the car, Rio."

She shook her head but didn't look at him. "No, I think it's a nice day for a walk. Besides, you might want to explode something on the way home, and I don't want to get in your way."

Luke slammed on the brakes and smashed his head into the steering wheel a few times, but no amazing bit of understanding regarding the female sex was knocked loose in the process. So he parked the car, jumped out, and went after her.

"Okay, what you want me to understand is that you can take care of yourself," he began tentatively.

She looked at him and rolled her eyes but said nothing.

"No problem. You can take care of yourself. See, that was easy."

She stopped walking, turned to face him, and poked a finger in his chest. Hard.

"Words. Those are just words. How is it that last night you watched me distract a giant duck—in fact, you told me to do it—and had no problem, but today you feel like you have to protect me from some thug dognapper?"

"Because that man wasn't human."

She threw her hands in the air. "Almost nobody in Bordertown is human. What does that have to do with anything?"

"He was an Iron Kin demon," Luke explained, pausing to glare at a few teenagers who were walking by, laughing at them. "If he got tired of shaking you, he could have picked up the Jeep with one hand and thrown it at you."

Rio blew out a breath and thought about that for a minute.

"Oh," she finally said. "Well, thank you, then."

"He was dangerous," Luke continued. "If you think for one second—"

He stopped, confused. She'd thanked him?

"You're right. I'm sorry." She put her hands on his shoulders, stood on her tiptoes, and kissed his cheek, leaving him floundering for what to say next.

"You're sorry?"

"I'm not an idiot, Luke. I know my limits. Okay, I sort of know my limits. He was a mental broadcaster, so I could read his mind loud and clear. I knew he'd taken the dog, and I knew which closet he'd stuffed her into. With no water, by the way."

She shuddered. "I even knew that he planned to feed her to the dragon lizards that live in the sewers. I think I might be pretty good at the investigation part of private investigation, but I'm no match in strength for most supernatural creatures. That's why we're partners, right?"

He shoved his hands into his pockets to keep from grabbing her and twirling her around right there on the street.

"So now we're partners?" he said in a mock growl. "Well, partner, we're never going to be able to pay the bills if you keep telling people that our services are free."

She walked over and climbed into the passenger seat of the Jeep, closed the door, and looked out the window at him, smiling primly. "I'd feel like an idiot sending her a bill for saving her puppy after you just admitted in her hearing range that you were going to buy some random person's grandma a new car because you'd had a temper tantrum."

"Temper tantrum? I thought we just agreed that I was being reasonable?"

She waited until he swung himself up into the driver's seat to respond.

"No. We agreed that you were being reasonable to protect me from an angry demon. We did not agree that the way to do it was to blow up half of an auto repair shop."

Luke tried not to stare at her. Her amber eyes were sparkling, her cheeks were pink with excitement, she was dusty from the explosion, and her hair was a tangled mess.

She was the most beautiful thing he'd ever seen.

"We spent all afternoon doing that," she said suddenly. "I hate to admit it, but I'm hungry again. How are you with spicy food? I have some friends that I'd like you to meet."

"I love hot and spicy," he said, and suddenly his mind went to very different places than dinner.

The predator inside Luke—the monster—lifted its head and growled, and he knew he was too close to the edge. He already had been forced to fight against his own savage instincts to keep from blasting the dognapping scumbag into a pile of greasy ash right there on the floor of his repair shop when the son of a bitch had dared to lay a hand on Rio.

Mine, mine, mine, the darkness inside him had howled, and he'd felt the rage clawing its way up from the pit of his stomach. So yeah, right now he was definitely in the mood for hot and spicy. The problem was, he was fighting to keep from thinking of Rio as his main course.

"Turn here," Rio said, oblivious to his internal battle. "Have you ever been to Hellacious before?"

He groaned, long and loud. "You're taking me to a demon-owned restaurant? Now?"

If fate was setting him a test, this was a good one. Right now, he was in the mood to blast any demon who even dared to blink in his direction.

"We can go somewhere else," she said, but she was clearly disappointed.

"Oh, no. Let's go to Hellacious. I hear they have great hot sauce."

When they entered the redbrick-fronted building, they headed straight for the restrooms to get cleaned up, and when they returned to the hostess station, Luke watched bemusedly as the demon couple who owned the restaurant rushed over to greet Rio and give her a hug.

"Thank you again for throwing that baby shower for Linda," the female of the couple said.

"It was my pleasure, Zephyr. How are she and the baby doing?"

And with that one magical word—*baby*—the two women were off and running in a conversation that lasted at least five minutes before Rio remembered Luke was standing there. He traded handshakes with the woman's husband in the meantime, trying to be on his best behavior.

No blasting Rio's friends, no blasting Rio's friends.

"Severius, but you can call me Seven," the demon said.

"Luke Oliver."

Seven raised one eyebrow. "I know who you are. What I want to know, and what everybody wants to know, is what your platform is going to be. If you're planning some kind of anti-demon campaign when you're sheriff, please have some integrity and put your cards on the table now, so we can organize against you."

Luke groaned. "I am not running for sheriff, I do not want to be sheriff, and I don't think there's anybody around big enough or tough enough to make me do it."

Rio finally stopped chatting about babies long enough to glance up at him from beneath her long, silky lashes. "I think you'd be a great sheriff," she murmured.

Suddenly he thought he might have to revise his thinking. She wasn't very big, but she was pretty tough, and he'd be damned if she didn't have him starting to rethink his position on the job. He groaned again, and Seven slapped him on the back.

"Let's find your table. It sounds like you need a beer."

"Do you have any whiskey?"

Rio closed her eyes in utter bliss as she took another bite of enchilada and fire-roasted salsa. Say what you would about some demon restaurants and the questionable origin of their roasted meats, Zephyr and Seven really knew how to fire-roast their salsas. When she opened her eyes, a man was standing next to her table, watching her, amusement in his pale green eyes.

Luke had gone to the kitchen with Seven to learn how to make a flaming dessert after the two of them had formed some weird male bond while talking about Quidditch. Luke had claimed the game was more fun to watch when they set the brooms on fire, and Seven had countered that the stakes were higher when the winners were allowed to drop their defeated foes over a cliff.

"Hard to keep a league running if you keep dropping teams off cliffs," Zephyr had observed as she passed by on her way to another table with a tray of drinks.

The word *league* had been enough to send Rio groping for her own drink, and she'd downed half the glass of Demon Pale Ale without stopping.

"It's always nice to observe someone enjoying her food," the man said, holding out his hand. "Chance Roberts."

Rio automatically started to hold out her hand in return, but then she yanked it back.

"I'm sorry, but I don't know you. And after the past few days, you'll excuse me if I'm a little leery of touching strangers."

It was a lie. Everybody in Bordertown had heard of Chance Roberts. Everybody in the freaking world probably had heard of him. He was rich. Astonishingly, obscenely rich. Not rich like *I can buy people new cars when I blow them up*, but rich like *I just bought Wall Street*.

All of Wall Street.

He'd invented a computer system that made all the others look like stone tablets and chisels. Of course, nobody outside Bordertown realized that there was magic involved. If they did, they probably wouldn't care, so long as their Twitter feed worked.

Chance indicated Luke's empty chair. "May I sit?"

Before waiting for her assent, he seated himself and offered her a smile. The man was great looking, she'd give him that. Tawny blond hair that looked like he spent a lot of time in the sun went perfectly with his deeply tanned skin. He looked a little rough—a little dangerous—and also like a man completely in control of every situation he encountered.

She had freaking had enough of arrogant men.

"No, you may not sit down. You may leave because my . . . friend is on his way back."

"If you're talking about Luke Oliver, I can see him through the kitchen pass-through window, and his back is to us. There's no need to be alarmed, Ms. Green. I only want to speak to you."

Rio looked around. The restaurant was very full, so it wasn't like he'd get away with trying to hurt her. She might as well listen to whatever it was he had to say, so he'd leave before Luke got back and decided to blow something up.

"Fine. What?" She almost laughed when she thought of what the nuns would think of her rudeness, but then she remembered that she never again had to worry about what they thought.

"You're very beautiful, has anyone told you that?" He laughed, and the sound was darkly seductive enough to turn female heads at several nearby tables. "I'm sorry, that was an idiotic question. Of course you must hear that all the time."

"Yes, I'm a freaking beauty queen," she drawled. "Now can we quit with the butter-Rio-up portion of the conversation and get to whatever your point is?"

Chance's eyes gleamed, and she had the feeling she was entertaining him. It ticked her off.

"Blunt. I like it. Here then, as you humans say, is the deal. I represent a consortium of people who are very interested in you. Especially now that it's almost your—"

"If you say twenty-fifth birthday, I'm going to scream," Rio warned him.

"Celebration of the anniversary of your birth," he finished smoothly.

He smiled, flashing a mouthful of beautiful white teeth, and a passing waitress nearly dropped her tray.

"Okay, you seem like a smart guy." She took a sip of her beer and then pointed a finger at him. "So why are you, one of the richest and most powerful men in the world, acting as a lowly messenger boy? I was a bicycle messenger until very recently, so trust me, I know about lowly."

Oh, he hadn't liked that at all. He clenched his jaw against whatever he had been about to retort and shook his head.

"Let's just say that my interests align with theirs in this matter."

Rio wanted to punch him. "Now I'm a 'matter'? Funny, I used to think I was a person. But that was before the Winter Court Fae, the League of the Black Swan, and now the famous Chance Roberts all expressed an interest in little old me."

His face had tightened minutely at the mention of the League, and Rio found that very interesting. Also, for such a powerful man, he didn't have much of a poker face. She put her anger aside and started thinking through the convoluted facts of the matter. Why was she wasting time baiting Roberts when she could be interrogating him?

"Why? What is it about my birthday that's important? Who exactly do you think I am?"

His gaze traveled down to her locket and then back up. A look of wonder spread across his face.

"You don't even know who you are, do you? How intriguing."

He started to laugh, and her blood pressure shot through the roof.

"I know exactly who I am," she shot back. "I'm the woman who is tired of this conversation. If you don't have any answers for me, then you can just leave. Now."

She felt Luke before she saw him, as if the air in the room had shifted, or gravity had tilted to concentrate on his approach. Luke was headed toward their table, and he was moving fast. She shoved her chair back and stood up to intercept him before he started destroying things or people.

"I've got it handled," she said firmly. "Don't blow up my friends' restaurant."

She put her hands on his chest to stop him, but it was like trying to slow down a speeding bullet train. He lifted her out of his way before he plowed over her, but she could feel the heat rising in his body and knew serious trouble was coming.

"Oliver," Chance said, rising unhurriedly from his seat.

"Roberts," Luke replied, blue flames already glowing around his fingertips. "What the hell do you think you're doing here? If you're bothering Rio, consider this your last meal."

Chance smiled, not giving a hint that he was the slightest bit worried. So maybe he did have a good poker face after all, because everybody else in the restaurant was scrambling to get out of the way.

"I didn't eat, unfortunately. But if it had been my last meal, I couldn't imagine a better place to enjoy it, or a better dinner companion. I was just having a conversation with your *friend*." He put a mocking emphasis on the word that made Rio start blushing.

Luke noticed, and all the muscles in his big body tightened as if in preparation for battle. Rio moved to stand between the two men and wondered if stomping her foot would do any good. Or maybe dumping her beer on their heads. She hated to waste good ale, though.

"Enough. I've had enough of all of this. Mr. Roberts, if you have something you want to say to me you can call my cell phone." She gave him the number. "But I'm warning you, if you don't have any more information for me, then don't bother to call. I'm tired of vague insinuations and even vaguer threats. There are an awful lot of people claiming to know something about my past and, I guess, my future, considering everybody's interest in my birthday, but nobody's willing to tell me anything."

She turned to signal Zephyr that she wanted the bill. "For now, I'm leaving. I need to check on my fox."

Roberts bowed to her in a surprisingly elegant motion and then walked out the door. The restaurant patrons slowly returned to their meals and conversations, and Seven walked over to the table smiling.

"This one is on the house," he said, and he shushed her when she tried to protest. "Trust me, it's worth it to us for the pure pleasure of watching Chance Roberts get put in his place."

"He tried to buy us out once, did we tell you that?" Zephyr said, walking up to stand beside her husband.

The demon couple frowned at the memory.

"Let's just say it was a very unpleasant few months. He has resources that I can't even begin to imagine," Seven said. "Even on the Demon Rift ruling council, we suspect."

"Is he a demon? I couldn't read him," Luke said.

Seven shrugged. "We don't know, either, and nobody else seems to know—or at least they're not admitting it if they do."

"He told me he wasn't human, but didn't go any further," Rio said. "Great. Just great. Now a guy who's buddy-buddy with the demon council is after me."

She hugged her friends and thanked them for the excellent dinner, which was now roiling around in her stomach like acid.

"I don't like that man," Luke growled as they left the restaurant.

She suddenly smiled. "I'm proud of you."

He raised an eyebrow. "For what?"

"You got angry, you read the situation as there was a man threatening me, and yet you didn't blow anything up. Not even a single car met its maker. This is real progress!"

He started muttering something under his breath, and she laughed all the way to the Jeep.

CHAPTER 15

Luke and Kit sat on the couch and watched in astonishment as Rio took yet another swig from the bottle of Summerlands Shiraz. Her second.

"Does that sort of thing happen to you all the time?" She was slurring only a little, so either she had an enormous capacity for very strong wine or it just hadn't hit her yet.

He shrugged, suddenly uncomfortable. "It happens more often than I would like."

Rio had persuaded him to stop by Bordertown Spirits, and a couple of thugs had rushed into the wine store while Luke and Rio had been there. The unlucky criminals had picked the worst possible time to try to rob the store. Luke had already been in a bad mood, and they were just making it worse. So he'd picked them up, knocked their heads together, and hurled them out the front door.

Then he'd pulled out his wallet to buy the bottles of wine Rio had selected.

"I didn't really do anything, and I didn't blow up even

a single bottle of wine," he pointed out, wanting some credit.

She started laughing so hard that she fell over sideways on the chair. "That's true. But you blew up their get-away car."

"Hey! I let the driver jump out of the car first," he muttered.

Kit yipped and laughed at him in her fox way.

"Traitor," he told her.

"Will you be buying him a new car?"

"Hell, no. *Criminal*," he said, wondering why that wasn't obvious.

"And you did incinerate that *Oliver for Sheriff* sign the woman was holding when we walked out."

Luke banged his head against the back of the couch. "Where did she *come* from?"

He made a gesture with his hand and started a fire in the fireplace. "Do they just lurk around, hiding signs in their pockets, and wait for me to show up? Isn't there any-body else in this town that people can ask to be sheriff?"

Rio took another long drink of wine. "Is that a sign in your pocket, sir, or are you just happy to see me?"

That set her off again, and she laughed until she was breathless from it. Luke loved watching her laugh. He was a little worried about the drinking, but he was also happy that the wine was making her relax and forget her problems for a little while. Also, she was freaking hot when she laughed. She put her whole body into it, throwing her head back and enjoying every ounce of amusement. He wanted to hold her against his body and feel the vibrations of her laughter travel through his skin.

"I think you should kiss me, Luke Oliver," she said, decisively, putting the bottle on the fireplace hearth and then launching herself at him.

Kit yelped and ran for cover down the hallway, and Luke found himself with an armful of warm, curvy, slightly drunken woman. When she started wiggling around in his lap and nestled her head on his chest, he groaned.

"You're going to drive me over the edge," he said fervently, trying to think of something—anything—to fight off the massive erection that was already starting to strain the crotch of his jeans.

"That's kind of the point," she said, giggling, and then she licked a hot trail of fire up the side of his neck. "Who needs edges? We are puppy and duck egg rescuers! We throw caution to the winds! We should eat, drink, and fuck merrily, for on my birthday, at least one of us might die."

A bolt of chained lightning sizzled through him at her sexy version of the old saying. He was surprised to hear her talk like that; he bet sober Rio would be surprised at herself, too. Although maybe that was the point.

"Did you need to drink wine to gear up to seduce me? Imagine how great that makes me feel," he said grimly.

She stopped feathering little kisses along his jawline, and he immediately wanted to take back his stupid question.

She pulled back far enough to look him in the eye, and her silly grin had vanished. "I don't actually get drunk on Fae wine, Luke. It relaxes me a little, so I can sleep, and it makes me feel happy and silly, but I could drink three more bottles of this and then head out for a day's work at my old job, if I'd wanted to do it."

Her lashes swept down to hide those beautiful golden eyes from him. "It's not drunken courage I need to seduce you, Luke. It's just plain old ordinary courage. You may not have noticed this, but I'm not very practiced at this kind of thing, and you have about a kajillion years' worth of experience."

Her eyes flashed amber fire. "Don't think I don't hate that, too. How many women have there been? Did you always use condoms? Did they even *have* condoms?"

She suddenly moved sideways so she wasn't sitting on his lap anymore, and he wanted to howl.

"That's a good question, actually," she said, pushing

her hair away from her face. "When were condoms invented?"

He pounced on her, pushing her back on the couch and stretching out his full length on top of her, while being careful to hold part of his weight on his arms so he didn't crush her. He bent down and caught the edge of her earlobe between his teeth and bit gently, nearly groaning again when she cried out and trembled beneath him.

"That's a terrible question. Any question either one of us could ask now would be a terrible question, in fact, but to answer what you're really asking, you are safe with me. It's been a long time, Rio, and I always used protection. Not to mention, I'm immortal, and human illnesses can't touch me; I'm also a wizard, so I can control the possibility of conception. For now, though, why don't we quit talking altogether?"

When she took a breath to answer him, he took complete advantage and captured her mouth with his. He took her mouth as if he were a conqueror: claiming her. Possessing her.

Branding her as his own.

Rio moaned into his mouth and made little gasping noises that inflamed his predatory instincts. He wanted to take and take and take—everything she had to give. All of it. All of her. Her warm body trembled under his and he settled his cock into the vee between her legs, exactly where he belonged.

"Luke," she whispered, when his lips left hers to travel down the side of her neck, kissing, licking, and gently biting. "Oh, gods, Luke, you're—I don't—I need you so much."

His breath quickened, and his arms tightened around her. The beast within him roared out a claim, and he realized that both he and the beast needed her surrender—but they needed something else from her, too.

"Rio, my name is Lucian," he growled. "I need you to say my name."

She met his gaze, her face glazed with desire, and he'd

never needed anything so much as he needed to sink his cock into her sweet heat, but he forced himself to wait.

"Say it," he demanded. Pleaded.

"Lucian," she breathed. "Kiss me again, Lucian. Touch me all over."

He leapt up off the couch and lifted her with one arm under her shoulders and the other under her lovely rounded ass.

"We're going to my bed. Now."

She pouted a little. "Then will you kiss me?"

He bent his head to murmur in her ear as they walked. "Yes, then I'll kiss you. I'll kiss your lovely lips, and then I'll kiss those perky nipples until they plump up and you squirm in my arms."

He shoved the door to his bedroom open so hard that it smashed against the wall and rebounded shut as soon as he'd passed through with his precious cargo in his arms. He tossed her on the bed and stood staring down at her, reveling in her parted lips and widened eyes.

"And then, my beautiful, brave, sexy woman, I'm going to kiss every single inch of your hot little body and tease you and taste you until you come, screaming, in my mouth."

Rio's heart stuttered in her chest. She'd unleashed the predator that Luke always kept so tightly controlled, and now she was going to see the power and passion that he'd hidden. Her secret, feminine heart rejoiced at the idea, but her courage faltered a little.

He pulled his shirt off, and she allowed her gaze to travel down the rippling muscles of his chest and the tight six-pack abs. His body was an incredible specimen of pure male perfection, and—at least for tonight—he was hers. She shivered at the thought, but then she crooked a finger at him.

"I think this would go better if you were a little closer."

He shouted out a laugh and leapt onto the bed, pushing her back and caging her in with his arms and legs.

"I have been dreaming about this moment since we were on that rooftop," he confessed, just before he kissed the skin above the neckline of her sweater. "Hell, if I'm being honest, since the first time you delivered a package to my office."

Her breath caught in her throat when she felt the warmth of his hand slide up under her sweater to the bottom of her breast. Time for her own confession.

"I had a similar reaction to you," she admitted. "I think I nearly bored Clarice to death talking about you for a while."

He stopped kissing her and stared down at her with a delighted expression on his face.

"Really? Tell me every sexy little detail," he said and, for the very first time since she'd known him, the tiniest hint of an Italian accent was present.

For some reason, that made her hesitate. This man—Lucian Olivieri—he hadn't wanted her before. What had changed?

He must've seen the shadow cross her face, because he tilted his head and then rolled onto his side next to her.

"What is it? What were you just thinking?"

"If you really had thoughts like that about me, why did you turn me down?" She wanted to look away, but courage demanded she face him.

His eyes darkened. "I didn't want to blow things up. There's a curse hanging over my head, Rio, and I should tell you all the details, so you can make an informed decision as to whether you want to stay in my bed or run screaming for cover."

"I'm not really the 'run screaming for cover' type, as you may have noticed," she said with some asperity. "So let's leave all talk of curses and birthdays for tomorrow, if you don't mind."

Then, because he was ticking her off, she leaned over

and bit the tendon of his neck where it met his shoulder, and he instantly grabbed her and yanked her on top of him.

"I have to warn you that I can't think when you do that," he growled. "Any nobility I might've had is very close to going out the window. All I can think of is driving into your hot, wet body while you wrap your legs around my waist and beg me to go harder and deeper."

She gasped, feeling heat and a rush of creamy readiness pool between her legs. The man was every primal, forbidden fantasy she'd ever had, wrapped up in the scents of spice and leather and magic. She wanted to rub her body all over his, push her breasts into his mouth, and beg him to suck on them until she exploded. She wanted him on her, around her, inside her—and her nipples peaked to hard, swollen buds at the mere thought of it.

She didn't know how to say any of that, though—it would've embarrassed her to death if she tried. Maybe she could work her way up to talking dirty another time. Instead, she grabbed him with both hands and pulled him closer.

"I need you to touch me right now," she demanded from between gritted teeth. "I don't know how to say this—I don't know how to *feel* this. My entire body is aching for you, and I'm going to explode if you don't do something *right now.*"

A blazingly seductive grin spread across his gorgeous face, and within five seconds flat she found herself stripped naked. He stood up to tear off his own clothes, and she got her first glimpse of the Dark Wizard of Bordertown in all his hard-bodied, erect, masculine glory.

A trail of silky dark hair arrowed down from his navel to where his erection jutted proudly out in front of him. It was long and thick and so hard that she couldn't take her eyes off it.

She finally tore her gaze away and stared up at him, suddenly feeling a little apprehensive.

"I think we have a problem." She had to stop to clear

her throat and lick her lips, and she noticed that he watched the stroke of her tongue with fiery and avid interest.

Suddenly, she felt every bit of her own nudity, and she yanked the quilts on his bed up and around her body.

"Don't even think of hiding those luscious breasts from me," he said, stalking forward.

The movement put his straining erection at eye level with her fascinated gaze, and she swallowed. Evidently this was not the right thing to do, because he groaned really loudly.

"I don't think so," she tried again, crossing her legs. "There is no way that's going to fit."

He threw back his head and laughed, and she could tell he was honestly amused.

"That's the wonderful thing about this, Rio," he said. "I'm going to make you so hot and so wet for me that we'll fit together just perfectly."

While that promise was still ringing in her ears, he pulled the quilts away from her body and took her breasts in his big hands. She drew in a shaky breath and blushed a hot pink when her nipples visibly got harder just from the touch of his gaze. When he bent down and licked a delicate path around one, she thought she might explode into a million sparkling pieces.

"It's so—why is it—is it a wizard thing?"

He grinned and then licked her nipple into his mouth and sucked on it, and she cried out from the intensity. She'd never felt anything like it, not even back before her nascent mind-reading skills drove her away from boys and then men for what she had feared was forever.

Luke switched his attention to her other breast, leaving his fingers to lightly pinch the one he'd abandoned, and she felt any attempt at rational thought vanish.

"These are so incredibly beautiful," he murmured, when he finally lifted his head, leaving her gasping and writhing beneath him.

He took her mouth again, and she met his attack with

one of her own. This was no surrender. She gave no quarter and took none. She wanted him fiercely, desperately, and without reservation.

He rolled onto his side and pulled her closer to him, and suddenly she felt his hand trail down her hip and then his clever fingers stroked into the center of her heat and she cried out.

"Oh, you like that, hmm?" He rubbed and stroked, first delving into her and then retreating to rub, at first lightly and then more insistently, on the little bud that smashed tidal waves of sensation and electricity through her body.

"What are you—I can't—" She couldn't talk; couldn't think; could only feel as wave after wave of pure, electric-blue flame rolled through her and left her powerless to the sensation.

He bent and captured a breast again with his lips as she exploded, and the stars fractured around her. She cried out again, and he drove his fingers inside her. Her body clenched around him, pulsing and coming, again and again, and the slight edge of his teeth against her nipple made her scream until her throat was raspy.

When she finally floated back down to earth from whatever precipice she'd plunged over, he was smiling at her with such smug male satisfaction that she very nearly laughed.

"I think we'll fit now," he said, and he was on top of her and driving his thick, heavy hardness inside her before she could catch her breath enough to debate questions of length or width.

He pulled her thighs up and around his hips with his hands and worked his way into her, slowly and carefully, his face showing the strain of his massive amount of self-control.

"It's—oh, my—it's so *good*," she said, dizzy with the feel of him taking her. Claiming her. Stretching her to plant the hard evidence of his desire inside the core of her being. Once he'd pushed inside her all the way to the hilt, until she felt his pelvic bone resting on hers, he started to pull out, and the slick tugging sensation nearly made her cry out again.

"I'm going to move a little faster now because I'm really close to losing control if I don't," he said hoarsely. "Is that okay?"

In answer, she frantically nodded and bucked her hips under him, wanting and needing something she instinctively knew that only he could provide. She wanted to explode again, but this time with him inside her. She could feel the delicious buildup of sexual tension as his hips sped up, and he thrust into her harder and faster, until she could feel the heavy weight of his testicles against her every time he drove himself all the way home.

"I'm going to come again, Luke," she whispered, clinging to his shoulders so she wouldn't spin off into space. "I'm sorry I'm doing it twice before you've even done it once, but it doesn't seem to be anything I can help."

"Never apologize to me for that," he said, breathing hard. "I want to make you come a dozen different times, in a dozen different ways, before dawn."

She didn't argue with him; she simply let the explosion take her. Light and magic and sound rushed around her and into her and through her in a symphony of passion and fulfillment, and all she could do was cling to Luke as her body and her heart both went cartwheeling into the stars together.

An inescapable truth flashed into her mind just before Luke's orgasm slammed into her with the power and force of a raging thunderstorm on a hot summer night. Her eyes flew open, and she stared blindly at the space over his shoulder, feeling the impact of the revelation every bit as much as she could feel his body, still wrapped around her and buried deep inside her.

She was falling in love with the Dark Wizard of Bordertown.

CHAPTER 16

Luke had finally discovered what the expression "died and gone to heaven" meant. Rio's body clenched and exploded around his cock, and suddenly it was as if someone had lit a rocket inside his brain. His tightly leashed control shattered, and he pinned her to the bed and fucked her harder and faster, driving into her body with all the power he'd been holding back, until she screamed again, clenching around him again, and this time he went over the edge with her.

His hips bucked against her as he came, and he could feel the jets of hot semen jetting out of the head of his cock, on and on, until he wondered if a man's body could somehow be drained completely by the unstoppable force and undeniable nature of simply coming. He wrapped his arms around Rio and rolled over, pulling her on top of him while he was still locked inside her. She was gasping for breath, her entire body shaking with passion and aftershocks, so he covered her face with kisses, drinking her in and soaking up the feel of her warmth on his icy heart.

She stripped him bare, this woman. Not just his body, and his hunger and need for her, but his heart and the darkness inside him, all the way to his soul. He knew beyond a shadow of a doubt that he never wanted to let her go. He'd fallen. He'd fallen in love with her, and were he a good man—a *better* man—he would be planning a way to keep her away from him, rather than futilely plotting how to try to defeat the curse and keep her forever.

Selfishness was no longer an option. Rio deserved more than he could ever give, because the curse hung over his head like the sword of Damocles and threatened not only his future but the happiness of anyone who was personally involved with him.

He could already feel his body hardening again, wanting her again, craving the fulfillment that he'd never felt before with anyone else. He tried to tame his unbridled reaction to her nearness. He didn't want to cause her any pain from his lack of restraint.

She folded her arms on his chest, propped her chin on her arms, and looked into his eyes, completely unaware of the epiphany that had changed his life forever.

"I have never felt this good in my entire life," she said dreamily. "Not even the time I broke into the convent kitchen and stole the five-gallon containers of ice cream, and we kids stayed up all night eating every bit of it."

Luke flexed his ass a little, pushing himself farther inside her, just for the pleasure of hearing her gasp and seeing her eyes go wide and unfocused.

"Can you do it again? Already?"

He loved the greedy touch of longing in her voice. "I can do it again, but I don't think we should. I don't want you to be sore tomorrow. I don't want you to have any reason for regrets, not now and not ever."

He twined his fingers in her hair, stroking it back from her face and enjoying the silky feel of it. She wiggled a little, and he closed his eyes from the pleasure of her body pressed against his.

"Luke. I don't care about that. I don't even know how many tomorrows I'll have. Right now, I want to make love to you in every way possible, all night long."

He started to protest again, but she cut him off by kissing him until he couldn't form a coherent thought.

"I was kind of wondering if you'd fit inside my mouth," she said, running her tongue across her lips.

After that, thinking of any kind was impossible for Luke for quite a long time.

✳

Rio woke up sprawled diagonally on Luke's bed, with a muscular male arm wrapped firmly around her waist and a long, hard body snug against her back. His hand was loosely cupping her breast, as if even after he'd done everything and anything possible to do, sexually, to another human being he still couldn't bear to lose contact with her.

She blushed fire-hot as she recalled some of the more exotic positions he'd enticed her into and some of the more erotic words he'd urged her on with. He'd claimed her in every possible way and made good on his word; there was no inch of her body that he hadn't touched or tasted, and she doubted there was an inch of his big body on which she hadn't done the same. She'd made up for years of celibacy in one night, and she wondered if she'd be able to walk.

Then she blushed again.

His arm tightened, and he stretched, moving her body with his, and then his fingers began to toy idly with her nipple. She caught her breath and then smacked his hand.

"Oh, no you don't," she said firmly, pulling away from him and sitting up. "I need to brush my teeth and take a shower, and then I need to go find my poor fox, who is probably traumatized, and feed her some breakfast."

As if on cue, Luke's stomach rumbled and then hers started up to match it. She glanced back at him over her shoulder and immediately regretted it, because the satisfied grin on his face made her blush even harder.

"I guess we worked up quite an appetite," he said, putting his hands behind his head and stretching some more.

He was utterly unconcerned about his own nudity, she'd

learned the night before, and absolutely fascinated with hers. With that in mind, she yanked the tangled sheet free of the end of the bed and wrapped it around herself before she fled to the bathroom, and his laughter followed her all the way there.

After Rio brushed her teeth and took care of the necessities, she stepped into the shower, almost moaning with pleasure as the hot spray pounded into her shoulders, relaxing her muscles. She turned and leaned against the glass tile of the shower wall, wondering if tough private-eye types could take a day off to lounge around and watch trashy TV.

She didn't hear Luke enter the shower, and she made a little squeaking noise when he unexpectedly put his arms around her from behind.

"Now that's a noise I didn't hear you make last night," he said, pouring shampoo into his hand.

For once, her automatic blushing instinct didn't kick in, so she had the hopeful thought that maybe she was becoming desensitized to embarrassment. But then he bent down and sucked one of her nipples into his mouth, right there in the shower, and she proved that theory wrong.

"Stop it," she snapped, but then she moaned as sizzling sensation traveled through her body and straight to her most sensitive places.

"I'm sorry, you're right," he said, stepping back a little but still grinning like a fiend. A sexually insatiable fiend. "We have a lot to do today. Turn around."

He gathered her hair in his hands and began to wash it, massaging shampoo into her scalp with firm pressure, and she almost moaned again. Her secret vice had always been how much she enjoyed a good head rub. Sometimes she went to get a haircut even when she didn't need one, just for the terrific massage her stylist delivered with the shampoo.

And Luke was a master at it.

"If you ever need a fallback job, I'm sure you could get a job at my hair salon."

He chuckled, a contented sound that sent tendrils of

warmth running through her. It occurred to her that there were people whose lives were just like this—they went to work, out to dinner, and came home to enjoy each other. Nobody was trying to kill them, recruit them, or torture them with mysterious snippets about their pasts.

She could even almost imagine her own life with Luke, if it could ever fall along that path. It would never be dull, and she'd never be alone again. She thought about the events of the past few days and added another item to the list.

She'd probably spend a lot of time buying people new cars.

Rio started laughing but then sputtered when water got in her mouth. Luke had switched to rinse mode.

By the time they were clean, dry, and dressed, Kit was waiting impatiently in the kitchen for them. She was seated on a bar stool, her bushy, white-tipped tail wrapped around her haunches and her chin resting mournfully on the counter, as if to ask where her breakfast was.

"Are you ever going to talk to me again?" Rio asked the fox. "Was your voice in my head just a fluke? You could talk telepathically because you were under extreme duress or something?"

Kit tilted her head and flicked her ears, as if listening intently.

"Maybe it was a onetime thing," Luke suggested, heading for the coffee maker. "You just never know with magic. Trust me, the weirder explanation is usually the right one with magical creatures."

Kit turned her head toward Luke and flattened her ears, like she was disagreeing with his comment.

"Hey, it was just a guess," Luke told her. "If you have something different to say, spit it out, little one."

Kit didn't move, but she perked up when Rio began to wash her bowls and refill them with fresh food and water. Rio placed the bowls back down on the floor, but when Kit didn't immediately jump down to eat, Rio turned to find the little fox watching her.

It is not easy to communicate this way. I am Yokai*; we*

meddle, we intervene and interfere, and sometimes we
help. But my mind does not comprehend what you call
morality in the same way that you do. I am here to help
you with a specific task, but I cannot tell you what or why,
because I do not know it yet.

"But you're good?" Rio felt like an idiot, but she had to
ask. "You're on my side?"

Yes. And no. It is complicated.

With that, Kitsune leapt lightly down and began to eat
her breakfast.

Rio blew out a frustrated sigh. Luke handed her a cup
of coffee and held up the butterscotch creamer in his other
hand.

"I think I'll try caramel today," she decided. "It seems
to be my week for trying new things."

Luke grinned, and she ordered herself not to blush.

"I especially liked that new thing where your tongue—"

"Stop!"

Luke laughed, but he stopped.

"What did she say?" He nodded at Kit.

"It's hard for her to talk to me. She verified that she is
Yokai. Something about her morality is different from
ours, and she's here to help me but she doesn't know with
what," Rio summarized.

"Did she say whether she's on your side? Because I
gotta tell you, if she's not, we can save money on fresh
chicken," he said, joking.

Kit raised her head and delicately lifted her upper lip
away from her front teeth in a silent snarl. Evidently she
didn't find him funny.

"Lighten up, fur-face," Luke advised. "I'm a whole lot
bigger than you are, and I like to blow things up."

Kit vanished. One moment she was eating her breakfast, and the next, she had completely disappeared. Rio
dropped the spoon she'd been using to stir coffee and
looked frantically around.

"You might want to be careful what you say," she slowly
told Luke, her eyes widening.

"Why is that, exactly?"

Rio pointed to where Kit was sitting, washing one paw, on the top of Luke's refrigerator.

"Well, this makes things interesting," Luke said calmly. "Now might be a good time for you to tell me if she said she's on your side."

"She said yes, but then she said no. It's complicated, apparently."

Her point made, Kit disappeared again and reappeared at her bowl of food, where she continued eating as if she'd never performed a magic trick right there in the middle of the kitchen.

"Yet another person, well, creature, in my life who knows more about me than I do," Rio said glumly. "I could throw a party and only invite people who know more about my past than I do, and we'd fill the Bordertown hockey arena."

Luke started assembling the ingredients to make another omelet, and it temporarily distracted Rio.

"Does Alice just stop by long enough to buy groceries and then leave?" A little pang of something that felt uncomfortably like jealousy struck, and Rio bit her lip. "Also, does she live here?"

Luke glanced up at her and then stopped what he was doing, crossed the space between them, and kissed her.

"Alice and I are old friends, nothing more. She stays here for the few days a month that she's actually in town, and we catch up. She manages to hear more eerily accurate scoop and gossip than anyone I've ever known, and she always shares any interesting information she learns with me."

He went back to his eggs but then looked up and hit her with a hard stare. "While we're clearing the air, what about Cage Whatsisname, the bike boy? He seemed like way more than a friend to me when I was—ah, when I happened to accidentally cross paths with you on multiple occasions in the past."

She caught a sheepish look on his face before he bent his head to chop vegetables, but decided not to ask.

"Cage may have wanted to be more than a friend, but I never returned the sentiment, and he promptly moved on. The last I heard, he was serving as Ophelia's operatic muse."

"Her naked muse?" Luke grinned at her. "I could use one of those."

"I'm the only naked muse you're going to see for a long time, Buster," she warned him, laughing.

For some reason, he scowled down at his omelet pan, which puzzled her until she thought back to what she'd said.

Oh. He didn't want her to think she had any claim on him. Of course.

"Hey, that's fine," she said lightly, pretending her heart wasn't beginning to crack like the eggshells he'd just discarded in the sink.

Discarded. Abandoned.

Like garbage down the drain.

She forced her face into something that might have approached a smile. "No expectations, right? You can get naked with anybody you like."

He was around the counter so fast she didn't even see him move, and then he had his hands on her waist, lifting her into the air. "Don't even think about it. There will be no naked anything for you with anybody but me. Do you understand me?"

Something feral and primitive stared at her from Luke's eyes, and she instinctively knew that she needed to tread very carefully until he could leash the darkness that was haunting him.

So she leaned forward and kissed him. It was a sweetly seductive kiss; she nibbled at his lips until he opened his mouth for her, and then she delicately licked and tasted until he responded, slanting his head and returning the kiss with all of the fierce passion he'd displayed during the night.

When he finally pulled back, there was a grim cast to his features, as if he had bitter news to tell and didn't know how to do it. Or maybe . . .

"Luke," she began, choosing her words with care. "I think I may have just read your thoughts, a little. Did you think about needing to tell me some bad news?"

His eyes widened a little, but he didn't seem either very surprised or very unhappy at her revelation.

"I need to tell you about my curse, Rio. I need to tell you everything, and then I need to give you the chance to walk out the door and never see me again, no matter how much I despise the thought."

Smoke drifted up, and Luke cursed and went to rescue his omelet, leaving Rio to watch, all alone, as her life and her plans and her heart shattered all around her. She'd been in his bed all night, giving him her body and her soul, and they hadn't even made it to breakfast before he was willing to say good-bye. She walked, dazed and almost blindly, across the room and out the back door before he could stop her, and then she stood in the rain and let the tears fall.

CHAPTER 17

Luke grabbed the pan, burning his hand in the process, which only served him right. He turned off the heat to avoid burning down his damn house and ran after Rio, but she was gone, and nothing, not even a trace of her scent, remained. Only the haunting image of her shock and pain, after he'd dropped that final bombshell on her, remained to taunt him.

He turned his face up to the cold, driving rain and wished bitterly that, for once in his life, he could have been the type of man for whom eloquent words came easily, but the glib conversationalist gene in his storied heritage had bypassed him completely. He didn't know how to talk to a woman he loved because he'd never done so.

He'd never before felt this way—that he might be falling in love with a woman—and now that he was, he had no map to guide him through the process. He was great at ordering people to do things. He was even pretty damn good at ordering people to leave him alone.

Cooperation had never been his style; he'd always simply

blasted anything that annoyed him and anyone who deserved it. And now, without even trying, he'd driven away the most incredible woman he'd ever known.

Behind him in the doorway, Kit howled. The sound of her song was so desolate that the tiny hairs on the back of his neck stood straight up and his already chilled flesh pebbled on his arms.

He suddenly laughed, standing alone in the rain, like the lunatic so many figured him to be. After all, it made sense that Rio had run away from both of them. He spun around and stalked back to his house, looking down at the little fox as he stepped past her.

"It's not like we didn't deserve it. You told her that you didn't know if you were on her side, and she thought that I told her I wanted her to leave. We deserve to lose her."

Kit howled again, but he pulled his door shut, forcing her to back up into the kitchen and out of the rain. The two of them stood looking at each other. Both miserable; both wet and dripping; both probably cursing the other for contributing to Rio's despair.

Luke had known enough about her history that he had no excuse for his thoughtlessness. Her parents—whoever they had been—had abandoned her at that convent. And now, even that pale shadow of a home had disappeared out from under Rio's metaphorical feet.

What a perfect time for him to dump the truth of his curse on her. He couldn't have timed his stupid blunder any worse if he'd planned it to cause her the maximum possible pain.

It was even worse than that, though. He had to be honest with himself. His fault lay in what he'd done the night before. He'd taken advantage of her inexperience and the vulnerability of her situation because he was a selfish bastard who'd only been interested in quenching his insatiable need for her.

It had been an unforgivable thing to do, especially from a man who knew he had no right to a future with someone like Rio. He was an immortal cursed to walk the razor's edge between salvation and damnation—forever. A man whose entire existence had been, and always would be, spent paying for the sins of the past.

His first instinct was to try a locator spell, but the little bit of common sense he had left after Hurricane Rio had swept through his life told him that she would never forgive him for tracking her down like a lost dog. So he turned his thoughts to something—anything—he could do while he waited to discover if she'd ever return or forgive him.

His upper lip lifted from his teeth in what was probably a good impression of Kit's best snarl. He knew exactly what to do. A practical task; one that would help Rio.

An easy mission.

He was going to storm the Silver Palace and drag the truth out of a certain Fae aristocrat.

Twenty minutes later, Luke was wondering how much trouble he'd be in for incinerating a half dozen Fae guardsmen, and whether it would be worth it, when a flunky finally officiously gave him permission to enter the palace. The flunky personally escorted Luke to Lady Merelith's quarters.

"It's not like I'm going to steal your silver, pal," Luke snarled, but the man never even blinked an eye. Probably, after life among the High Court Winter Fae, the little guy wouldn't be afraid of much that didn't walk the icy realms. There was plenty enough and more to be terrified of right here.

Luke had been in the Winter Court Palace several times before, but familiarity, though it didn't breed contempt, didn't breed admiration or liking, either. The place's icy lines and sterile decorations always made him think that here was a home without a heart. It was an easily recognizable flaw when the one doing the noticing suffered from the same problem.

Rio could have been the heart of his home, Luke realized, and the rhythm of his pace faltered enough that the flunky cast a chiding glance back over his epauletted shoulder.

Merelith inhabited an enormous suite on the east wing of the third floor. By the time they got there, and more of her flunkies, this time dressed like the Royal Guard, screwed around for a while and then finally allowed him into her presence, Luke was about a mile and a half past reasonable.

Which was fine by Merelith, apparently, because she didn't bother much with small talk, either.

"How did you get in here? Get out." She didn't even bother to look at him, which raised the thermostat to red on the How to Anger the Wizard meter.

"Make me. What do you know about Rio and her parents?"

Her eyes narrowed, and the four guardsmen flanking her immediately drew their swords and pointed all four of them, plus the requisite daggers, straight at Luke. Luke bared his teeth at them, and then he started to laugh.

"Merelith, do I look like somebody who'd be afraid of your boy toys and their little pointy sticks? They're very decorative, but I've had a bad damn day. I'm soaked from the rain, and I'm standing here dripping on what I'm sure are very expensive carpets. Is this really something you want to prolong?" He held up his hands and made sure she saw the blue flames sparkling between his fingers. "I'd be happy to redecorate for you. Kind of minimalist in here, don't you think? Little cold? What would you think about a nice roaring fire right here where your men used to be standing?"

The guardsmen all simultaneously tensed and leaned forward, eager to slit him from stem to stern, no doubt.

"Wow, it's like watching synchronized swimming without the water. Now we just need Michael Phelps," Luke drawled. "Did you hear the rumor that he's probably a Water Fae?"

Merelith sighed. "Lucian Olivieri, you make it very hard for a person to be pleasant to you."

Her voice was as icily arrogant as ever, but Luke's

wrongness detector was buzzing. The Fae wasn't one hundred percent on her game today; she lacked some indefinable quality of command or control that he'd never seen her without before. Luke suddenly looked around. Something was off. The usual luster of the room had dimmed to a dull sheen. He'd visited Merelith on a few occasions on investigative business. Whenever he had been in her sitting rooms before, it had felt uncomfortably like he'd entered the inside of a highly decorated ice cube.

Now, however, the effect was more like that of the interior of an old tin box.

"What's wrong? I don't mean to be blunt, and you know I can play Winter Court etiquette with the best of them when I'm really motivated—"

"Which is almost never," she interrupted icily.

"Granted," he agreed. "But it's almost Rio's birthday, and suddenly everybody in the known universe is interested in her, and I don't like anything about that. I need to help her, and in order to do so, I need to know what's going on. You gave us the impression that you knew something about her, when you were at my place, so talk."

One of the guardsmen raised his dagger and rushed Luke, screaming something about Luke's "effrontery," and Luke smashed him to the ground with a bolt of enhanced gravity designed to break several of the man's bones.

"I don't even know what 'effrontery' means, and that pissed me off," Luke said, mocking the rest of them, daring them to try something.

Anything.

"Is this the wizarding world equivalent to trying to start a bar fight?" Merelith stared down at the broken guardsman with distaste. "And you. Did I order you to attack this man, who is a guest under my roof, however uninvited and unwanted?"

She pointed to the others. "Get him out of here."

The remaining three guardsmen picked up their fallen companion and filed silently out of the room, leaving Merelith and Luke alone.

"Why would you possibly think I would tell you anything, especially after you just damaged my guard?" Merelith never raised her voice, but she didn't need to do anything overt like that. Menace ran through her veins like blood, and Luke wondered why he wasn't afraid.

Maybe because he'd finally reached the point where he had something to lose.

"Because you owe me. Do I really need to call you on the debt that your honor should have seen paid?"

Luke played the game. Fae were big on defending their honor. He didn't give a rat's ass if she ever paid him for basically playing taxi service to her niece, and if she did, he'd do with it what he always did—donate it to the poison control hotline.

Those gifts always gave him a great deal of satisfaction. It was like spitting in his ancestors' collective eye.

"Do not question me on my honor, wizard, or you will regret it very bitterly. Payment is on its way to you, as agreed, but I have been somewhat . . . occupied."

Luke wanted to blast something, but for once in his miserable, impatient, cursed life, he took the time to consider his options. He studied—*really* studied—Merelith's face for a hint of what she was feeling. That would usually be a stupid waste of time with her, or with any Fae, but this time something was different.

Merelith's face was showing emotion, and that was very, very wrong.

He could see faint lines of strain around her perfect eyes, which meant that either she was in true pain or her magic had become so badly flawed that it was failing to preserve an illusion of beauty that she had previously maintained for all the years he'd known her. He knew enough of the Fae to discard the second option. Her beauty was no illusion. Neither was the terror she inspired in any sane man.

Therefore, something was wrong, and only one name came to mind.

Elisabeth.

"Where is she? Where's Elisabeth? Is she all right?" He strode right past the startled Fae and slammed open the door to her inner sanctum. It was a door he'd never seen opened before, and he didn't know quite what to expect. What he found was gut-wrenchingly devastating.

Elisabeth lay in the middle of an enormous bed, swaddled in silk coverlets, so pale and still that he was sure she must be dead.

"What did you do to her?" He whirled around and confronted Merelith. "If you hurt her in any way, I swear to you—"

He abruptly shut his fool mouth, because the truth of it was plainly apparent on Merelith's drawn and tired face. She was hurting over this. Hurting in a way that he'd never seen before, not even when her youngest sister—Merelith's favorite—had made a bad marriage and been exiled. Or murdered, Luke had always secretly suspected, but that wasn't important now. It was simply his brain babbling and taking cover under an onslaught of trivia so Luke didn't have to face the tiny body on the bed.

"When did Elisabeth die?" Luke managed to force the words out, even though his throat was closing up and his eyes were burning.

Merelith's face softened for a second as she watched him, but then she resumed the blank stare that had replaced her icy mask of indifference.

"She is not dead."

Luke's knees weakened with relief, and he didn't even care that Merelith saw it.

"She is very ill, and we do not know why," the Fae continued. "None of our healers can help her, not even I, and I share a blood bond with her. I have had five different human doctors examine her and take specimens of her blood, hair, and urine back to their laboratories outside Bordertown, in case the illness could have been related to Elisabeth's human heritage, but none of them could find anything."

A single tear pooled in Merelith's right eye and slipped

down her face, and it was all the more jarring since Luke was almost certain that she was completely unaware of it.

"I let them live," she said, almost as an afterthought. "The useless human doctors. In case that's the next accusation you want to hurl at me."

The only accusations Luke wanted to hurl were at himself, but he figured he'd join Merelith in her anguish only when he'd run out of other options. He was a wizard, damn it. He should be able to find a cure for a sick kid.

"When did it start?" He crossed over to the bed and stared down at the tiny girl, who seemed much smaller than she'd been when he'd retrieved her from Dalriata's office.

She was so pale—impossibly pale—a color that no human skin should ever be. Her pulse and breathing had slowed so much that it was almost as if she were under a sleeping curse.

"Sleeping beauty," he murmured, reaching out to move a strand of her hair that had fallen in her face.

Merelith glanced sharply at him. "That is a very old curse, indeed. I'm surprised you have heard of it, beyond the fairy tales that infuse contemporary culture. I thought of it, of course, but the counterspell has had no effect. Whatever this is, it is not that."

Merelith sank down to sit on the bed next to her niece, graceful even in her extreme distress.

"She wanted to see Rio. She asked me if Rio and the fox could visit her, and I said no," Merelith admitted, the perfect silken perfection of her voice finally cracking. "That was the last thing I said to her before she fell into this coma, or curse, or whatever it is."

"She knows that you care about her," Luke said, briefly putting a hand on Merelith's shoulder even as he wondered why he cared that she was hurting so much.

It was a touch she never would have allowed, and he never would've attempted, but for their shared burden of grief over one small, half-human child.

"You are a wizard," she began, slowly, then picking up

speed as the idea formed. "You will be able to find a way. Heal my niece, and I'll tell you everything I know about Rio."

Luke scowled. "You damn Fae. Even in the worst situations, you're still trying to negotiate and bargain. You didn't need to do that, and you don't need to threaten me either. I will do everything I can to try to help Elisabeth. For her sake, not for yours."

He knelt down by the side of the bed, leaned over, and sniffed at the puff of breath that barely touched his face when Elisabeth shallowly exhaled. There was no odor, no hint of a sense that might tell him of a sickness or a poison.

"Is this coma, or sleep, her only symptom?"

"She grew ever more tired when we brought her home, and within the space of six hours had become as you see now."

He fought the urge to lash out at her for not calling him earlier. For letting her pride get in the way of seeking out help for Elisabeth, who now might be too small and too frail to fight this off—whatever *this* was—any longer.

"I need a sample of her blood, and a lock of her hair, if I may." He tried to be formally correct, knowing that to ask for such things, when the request came from a wizard, was no small thing.

Especially to the Fae.

Merelith offered no arguments, though. She simply nodded and walked away, presumably to find the necessary tools.

"I'll do everything I can for you, I promise that," Luke whispered to the still, silent form on the bed. "Come back to us, Elisabeth. Your auntie Merelith needs you, and Kit would love to play with a nice girl like you. I promise I'll bring Rio to visit, too, if she ever forgives me."

He bent his head and rested it on the edge of the bed, praying to any gods who would still listen to someone with a soul as dark as his. "Please spare this child. Please help me find a way to help her."

When he looked up, Merelith was standing there, staring down at him with an expression of utter astonishment.

"I had not expected this of you, Lucian Olivieri," she whispered.

He blinked hard, because his eyes were burning so much. He must've gotten dust in them, and he didn't want Merelith to see it. When he had it under control, he stood up and nodded to her. The healer she'd brought with her gently drew a vial of the child's blood and snipped a long strand of her hair, packaged both, and handed them to Luke.

"You will do your best," Merelith said.

The words were not a question, nor were they a request, but rather pure command, coming from one who was second in line to the winter throne.

Luke nodded. "I always do my best. I'll contact you as soon as I know anything."

Luke didn't waste time saying anything else but headed for the door.

Merelith's voice stopped him. "Your Rio is in more danger than she knows. On the anniversary of her birth, she will be claimed—one way or the other. Keep her safe until we can talk again."

"Keep her safe from whom?"

"Everyone."

The word haunted him all the way home.

CHAPTER 18

Rio sat at the Roadhouse's bar next to Miro eating jelly beans and nachos. The candy was his, and the nachos with extra jalapeños were hers. It was a meal they'd shared once a week or so for the past few years.

"He doesn't deserve you," the ogre said glumly, tossing another of the hated black jelly beans into the trash can behind the bar.

Rio, who had shared only a highly abbreviated version of what had happened between her and Luke, wasn't sure she agreed, but she soaked up the sympathy anyway.

Clarice thumped a small fist on the bar. "Oh, for Pete's sake, Rio. Have a fling. Live a little. Make sure you discover all the special wizarding tricks he can do in the sack."

Rio didn't have the energy to pretend to be surprised. Clarice was never anything but blunt when it came to talking about personal relationships.

Miro's blocky cheeks turned a delicate shade of rose-tinted green. He was a bit of a prudish ogre.

"I think Luke might be important to me," Rio admitted.

"Then fight for him, or lose him forever," Clarice said

unsympathetically. "Those are your options. I have waited for all the years I've known you, since the night you stole the ice cream for us in that damn orphanage, for you to find someone I thought was good enough for you."

Clarice stood on tiptoe, reached across the bar, and smacked Rio on the side of her head.

"Ow! What was that for?" Rio rubbed her head and scowled at Miro. "Nice job protecting me, Mr. Head Bouncer."

Clarice wagged her finger in Rio's face. "That was for being a numbskull. This wizard actually might be good enough for you. You know that, or you never would've trusted him this far. Go after him, or you will regret it."

Miro nodded solemnly, then tipped about a quarter of the bowl of jelly beans into his mouth. When he was done chewing, he belched and then looked at Rio.

"You should. And if he treats you bad, I will rip his limbs apart and use them for pool cues."

Rio nodded slowly and then put another slice of jalapeño in her mouth as an easily visible excuse for not talking. Sometimes it was good to have friends, even if she didn't let them very far into her life or heart. She had to fight to protect herself—she'd always been very careful to do so. She'd kept any hint of her true emotions hidden down deep beneath her disguise of amiability, or so she'd thought, but Clarice, and now Miro, had always seen beneath her masks.

Maybe it was because she and Clarice had shared part of their childhood. Clarice had been in and out of the convent so fast that her name had still been written in crayon on a piece of masking tape on her locker by the time she'd been adopted. She'd been exactly the kind of child that so many parents were looking for: happy, bubbly, and eager to please.

Rio, who had been none of those things, had somehow never resented Clarice for her happiness or her new family. And when they'd run into each other again in Bordertown High School, they'd become fast friends.

These days, Clarice ran through boyfriends the way

Miro ran through jelly beans: in bulk, with great enjoyment, and sometimes with more than one at a time. She never kept any of them around for very long, and they all wound up being great friends after the relationship was over.

As in so many other things, Rio was the exact opposite of Clarice in that, too. Rio had always worked hard to preserve her independence, but she hadn't noticed exactly when independence had turned into solitude, or when solitude had turned into loneliness.

Her life had been passing her by as quickly as the scenery did when she flew down the streets of Bordertown on her bicycle. Now she'd suddenly acquired a magical fox who might or might not be an ally and attracted an assortment of dangerous people who either wanted to recruit her or hurt her. Her life didn't make any sense at all.

Except—she'd thought that at least one tiny corner of her life had been beginning to make quite a lot of sense. Her feelings for Luke. Her lips quirked up a little when she realized that she'd just thought of the tall, imposing man as a "tiny corner" of her life. He'd really hate that.

After all, Luke had alluded to the curse before and the danger he would face if he were ever to turn dark. Maybe he'd had the right to expect that she would understand what that meant.

But then he'd made love to her—he'd *claimed* her, in such a primal way. How could he have even considered casting her aside after that?

How could he even think she would let him?

Suddenly, she was angry, and angry was far, far better than devastated.

"I'm going to kick his ass for him," she announced.

She wasn't going to let this man go so easily, wizard or no. He was *her* wizard, and he'd better darn well realize it.

She pushed the plate of nachos aside, put her money on the bar, and smiled at Clarice and Miro.

"I love you guys. Thank you for listening to me, and thank you for kicking my butt when I needed it."

Pretending not to notice the shocked expression on

Clarice's face, Rio gave Miro a quick hug and then started to leave, but found her way blocked by half a dozen goblins.

"We need to talk to you right now," the tall one in front rumbled.

"Not you, too." Rio threw her hands in the air. "I have absolutely had it. If you tell me that the goblins are also interested in my twenty-fifth birthday, I am going to lie down on the floor right here and have a kicking and screaming temper tantrum."

Miro glanced down at the floor and shook his head. "I wouldn't advise it. Floor's not too clean."

Rio noticed that the goblins had all backed up a step and were cautiously watching her, as if she might do something scary. This, coming from goblins, who were famed for their ferocity and destructiveness, should have struck her as amusing. It said a lot about the way her life had been going recently that it didn't.

"Then let us wish you happy birthday with all possible speed," offered the goblin, flashing a set of very frightening teeth.

"That wasn't why I wanted to talk to you, though, human. You helped my cousin Janet find her puppy, and I wanted to say thank you. If you ever need a favor, the goblins in my Oblong will answer your call."

Rio's mouth fell open a little. A goblin's Oblong was his immediate family group, and it usually consisted of around 110 members. The word *Oblong* referred both to the family group and to the communal residence they shared.

The offer that they would answer her call was a substantial one and conveyed great honor in the goblin world.

Rio belatedly remembered her manners, and she bowed, hoping to convey the proper respect. The goblin lord, for that was what he must've been in order to have the ability to offer such a thing, grinned and gnashed his teeth with satisfaction.

"You do me great honor with your words," she said carefully, remembering what little she'd learned about goblins and how easy they were to offend. "Please forgive the rudeness I showed when you first approached. My life has not gone according to plan this week, and I am somewhat disgruntled about it."

The goblin chortled, and his companions did the same. "We, of all creatures living, understand about life not going according to plan. Any rudeness is forgiven, and the offer stands."

Rio bowed again. "There is no debt owed," she tried to explain. "We were glad to help your . . . cousin?"

"She is my third cousin, and very beloved by my mother. The offer stands. For some reason, Janet values that furry creature above and beyond its value as a potential dinner." He shook his head in bewilderment, a reaction apparently shared by all of his buddies, considering the way they were shaking their heads and muttering.

Rio worked hard to contain her relief that poor Penelope was safe from their cooking pots, and the goblins trundled off back to the roulette wheel, which fascinated them.

"It's a good thing I saw that with my own eyes, or I never would have believed it," Clarice said, shaking her head. "I wasn't even sure he knew how to talk, other than the same two words he always says: *More beer.*"

Miro had turned around on his bar stool during the exchange, and he gazed thoughtfully after the goblins.

"This is a big honor from the little man," he said, from the perspective of his nearly giant-sized height. "Goblins are good to have at your side in a battle. Nasty street fighters, and they never give up."

Rio sighed. "Well I'm hoping things haven't deteriorated so badly that I need an Oblong of goblins on call just in case I get into a street fight."

"Maybe, maybe not. Considering the stuff that's been happening to you lately, you might be heading for one hell of a birthday party," Clarice pointed out. "You know, the more I think about it, the more I believe you're perfect for that private investigator job. Not just because of your mind-reading talent, either. Wherever you go, you manage to make friends, or at least allies. It seems to me that that would be a big part of the PI business—networking and contacts."

Clarice dried a few more glasses, obviously deep in thought. "Everybody likes you, Rio, and for good reason."

Miro nodded. "It's true. If you go into business with Oliver, he gains every bit as much as you do."

Rio was ridiculously touched by their comments, but she didn't want to get all girly about it, so she just bit her lip and smiled. "Well, Maestro was probably lying to me anyway about knowing who my parents were. Also, from what I've seen of the way the League of the Black Swan works, I don't want anything to do with it. So I think I'm going to refuse his recruitment offer."

"Perfect. We've plotted out your future," Clarice said. "Changing the subject entirely, what kind of cake do you want for your birthday?"

Rio groaned. "Surprise me. And no presents! I love you both, but I've gotta bounce. I need to go talk to a wizard."

Clarice grinned wickedly. "For your present, maybe he can wrap a bow around his—"

"I'm leaving now. La la la, I can't hear you," Rio shouted, putting her hands over her ears.

But the visual kept her warm all the way to Luke's place.

Luke smashed his foot into the side of his desk, accomplishing nothing except for denting the metal and hurting his foot. Nothing worked. None of it. None of the spells or potions or powders he'd carefully collected for so many years. Her blood had given him no clues, no matter how many different ways he'd tried to analyze it.

He would not—*could* not—accept that Elisabeth would die because of his incompetence.

His office door slammed open and he whirled, snarling, ready to incinerate whoever dared to interrupt him, but it was the one person he hadn't expected. Protest and anger sharpened into sensual emotions bordered by need and hunger. For her.

"Rio."

She *glowed*. Her eyes flashed amber fire as if she were lit up from within; she was brilliantly incandescent. Unbelievably beautiful.

"I'm not letting you leave me over some stupid curse," she declared.

She was furious. Defiant.

Spectacular.

She was the dream he'd never even known he'd been having, come to vivid, three-dimensional life, and he wanted her so badly that he ached with it.

She glared at him. "You can't just make love to a person all night long and then suddenly decide to be noble."

She pronounced the word *noble* as if it meant *cowardly*. He suspected there were times that the two might be interchangeable.

He needed her. *Now.*

He waved his hand, and the office door slammed shut and locked behind her. He finally let it all go. Let down his safeguards. Smashed the barricades to his emotions aside. Unleashed the helpless fury he'd felt ever since she'd left him that morning. The rage—an electric, visceral fury—had intensified when he found Elisabeth. All afternoon, while he failed over and over again, he'd fought to keep it under control.

Control shattered. Rage lost the battle to desire—hunger—need.

Luke handed the reins to Lucian, and the beast he kept caged inside him roared its way to the forefront. He waved his hand again, and shutters slammed shut over the large office window.

Rio flinched a little, but he was pleased to see that she stood her ground. She had courage, his woman.

"I need you," he ground out.

"Well, you should have thought of that—"

He snarled, cutting off whatever defiant remark she'd been about to finish. "Take off your clothes."

She actually growled right back at him. "Are you out

of your tiny little mind? After what you said to me this morning? Don't even think—"

He prowled across the room toward her, throwing off his shirt as he went, sweeping his hot gaze from her head to her toes and letting it linger on her beautiful breasts until she blushed again.

"Take them off," he repeated, his voice low and menacing.

A distant part of his brain recognized that he could not—he *would not*—take her without her consent, but he'd be damned if he'd let her go without a fight.

He clenched his hands into fists at his sides to keep from touching her, his cock so hard it was already straining the fabric of his jeans. He ached for her; he *throbbed* for her, and nothing would calm the savage monster inside him until he was driving his cock into her hot, wet heat.

"You have about ten seconds to run away before I rip your clothes into shreds," he warned her. "Run now, tell me no, give me some indication that you don't want me, but do it *right now*, because in less than a minute I plan to be fucking you right here on my desk."

She gasped, but she didn't back away. She *didn't run away*.

Deep in her amber gaze he found the acceptance he wanted and needed so badly, but he didn't pounce until she raised her hand and touched his face.

"I need you," he repeated, broken and desperate.

"I need you, too," she said, and the words were the tinder to the flames burning his body.

He shoved his jeans down and kicked them off, groaning in relief as his cock sprang free from its denim restraint. He was so hard that the head of his erection pointed straight up into the air, and he could almost feel individual veins and nerves pulsing with hunger and need.

"Now," he said, because that was all he could manage. It was the only word he could find in the roaring conflagration of his mind.

Hunger dominated reason; need overpowered caution. He

bunched the front of her shirt in his hands and ripped it down the middle. Her breasts, barely hidden from his sight in a scrap of blue lacy fabric, begged him to touch them and lick them and suck on them, so he lifted her by the waist and took one hard little nipple into his mouth and sucked, hard.

She cried out and tried to put her legs around his waist, but it wasn't enough, she wasn't naked, and so he lowered her back down to her feet and stripped her clothes from her with so little care that soon they were lying in shreds on the floor.

"Need you now," he growled. "Need to fuck you now, so hard and so deep that the memory of me is burned into your soul."

She captured his face in her hands and pulled his head down to kiss him, and the monster inside him, never balanced so far over the abyss as at right that moment, shivered with pleasure.

"Make love to me," she said, and he was lost, because she was right, it wasn't about fucking, it was about loving.

He dropped to his knees in front of her, right there and then, and took her sweet, wet heat with his mouth. He licked her and speared his tongue into her, reveling in the creamy evidence of her desire for him, and then he fastened his lips to the little bud that brought her so much pleasure and he sucked on it, just as hard as he'd sucked on her nipple.

This time she screamed.

He immediately stopped what he was doing and stood up.

"No. You will not come until your body is locked around my cock," he ordered.

Her head fell back and she panted with short, quick breaths, and he stared at her, frozen and struck mute by her rosy loveliness, but then she opened her eyes and glared at him.

"Now, already," she demanded.

His incredible, wonderful, amazing woman wanted him *now*.

"Yes," he growled.

He picked her up and positioned the head of his cock at her slick entrance and then he pushed forward at the same time he lowered her body, letting gravity help him to thrust as far into her as he could go.

"Mine," he said fiercely, loving the passion that glazed her eyes and the way she clung to his shoulders as if to a lifeline in a storm-tossed sea.

"Oh, Luke, oh, Luke, oh, *Lucian*," she said, crying out again when he started walking, still fucking her, over to his desk.

The rhythmic movement seated his cock even more deeply inside her, until he was sure he was going to explode before another heartbeat passed. He reached his desk just in time, and shoved everything off it with one hand and then gently lowered her onto the desk while he was still deep in her body. She lay back on the desk, her arms over her head, and the visual feast of having her nude beauty spread out in front of him nearly made him weep.

"I need you," he said, and the welcome in her eyes and her body began to heal his damaged soul.

"I need you, I need you, I need you," he said, thrusting into her again and again, because it was the closest he could come to saying he loved her. The only words that he was brave enough to say.

"I need you, too," she said, barely able to catch her breath.

"Come for me," he demanded, and he pushed his thumb against that magical little bud, rubbing and stroking, and he fucked her and fucked her, so hard, and so deep, and so right.

And then somehow, without him knowing how or why, he wasn't fucking her at all.

He was *making love* to her.

"I need you," he said, torn apart by the realization. "Come for me now."

Her eyes widened, and she shattered around him, screaming his name.

His *real* name.

"Lucian, it's too much, it's too much," she screamed,

shaking and writhing on the desk in the throes of the passion he'd given her.

He'd given her. She was his, and she always would be.

He pulled her up and into his arms, and his cock, already swollen beyond the bounds of endurance, demanded relief. He let the release smash through him, shouting out his triumph and pleasure as he came, long and hard, deep inside her.

Rio's head lolled on his shoulder as her body went boneless in his arms, and he finally allowed himself to think the words he couldn't say.

I love you.

The power of the thought conquered him, sweeping through him with the crystalline power of the purest magic he'd ever encountered, and he stumbled, almost falling, before he managed to catch his balance and make his way, still holding her, to his bedroom.

He spared a moment as he made his way down the hall to be grateful that Kit was nowhere to be seen, probably sleeping in Rio's room, and then he was falling into bed, still holding Rio as close as he could, his cock still buried deep inside her.

"I'm not letting you go without a fight," she murmured sleepily. "Miro agrees. He said he'll use your bones for cue sticks if you hurt me, plus you should know that the goblins owe me a favor."

Luke pulled the covers up and over them and then settled her against his chest. "You do meet the most interesting people, Rio Jones Green."

But she was already asleep. Luke stayed awake watching her for a very long time.

"I love you," he whispered, and the curse—or, as he thought of it, the monster who'd crouched inside his soul for so long—agreed.

He carefully untangled Rio's limbs from his own, kissed her forehead, and headed back to his office. Maybe now, confident that she returned at least some part of his emotion, he would finally be able to think.

CHAPTER 19

Rio found Luke in his office at dawn, and she handed him a mug of coffee. The long, high table in his office was covered with bottles, vials, and jars, all filled with various powders and liquids. The hair on the top of his head was standing almost straight up, as if he'd been clutching his head all night long. She glanced around and froze when she saw the evidence of the previous night's encounter. Everything from the top of his desk was still strewn across the floor nearby.

She was the new, nonblushing Rio, however. She ignored the mess and her embarrassment and instead concentrated on what he was doing now.

"New case?"

He stared almost blindly into his mug and then placed it on the table, reached out and took hers and did the same with it, and then pulled her into a tight hug and kissed her soundly.

"Good morning."

"Good morning to you, too," she murmured, perfectly content to stand right there for the rest of the morning.

But he let her go, picked up his coffee, and drained it in a few long swallows. "I need to tell you something, and it's going to be hard to hear. I think you should sit down."

Panic and anger flared. "If this is some kind of twisted routine with you, that you have sex and then have unpleasant talks the next morning, I'm not—"

"It's not about us," Luke said, flashing a brief, reassuring smile before his face resumed its stern lines. "I've never used the expression before, but this time it applies: This is literally about life and death."

She didn't like the sound of that. At all. Her mind immediately started tumbling in a thousand different directions, trying to figure out what could be wrong. "What?"

"It's Elisabeth," he said gently. "She is in very bad shape."

Of all the crises she'd been considering, one involving Elisabeth hadn't even been in the mix.

"What's wrong with her? I thought she was fine when Merelith came to get her. Is she hurt? Was she in an accident?" Rio put her coffee down again and drummed her fingers on the table, unable to stand still.

"We should go to her. Where is she?"

"That's just it. I saw her yesterday. I went to the Silver Palace to see if I could get Merelith to talk to us about your parents, and I saw Elisabeth while I was there. She's in a coma, Rio, and she's barely breathing—she's barely alive. Neither the Fae healers nor the human doctors can figure out what's wrong there."

He swept out his hand and knocked half the bottles and jars off the table and sent them crashing to the floor. "None of this is going to work, either. Her blood tells me nothing. Her hair tells me nothing. I have no idea why that little girl is sick, but she's fading fast, and she's going to die if I can't figure it out."

"Then you'll figure it out." She said it with all the calm certainty in her heart.

Luke could do anything, and he would do this. It was that simple. Elisabeth needed them, and they were going to make her well.

He stilled, and then he captured her with his hot, blue gaze. "Maybe there's a way. Maybe if you could somehow reach her telepathically, in spite of the coma, you could help me figure out what's wrong. Where it hurts, or what the symptoms are, or something."

"Yes," she said instantly. "Let's do it. I'll try anything."

She pushed away the niggling fear that nothing she could do would be enough, or that she might actually make it worse.

Kit suddenly appeared in the doorway, and she didn't look happy.

"I already put your breakfast down," Rio told her. "It's fish this morning."

Kit snarled, but she was facing Luke, so Rio figured it wasn't about the fish.

"I know. Don't you think I know?" Luke ran his hand through his hair again, making it stick up even more wildly, as he stared with frustration at the little fox. "It's dangerous for Rio to be anywhere around the Winter Court right now. I know. But that little girl's life hangs in the balance, and I can't think of any other way to try to reach her."

"The two of you had better stop talking about me and start talking to me," Rio snapped. "I'm going. If there's even a chance that I might be able to help her and I don't take it, I could never live with myself."

Kit crouched down on the floor, as if ready to leap, and she growled, but this time at Rio.

"I'm going," Rio repeated firmly.

"There's no way I can get you in there without a big battle or long explanations that I just don't have time for," Luke told Kit. "You're *Yokai*, and they may not like that. You'll have to stay here. Merelith did say that Elisabeth wants to see you, so once I explain it to her, I'm sure we'll be able to bring you with us. But for now, I'd never get past the front door."

Kit snarled again and then turned around and stalked back into the house.

"I think she's letting us get away with it for now," Rio

said. "Or maybe she'll just suddenly appear in the middle of Merelith's place, like that trick she did in the kitchen."

She grinned at Luke. "Now that's something I'd like to see."

Luke stared after Kit for a moment, but then he shrugged, as if dismissing the topic.

"We're going to travel by Shadows again," Luke told her. "It can be a little disorienting."

"I remember. That's how you brought me here the night the Grendels were chasing me."

He nodded and then wrapped his arms around her waist. She could almost see a dark, shadowy space just before they stepped into it, but it struck her that she didn't actually know if she'd seen it in reality or if she'd seen it through the prism of Luke's thoughts. The new and disturbing possibility that she was able to read Luke's mind was something she'd tried deliberately not to think about, and now wasn't the time, either, because they were walking into the darkness of his peculiar mode of travel.

After a brief disorientation, they took another step forward, and Rio realized they were standing about a hundred feet away from the Silver Palace.

"What? You couldn't get us right up to the doorway?" She was trying for a little humor—anything to lighten the burden of despair that was crushing Luke—but he only shook his head.

"The Fae have safeguards in place to keep anyone from showing up on their doorstep through magical means. This is as close as I could get us, and now we're probably going to have to do battle with the flunkies before we can get to Merelith," he said grimly. "If ever I were in the mood to blow something up, it's now, so maybe you should keep an eye on me."

She had a better idea. She slipped her hand into his. "We'll figure this out, and Elisabeth will be just fine. I promise."

He kissed her then, fast and hard, and they headed for the Winter Court Palace.

*

Elisabeth was awake.

Rio wanted to jump up and down with joy, but she noticed that Luke's grim expression didn't change much. He'd managed to keep from incinerating anybody on the way in, which had been exactly as difficult as he'd predicted.

"Has she eaten anything? Has she had water? How is her temperature?" He fired the questions at Merelith as he paced the sumptuous silver-and-white room.

The Fae's eyes dimmed. "No. In fact, she only woke up a little less than an hour ago. She refuses food and won't drink any water, but she did accept a little papaya juice. Should we be worried?"

Rio barely managed to contain her shock at hearing a member of the High Court admit to having an emotion like worry, but she must have given something away with her expression, because Merelith's icy gaze snapped to Rio.

"Uncanny," Merelith whispered. "If someone else had told me, but then—who would've dared?"

It was almost as though she were talking to herself, and when Rio started to ask her about it, the Fae turned away. Rio filed it under things to ask later, when they were sure Elisabeth was well, but questions burned in her brain, and the ominous sound of the ticking grandfather clock in the room haunted her with a reminder of the countdown to her birthday.

Luke, oblivious to the interchange, was still firing questions. "What did she say? How does she feel? What part—"

Merelith finally cut him off and gestured to the door. "Why don't we go in and you can see for yourself, wizard. Elisabeth does want to see Rio and her fox."

The Fae looked around the room and then frowned. "Where is the *Yokai*?"

"Kit wanted to come and see Elisabeth, but Luke was afraid it would waste too much time trying to persuade your guards to let her in with us," Rio explained.

Merelith nodded slowly. "That may indeed have been the case. I will make sure they know to allow her to enter, should you visit at Elisabeth's request in the future."

They all ignored the elephant in the room—the question of whether little Elisabeth even had a future. Rio shoved the thought out of her mind as soon as it appeared.

"Can we see her now?"

Merelith opened the door, and the three of them walked into an enormous bedroom that looked like Marie Antoinette's interior designer had decorated it. There were even chandeliers. Rio, who'd grown up feeling lucky when she managed to get one of the soft cotton quilts for her cot instead of being stuck with one of the scratchy wool ones, gaped at the splendor like she was a country mouse.

"Rio. You came." The faint, frail voice came from the direction of the biggest silk-covered bed Rio had ever seen.

All thoughts of silk and chandeliers fled Rio's mind when she saw Elisabeth. The girl was clearly very, very ill. She'd become a skeletal caricature of her former self— emaciated, as if an evil incubus had drained her life force in the short amount of time since Rio had last seen her.

Elisabeth's cheeks burned with two bright red spots of color, and Rio recognized it as a very bad sign. She'd seen fever like that in children before, and there'd often been a funeral in the convent's small cemetery shortly afterward. She had no idea how human fever affected the Fae, or if Elisabeth's half-human, half-Fae body was reacting in a doubly bad way to whatever it was that was making her ill, but Rio didn't need to be a doctor, or even a wizard, to know that the child was rapidly approaching the end.

And Rio didn't let one ounce of any of that thought process show on her face. Instead, she flashed her brightest smile and strolled over to the bed as if Elisabeth had all the time in the world to chat.

"Elisabeth! You look so beautiful in that lace nightgown," Rio said enthusiastically. All the time in the world to talk about nightgowns, she reminded herself. "I wish I'd had something like that when I was a little girl. My most exciting pajamas were the Donald Duck ones I once scored at the Bordertown Goodwill thrift shop."

"I like Donald Duck," Elisabeth said, smiling so beautifully that Rio's heart cracked into several jagged pieces. "But I like Minnie Mouse better. She's my favorite. I would love to have some pajamas with Minnie Mouse on them."

"I do not understand humans," Merelith said, but she was smiling instead of sneering, and Rio felt a moment of kinship with the Fae when she realized they were both putting on an act for the desperately ill child.

"Why would you want a rodent or a waterfowl on your nightclothes?"

The Fae looked honestly baffled, and Luke, Rio, and Elisabeth all started laughing.

"They're cartoons, Auntie Merelith. I'll show them to you when I get better." Elisabeth sighed and closed her eyes, and then she leaned back against the mound of propped-up pillows behind her.

"Will you try now?" Luke quietly murmured the words, so that Elisabeth wouldn't hear.

"But she's awake. She can tell you herself," Rio protested.

She was still afraid that she'd try to fish around in the child's brain and maybe make things worse. She didn't know what she was doing—she was a bike messenger, not a neurosurgeon.

Luke was shaking his head before Rio even finished her sentence. "She's just a little girl. She probably doesn't understand what's happening to her, and to interrogate her about it would frighten her even more than she already is."

Merelith stepped closer. "What are you talking about?"

"I want Rio to listen in on Elisabeth's mind and see if she can learn anything about this illness that might help us."

Merelith considered the idea, and then she nodded.

"Yes. I give my permission. Besides, since it is you—" Merelith interrupted herself, and whatever she had been about to say to Rio remained unsaid. "Yes, please try it now."

Rio approached the bed, climbed up on it, and curled up next to Elisabeth. She stroked the little girl's hair away from her brow and nearly flinched at the searing heat that was pouring off Elisabeth's skin. No child could survive fever like this. It was hopeless to even try.

What if she made things worse? The thought of hurting the little girl was causing the familiar stabbing pains in Rio's lungs. She'd be in a full-blown panic attack soon. Just as Rio was contemplating how far she'd get if she started running, Elisabeth opened her eyes and smiled.

"My mommy is trying to get here, but Auntie Merelith thinks she won't make it in time to see me before I go to heaven."

The words sliced through Rio like a blade, and she had to fight to keep the tears from welling up in her eyes. She'd do anything to keep Elisabeth from seeing how desperately sad she was, or even how hopeless she felt.

Merelith's gasp, though, told Rio that the Fae had heard her niece.

"I never said anything of the sort, and you know it. You're not going anywhere. I won't allow it," Merelith said haughtily, playing the role of the autocratic Fae princess to amuse her niece.

It worked. Elisabeth giggled, but then a gentle sadness returned to the little girl's face. "I heard it in your mind, Auntie Merelith. It's okay. I know you don't want me to be sad, and I know that Mommy is having trouble getting back here because there might be a war."

She'd heard it in her aunt's mind? Was Elisabeth like Rio?

Elisabeth reached out with one small hand and touched Rio on the arm, scattering her thoughts of whether the child was a mind reader.

"I did want to see Kit again, though. Do you think you could bring her soon? I don't think I have much time," Elisabeth said softly.

The little girl's face changed then, and her gaze turned inward, as if she were seeing something too far away for the rest of them to be able to understand. After several long seconds in which her breath came far too slowly, Elisabeth looked up, searching for Luke.

"Mr. Oliver, I know you're a wizard, and everybody says you're also a very smart man who's going to be the sheriff. If I ask you a question, will you promise to tell me the truth?"

A wave of black despair crashed over Rio, and it took her a moment to realize that the emotion was coming from Luke. His pain poured out of him and into her like wine into a jug—first filling and then overflowing—and she could tell that he didn't even know he was doing it. She dug the fingers of the hand that Elisabeth couldn't see into the bed to try to ride out the wave of pain.

"I'll always tell you the truth, little one," Luke said, grinning as if he weren't being crushed by the landslide of his pain and sense of failure. "What's up? You're wondering who's on my PJs? I gotta admit, it's SpongeBob SquarePants. Yellow is my color."

Elisabeth giggled a little, but every bit of color had drained from her face, and every adult in that room knew that the end was very near.

"No, silly," Elisabeth said. "I was just wondering, do you think that maybe, if I die, I can talk to the angels and convince them to stop the Fae war? I don't want my mommy and daddy or Auntie Merelith to get hurt."

Her voice trailed off to a whisper, and she started coughing.

Luke knelt down beside the bed, and Merelith swiftly crossed to the other side and took her niece's hand in her own.

"I'm trying to be brave. Big girls are brave. But I don't want to die," Elisabeth said, her beautiful eyes welling up with unshed tears. "I'm afraid."

"You're not going to die," Luke said fiercely. "I'm the best wizard in the world, and I won't allow it."

The child tried to smile, but even that slight effort was

beyond her now. Instead, she turned her head and looked up at Rio.

"Pretty," she said, her eyes going dim.

The words triggered a memory that was sharp enough to slice through the pain buffeting Rio from both her own heart and Luke's.

She pinned Luke with a stare. "Did you hear that? She said *pretty*."

She could tell he didn't get it, but it was okay, because now she did.

"*Pretty.* It's what you kept saying to me when that Grendel venom had poisoned you. Is it possible—is it possible at all—that the Grendels scratched her when Dalriata had her?"

Luke was shaking his head. "I never even thought of that because the symptoms are so different. If this is Grendel venom—"

"The Winter Court Fae react very badly to many types of venom," Merelith interjected. "And who knows how her human half would react? Is it possible?"

Rio didn't wait any longer. She put her hands on either side of Elisabeth's hot little face, and she sent her thoughts winging deep inside the child's mind. She'd never tried anything quite so delicate before, and she was still desperately afraid of the possibility of harming the girl, but she wasn't about to let Elisabeth die because Rio was too much of a coward to even try.

She looked, and she *Looked*, and she saw. Flashes of what Elisabeth had felt and seen and done.

Trying to run, terrified, when she'd been abducted.

Sitting quietly in an empty office and crying for her mommy.

Refusing to eat a sandwich.

Crying; she'd been so afraid of the creature who was picking her up—her shoulder hurt—crying again.

Rio released her hold on Elisabeth's mind, and hope and relief rushed through her in equal measures.

"Yes. The Grendel scratched her accidentally. It was actually trying to be very careful with her, but Elisabeth has a clear memory of feeling a tiny pain on her left shoulder."

"We didn't see anything," Merelith began, but then she stopped wasting time talking and gently pulled the girl's nightgown down and off her left shoulder. Sure enough, there was a tiny pink scratch, no bigger than half an inch, but it was swollen and angry looking.

"That wasn't there before, I swear it. If my negligence is what causes this child to die—" Merelith collapsed on the bed next to Elisabeth, pulling the child into her lap. Silvery tears streamed down the Fae's face.

"She's not going to die," Luke said firmly. "Rio, hand me that cup of juice."

He was already digging in the pockets of his coat, and he produced a small vial of powder. He dumped about half of it in the juice and stirred it with his finger, then handed it to Merelith.

"This isn't exactly right, but it's close enough. It will bring her back from the brink and give me plenty of time to mix exactly the right antidote for her."

Merelith was already urging the child to drink. Drop by agonizingly slow drop, the juice was making it into Elisabeth's mouth, and she was swallowing it down. Within three minutes, color had begun to return to the child's face. Within five more, Elisabeth opened her eyes and smiled up at them.

"I think I would like to have a hot dog, please," she said.

Rio started laughing and crying at the same time, and Luke shouted out a joyous whooping sound. Merelith hugged her niece tightly, rocking back and forth, and then she sang out a word that Rio didn't know, and silvery bells sounded in the distance.

"I have just called for all the hot dogs you could possibly eat, and pancakes and tea cakes and jam," Merelith told Elisabeth. "We are going to have such a wonderful

day. I will send all of my guardsmen out to find you pajamas with rodents on them."

Elisabeth's laughter pealed, sounding a lot like the
little bells. "Oh, Auntie Merelith. You are too funny."

Luke put a hand on Rio's shoulder. "We need to go. I
have to do that thing in the office."

"Will you please bring Kit back with you for a visit?"
Elisabeth asked, smiling up at Luke, and Rio actually felt
the sunlight break through the darkness inside him at the
sight of the little girl's happiness and obvious recovery.

"The wizard is going to whip up some very special medicine, which will make you completely better, and then
we'll bring it back to you, and we'll bring Kit with us. She
misses you, you know. She loves little girls," Rio told
Elisabeth, who smiled even more radiantly at the news.

Rio had to turn her head a little so the child wouldn't
see her tears.

As Luke and Rio started to leave, Merelith stopped
them. "Luke. I know you travel with the Shadows. If it will
speed your way to aid my niece, I will open a space for
you to return to your office and then travel back here to
my rooms."

"That would help a lot," Rio answered for him, when
he looked like he was weighing the pros and cons of the
offer. "Thank you."

Merelith's glance was weary but almost fond as she
looked at Rio. "You have just thanked me again, young
one. Will you never learn?"

"There's a good chance I won't," Rio said cheerfully,
too happy to be insulted or worried.

The Fae just shook her head. "Stand in the exact center
of the blue carpet, on top of the largest fleur-de-lis, and
you'll be able to access your Shadows there, just for today."

Elisabeth's eyelashes fluttered closed, and Merelith
looked up in alarm.

"It's okay to let her sleep now," Luke reassured her.
"She probably needs some real rest. Wake her up within

the hour and give her a good meal, fruit and protein, but don't let her eat too much of it. We'll be back by early evening with an antidote tailored specifically to Elisabeth. I still have a sample of her blood that I can use to be sure it's right."

Merelith nodded, the strain relaxing out of her tight posture. "I will never forget this. You may be sure of that."

Luke nodded, and Rio smiled, and then they headed for home. Traveling through the Shadows didn't even bother Rio this time because she was so happy she felt as though she could have floated across Bordertown and back to Luke's all on her own.

"You did it," Rio told him, when they arrived back in his office. "I knew you would."

"No, *we* did it, and I couldn't have figured it out without you." Luke bent his head to kiss her, and all the terror, pain, and joy of the morning swept them both into a whirlwind of sensation.

It was a very long time later when she finally pulled back, gasping and laughing a little, to catch her breath.

"Now it's my turn to make breakfast, while you make an anti-Grendel antidote," she told him.

When she opened the door and walked back into Luke's house, she noticed two things right away. First, all the walls had been painted a virulently hot pink.

Second, Meryl Streep was sharpening knives in the kitchen.

CHAPTER 20

Luke figured he'd grab some fresh coffee before he got started, so he took their discarded mugs and headed into the house after Rio. He almost ran into her back before he realized that she'd stopped dead in the middle of the doorway, so he looked past her and then almost dropped the coffee cups.

"What in the hell is that?

Rio bit her lip. "It appears to be Meryl Streep sharpening knives, but I've been fooled before, so I'm going to go with Alice is back."

He wondered if he needed to find some guys to hang out with so he could have friends whose conversations he actually understood.

"No," he said carefully. "I would like to know why the walls of my house look like the inside of an Iguanosaurus exploded all over them."

"I saw one of those in the Caribbean once," Meryl Streep said, shuddering. "Nasty creature. Easily nine feet tall."

"The pink paint is on the ceiling, too," Rio pointed out helpfully.

"I'm just guessing, but I think you may have annoyed the fox," Meryl Streep said, as she began to chop vegetables. "I'm making chili. Beef and sausage okay, or does anyone have any preference?"

"I love chili," Rio said, crossing over to the counter and taking a seat. "Also, I loved you in *The Devil Wears Prada*. Is there anything I can do to help? I was going to make breakfast, but it can wait."

"I brought scones," Meryl Streep said, pointing to a blue box. "Feel free to nosh while we catch up."

"My *walls* are *pink*," Luke said, being sure to enunciate clearly, in case they hadn't heard him the first time.

Kit trotted into the room and hopped up into Rio's lap, putting her head on Rio's shoulder, and he could have sworn that the fox cast a smug look at him. Rio hugged and petted the little animal, ignoring Luke completely, so he closed his eyes and counted to ten.

When he opened his eyes, the walls were still pink.

"Is this because you're pissed off that I took Rio to the Silver Palace without you?"

Enormous purple-and-yellow-striped flowers appeared on the walls, and they were so shiny that the glare was driving spikes into Luke's skull.

"I'll take that as a yes," he ground out. "I'm sorry. I *said* I was sorry, so get off your furry little butt and change my walls back to what they were."

Meryl Streep frowned. "You don't really sound like you're sorry, love. You sound like you're ready to blast something."

"Meryl Streep doesn't have a British accent, *love*," he retorted.

Meryl grinned, and suddenly Alice was standing there. "Sorry. I forgot."

"She was only trying to protect me," Rio said. "Weren't you, sweetheart?"

Kit snuggled closer to Rio, and Luke glared at her. Suddenly Rio's cheeks turned pink.

"What did that annoying *Yokai* just say?" he demanded.

"There's no way I'm telling you what she just said. There is nothing in my job description that says 'fox translation service.'"

She put Kit down on the floor, and it was Luke's turn to grin smugly.

"In fact, I will quit feeding you if you don't stop saying things like that," Rio said hotly to the fox.

Whatever Kit said, it must have been good, because Rio's cheeks blushed even hotter, and she threw her head back and groaned.

"Okay, fine. Kit said to tell you that if you want to talk about furry butts, she's not a big fan of having to see *yours* walking down the hall in the middle of the night," Rio said with her eyes tightly closed.

"While that sounds like a lovely story, why don't we cut to the chase?" Alice pointed at Luke. "You. Apologize like you mean it."

Then she pointed at Kit. "You. Change those walls back, or you're not getting any of this lovely sausage, not even the bit I bought especially for you."

Rio made a noise that sounded suspiciously like muffled laughter, but Luke decided to be the bigger person and ignore her. He apologized as gracefully as he could manage to Kit, and pink, purple, and yellow disappeared from his walls.

Rio whistled. "Wow. That's pretty impressive."

Alice shrugged. "*Yokai.* Now, which do you want to hear first? The story about how the League has new offices in town? Or the one about the bolt of lightning that took out Dalriata and his entire office building in the middle of a cloudless morning?"

Luke took a chocolate croissant out of the box, tore off a corner, and gave it to Kit as a gesture of truce. "I'd wondered how long it would take Merelith to retaliate."

Rio's face had turned pale. "Oh, no! *Abernathy.* Alice, did you hear anything about the doorman? His name was Abernathy. I hope that he's okay."

Alice stopped chopping and dicing and put her knife

down on the side of the cutting board. She rubbed one hand over her face, and Meryl Streep reappeared and then disappeared, leaving only Alice behind. Luke realized that he was so used to her disguises that sometimes he didn't even see them, even when she was wearing them. She was always simply Alice to him.

"Abernathy is just fine. I called him away for a lunch date just before the lightning bolt struck," Alice said, smiling warmly at Rio. "He's been a friend of mine for a long time, and I'm glad to know you cared about what happened to him. Not many would spare a thought for a mountain troll."

"I only met him that one time, but he seemed like a very nice person," Rio said. "But wait. You said you called him away to lunch just before it happened. Did you know in advance—"

"Better not to ask," Luke advised. "Alice always knows things, and Alice never tells. It's part of her charm."

They filled her in on what had happened with Elisabeth, and Alice insisted on opening a bottle of champagne to toast the little girl's health.

"That poor kid is going to need all the friends she can get. Things are not looking good for her mother. I heard she might have been taken as a hostage in Europe. And after what happened to Merelith's other sister—well. It's just not a very lucky family when it comes to the female heirs to the throne," Alice said.

"Merelith told us that Elisabeth could never inherit, so at least she doesn't have to worry about that," Rio said.

Luke frowned, still thinking about Dalriata's building. "Merelith isn't the type to worry about collateral damage. I hope no innocent people were harmed or killed."

Alice shook her head. "No, Dalriata owns the whole building, and it was mostly empty, except for himself, a couple of his thugs, and that nasty woman he kept chained to the front desk."

"She didn't seem like a prisoner to me," Rio said, her brow furrowing.

"She was no prisoner. She probably chained herself there. She and Dalriata had a weird on-again, off-again relationship, and every time he tried to dump her, she hunted him down."

Alice shook her head. "Very unhealthy. The woman needed to watch more daytime talk shows to gain a little self-esteem."

Luke grabbed his coffee mug and filled it, took another croissant, and started to head back for his office to make Elisabeth's antidote.

"Luke, stay a moment," Alice said, her voice uncharacteristically solemn. "There's one more thing I learned, and you're both going to need to hear this."

Rio buried her head in her hands. "Every time somebody tells me I need to hear something, another piece of my life crashes and burns."

"I'm sorry to say that this is more of the same. The whole incident with Dalriata taking Elisabeth? It was part of a plot by the League to frighten Rio into joining."

Luke swore a blue streak under his breath. "I'm going to kill that son of a bitch. When I find Maestro, I'm going to tear his head off and offer it to the Bordertown bowling league."

Rio glared at him. "Don't even say the word *league*. Don't even think it. Not softball, not bowling, and definitely not League of the Black Swan. What kind of monster would use a little girl like that?"

Luke didn't bother to answer. Rio had lived in Bordertown all of her life, so she knew all about monsters. The question had been rhetorical at best and hopelessly futile at worst.

"It's only two days until my birthday. I need to find out what is going on before I lose my mind worrying about all of this," Rio said.

"The League's new offices are over on Asimov Avenue. That might be a place to start," Alice said, pouring two jars of tomatoes into her large pot and turning the heat on low to simmer.

"Will you go with me? Luke has to make this potion for Elisabeth right now, and nothing is more important than that. But I'm a little nervous about facing Maestro and his shadowy League by myself," Rio admitted.

Alice glanced at her watch and then regretfully shook her head. "I'm sorry, love. I'd be happy to do it, but I've only got about forty-five minutes to get to the airport, and I'll still just make my flight to Hawaii by the skin of my teeth. I've got a job I committed to do, and in my business, my word is everything. If I don't show up, it's a real problem."

Rio nodded. "I understand. Be careful in Hawaii. I'll head over to Asimov by myself. I need some answers, and I need them now."

Kit, who'd been sitting by her water bowl, yipped in protest before Luke could do the same, and Rio smiled down at her.

"Yes, you can come with me," Rio said to the fox.

"Well, there you go," Alice said, washing her hands and drying them on a kitchen towel. "Kit can go with Rio, Luke can make the potion, and I can go to Hawaii. Let this chili simmer, please, and you'll have a lovely dinner in about four hours."

Luke waited until the door had closed behind Alice before he started yelling.

The first thing that Rio did was walk around to the stove and turn off the burner beneath the pot. She had a feeling it wasn't going to be the kind of day where she could wait around for hours for chili to simmer.

"You do realize that there's no way I'm letting you go confront Maestro by yourself?"

Luke's eyes flared a hot blue, and she caught her breath as she truly began to believe that she was important to this man, perhaps important in a way she'd never been to anyone else in her life. Her own world was beginning to revolve around his presence, and it terrified her even as it comforted her.

She needed to establish boundaries or she would be floating, lost and untethered, in this new emotion. She couldn't allow herself to lose her independence, no matter how heady the feeling, and she couldn't let him begin the relationship believing he could give her commands.

"I'm not a child, and I'm not an idiot. All of this affects my life. You may think I'm taking it pretty well, since I haven't had a meltdown, but do you realize that it's been only a few days since my life was entirely different?" The reality of what she was saying crashed down around her head, and her breathing sped up.

"I had a nice apartment—okay, it was a tiny apartment, furnished with milk crates, but it was mine—and I had a job that I usually enjoyed. I had a nice, quiet life, with nobody trying to abduct me or kill me, and I certainly didn't have magical foxes or wizards hanging around." She realized she was shouting by the time she got to the end of her mini-diatribe, and she forced herself to unclench her hands and take deep breaths before the hyperventilating kicked in.

Kit trotted up and twined around her ankles, offering comfort, and Rio leaned down to scratch behind the little fox's ears. Luke stared at the two of them for a moment, and then he shook his head.

"You're wrong. I'm not trying to run your life. I'm only trying to tell you what to do," he said, and then his mouth fell open and a quizzical expression crossed his face.

"Oh. *Shit*."

They both started laughing, and he ran a hand through his hair in his familiar gesture of frustration.

"I'm only trying to help, Rio. I need to keep you safe."

She softened. "I know that, Luke. It's your big bad need to protect everyone—"

"To protect *you*. Everybody else can go hang," he growled.

"But I need answers, and I'm running out of time. You need to make Elisabeth's antidote. You admitted you have no idea exactly how her metabolism works because of her mixed parentage. So that means you have no idea if the stopgap antidote you gave her will last as long as you think it might, right?"

He stopped pacing up and down the room and scowled, but reluctantly nodded.

"Then you need to work on mixing an antidote that's tailored to Elisabeth, and I need to go talk to whoever happens to be at the League's new offices. I doubt it will be Maestro anyway. He's doing a really good job of hiding from us lately."

Kit suddenly hopped up on the back of the couch and snarled at Luke.

"Yeah, I know. I know you're going with her. But you'll pardon me if I'm not all that reassured that Rio's only protection will be a forty-pound fox who moonlights as a really bad interior designer."

Kit snapped her teeth in Luke's general direction, and suddenly the walls and ceiling were Day-Glo orange.

Luke snorted. "You've just proved my point. What are you going to do if Maestro threatens Rio? Color-blind him to death?"

Luke took a step toward Rio, and suddenly a furry projectile rocketed through the air toward him, flew over his shoulder, and landed on the other side. Luke and Rio both froze, stunned.

"Luke, there's a red scratch on your neck that goes all the way around the side," Rio said slowly. "Was that there before?"

Luke put a hand to his neck and then winced, as if it stung.

"I think your fox just gave me a demonstration of her nonartistic skills," he said wryly.

Kit looked away from both of them and began to wash her paw.

"That wasn't very nice," Rio scolded her, but then she felt ridiculous.

Who was she to scold a magical creature, let alone one who might actually be a Japanese celestial figure? Rio's life was tumbling into the rabbit hole, and she had no idea which way was out.

"*Please*, then," Luke said, gritting out the words. "Will you please wait for me to mix this antidote, and then we'll go together? The elixir will need time to process before we can take it to Elisabeth. We'll leave it to cook, we'll throw the chili in the Crock-Pot and leave that to cook, and then we'll go beat some answers out of the League of the Black Swan. This is an extremely dangerous organization, Rio. They've been making their enemies disappear for centuries. Don't underestimate what they'll do when they want something."

Rio took a deep breath and nodded. There was a thin line between courage and stupidity, and she didn't particularly have any desire to cross it. If a perfectly good wizard was offering to go with her to confront one of the scariest organizations that had ever existed in the history of the world, who was she to say no?

"Where's the Crock-Pot?"

CHAPTER 21

The early afternoon sunlight slanted into the office window, and Rio watched as Luke mixed liquids and powders into various vials, measuring proportions by sight and feel, apparently, because she hadn't seen him use a single measuring tube or beaker. The aroma of dried flowers and herbs, combined with the sharp electric scent she'd come to associate with his use of magic, infused the air. His long, capable fingers arranged items on the table with careful precision, and she realized that she was watching his movements so closely that she was nearly hypnotizing herself.

"When did you become a wizard?" she asked, suddenly curious about his background; after all, he had a lot more of it than the average person. "This is something you're born with? Magical ability?"

Luke didn't look up from what he was doing, but he shrugged a little. "I think that's how it usually works. I don't know if that's what happened with me. Considering my family, if I had any innate magical talent, it would've all been black magic."

Rio shivered a little at his blunt statement. She'd made it a point to stay far out of the range of any black magic practitioners; she'd even refused to deliver packages to certain streets that were known enclaves. Some of her friends at Ophelia's had liked to experiment, as if they'd been trying out a new kind of cocktail or designer drug, but something deep inside her had recoiled from allowing even the slightest hint of a black taint anywhere near her.

Now, though, she was sleeping with a wizard who'd been born to an evil family and cursed with more of the same. When she decided to jump, she didn't waste any time.

Luke, meanwhile, scowled down at the table as if it were an enemy he needed to destroy. "Look at this. All of this is the legacy I inherited. I spent years studying and learning, so I could be an expert in antidotes to every poison I came across. Where do you think I might've gotten that exciting ambition?"

Rio didn't know an awful lot about the Borgias, beyond the vague idea that they'd been a really famous family associated with some pretty awful things. She knew poisoning had been a specialty of theirs, and she thought she remembered that one of them had bribed and blackmailed his way into being a pope. She'd never been all that interested in European history, but now would be a good time to begin to develop some curiosity.

Maybe what she ought to be doing while he worked was head to a library. She could check out books on the Borgias and on Japanese mythology in order to help her understand Luke and Kit. Maybe the Bordertown Public Library had a book titled *The ABCs of Evil Conspiracy-Type Organizations* to help her understand the League, too.

"What happened? The curse? Do you know how that started? If you don't want to talk about it, I understand." There were plenty of things about her past that she didn't want to talk about, like her entire childhood, for example.

He capped a glass vial and shook it vigorously and then placed it upright in a wooden holder. The silver liquid inside bubbled and frothed, sparkling in the sunlight.

"Done," he said, and she could see the satisfaction on his face. "This should be exactly what she needs to remove any remaining traces of the Grendel poison from her system, for now and for always. I'm also pretty sure that she'll have no residual effects from it."

Rio heaved an enormous sigh of relief. "That's wonderful news. She's so lucky that you're the one Merelith called."

But then she slowly lowered her coffee cup to the table as a horrible thought occurred to her. "You don't think that was all part of the master plot, do you? The League would contact you because you would know how to deal with poison if it happened to Elisabeth?"

Luke narrowed his eyes, but then he shook his head. "No, I don't think even the maestro is that devious. I'm pretty sure that Elisabeth's poisoning was completely accidental and unplanned. Even in its worst days, I've never known the League to participate in any way in harming children."

"Dalriata paid a very high price for his part in what was essentially some kind of twisted business deal," Rio said, feeling a twinge of unwanted sympathy for the man. He'd been a heartless criminal, but had he deserved to die for his minor role in all of this?

She didn't know, and she was suddenly glad that life-or-death decisions were not her job. She'd never do well in any kind of government role, because she saw all sides of a matter and could argue convincingly for each. Clarice had always told her she was too softhearted.

"The players in all this are the types who are used to dealing with very high stakes," Luke said, sounding troubled. "What bothers me about that right now is why they're all circling you."

"It must be about my parents. People keep bringing up my birthday," Rio reminded him.

Luke rubbed a hand over his face, thinking, but then he nodded. "I think you must be right. At first, I wondered if you'd somehow seen something that somebody didn't want you to see during the course of your job, but that doesn't really make sense given the circumstances. And of course your birthday wouldn't matter at all, in that case."

Rio looked at the potion, mostly in order to be able to quit thinking about herself and all the unsolvable puzzles surrounding her. The vial was only about three-quarters full. Such a tiny amount of liquid to be able to cause such a wonderful effect.

"How long until it's ready to take to her?"

"A couple of hours. Long enough for the magic to infuse into the potion, but not so long that it begins to lose its efficacy."

"Should we eat lunch?" It would be better to face the League on a full stomach, after all. A few hours wouldn't make much difference after all these years.

Luke started laughing. "Have I mentioned how much I like that you're not one of those women afraid to eat?"

"I never understood that," she admitted. "You eat, you use your body, and then your muscles need more fuel. It's really a very efficient process. But I can't ever say that out loud, because it turns out that not everybody's metabolism works as well as mine. I'm really pretty lucky, Clarice tells me, and she also offers dire warnings of what will happen to us when we get older and everything slows down. For now, though, I like to eat."

"Good genes," Luke said, and then he smacked himself in the forehead with the heel of his hand.

Rio shrugged, but for the first time in a long while she felt a little twinge of pain at the reminder that she didn't know anything about the *origin* of her genes. Maybe, finally, she was about to find out. There were only two days till her birthday. She had a feeling she was definitely going to learn something then.

They pulled together an easy lunch of fruit and sandwiches, raiding Alice's groceries with abandon and giving Kit a plate filled with sliced meat, leafy spinach, and strawberries. The little fox had a particular fondness for any fruit with the word *berry* in it, Rio had discovered.

"So. You want to hear about the curse. Are you sure? It's a pretty ugly story," Luke said, looking resigned.

He bit into a pickle spear, and Rio felt herself blushing a little as she thought about how he'd used his lovely white teeth when he'd been nibbling on her neck the night before. Luke raised an eyebrow, and then his eyes darkened, as if he'd picked up on what Rio had been thinking.

"If you keep looking at me like that, we won't be talking," he said, and his voice had gone low and deep.

Rio glanced at the clock on the wall. "How long did you say we had until the antidote was ready?"

He caught her halfway down the hall and grabbed her and tossed her over his shoulder as if she weighed nothing. She laughed and fought him, and sometime between closing the door behind them and tossing her on his bed, Luke managed to take off his shirt. She let her gaze travel over his beautiful chest, letting it pass over the scars of old battles and linger on the sexy masculine muscles of his chest and abdomen.

"I've never seen you go to a gym or work out," she said. "How do you stay in shape like that?"

He shrugged and then sat down on the bed next to her and became very interested in removing her shirt. "I have good genes, too, at least when it comes to the physical stuff. I also usually do an hour a day of some kind of training, depending on my mood. I was friendly with a martial arts sensei in the 1700s who taught me a great deal."

She blinked. "It still gets me when you toss out things like that. 'In the 1700s.' Like most people would say 'in the nineties' or 'a few months ago.'"

Luke's face darkened, and she knew the ghosts of his past were haunting him.

"I think we need to finish the conversation we were having, Rio. Let me tell you the rest, and then we don't ever need to talk about this again, I hope."

"We don't need to talk about it at all. I didn't mean to bring it up. I have my own bad memories that I don't want to stir up. Please, just forget it." She tried to pull off her shirt, anything to distract him, but he stopped her and sat on the bed next to her.

"No, I'd rather tell you. I want you to know about me. It feels important that you do," he said, and she reluctantly nodded.

If he thought it was important, she couldn't deny him the right to be heard. He already meant too much to her.

"There's really not all that much of the story that I know. My mother had been involved in poisoning a member of one of the family's rivals. But this time, it wasn't the business rival himself; it was the man's cherished daughter. He was destroyed by it. His wife committed suicide, and his son—the girl's brother—became a hopeless alcoholic, although we didn't use that word back then. The family lost everything."

Rio touched his arm, aching for him, but she said nothing. She didn't want to interrupt the flow of words. Sometimes it was better to lance the wound and let the infection drain out.

"You realize, of course, that I only heard this third- and fourth-hand from the servants of my adoptive family. The Borgias found me a home, after my mother was forced to deny my existence." He stared off into the distance, as if watching the horrific scenes from his past play out on a movie screen in his mind.

"It took him years to do it, but before I was ten, the father found what he was looking for. He found a way to deliver a horrible curse, but instead of using it directly against the family who'd cost him everything, he thought that he would take their precious little boy away from them." Luke laughed, and the sound was so filled with pain and bitterness that Rio shivered and wrapped her arms around him. He stroked her hair while he continued.

"The curse's exact wording is something I forgot a long time ago, but I can never forget the result. He cursed me to suffer the consequences of my family's evil. He cursed me to always walk the line between salvation and damnation. He used my blood to seal the magic, and the poor, mad bastard promised me to the forces of darkness."

Luke laughed a little. "It sounds so overly dramatic today, doesn't it? He promised the child to the forces of darkness. Sounds like a cheesy horror movie. But everything about it was deadly serious. The only way I could ever keep from becoming soulless and damned would be by constant vigilance. Constant demonstration of my commitment to help others, instead of harm them. To be selfless instead of selfish. In other words, I would survive this life with my soul only if I could become the exact opposite of everything the Borgias represented."

He pulled her into his lap, embraced her tightly, and rested his cheek on the top of her head. When he began his story again, she could feel the vibrations of his words rumble in his chest, as if the horrible truth had been trapped in his heart and was clawing to break free.

"He wanted to return the pain, didn't he? A child for a child?" Rio said, shivering. It all made a certain horrible sense, especially when viewed from the twisted perspective of a madman.

"The Borgias didn't care about me at all, of course," he said flatly. "My mother had tried to visit me in the early years, but her family forbade it as soon as they caught on. They continued to fund my existence, probably to buy my adoptive family's silence, but any personal oversight disappeared."

He laughed, but it was a hideous, grating sound. "I suppose I'm lucky. It would have been easy enough for them to make me disappear, like they usually did with unwanted problems."

Rio almost couldn't believe what she was hearing, but she knew it had to be the truth. History was full of powerful dynasties amassing wealth and accomplishment through horrible, ruthless, bloodthirsty means. It made her glad, for just a minute, to be a lowly bike messenger.

Luke was quiet for a while, but she had a few questions.

He needed to finish the story, clean out the poison that had infected his soul for so long.

"How did he find you? If they hid you with this adoptive family? How did he know where you were?"

"Bribing servants was easy enough, especially for a man with a personal vendetta. That's the worst part of it, you see," Luke said, in a monotone that frightened her a little. Maybe he'd reached and gone beyond the limit of what he could dredge up for one day.

"Luke, wait—"

But he ignored her feeble attempt to stop him.

"The Borgias had needed a way to get the poison into the family, hadn't they? Only someone the family trusted would have been able to get that close, back in those days."

Luke's hands convulsively tightened on Rio's body, and she had a horrible premonition of what he was going to say next.

"Oh, no," she whispered.

"Oh, yes. The man who cursed me was my own father and—worse—he knew it."

Rio held him in her arms until the storm passed. He didn't weep or sob or scream or cry, although she would have done all of those things. His big body simply shook as if he stood, alone and unprotected, in a gale-force wind, while harsh choking noises ripped up from his throat.

"You're not alone. You'll never be alone again," she said, over and over, while she held him. "I'm here. I promise I'm here."

He couldn't cry or wouldn't cry, but then again he'd had centuries for the tears to have been burned out of him. Rio was only approaching her first quarter century, and she had plenty of tears left. By the time he calmed down, his shoulder and side were soaking wet from her tears.

"Aren't you ready to run away from me yet?" He took her shoulders and stared into her eyes.

"Never," she said, trying to smile.

He captured her mouth, then, and kissed her as if he were drowning in her.

"I need you, Rio," he whispered. "I've always needed you, even before I met you."

"Tell me all about that," she invited, gently biting his neck and then placing soothing kisses where her teeth had been.

He shuddered and pulled her closer. "Enough talking."

She agreed wholeheartedly, so she put her arms around his neck and pulled him to her and then raised her head for his kiss, wanting so badly to burn away any remnants of his pain with her touch.

He happily complied, diving into the job with the same dedication he brought to everything in his life. She sighed with relief and pleasure. If kissing was its own form of magic, Luke was a master practitioner. His tongue delved into her mouth, dancing with hers, teasing and taunting and seducing.

Her body yearned toward his. She could feel the heat and delicious anticipation already beginning to build in the form of a flush on her skin and an insistent thrumming ache deep within her. She wanted to touch and taste; she wanted to go slow and revel in the music of the song they created between them. She wanted to make him forget that he'd ever been sad, or abandoned, or cursed.

"I can't believe you're here," Luke admitted, raising himself on one elbow and looking down at her. "You feel like a dream of beauty I once had. When I woke, I was so bereft at the loss that my cheeks were wet from tears."

The words struck her with the power of a promise, and she cherished them and loved that he'd been so open with her.

"Big, tough wizard crying like a baby," he said, mocking himself, and she knew he wasn't only referring to the remembered dream. "Real romantic, right?"

She traced her finger over the curve of his sculpted lips and shushed him. "Maybe the most romantic thing I've ever heard."

A thought occurred to her, though, and she laughed.

"Except for 'You were hurting, and I wanted to help, but I didn't know how, so I blew something up.'"

His face flushed, and she fell back on the pillow, laughing even harder. "You just blushed! After days of making me blush every time I turn around, I finally did it to you!"

"Maybe I can make you blush again," he murmured.

He traced the curve of her bra with his fingers, so gently that she shivered under his touch. "You are so beautiful. I can't believe I can touch your lovely porcelain skin and you won't shatter under my rough handling."

"Sometimes I like your rough handling," she admitted shyly.

"Sometimes I want to cherish you," he said.

With a thousand touches and kisses, they delighted in each other; and she gradually discarded her clothes and shed her inhibitions in the soft light of the afternoon sun that lit the room from the edges of the heavy window blinds.

"I love touching you," she confessed, reaching out to stroke the silky trail of hair that traveled down his abdomen to his erection, which was very hard and happy to see her, judging by the way it seemed to strain to reach her. "Maybe this part of you loves it when I touch you, too."

"All of me loves it when you touch me," he said hoarsely.

She followed words with action and gently stroked the long velvety length of him, and he moaned as if in pain. She'd learned better by then, though, and she recognized the sound as proof that his control was near to shattering.

"Love me now," she whispered. "I want to feel you inside me."

He immediately rolled over on his back and pulled her on top of him, surprising her, and kissed her for a long, luxurious time, stroking her back and arms and bottom with his big hands.

"Let's take this slowly," he said. "Why don't you set the pace? I want to see you riding me."

Heat intensified in her nerve endings at the idea, and

she moved her legs to straddle him, then lifted her hips so she could place his erection exactly where she wanted and needed it. She slowly, ever so slowly, slid down the hard length of him, and let her head fall back as she gasped with pure, liquid sensation. His strong hands on her hips didn't let her rhythm falter, and together they found the pace that was almost certainly guaranteed to drive her completely insane.

For a while, she knew nothing but the feel of him, as a sensation like starlight rushed into her from their joining, sparkling and sizzling throughout her body and focusing intensely on her most sensitive places. Time slowed to a stop and nothing existed but the vast, unimaginable pleasure of having him rock into her, over and over, until she was dizzy with desire and need.

"Faster," she panted, when his long, sure strokes were forcing her to hover right on the edge of the explosion she knew was coming.

"No." He held her in place with one hand on her hip, and then he raised his head and captured her breast with his mouth. A jolt of sensual bliss seared through her, and she bucked against him, desperate to feel him even deeper inside her.

"Now," she ordered. "More. Now."

"No," he said again, but this time he reached between their bodies and stroked her just exactly where she needed it, and she didn't need to wait for him because she was flying into the stars, shaking and pulsing around him, clenching his hardness with her feminine muscles, which only made her shatter apart even more.

"I'm coming now," she announced, breathlessly and needlessly, and he laughed, the sound so full of joy and masculine triumph that it made her come even harder.

"I know," he said, and then he rolled over, still inside her, and unleashed the frenzied power that he'd been holding back.

He drove into her so hard and so fast that her body reacted violently, coming and coming in an unending wave of orgasm that blew through her defenses and any sense of self-restraint, and she screamed his name while he pounded into her.

"Lucian, yes, oh please yes, more oh more oh," and then any pretense at coherency dissolved as he thrust one final time and came deep inside her, and the feel of his big body shuddering in her arms tipped her even further into the tornado of sensation.

"I will never be able to get enough of you," he said, low and fierce, and then he rolled onto his side and, pulling her close, immediately fell asleep.

Rio smiled, knowing he was exhausted from the emotional catharsis and then the amazing lovemaking, but then she caught herself falling asleep, so she glanced at the clock on the bedside table.

"Luke, it's almost time. The potion will be ready in about an hour, and we need to get it to the Silver Palace. Plus, I'm starving. We kind of skipped the eating part of lunch," she said, grinning.

He pulled her to him and kissed her again—thoroughly, lingeringly, and with the promise of forever. For some reason, she was suddenly afraid. Too much had happened too fast, and she, who had spent her lifetime avoiding attachments, had fallen so hard and so fast for Luke, but it didn't seem real.

It seemed impossible.

CHAPTER 22

The pounding on the office door was their first clue. This was no polite and gentle knock. This was a thunderous demand that they open the door right now or else. Rio glanced at Luke in alarm and saw that he was rolling up his sleeves, his hands already glowing with the familiar blue fire.

"Somebody wants to get blasted," he said calmly. "I happen to be in a particularly good mood and had no immediate plans to blow anything up. I'm always glad to change that."

The pounding came again, and the heavy metal door actually shook in its frame.

"If that's another Grendel, I'm going to scream. I am sick to death of Grendels and their venom, and all the problems they cause," Rio said, but then she grinned at Luke. "Maybe we could get Dr. Black to declaw them. It's inhumane for cats, but I'd be willing to make an exception for Grendels."

The pounding stopped, but almost simultaneously Rio's cell phone started to ring.

"Unknown number," she told Luke. "Huh."

She answered it. "Hello?"

"This is Chance Roberts. As I suspect you know, I am standing outside Oliver's office. If one of you doesn't open the door in the next five seconds, I'm going to have the contingent of demon war guards who are with me rip the door off its hinges," he said in a level tone. "Do you understand this? Or do I need to speak to Oliver directly?"

She glared at her phone and then at the door.

"It's Chance Roberts," she told Luke. "He's the one doing all of the pounding. Also, he apparently thinks I'm an idiot.

"I don't know, Mr. Roberts. I'm not very bright. You might want to rephrase that, using one-syllable words," she said into the phone. "Me dumb bicycle messenger."

Luke started laughing, and then he waved a hand at the door, and it flew open. "Oh, Roberts. You are in trouble."

Roberts, wearing another fancy suit and a beautiful long coat that made Rio drool with envy, stood at the doorway.

"Is some magical booby trap going to explode in my face if I step over this threshold?"

"Try it and see," Luke taunted.

Rio rolled her eyes at Luke and then glared at Roberts. "What exactly do you want?"

A deep rumbling voice sounded from behind Roberts, and Rio stepped closer to the door to peek out. Wow. So this was the demon war guard, the stuff of legend and nightmare. She'd heard they didn't venture outside Demon Rift, but apparently that had been wrong. Or else they were making a special exception, and she had the feeling it had something to do with her.

"I'm not paranoid. Everybody really is out to get me," she said, and then she started laughing and backed away from the door. "Let him in, Luke. We should find out what this is about."

Luke sighed, but he gestured to Roberts to come in. "You have five minutes. We have someplace we need to be."

"This is more important," Roberts declared, arrogant as ever.

"No, it isn't," Rio said hotly "There's a sick little girl's life at stake for us. What do you have to say that could possibly be more important than that?"

Roberts took a moment to frame his reply, and Luke jumped into the silence.

"I heard you were thinking of partnering up with Dalriata. Guess that's not happening anymore, huh?" Luke grinned and carefully put the precious vial in the inside pocket of his jacket.

"How did you—never mind. The king and the Demon Rift governing council would like to speak to you, Rio."

Rio stumbled back a step and caught herself against the desk, as the invisible pieces of the puzzle surrounding her all but swirled through the air, buffeting her but leaving her no closer to understanding.

"The king and council can go fuck themselves," Luke snarled. "She's not going anywhere near that place with you."

"So that's what you are," Rio said slowly, solving at least one part of the mystery. "You're a demon. You're too smart, too rich, and too powerful to be acting like a little messenger boy for them, unless you have something at stake. And nobody who's not a demon has anything at stake in this business. There are plenty of demons in Bordertown. Why do you hide it?"

Chance's face had gone a little pale beneath his tan. "I'm not hiding it any longer. I knew associating myself with this task would put the connection between me and Demon Rift into too many minds, but I had no choice. After all, who else would they ask but me? I am, after all, uniquely suited to the job."

"I don't think so," Rio said, pointing to the doorway where three of the demon war guards stood at attention. "If you were uniquely suited to this *job*, as you call it, of inviting me to *visit*, then you wouldn't have needed your bully boys out there to help you do it, would you?"

"He's afraid of me," Luke said smugly.

She noticed his hands were still glowing with flames, like he was trying to hold himself back from blasting Chance and everyone who had come with him.

Chance glared at Luke, and Rio noticed that the demon's eyes had lightened to a pale yellow. "There is nothing about you that frightens me, you pathetic excuse for a cut-rate magician," he snarled.

Luke strode forward until the two were right up in each other's faces. Rio expected the chest pounding to start any minute.

"Then why'd you have to bring your babysitters?" Luke demanded. "Seems like overkill to face down a cut-rate magician, *Chancy*."

Chance, finally losing either his patience or his self-control, shoved Luke back with a hard shot to the shoulder.

"That's *Prince* Chance to you, and the war guards aren't for me," the demon said from between clenched teeth. "They're for *her*."

He pointed at Rio, and she felt the bottom drop out of her stomach. Something in the tone of his voice, or maybe she'd even heard a stray thought, suddenly terrified her. She was more afraid than she'd ever been in her life of what he was about to say. She started to back away, wondering where she could run, and how far and how fast, but just then a streak of red shot past her and landed in front of Roberts, snarling.

It was Kit, and yet somehow it wasn't. The little fox had grown to four or five times her normal size. She was huge—the size of a mountain lion or maybe a bushy-tailed Great Dane. She still looked like a fox, if there had ever been a fox with such long, sharp teeth.

Roberts froze, and Rio could have sworn that he sniffed the air once before an expression of understanding crossed his face, and he bowed, ever so slightly, to Kit.

"Please tell the *Yokai* that I have no intention of harming you," he said to Rio. "I only want to get to know you and invite you to visit my home."

Roberts smiled, and it almost looked sincere. "After all, you are my sister."

※

Luke watched, unable to move fast enough to catch her, as Rio slid down the side of the desk until her butt hit the floor, and then sat there, bent over, sucking in gulps of air. Kit backed up, still snarling at Chance, until she was standing right next to Rio.

"I'm going to break you into little pieces with my bare hands for daring to show up and spout such a load of bullshit. There is no way that even a microscopic amount of Rio's DNA came from Demon Rift," he snarled at Roberts.

He started toward Rio and her suddenly overgrown fox, but she held up a hand and shook her head. "I'm fine. I just need a minute."

Kit apparently agreed, because she quit growling, sat down, and licked the side of Rio's face.

But the rage that had flooded Luke when Roberts made his impossible claim needed an outlet. He could feel the darkness hovering, waiting to snatch him with jagged claws. He forced himself to fight it—Rio deserved better than that from him. She needed him, more now than ever.

So instead he smiled, but it didn't feel like a particularly nice smile. Chance paled and backed up a step.

"Oh, that's not good," Rio said, staring at Luke with wide eyes. "Don't even think about it, Luke Oliver."

"Too late," Luke said cheerfully.

He blasted Roberts so hard with a fireball backed by kinetic force that it lifted the demon prince, if that was really what he was, off his feet, into the air, and back out the office door. Roberts smashed into the wall of guards, and several of them went tumbling backward to the sidewalk with him.

"I hate to be predictable, but I'm going with Bowling for Demons here," Rio said, still apparently content to remain sitting on the floor. "Although, you do you realize you might have just hurt my brother? I wonder if the appropriate thing to do here would be to defend the family honor."

Her laughter had a touch of hysteria to it that Luke didn't like at all, but he didn't know how to fix it, so he stomped over to his office door, looked down the street both ways to be sure the coast was clear of innocent bystanders and innocent grandmotherly sedans, and then he blasted the hell out of the black stretch limo that was parked in front of his office.

Then he turned around, reset the wards to his office with a simple hand gesture, and pulled Rio to her feet.

"It's probably a lie."

"It doesn't feel like a lie," she said calmly.

But he knew her well enough by then to recognize the intensity of the terror hiding under her impressively nonhysterical surface. She was scared to death, and he didn't blame her. He wanted to set Roberts's skull on fire for doing this to her.

He settled for kicking the side of his desk, leaving another dent to match all the others he'd left there in the past. "This doesn't make sense. I have to admit, I was starting to suspect something just as impossible but nothing like this. Or, hell, actually a lot like this."

She looked up at him and, for the first time, he wondered if the amber in her eyes would lighten to yellow when she got angry. The realization hit her before he could say it.

"You thought I might be related to Merelith and her missing sister."

He studied her face and saw what he thought were hints of resignation. "Apparently you thought so, too, because the one thing you don't seem to be is very surprised by all of this."

She looked anywhere but at him, and he had a fleeting idea that she was putting on an act, but then dismissed it. She was too honest to hide from him like that.

"There was too much," she said. "I keep a book with

me when I do bike runs. There's always downtime, and I'm always reading. Usually mysteries. The clues in this one—the mystery of my life—well, they've been shouting at me for a while now."

"Merelith's reaction," he said.

Rio nodded. "My birthday, Elisabeth and her mind-reading ability, and even how I could look into that little girl's mind, in a way I've never been able to do with anyone else before, not even Clarice, and she's my best friend."

"But maybe if you're related to Elisabeth—"

"Then it would make sense because we'd have similar thought patterns," she said, finishing his sentence. "We have another thing in common, too. We're both—what did Merelith call it? Halflings?—Half-breeds. Half Fae, and half something else. At least Elisabeth got a nice half."

"It might not be true," he said, but even he didn't believe it anymore.

"Maybe it's not. Maybe all of this is just a nightmare, and I'm going to wake up in my own bed in my own apartment and get on my bicycle and go to work any minute," she said lightly, and everything inside him violently rejected the idea that he'd no longer be part of her life.

"Don't even think about leaving me," he warned her, but she laughed at him, bizarrely lighthearted, as if he'd been joking.

Then she put her hands on his shoulders and rose on her tiptoes to kiss him, which distracted him completely from concerns about what Roberts and his demon guard were doing outside.

"I need you to know something, Lucian Olivieri," she said, her voice low and fierce. "No matter what happens, I need you to know that being brave enough to spend this time with you was the best thing I've ever done in my life."

Her kiss was long and hard and drowning deep, as if she were pouring all of her desperation at the situation directly into his heart by way of her lips.

"Now go take that medicine to Elisabeth—to my

cousin—right now before it goes bad and you have to start over."

He blinked at that, still a little stunned both from what she'd said to him and from that kiss. His body had kicked into some weird adrenaline thing—a fight-or-flight-or-fuck reaction—and so it took him a fraction of a heartbeat longer than it should have to realize what she was up to, and by then it was too late.

She was running out the door.

He leapt after her a split second after she made it outside, but a dozen or so of the guards were ready and waiting. They let Rio slip between them to get to Chance, who was safely behind the wall of war guards, but then they blocked Luke, hard. Kit, who'd followed, hot on his heels, hurled herself at the guards but bounced back, snarling, when one of them smashed his shield into her.

Roberts had been waiting for Rio. Luke saw him take her hand and help her into the waiting chariot. Luke wanted to blast him, but he couldn't take the chance of injuring Rio, so he stood there helplessly while the four flame-red horses leapt into the sky and took the chariot, the demon prince, and Luke's entire world with them.

He threw back his head and howled, and Kit stood next to him and did the same. Then he rolled up his sleeves, because his magical fire was climbing his arms and smoldering hotter than he'd ever felt it before in the centuries of his curse, and the shirt was already beginning to char.

"Where's Miro? Somebody had better alert him that there's about to be barbecue over here." He counted off the number of demon guards who'd dared to stand between him and his woman. A full dozen. "A *lot* of barbecue."

The berserker rage took him after that, and he didn't stop fighting until all the demons who wanted to fight back were either groaning in pain or running away. When Luke came back to his senses, he was sprawled on the ground, alone, and Kit, back to her normal size, was waiting anxiously and nudging his face with her cold nose.

"We've got to go get her," Luke told Kit.

Kit whined again, and then she nudged him in the chest, and Luke felt something poking him. Reason returned fully as he remembered that it was the vial of Elisabeth's antidote, miraculously unbroken. A black chasm of unwanted choice opened up before him. There was still time to take the potion to Merelith before it started losing efficacy. On the other hand, every minute he delayed was another minute that Rio was with Chance Roberts in Demon Rift.

How could he possibly choose between two horrible options? Which one of them would he leave in danger even a single minute longer?

Kit nudged at his chest again, and Luke sighed.

"I know, I know. You're right. There's really no choice at all. If I take any possible risk with that little girl's life, Rio would never forgive me. We'll get the cure to Elisabeth, and then we're going to give Demon Rift a surprise the likes of which they've never seen before."

He stood up and brushed himself off. "So, *Yokai*. Have you ever traveled through Shadows?"

CHAPTER 23

She hadn't fallen apart. Rio wrapped her arms around herself to keep from shattering into a million tiny pieces, and she kept reminding herself that she *hadn't fallen apart*.

She'd spoken so calmly about Chance's revelation that Luke had bought into her façade, and he'd even talked to her about his suspicions about Merelith, having no idea that everything Rio had been saying to him was a load of unbelievable duck shit.

She'd had suspicions that she might be related to the freaking queen of the freaking fairies? Not in a million years, she hadn't. Rio hadn't known much about the story of the Fae princess who'd loved a demon prince, and certainly nothing she'd ever done, seen, or heard had in any way—not even the slightest possible way—led her to believe that she might be involved with the story.

She was *human*. She'd always been human. Sure, with a little extra, but most people in Bordertown had that. How was it that nobody had ever recognized her as a kindred creature in all of her years of living among the many and varied Fae and demon residents of the city?

Never once had anybody told her she reminded them of someone. Never once had she looked up to see any of the Fae or any demons staring at her suspiciously. None of the magic detectors in the hundreds of buildings she'd entered for her own job had ever registered her as anything but garden-variety human.

But she wasn't. Human. Which led her to wonder— what exactly was she? Fae-demon pairings were so rare that she'd never actually seen or heard of one, even in Bordertown. Even the idea of a child of such a union was pretty much universally reviled.

If any of this crazy story was true, did that make Rio a freak? A mutant? Was it a good thing? Bad? Was she the next step up the evolutionary chain or the living, breathing equivalent of a defective product?

She glanced at the man who'd claimed to be both a demon prince and—even more fantastically—her brother. What happened next? Was he taking her to Demon Rift to meet the family—or to be destroyed?

Dodging Luke to climb into the carriage had been probably the stupidest thing she'd ever done, and she knew it, but she hadn't leapt into the situation—or the carriage— totally out of the blue. Luke might violently disagree with her reasoning once he heard it, but she'd reacted with at least as much intellect as instinct.

The thing was, alone among all of the players in the bizarre drama that her life had become, Chance had told her the truth. Sure, it had taken him a while, but he'd come right out and said that she was his sister. Nobody else had come close.

Maestro had said he knew who her parents were, and he'd chosen to play stupid games with that vision and the cake. Merelith had hinted around the subject but never told Rio a damned thing, even when Rio had pretty clearly demonstrated that she could be trusted.

That had been Rio's *cousin* she'd helped rescue. Her cousin, who'd known a kindred soul from the minute the electric spark of recognition had traveled between them back at Dalriata's lair. She shivered at the thought of the man's fate, but she was angry on her own behalf, too. Merelith had obviously had time to organize a massive strike against the enemy, but she hadn't taken five minutes to tell the truth to her long-lost niece who'd been *standing in the same room with her.*

Rio decided to quit wasting time mentally justifying her actions to Luke, since he wasn't even there, and even as she had the thought, another one slammed into her with the force of a tornado: Luke could never be part of her life again. Dealing with the Fae and the demons—trying to balance his protective instincts against Rio's need to learn about her two very different heritages—had enormous potential to send him crashing over the abyss into the darkness of his curse.

In order to protect him, she needed to leave him.

The realization threatened to shatter both her heart and her ability to function, so she fought ruthlessly to push it down and away and concentrate on the here and now. She was riding in a flying carriage with her demon brother.

She was a demon. Half demon. Demoness?

She'd never been so close to losing it, and talking would be impossible, so she dug her fingers into her legs through her jeans and looked out the window. The view was incredible. She'd never flown in a plane or helicopter, or even in a balloon. The sensation was dizzying and joyous all at once, and she wanted to laugh or sing at the amazing feeling of freedom from all of her Earth-bound worries.

She couldn't help it, and she knew it was more of the country mouse stuff, but she'd never been inside Demon Rift, she'd never ridden in a flying carriage pulled by demon steeds, and she'd certainly never been told that her brother was a prince.

A demon prince who just happened to be one of the richest men in the world.

She started laughing.

Chance, who'd been silently staring at her with those glowing yellow eyes, tilted his head in an abrupt, almost animalistic movement. Kit had a habit of tilting hers in that exact same manner.

Her . . . brother . . . frowned at her. "What is funny?"

"This entire situation is funny, don't you think? Speaking specifically, however, I was thinking about the times I've had to eat macaroni and cheese for a week because bike runs were slow and I had to make the rent. If only I'd known I had Mr. Super Billionaire for a brother, I could have hit you up for a loan."

She leaned back against the seat and then jerked forward and stared at it, suddenly hoping that it was cow leather and not some weird skins-of-my-enemies demon upholstery.

In the back of her mind, a constant refrain was pounding at her:

Luke Luke Luke Luke.

She pushed it away, determined not to let pain shatter her when she was about to enter the demon realm for the first time in her life. She needed to be on the alert for danger, not falling apart.

An expression of faint distaste crossed Chance's handsome face too quickly for her to label it as a sneer, and she tried to remember what they'd been talking about before her traitorous emotions had tried to overwhelm her with grief.

"Naturally, I will open the appropriate bank and credit accounts for you," he said.

Oh. Right. Her joke about hitting him up for a loan. Anger flashed hot, then died down to ash. She couldn't take it personally. It was the way rich people usually thought about those who weren't rich. Like the rest of the world was just lurking, waiting to ask for a handout. But just because she couldn't take it personally didn't mean she couldn't correct his false impression of *her*.

"Let's get a few things straight, Chance."

He glared at her, but she leaned forward and started ticking items off on her fingers. "First, I'm not even sure I believe one hundred percent that we are related, and if we are, I'm pretty sure that you're only my half brother, right?"

He nodded.

She moved on before he could start talking again and make her want to punch him. She was trying to be reasonable here, and she had a feeling that Luke was already blowing things up back at his place.

Luke Luke Luke.

A twinge of pain stabbed into her at the thought of what Luke must think of her for leaving like that—she definitely owed him an explanation, but she'd needed to know about Chance and his claims. Elisabeth needed the antidote, but Rio wasn't necessary for that, and it was probably better that she didn't go along, in case she started to feel the overwhelming urge to smack Merelith across the back of the head.

For now, Rio was exactly where she needed to be. The countdown clock was moving faster and faster, rushing by at the speed of magic-fueled light, and now that she had some concrete information—or at least an allegation—she was going to pursue it.

"Is there more?" Chance's voice broke into her reverie, and she realized he'd been waiting for her to continue.

He probably hadn't had to wait for anybody for years.

She smiled at him, enjoying the thought. "Second, if it turns out that you are my brother, I would like to get to know you."

The condescending expression on Chance's face was replaced by one of surprise. His slightly widened eyes and flattened lips told her that it was a cautious surprise, but it was still surprise.

"Third, you will not open any accounts for me— appropriate or inappropriate. I don't want your money. I don't want a job from you. I don't want presents from you."

Now he was scowling again. Well, too bad for him.

"Finally, and I know this is going to sound naïve, but I hope that someday you can learn to be on my side, and I can do the same for you."

Her voice started to tremble, and she willed herself to keep it together and finish her thought. "When I was a little girl, I used to dream about having a brother. Some of the kids would come into the convent with their brothers or sisters, and I was always so desperately envious. I know we're not kids anymore, but if you are my brother, I hope we can be friends."

She had to stop then and look out the window, so she could try to get her voice under control and fight back the tears that were burning her eyes. It was stupidly naïve of her to even hope this, let alone say it out loud, so now he'd know exactly which weapon to use to get to her.

She knew all that.

But it was almost her birthday, and she might be able to celebrate it with a family member for the first time in her entire life. It was one of the reasons she'd stepped into this carriage in the first place.

"I have negotiated with some of the toughest businessmen and government leaders in the world," he said, finally breaking the silence in the carriage.

Caught off guard by the randomness of the statement, Rio turned to look at him.

"I have battled my way up the hierarchy of challenge every year, in order to defend my position as prince and heir to the throne of Demon Rift," he continued, and he drummed his fingers on the edge of the seat in a nervous gesture that looked very familiar to her.

Shock rolled over her when she realized it was familiar because it was one of her own.

"And now, here you are. Young, small, poor, and almost powerless, and yet you have disarmed me more quickly than has ever happened to me in my life." He lifted one hand as if to touch her but then let it fall back down to his side. "I will try to be this person—this brother—for you, although I do not know how, and my instincts are screaming at me that you will betray me. Half of you is Fae princess, and they can never be trusted."

He shook his head. "Will blood tell, and if so, which blood?"

Rio knew a rhetorical question when she heard one. Words alone would never convince him of anything, but she squared her shoulders and took a deep breath. "I know I sound stupid. I know we have no reason to trust each other. But if I really am your sister, then you need to know that I'm going to do everything I can to be on your side."

The carriage tilted as it started its descent, and the moment was over, but Rio could tell by the way Chance kept staring at her that she'd given him something to think about.

A thought crossed her mind, and she grinned. "Now all my girlfriends will want to meet my brother."

He laughed, and she could tell that she'd surprised it out of him.

"Does this mean that I also get to approve or disapprove of your boyfriends?" He leaned forward. "Because I must tell you that I am not a fan of your current choice."

She shrugged and tried to ignore the pain that sliced through her at the thought. She also tried to ignore the hot bundle of nerves jumping around in her stomach now that they were about to land. "That depends. Are you my big brother or my little brother?"

Chance looked down and pretended to brush a speck of dust off of his impeccably clean pants. When he looked up again, his mask of arrogance was back in place.

"I'm your older brother. My mother died many years before my father disappeared with his Fae . . . mistress."

She could tell he'd been about to use a different word—a far more derogatory word—but he'd changed it at the last minute for her sake. She didn't know whether to be relieved or not. She knew the demons had no love for the Fae, and she had no idea how the royal family or the ruling council were going to feel about meeting a half-Fae, half-demon potential heiress to the thrones of both realms.

The world tilted sideways and started to go black, and

she realized with some surprise that she was on the verge
of fainting. None of this could possibly be happening to
her. Not to the little unwanted orphan girl who'd been on
her own, scrambling to survive, since she was fifteen
years old.

Absolutely not; no way, nohow was this happening
to her.

"We are here," Chance announced, as the carriage
bumped to a gentle landing.

Holy crap, this is happening to me.

Someone outside opened the carriage door, and then
Chance stepped out and held out a hand to help her down.
She almost stumbled and was glad he was there to catch
her when she got her first view of Demon Rift.

It was absolutely spectacular.

She didn't know what she'd been expecting, but the
reality was nothing like anything that her imagination
might have conjured. The city was made of pale blue
marble veined with gold, and it was so beautiful it looked
like a Renaissance master painter had designed it.

She must have sighed or gasped or made some kind of
sound, because Chance gave her a wry look. "Not the fire-
blasted, postapocalyptic landscape you were expecting?
You humans have an interesting prejudice against the word
demon."

Realization at what he'd just said dawned and then
struck both of them as funny at the same time.

"Isn't the whole reason I'm here because you want to
tell me that I'm not human at all?" Rio finally said, wiping
her eyes.

"Damn. I can't use my best 'you humans' lines with
you," he said at the same time.

So as it turned out, two of the royal heirs to the Demon
Rift throne and ruling council were laughing together like
fools when the official welcoming procession met them at
the gates of the palace. From the wide-eyed stares and
frantic whispers that quickly surrounded them, Rio had

the feeling that nothing had made Chance laugh so hard or so openly in a very long time.

A man dressed in a very formal and fancy blue-and-white uniform, carrying a long, slender horn, blew out a note and then held it for so long that Rio started to wonder if he didn't have actual lungs. Just when she was getting a little worried about his health, he let the note trail away.

"Welcome to your home, El'andille na Kythelion na Demon Rift," the herald said in a booming voice, disproving the no-lungs theory. He bowed low to her and then moved aside so a group of elder demons who'd been standing just behind him could approach.

Rio knew she was probably breaking all kinds of protocol, but in that exact minute, she didn't care. She spun around to face Chance and tightly grabbed him by both hands.

"I have a name? I didn't think to even ask you about that," she said, laughing and crying all at once. She could taste the salt of her tears as they ran down her face and into her mouth, but she couldn't help it. *She had a name.*

Still holding Chance's hand, she turned to face the people who claimed to be part of her family.

Her family.

"Say it again, please, sir. Tell me my name."

The herald blinked and looked to Chance and then back at the others for permission, but when first a few, and then all of them, nodded and some even smiled a little, the demon gave a self-conscious tug to his shirt and stood even straighter.

"Your name, my lady, is El'andille na Kythelion na Demon Rift, and you are most welcome here." He bowed again, even more elegantly than before.

"El'andille," Rio whispered. "My name is El'andille, and I have a brother."

The oldest demon she'd ever seen, whose beard trailed down all the way to his finely worked gold-and-silver belt, cleared his throat and harrumphed a little bit, and then he tilted his head and shot an incredulous look over Rio's shoulder at Chance, who shrugged.

"I know," Chance said. "She has that effect on people."

Rio had no idea what they were talking about, but she didn't waste time worrying about it. She stepped forward, finally releasing Chance's hand, and then she offered her most formal bow and hoped the demon etiquette book she'd read wasn't too outdated.

"Thank you for this welcome. I'd love a tour. I want to see *everything*."

"El'andille na Kythelion na Demon Rift, would you care for refreshments before we begin our tour?" The old man gestured, and the crowd parted to make room for them to enter the palace. "We have a lovely batch of ale just up from the brewery."

"I'd love that," Rio said, thinking privately that she was probably going to be very much in need of a tall glass of ale before too much longer. "And please call me Rio."

"Rio, then, for now," the old demon rumbled. "We have many gifts for you, young one, to welcome you back to your home."

Welcome her *back*? Had she ever been there in the first place? If so, why had she been kicked out? Who'd put her in that orphanage? What were her parents' names? Rio had so many questions careening around her mind that she was making herself dizzy and not a little nauseated.

If they wanted her *now*, why hadn't they wanted her *then*?

"She doesn't like gifts," Chance called out. "She already warned me not to give her any."

Rio froze, not wanting to cause an international incident by refusing a gift from the person she was starting to be sure was the demon king.

"Ah, I only meant I didn't want any gifts from *you*. Or any money. Definitely no money, or—what did you say? Accounts? Yes, no accounts," she said, sure she was babbling like an idiot.

"You already bicker like siblings," the demon king said, his beard quivering a little.

She almost thought he was trying not to laugh, but that couldn't be possible. She'd heard too much about the grand and dour demon king to believe that he could have a sense of humor. Or maybe she was wrong about who he was, but she was too intimidated to ask, just yet.

"Do demon siblings bicker?" she asked, instead.

"Just like any other children," the old man said, nodding sagely. "Bicker, fight, and cut each others' limbs off in the annual challenge games. We are no different from the humans or the Fae."

Rio swallowed and hoped she wasn't turning pale. Cut each others' limbs off. Just like in the convent, really. Food fights, leg amputation; it was all in a day's fun.

No difference at all.

It was probably perfectly safe for Rio to be alone and unprotected in a place where her own brother might have hacked off her arm or leg if she'd grown up here. No worries. No problem.

Luke was going to *kill* her. Heck, for that matter, *Clarice* was going to kill her.

"I think I'd really love to have that ale now," she said, flashing her best don't-chop-my-leg-off smile.

"Perfect," the demon who might or might not be the king said, beaming. "And then we will tour the fighting ring."

Oh, goody.

CHAPTER 24

Luke watched Elisabeth drink every single drop of the elixir before he finally pronounced himself satisfied. He left the little girl happily romping with Kit, who was playing puppy and enjoying belly rubs while she was at it, and gestured to Merelith to follow him out of the child's silver-and-pink room.

He advanced on the Fae the minute she closed the door behind her.

"Rio is your niece? Elisabeth's cousin? And you didn't bother to mention any of this? What kind of heartless monster are you?"

If possible, Merelith's face turned even paler than it normally was. "You learned the truth?"

It was the kind of nonanswer that Fae aristocrats normally got away with, and it pissed him off even more.

"Don't play with me," he said savagely. "You've been dropping all of those heavy-handed hints, but we hadn't quite pulled it together, until the heir to the Demon Rift throne dropped by *to say hello to his sister.*"

"No!"

Luke continued, his voice a slashing weapon. "Chance Roberts just stole Rio away from me and flew her in a big-ass chariot over to Demon Rift, but he was kind enough to leave a dozen or so of his war guards to occupy my time."

Merelith stumbled back a step. "No! She cannot—they cannot have her. I will not allow it. I owe her mother that much."

Luke sneered at her.

"Save it," he advised. "I know exactly how deep your family sentiment runs, after seeing what you've done to Rio over the past few days. The only reason you want to get your hands on her is that nobody knows what kind of powers she's going to have. A hybrid of demon royal family and Fae royal family? She could be the most powerful being that any of the three realms have ever seen."

"Or the two sides could cancel each other out, and she might have no powers at all," Merelith snapped, but it was clear that she didn't believe it.

"I'm going after her, and when I find her, you're going to give us both some answers."

Luke strode to the center of the damn fleur-de-lis, and then he called to the Shadows.

"Kit," he shouted, and Kit came running out of Elisabeth's room.

"It will be El'andille's birthday at midnight tomorrow night, and then we will all have our answers," Merelith said, her hair floating on the waves of her magic as she grew angrier. "But know this, wizard. Winter's Edge will not allow Demon Rift to have her. No matter what happens at midnight on her birthday, the unlocked potential she carries is too dangerous for us to allow it to be used against us."

Luke snarled and took a step toward her, his hands itching to throttle the arrogance off her face. She pointed one slender finger at him, and he was suddenly enclosed in an impermeable shield that consisted entirely of her magic.

"Do you think you can threaten me here, in the seat of my power?" Her voice rose in intensity until it thundered at him from all corners of the room. "She will join us, or she will die. If she remains in Demon Rift until the hour of her birth, we will march on the demon realm and declare war. Are you sure you want to get in the middle of that, little wizard?"

Before he could answer or counter with his own magic, no matter how futile that might be, Merelith twirled one finger in the air and the Shadows came at her call, hovering near him and Kit.

She laughed at his surprise, and her laughter hurt his ears. Kit, at his side, whined and ducked her head. "Yes, I know a few of your tricks," Merelith said.

Elisabeth picked that moment to wander into the room, and her aunt immediately dropped the terrifying glamour and suddenly became nothing more than a concerned aunt. She wrapped her arms around the girl and pulled her close.

"Good-bye, Mr. Oliver. Good-bye, Kit," Elisabeth said, waving, and he was forced to smile and wave back, so as not to scare her. "Thank you for my medicine."

"Run along to your room, dear, and I will send for some juice," Merelith said, and Elisabeth waved again and then dutifully left the room.

As soon as the door had closed behind her, Merelith dropped her pretense.

"Remember what I have said, Lucian Olivieri. I owe you a debt for what you have done for Elisabeth, and I will endeavor to repay it, but I will not forfeit my claim on my sister Berylan's lost daughter or her potential powers."

With that, she *pushed*, and the Shadows took Luke and Kit and hurtled them through space. When he stepped out of the vortex at the entrance to Demon Rift, he realized that at least he now had the answer to two questions about Rio's past. He knew her mother's name, and he knew Rio's birth name.

El'andille. It was lovely, but he liked Rio better. Rio was *his*. El'andille belonged to the royal intrigue, in all of its deadly, backstabbing, deceitful glory, of two different courts.

Yes, he definitely liked *Rio* better.

He took a deep breath and stared up at the city's blue marble walls. By now, Rio probably knew her father's name as well.

"Hello, guard," he called out. "My name is Luke Oliver, and this is Kit, and I am here to escort a friend of mine back to Bordertown."

A squat, heavy guard trundled out to meet him. "We know who you are, Luke Oliver. Do you begin your campaign for sheriff here?"

Luke didn't know whether to smile or blow something up. He'd never been as tired of hearing about anything as he was of hearing about that damn sheriff's job.

"I am not running for sheriff," he said from between his teeth. "I am here for Rio Jones. Or she might have said Rio Green. Or even Rio something else. None of it matters; they're all names for the same person, and I am here to get her. Right. Now."

The demon's eyebrows beetled together, and he stomped his feet three times in the traditional warning that offense was about to be taken. It was a serious matter, in spite of the comical nature of the gesture. When a demon took offense, somebody was usually lying bloody on the ground soon afterward.

"I don't mean to cause insult," Luke said cautiously.

He realized it might be a bad idea to cause Rio trouble with her new family on the first day she met them, but his concern for her safety far outweighed his concern for demon family protocol.

A new guard, who was much bigger than the first one, marched up to them and pounded the butt end of his spear on the ground three times. Again with three times. Luke got the feeling he was soon to be in big trouble here.

"She does not want to see you," the newcomer growled. "The princess is occupied, and she ordered us to tell you that she would see you later, and that you are not to enter the palace."

Luke didn't know who looked more surprised; the first demon guard or himself.

"The princess?" The first guard squeaked a little and stared up at the big guy. "So it's true then?"

"Yes. The princess has returned to Demon Rift," the guard intoned, with a sense of drama that made Luke want to salute him or punch him.

He was leaning toward punching.

"I don't believe you," Luke challenged the big guy, stepping forward and getting in his face.

The demon remained calm. "She said you wouldn't. She said to tell you to watch out for a tree, and that you would understand her meaning, and you would go away."

Luke started to tell the two of them they had no freaking idea what she was talking about, and then a snippet of memory about Rio and movie lines flashed into his mind. It was true, then. She didn't want to see him. The curse, crouching inside him like a beast waiting for a chance to explode into the world, howled out its fury when a searing wave of pain struck Luke so hard and so fast that it nearly crippled him.

She didn't want to see him. Maybe she was even leaving him, forever, now that she had a new family.

"Believe me now, don't you?" taunted the demon.

"Now would be a good time for you to back away from me," Luke said calmly, his words coated in ice.

The flames started in his fingertips and then wove their way up his arms, spreading and spreading until blue flame covered his entire body. The guards pulled their weapons, but in their surprise they hadn't done so quickly enough.

"I find that I have a need to destroy something, and I'm guessing you would prefer that it not be you," Luke said. He pointed at the little guardhouse from which the two had come. "Is there anybody left in there?"

The first demon—the little one—frantically shook his head. "No, it's only us. You need to leave now."

The other demon elbowed the first one, but Luke only vaguely registered it because he was done with them. Instead, he focused the howling pain threatening to crush him into a blast of heat, and he hurled it all at the guardhouse.

"Ignatio!" He shouted the word of power as he destroyed the building, leaving nothing but a charred piece of ground, and then he turned, slowly and carefully, and walked back into the Shadows.

It wasn't until he arrived in the middle of the road in front of his house that he realized that he was alone. Kit had abandoned him, too.

They'd toured the palace and some of the grounds, and all of it was amazing, but now Rio was tired and starving and very appreciative that they were finally sitting down to eat. She'd filled her plate with so much food that Chance had given her one of his patented sneers, but she didn't care. She needed fuel.

When her stomach was full, she felt a little bit calmer, so Rio didn't even flinch when the guards marched in with reports about the confrontation with Luke and the fact that he'd destroyed the guardhouse. The king, for she'd learned that indeed he was the king and also her grandfather, merely nodded and fixed his gaze on Rio.

"I apologize for my friend's actions," Rio said carefully. "I promise you he will pay for the damage. He buys people new cars all the time, so replacing a guardhouse shouldn't be any big deal."

Chance, who was lounging on a benchlike couch across the room from her, snorted. "Are you sure you know what you've gotten yourself into with this wizard, little sister? He seems a little dangerous."

Rio didn't know whether to laugh or just fall off the bench. "*You're* talking to *me* about dangerous? When you just took me on a tour that included regaling me with the stories of all the challengers you defeated over the years in that ring? I'm surprised there wasn't a box filled with hacked-off arms and legs somewhere in a corner, just so you could admire your own prowess."

The king laughed, and Chance scowled at her, but then he tilted his head, as if considering the idea.

"It is true that it would serve as a deterrent to hopeless challenges in the future," he began, and she jumped up, shaking her head.

"Don't even think about it. It was a stupid comment, and I will not be the one responsible, as my first act as a new member of the family, for beginning the body-part box."

"And yet it is an idea fit for a demon princess," her grandfather rumbled, looking proud.

Her grandfather. The king. She still had no idea what his name was because demon names did not translate out of the demon language very well. They'd given her a suite of rooms, complete with a library and tutor, and expected her to begin studies of their language, culture, and traditions as soon as possible.

She took a deep breath and asked the question for which she'd been building up her courage for the past three hours. "What were my mother's and father's names?"

The guards lining the walls of the huge dining room all seemed to turn into stone simultaneously, as if they wished to be anywhere else but there.

"We do not speak their names," the king roared, and it took a few minutes for the walls to quit shaking, but Rio had had enough of being intimidated by arrogant men.

"Then find me somebody who will, because I want to know about my parents," she shouted right back at him.

This time, even Chance looked like he wished he could disappear. The king, however, drummed his fingers on the tabletop—apparently it was a gesture her entire family shared—and stared at her as if she'd finally become worthy of his notice.

"You dare stand up to me? You truly are my granddaughter, are you not? Of course, I'll have to throw you in the dungeons for a week or two to teach you a lesson," he mused out loud.

"More ale," Chance called out, and the servants in the

room ran out, probably glad to have an excuse to leave. The guards, however, stayed where they were.

Rio tried not to panic. "I'm sorry for shouting at you. All of this is very overwhelming. I can't stay here, in the dungeons or not, although I'd like to return to visit quite often."

Chance shot a surprised look at her that she couldn't interpret, and the king started laughing.

"You're not going anywhere. We have no idea what powers you might inherit at midnight on your birthday, and you are far too deadly a weapon for us to allow you anywhere near Winter's Edge. You will stay here. Permanently. You are the princess of Demon Rift, and you will behave accordingly."

Before Rio could argue, or flee, or start shouting at her grandfather again, Kit magically appeared on the bench beside her. The *Yokai* was back to being enormous, and she wrapped her tail around herself and sat calmly, as if she'd always been there, and stared at the demon king.

The king shouted something in his own language, and suddenly two lines of spears appeared in his guards' hands, all raised and pointing at Kit.

Rio jumped up and put herself between the guards and her fox.

"No," she shouted. "You leave her alone. She's my friend."

The king grumbled but gradually settled himself back down in his seat, never taking his eyes off of Kit. "She is friends with the *Yokai*?"

Chance, to whom the question had been directed, nodded. "Wizards, *Yokai*, goblins, ogres, and even humans. It's the strangest thing I've ever seen. I heard a rumor that there was a mountain troll claiming Rio as a friend."

One of the guards muttered something and shuddered, and the king's sharp gaze snapped to him.

"You. What did you say?"

The guard bowed, and his face flushed a hot, dark

purple. "My apologies, sire. I was just mentioning that Alice put out the word that she claimed Rio as friend."

"Alice? Alice!" The name swept down the line of guards like a hailstorm, and Rio was bewildered to see so many enormous, terrifying-looking demons tremble at the name of the woman who'd spent part of her day making chili for Rio and Luke.

The king narrowed his eyes. "She may become the first demon in our history to create connections across species, perhaps, but be that as it may, she cannot leave until we have finished her education. Perhaps in two or three years' time—"

"Years? Are you out of your mind?" Rio realized she was shouting, but she couldn't help it. "You can't keep me prisoner here after you've admitted that I'm part of your family."

"Actually, he can," Chance said, frowning a little. "I have a cousin who has been in the dungeon for nearly twenty years for offending the king during a formal dinner."

"You can't start out our relationship like this," Rio pleaded, pinning her hopes on Chance. "You're my brother, and we said we'd try—"

"I serve at the king's pleasure," Chance said, icily cold, cutting her off. "If your *Yokai* wishes to visit the dungeons with you, she may."

He stared, hard, at Kit, and Rio almost thought he was trying to tell the fox something, but she didn't have much time to wonder. Kit suddenly jumped up off the bench and nudged Rio's hand until she automatically lifted it and scratched Kit's ears. Chance, the king, the guards, and the dining room itself all vanished, and Rio found herself standing on shaky legs in the middle of Luke's living room, watching him methodically hurl blasts of blue flame at his scorched walls.

Kit's voice rang in her mind.

It was time to leave. I would like some sausage now.

CHAPTER 25

Luke thought he was having a hallucination when giant-sized Kit bounded past the corner of his eye toward her food dish.

"I'm going to need to start buying a lot more fox-friendly food if you're going to stay that size," he began, turning toward her, but then he stopped.

Stopped talking, stopped thinking, stopped breathing.

Rio was back.

He crossed the room in a half second and then she was in his arms and the world's colors started to return, little by little. He was shaking, or she was shaking, or both of them were, with relief and fury and too many emotions to name, let alone feel.

"You came back," he said, and then words weren't enough, could never be enough, and he kissed her.

He captured her mouth like a conquering warrior, staking out his claim. Invading and possessing. Drinking her in, inhaling her essence. He needed more and more and more of her, and the beast inside him truly began to calm only when he realized she was staking her own claim on him.

"I came back," she finally said, when he released her mouth from his kisses.

"We should talk about that stunt you pulled, but I'm too glad to see you to even think about arguing with you," he growled in her ear.

Kit yipped somewhere behind him, and he waved a hand at her. "Yes, yes, you are my hero, now go take a nap while I have a chat with Rio, unless you want to see my furry naked ass again."

Rio offered up a ghost of a smile, and not the laugh he'd hoped for.

"What is it?"

She shook her head. "I don't want to talk about it yet. Is that Alice's chili I smell?"

He nodded. He hadn't paid much attention to it before, but it was true that the aroma was tantalizing, now that he thought he might be able to eat again sometime in this lifetime.

"Maybe we could eat some of that while we talk?" She was too quiet and listless, and Luke's concern grew when she pulled away from him, stumbled over to the table, and practically fell into a chair. "I wish I knew what to do next, Luke, I really do."

"What did they do to you?" He followed her and lifted her head so he could check her pupils. "Breathe on me."

She pulled her head out of his hand. "They didn't poison me. They're not subtle like that. The king—who happens to be my *grandfather*; imagine trying to wrap your head around that—threatened to drop me into the dungeon for a couple of weeks to teach me a lesson."

"He did what?" Luke looked wildly around for something to incinerate, but Rio touched his hand.

"No blowing up cars. I heard about the guardhouse, you idiot. I told them you'd pay for it." A grin touched her lips.

"It was an interesting conversation. Alice has quite some reputation, by the way."

Luke bent to kiss her again, and then he strode over to the kitchen to yank bowls and utensils out of cupboards and drawers.

"Kit would like some sausage," Rio said, folding her arms on the table and putting her head down. "You know, I'm suddenly as exhausted as if I'd been running a marathon. I wonder why that is?"

"Oh, I don't know. Maybe because you've been run through the magical and emotional wringer lately? Finding out you're related to not one, but two royal families? It makes sense that you'd be tired."

Luke spooned chili into bowls, then filled a plate with sausage and gave it and a bowl of fresh water to Kit, who had returned to normal size.

He put the chili down on the placemat next to Rio, but she didn't even move, and he realized that she'd fallen asleep, right there at the table. He deposited his own bowl on the table and then gently lifted her into his arms.

She barely opened her eyes, but she frowned at him. "I won't be able to keep you, Luke. The curse—it's too dangerous now for you to be with me."

Luke's heart turned over in his chest, right there in the middle of his dining room, as he held Rio in his arms and she slipped into a deep sleep. He'd spent hundreds of years not getting close to anyone, for fear of what being near him and his curse might do to them. Now, for the first time in his long, tortured existence, this amazing woman was worried about any pain that being with *her* might cause *him.*

"Time to rest, Princess El'andille," he whispered. "Too bad I'm not Prince Charming, but I have to warn you that I'm never going to let you go."

He held her in his arms for the rest of the night, never once falling asleep himself, and plotted ways they could escape the potentially deadly consequences of Rio's new-found heritage. By the time dawn's first rays of sunshine tried to peek into the room, he thought he'd finally worked out a workable plan.

Now he just had to persuade Rio to agree to it.

Rio woke up in Luke's arms—a new habit she'd grown to love far too much.

"I need you," he said, and his blue eyes shone with heat and hunger.

"I need you, too," she whispered, and it was all the answer he needed.

In seconds, they were both undressed and lying wrapped together, and he was seducing her with long, slow kisses that began with her mouth, moved down to her breasts, and then began to fall all along every inch of her sides and belly and arms and legs. She caught her breath when he approached too near to her center and hot breath passed nearby. She needed him.

She *needed* him.

"Luke, I—"

"I'm going to taste you now," he announced, and then he parted her legs and moved between them, lifting her legs so they straddled his shoulders.

He speared her with such a look of determination and desire that her words dried up in her throat, because apparently all the liquid in her body was heating and rushing to the very place he was bending his head to kiss.

At the first touch of his tongue, she cried out and fisted her hands in the quilts, knowing only that she needed to hang on for this ride that threatened to take her deeper into sensation than she'd ever gone before. He licked and sucked on her, destroying her, sending sizzling heat shooting through her body; every nerve ending expanded and contracted in time with the touch of his tongue.

Her hips moved rhythmically beneath him. She couldn't help it; they moved on their own, trying to rush the pace and force the issue. Every inch of her body was straining and focused on what he was doing to her with his mouth.

"Touch your breasts for me," he said hoarsely, and she blushed again, but she touched her nipples, softly at first, and then pinching them the way he had done during one of the many times he'd driven her to incredible orgasm.

He shot her a look so filled with masculine pride and possession that she almost laughed, but then he bent and fastened his lips around the most sensitive place on her body and she exploded beneath him. By the time she'd quit shaking, he was already moving up on the bed and then rocking into her, his hardness providing the perfect counterpoint to her sensitive flesh, and soon his steady, deep thrusts sent her over the edge again, and this time he tumbled over with her.

"I love you," he said, so quietly she almost didn't hear him, so she could pretend he hadn't said it at all.

But then he took her face in his hands and said it again. "I love you, Rio."

Caught by his gaze—trapped by his honesty—she couldn't lie to him. "I love you, too, but we can't be together. My families, the curse—"

"I have a plan," he said, grinning smugly.

He rolled over on his back, laced his hands together under his head, and began to whistle.

She poked him in the chest. "Are you going to share?"

"We're going to get out of Dodge."

She sat up and stared down at him in bewilderment. "What?"

"We're leaving Bordertown."

CHAPTER 26

"Get up, get dressed, and let's get going," Luke said, jumping out of bed after planting a resounding kiss on her lips.

Rio didn't move. She just watched him warily, like a zoo visitor might watch the tiger from behind the glass, and wondered if he'd been drinking Grendel venom. Doing shots of the stuff, maybe.

"Luke. Luke! Listen to me. We can't leave Bordertown. What about your business? Your house? Your things? And where would we go?"

He paused in his apparent quest to throw the worst combination of clothing possible in a backpack. "I have a plan. I don't care about the business. Alice will send me anything from the house that I want, and she can have the house. All I need is you, and we can live anywhere in the world that you want."

Luke threw one yellow and one blue sock and a red T-shirt into his bag, but then he finally seemed to realize that she wasn't moving. He shoved the silky dark hair out of his face, and she was caught off guard and wondered what a man as beautiful as a fallen angel would look like in one blue and one yellow sock.

Probably just as gorgeous. It was ridiculously unfair. Also, she didn't want to talk about her new families and their schemes before she'd had even her first cup of coffee.

"Is it only me, or does this feel like I'm caught in a magical episode of a soap opera?" She experimented with a sultry TV pose, letting the sheet drop down low, and had the immediate satisfaction of watching his eyes glaze over and his erection bob up to instant, interested attention.

He groaned and covered his eyes, which left all of his other glorious parts still naked. "Rio, I'm trying to be serious. If we stay here, your life will be a continual battle between trying to balance the demands of one family against the other. They'll want to use you, and if they can't use you, they'll kill you," he said seriously, and his erection and her silly mood both wilted at the thought.

"I know, all right? I know. I just wanted to be able to have a family for a little while. Is that so wrong?" She sighed. "Maybe the Fae court—"

"Rio, Merelith told me as much, right to my face."

"The king told me he planned to lock me up in my new suite of rooms in the palace for 'two or three years' until I was properly educated," she reluctantly admitted, feeling torn in two despite the threats. "I know it sounds childish to say, but it's not fair that I've only just found them, and now I have to lose them again."

"Tell me what you want to do. Whatever you want, that's what we'll do," he said, holding perfectly still; a predator weighing options in order to make the most lethal decision. Except he'd just said he'd leave the decision up to her—nothing he could do would be better proof of his feelings for her.

"We should go," she said slowly, and then with more conviction. "We should go. To hell with them. They had twenty-five years to find me. I'll call Clarice once we're settled somewhere."

His smile was almost blinding. "Come on, then, the

sooner the better, before one or both of your families sends armed guards to collect you. I could blast them, but it would attract a lot of attention, and we're trying to do this quietly."

Rio loved watching him move; even watching him do something as mundane as shoving clothes in a bag was a treat. Especially since he was doing it naked. She smiled as the muscles in his back bunched while he reached up to the top shelf of his closet for a single electric-blue Converse shoe, considered it for a second, and then tossed it back.

"You know, they have clothes and shoes in Paris," he said, tossing his backpack on the end of the bed. "Why don't we go there first?"

"I don't have a passport," Rio said, wondering why the idea of leaving town was freaking her completely out.

"I'm a wizard, Rio. I can manage a passport." He pulled the quilts away from her, then grinned wolfishly at the sight of her breasts. "You know, we might have a little more time."

"No! I'm up, already."

She escaped to the bathroom and the shower. By the time she was clean and dressed, the idea had caught fire in her imagination. More important, she'd woken up enough to appreciate the full extent of what he was offering her.

Luke was willing to give up his entire life for her. How could she not be willing to do the same?

"Let's leave now," she said, when she found him in his office, sorting through potions and powders. "Or as soon as you're done with what you need to do. The sooner we're gone, the sooner we can start over somewhere else."

Luke nodded, still sorting, and she went to find Kit.

"Sleeping in Alice's room? Do you think that will be okay with her?"

Kit was curled up in a snug little ball in the middle of a gorgeous jade-green silk comforter. She stretched her head up to have her ears scratched, and then she stared at Rio with her beautiful emerald eyes.

Are you leaving?

"Yes, we're leaving. If I stay, my families will tear me—or all of Bordertown—apart trying to control me."

Rio stroked Kit's silky fur and realized she didn't know if the little *Yokai* would be willing to go with her. She swallowed, hard.

"Kit, I'd love it if you'd come with me. I know foxes can't roam around in human places as easily as they can in Bordertown, but we can buy you a pretty collar and pretend you're a pet, some kind of dog. I think an Akita looks like a fox." Rio was babbling, but she was afraid that if she stopped talking, Kit would have a chance to tell her no.

My task is not done, but I am still not sure what it is. I will remain with you for now.

Rio hugged Kit, and Kit allowed it, and then the two of them went to find Luke so they could begin their new life together.

★

Luke finished sorting through the most important bottles in his collection, selecting some to go with him and carefully boxing more up for Alice to send. Now he could leave his office, secure in the knowledge that nobody who might manage to break in after his wards had faded would be inadvertently poisoned.

Rio appeared, carrying only the backpack she'd first arrived with, and Kit trotted along at her heels.

"We're going to need a collar. Green, I think," Rio said, grinning down at Kit.

"I'm glad you're coming with us, fur-face. I need your superior help to keep Rio safe, after all," Luke said, and for the first time, he heard Kit's voice in his mind.

I know.

Luke's mouth fell open, and Kit laughed her little fox

laugh at him, with her tongue hanging down from the side of her mouth.

"She talked to me," he sputtered. "Smug little—"

"I heard her," Rio interrupted, grinning. "You two deserve each other. Stupid arrogant wizards and *Yokai*."

"We should go. Now," he said. "The best exit from Bordertown to the human side of things is through the High Line park. Also, the park was built out of an old abandoned railroad line, so the Fae can't get anywhere near it because of the metal."

"That's half of my relatives, at least. Strange that I never had a problem with metal. Must be my demon half." Rio forced a smile, and he appreciated the attempt. "I guess we'll worry about Chance and the demons when they show up."

Within five minutes, they'd locked up the place and were in the Jeep. Rio kept glancing nervously around, and he wanted to reassure her but knew she'd only feel safe once they made it out of Bordertown. He pulled into a parking lot owned by a black bear shifter who owed him a favor, tossed the attendant the keys, and told the boy that Alice would pick it up. He thought the kid would wet himself at the news, but Luke managed to wait until he and Rio had walked a half block away before he started laughing.

"So everybody knows Alice," Rio said. "Someday I'd like to hear more about her."

Luke took her cold hand in his. "I'll tell you all I know. She's one of the most secretive people in the world, I think."

He gestured. "There's the entrance to the park."

She stopped and stared for a moment. "Oh, Luke, it's gorgeous. Is that hotel actually stretched over the top of the park?"

"Yes, that's the Standard Hotel. There are a couple of other buildings that cross the park, too."

"It used to be a railroad?"

"For freight. It was an elevated line that brought freight cars directly to factories and warehouses. Once it was abandoned, it became a horrible urban eyesore. In fact, the Manhattan city government wanted to tear it down."

She started walking again, still admiring the sight of the oasis of plants that existed not only in Bordertown, where such things were magical and common, but in the steel and concrete jungle of Manhattan, where the humans seemed to systematically destroy all plant life so they could build more and more buildings.

"What happened? Did Bordertown take it over?"

Luke laughed. "No, we had little to do with it, other than some discreetly disguised contributions. This was all done by the humans. A talented team of landscape architects and traditional architects worked together with a lot of volunteers and donors to make this a remarkable place."

She glanced up at him. "Sounds like you come here a lot."

He shrugged, feeling sheepish at being caught out. "The view over Tenth Avenue is a good place to sit and think and eat my lunch, sometimes."

"Sounds . . . normal," she said wistfully.

"The view over the Seine is pretty incredible for picnics, too," he told her. "When we get to Paris, I'll take you—"

"I don't think you'll be taking her anywhere." The voice came from behind them, and Kit's snarled warning came too late.

Luke whirled around, already reaching for fire. "Maestro. Nice of you to return my calls."

The man looked more exhausted than Luke had ever seen him, but he ruthlessly repressed a twinge of sympathy. The maestro had put Rio through hell. He deserved whatever bad things happened to him.

"What? No cake?" Rio's face was harder and colder than Luke had ever seen it. "No fancy roulette wheels?"

"I've been in Europe, trying to buy us time," Maestro said wearily. "The Fae are arming for war, but this time it's against each other. Internal factions are ripping the courts apart, and the only chance I can see of stopping it is to find a ruler powerful enough to control all of them."

His gaze traveled to Rio and stopped.

"Oh, no," she said, her eyes enormous. "You're out of your mind if you think that I'll have anything to do with this."

"You're not using her, Maestro. I'll kill you and any of the League who even try." Luke didn't raise his voice, and the man knew what that meant.

"Still okay to touch silver?" Maestro held out a hand, and it was suddenly holding a silver knife. "Want to try mine again and see?"

Before any of them could move, Kit's jaws fastened on Maestro's wrist, and there was a distinct *crunch* as she snapped his bones. Maestro shouted, Rio caught the knife before it hit the ground, and then suddenly Kit vanished and then reappeared safely behind Luke.

"Nice job, Kitsune," Luke said, drawing out her name so Maestro would know what he was up against.

The man had already healed his own wrist, so it wasn't a permanent injury or even one that delayed him much, but Luke figured it had proven a point.

"The *Yokai* doesn't like me much."

"None of us like you much. Don't mess with us," Rio said, steely-eyed. "I'll just keep this knife as a souvenir of what happens to people who try to mess with my family."

Luke's heart leapt in his chest. She'd called him her *family*.

"We can help you," Maestro said.

"You just want to use me," Rio countered.

"Everybody wants to use everybody, child," the old web spinner said wearily. "Right now, I only want to protect you and Bordertown from what's going to happen to you at midnight."

Luke backed him up against the wall of the building. "You know something, don't you?"

"I know many things. Come with me to our offices, and I'll tell you."

Rio shook her head and pointed to the High Line. "No. Tell me there, in the park, or don't tell me at all."

Maestro contemplated her for a moment and then nodded. "Yes. That will work."

"Fine." She turned and headed for the park entrance,
Kit at her side, leaving them to follow, but then she glanced
back over her shoulder. "We need food. Don't forget Kit."

Luke grinned and then headed after her, in case any of
her demon family had decided to hang out at the park
today.

"You're buying," he told Maestro. "I have to go after
my woman."

"It's a mistake, you know. You and her," Maestro said
quietly, almost under his breath.

"Save it," Luke advised, not bothering to slow down.

This "mistake" was going to last for the rest of Rio's
life.

CHAPTER 27

Rio waited for Luke in the park, but the stunning surroundings didn't match her mood, the situation, or the conversation they were about to have. Kit, still walking next to her, had transformed again, and now she looked like a pint-sized collie.

The people they passed—although now perhaps Rio needed to say the *humans* they passed, since she was no longer one of them—didn't see anything but a lovely dog when they looked at Kit, judging by their compliments and comments, so that was good.

Rio nodded her thanks but didn't stop to engage in conversation. There was no point in trying to make friends or strike up acquaintances now, when she might never see this park or anyone in it ever again.

Melancholy struck, hard, and Rio tried to swallow her fears, but the lump in her throat and the pain in her chest were making it tough. What if she never made it back? What if she'd never see Clarice again? And Chance . . . Although he hadn't done much to impress her yet, she'd had the feeling that there might be hope for the future.

Elisabeth, Miro, even Mrs. G, who'd probably had no choice but to do what she'd done.

She headed toward the Manhattan side of the stretch of park and made it about halfway across the path, inhaling deeply to enjoy the delicious aroma of flowers and foliage, when the headache and then the first tingle hit. She ignored both and took another step, and *bam*, the sensation struck again. It was a shiver across her skin, like static electricity that had somehow dispersed from an isolated shock into a full-body assault.

Kit started to whine, softly at first and then more loudly. When Rio tried to take another step as a sort of experiment, Kit sank her teeth into Rio's pants leg and pulled, bracing her small body with stiff legs, and her voice sounded loud and clear in Rio's mind.

No.

"Looks like she doesn't like that side of the park," Luke said, approaching from her left. When she turned to face him, she inadvertently brushed her right shoulder against the electric fence or whatever it was, and Luke's face went slack with fear.

"Rio, no," he shouted.

He leapt forward toward her at the same time that Kit yanked especially hard, and between the two of them, Rio fell back and away from the bizarre electrical current and sprawled on her butt on the path right there in the middle of the High Line.

"What the hell was that?" Luke muttered, stalking up and down the path in the exact spot where Rio had first felt the unpleasant electric charge.

Kit took up a position in front of Rio and barked at her when Rio tried to stand up.

"What is it?" Rio asked the *Yokai*, frustrated beyond belief that everybody was overreacting because she'd stepped into a freak electrical current.

Luke returned and crouched down next to her, taking her chin in his hand and staring intently at first one, and then the other side of her face.

"What?" she demanded.

"Rio, you started to disappear," he said, and he was visibly shaken.

She swallowed whatever smart-ass remark she'd been about to make, because he looked like he'd seen a ghost, and the ghost had been Rio.

"It was like nothing I've ever seen before. You started to fade in sections; not like traveling through Shadows, or jumping the way Kit leaps through space, or any kind of magical transport I've ever seen or heard of," he continued, compulsively running his hands up and down her arms, as if to make sure she didn't disappear again.

He finally pulled her up from the ground when they started to get strange looks from passing humans, but he and Kit walked between Rio and the danger zone all the way to the other side—the Bordertown side—of the park.

Maestro waited there, seated on a bench with bags of food at his side and his hands folded together in his lap.

"I'm guessing you've discovered the truth now," he said.

"What truth is it this time? That I'm strangely sensitive to human-built electrical currents?" Rio rolled her eyes. "You're all overreacting."

"No, child. The truth that you will never be able to leave Bordertown, at least not by way of the human world. Demon Rift and the Fae realms are open to you."

She sat down, hard, on the bench next to him. "What?"

"Julian and Berylan made sure of that, when they warded you against discovery," Maestro said.

Rio knew her face looked blank, but she had no idea what he was talking about. "Who?"

The old man's face softened for just a split second before he resumed his usual expressionless mask. "Julian na Demon Rift and Berylan na Kythelion. Your parents."

Rio didn't hear anything else, although she knew he was still talking. It was too much, finally. Too much to accept, too much to comprehend, too much to believe.

Their names. She finally knew their names, and the

sound of them had hit her hard with the force of returning memory. Something tickled at the edge of her consciousness—something to do with those names—but she couldn't quite capture it. Luke tried to talk to her, but he was only interrupting the process, so she impatiently waved him away and turned her mind even further inward.

Julian na Demon Rift and Berylan na Kythelion. Her parents. They'd loved each other; at least enough to have defied *their* parents and conceived her. They'd named her, too: El'andille na Kythelion na Demon Rift. Even the sound of it was beautiful and regal and elegant—everything that Rio was not.

She'd never felt the lack of those qualities so keenly before today.

And now she'd learned, from the very person who'd put the *Ruin Rio's life* plans in action, that her own parents had damaged her in some way. Cursed her to a life lived only in Bordertown and her families' realms. The same families who had treated her parents so badly. It didn't make sense.

She looked at Luke and started to laugh. The two of them were almost fated to be together. They were two of a kind—*the cursed*—both of them trapped in fates designed by the cruelest possible architects: their own parents.

"Tell me," he said, watching her from eyes darkened with concern.

"I will. Later," she promised.

Maestro stared at the flowering bushes nearest the bench. "These do not bloom on the human side of the park. Perhaps there is a bit of wisdom there, El'andille. Some of us need magic to bloom, and you have not begun to reach or understand the full extent of your powers."

"El'andille," Luke repeated softly. "It's a beautiful name, Rio."

"I prefer Rio," she said quickly, not even knowing yet if it was the truth for always, but it was absolutely the truth for now.

El'andille was a person she didn't know yet and might

not have the opportunity to get to know. Rio was the woman who could stand up for herself against Fae princesses, demon kings, and enraged mama ducks. El'andille might have magic, but Rio had guts.

Right now, she needed guts.

"Tell me," she told Maestro. "Everything you know."

He nodded. "They met at a formal function, during which they were meant to offer the usual glib reassurances that the wars of the past would never happen again, that both realms lived for nothing but peace, et cetera, et cetera."

"But it didn't work out that way, I guess," Rio said.

"No, it did not. Three oracles took to their beds after that night, never to rise again, and another six hung up their shingles and took work in shops. It was always said that nobody could ever have predicted it, but the truth was that anybody who saw them dance that night should have known exactly what would happen next," Maestro said, and he smiled as if remembering the sight.

"Your mother was the most beautiful woman I have ever seen, and your father was her match, with the sharp-edged masculine beauty that only the Demon Rift royal family has ever displayed."

Luke sat down next to Rio and handed her the other half of Kit's sandwich.

"Hey, I look okay in a tux," he said, sounding vaguely disgruntled.

She smiled and kissed his cheek. "I'm looking forward to seeing that."

Maestro frowned. "Do you want to hear this or not?"

Rio sighed, not sure if she did, but she nodded.

"There was nothing for either of them, after that, but each other. The royal families nearly went to war over it. In the end, both were disinherited, disowned, and driven from their respective realms. They came to live in Bordertown, but Berylan was already pregnant with you by that time. The pain of losing her family, combined with the fear that the demons or her own kind would find and kill them, was too much for her. She became ill and died soon after childbirth, and Julian disappeared shortly after that. You were never seen again; most assumed the baby had died, including me, I might add. I'm sorry, but that's all I know, other than about the ward, because Julian came to me for help finding someone to set it shortly after you were born."

Rio had listened silently while the tragedy unfolded in his words as if it were happening all around her instead of being the story of her past, a quarter of a century distant. She, Rio, had been *assumed dead*, after her mother's own family had hounded Berylan to an early grave. Her father had disappeared, which meant he was probably dead, too. Shock, rage, and sorrow buffeted her, nearly driving her to her knees, but Luke put his strong arms around her and held on tight while she weathered the storm.

Ultimately, Rio's heart was too full to hold anything but the pain, so the rest of it broke on the rocky shore of her numbness. Too much, indeed. She wondered if this was what a mental breakdown felt like.

"How did you not know any of this? You were here in Bordertown then," she said to Luke.

He shook his head. "I was in and out, and I was keeping a very low profile back then, avoiding both courts entirely. When I had anything to do with demons or Fae, it was with the lowlifes. I never heard any gossip about the royal families, that's for sure."

"You didn't know Alice yet, either, so you weren't nearly as informed as you are these days," Maestro said.

"True," Luke agreed, but then he glared at the man. "Is there *anything* you don't know?"

Maestro sighed. "Every day that I am still alive, I realize that there is more and more that I do not know. Like what's going to happen tonight at midnight, for example, when Rio will either inherit unimaginable power from both lines of her heritage or be slain when both of her families conspire to kill her."

Luke snarled at the man. "I will never let them harm her, and if you've got any balls left, you'll help me protect her."

"I've been trying to protect her," Maestro snapped. "Why do you think I'm trying to recruit her? The League is neutral; she'd be safe from both families for a short time."

"*She* is right *here*," Rio told them. "Stop talking *about* me and start talking *to* me."

Luke leaned over and rescued a wrapped sandwich from Kit, then broke pieces off it and started feeding them to the fox. "What do you want to do, Rio? I'll support you in anything, so long as you don't plan to leave me behind."

Maestro shook his head, but they both ignored him.

"They drove my parents to an early grave, and I grew up in a convent orphanage because of it," she said, standing up and brushing off the seat of her jeans. "I need to learn everything about them, so I can decide whether to forgive and forget or find a way to pay them back."

"Revenge isn't a goal worth building a life around," Luke warned her.

She nodded, accepting the statement as true without committing to it, and then she held out her hand to Maestro. "I'll give the League one year, if you can keep my families from going to war. I won't kill anybody for you, and I won't break any laws, or even any ethical guidelines. If you can live with that, I'll sign up right here and now."

Maestro stood and they shook hands on the strangest and, probably, the most dangerous deal she'd ever made.

CHAPTER 28

Luke figured Rio had about twelve hours left to be part of her old life, and he was determined to give her every opportunity to do exactly that. He managed to sneak in a few phone calls, and by the time they'd walked up and down the length of the Bordertown side of the High Line park twice, everything was in place.

"We have plans," he announced.

"I know," she said glumly.

"No, not midnight plans. These are *spend the rest of the day having fun* plans," he said, grinning.

She sighed, and the desolation in that sound was enough to break his heart. "Do you really think I'm in the mood for plans? Or fun? After what I just learned?"

Luke stopped walking and pulled her into his arms. "I know you're devastated. I also know that you're going to have the next year to sort through facts and fictions, and we'll figure all this out together."

"But still—"

"Clarice said to tell you dancing, O'Malley's, and the gold dress that matches your eyes," he said, but then he thought about O'Malley's, and about how beautiful Rio was, and he scowled. "Although maybe not that, exactly. I don't want Sean O'Malley or any of his brothers anywhere around you."

"Sean O'Malley is a great-looking guy who needs to find the right woman, but that woman is definitely not me," Rio said.

He could tell she was thinking about the idea of going out, but after a minute or so, she shook her head. "I just can't do it. All I want to do right now is sleep and eat and gear up for tonight. I wish I had some idea of what might happen or how to prepare."

"I tend to carbo-load in preparation for a major magical event," he said, tongue firmly in cheek, and was rewarded with a glimmer of a smile.

"I can't imagine how I could make it through this without you, but I can't believe how selfish I am to say that, or even to feel it," she whispered. "What if the stress of tonight activates your curse?"

"Then we'll be cursed together, and your families in both Winter's Edge and Demon Rift had better watch their asses, because we'll be coming for them." He knew he'd probably ruined the atmosphere of lighthearted fun he'd been trying to create, but just the thought of taking on the assholes who'd ruined Rio's parents' lives was enough to make his entire damn day.

She flashed a menacingly deadly smile, and he almost started to worry. Maybe being around him was teaching her to be bloodthirsty. Next thing he knew, she'd be blowing up cars and hurling fireballs.

"Why would I want to blow up cars?" She looked puzzled, and then her eyes widened and she gasped as she looked up at Luke.

"You did it again, didn't you?"

She nodded. "Just that snippet about next I'd be blowing up cars and hurling fireballs. I'm so sorry! I'm not trying to intrude on your privacy or your mind. It just . . . happens."

He frowned down at her, while humans passed them

by on both sides, barely sparing a glance at the couple standing stock-still in the middle of the path.

"What am I thinking now?"

She closed her eyes, and then she inhaled sharply and her cheeks flamed a vividly hot pink. "You—you—is that even possible?"

He leaned closer, so he could whisper in her ear. "I think if you are very, *very* flexible, and I—"

"Luke!" She cast a scandalized glance around. "Stop it immediately. There are people walking here."

He clasped her hand in his and started walking, ready to leave the park, retrieve his Jeep, and head for home so they could eat, sleep, and maybe try out the idea that he'd just been thinking about. Or an even simpler one, that involved Rio naked, bent over the back of the couch, and him driving into her until she lost her mind and screamed his name.

"Luke," she said, gasping, and he realized she'd done it again. She must have pulled the visual right out of his mind because she was blushing so hard her skin was practically on fire.

"Oh, Rio. I am so going to love this new skill of yours. Do you want to know what I'm thinking about now?"

"No! Kit, bite him," Rio commanded, but Kit laughed her little laugh, changing back from dog into fox as they walked down the stairs into Bordertown, and then she trotted about ten paces ahead of them all the way back to the parking lot.

Luke called Clarice back and postponed their plans and asked her to organize a birthday bash for Rio—for tomorrow night. He and Rio both might be dead, but if they survived tonight, they'd be seriously in need of a party.

"Luke," Clarice said, stopping him just as he was about to hang up. "Take care of her. Whatever is about to happen tonight—and I don't want to know—but please. Take care of Rio for me."

"I swear to you that I'll either protect her or die trying," he told her.

"I'd prefer option A," she said dryly. "You wizards are pretty dramatic."

"I think we're going to be great friends," he said, grinning.

"You still owe me a car."

When he hung up, he was still smiling.

"She has that effect on men," Rio said, rolling her eyes.

"Would you like to know the effect you have on me? Why don't you read my mind again?" He leered cheerfully, and she burst out laughing.

The sound was like balm to the cracked and scorched places in his soul.

Mine, mine, mine, mine.

"Yes, yours," she agreed. "Now give me the keys, I'm driving."

For the entire way back to his place, Luke couldn't wipe the smile off his face.

CHAPTER 29

Twenty minutes to midnight

BLACK SWAN FOUNTAIN SQUARE

"Here's the thing about the easy times. They sweep by in life far too quickly," Rio said, smoothing the sides of her dress with her hands. "I can't believe I'll be twenty-five in twenty more minutes."

"You look spectacular, and I enjoyed every minute of today. There was no sweeping," Luke said, and the gleam of honest appreciation and even more sincere desire in his eyes—in spite of all the ways they'd tried to quench their hunger for each other all afternoon and evening—was enough to warm her up all the way to her icy cold toes.

"I'd feel better in my jeans and boots."

Clarice had insisted on stopping by with The Dress, telling Rio that if she wouldn't wear it on her own twenty-fifth birthday, then there must be something wrong with her. Rio had sat her down, poured her a stiff glass of whiskey, and then told her everything. It had taken longer for Clarice to quit saying "You're a princess?" than it had for her to stop saying "You slept with Luke Oliver?" but she'd finally moved on.

After that, she'd held Rio's hand while Rio had cried about losing her parents before she'd ever been able to know them, and Luke had gone outside and incinerated Helga's new van.

"We need to get you a new hobby, by the way," Rio told Luke, but then she handed him another bottle of water. Preventive medicine, in a way. "This one is costing you a fortune. Helga told me that she's looking to trade up again, and this time she wants a better sound system."

Luke grimaced, and Rio started laughing. Only in Bordertown would people be so sanguine about a neighbor who regularly detonated their automobiles as a bizarre kind of stress relief.

Anyway, The Dress. It was a shimmery gold silk that matched exactly the amber flecks in her eyes, or so Clarice had told her, but even fashion-challenged Rio had to admit that when she'd put it on, she felt sexier, more beautiful, and more powerful than she'd ever felt in anything she'd worn before.

And Luke loved it. He'd been reduced to stuttering incoherence when he'd first seen her, in the dress, with actual makeup on, and with her hair framing her face in gentle waves. Clarice was a miracle worker, and Rio'd needed to fight Luke off to keep him from ripping the dress off her, right there in the dining room. They'd discovered, though, that silk slid up legs and hips really easily, and at least one of Luke's fantasy visuals from earlier in the day had been fulfilled.

"You *look* like a princess, so maybe the people who don't know you well enough to see your inner royalty will pause, at least, before they try to pull any tricks," Luke said, folding his arms over his chest in his best bodyguard impersonation.

"Here comes Merelith, so let the tricks begin," Rio whispered, and then she began her own impersonation, the one where she pretended to actually feel like the heiress to two separate thrones.

The Fae led at least two dozen of her guardsmen, and

they marched toward Rio in icy and terrible beauty. She could imagine herself after a decade with the Winter's Edge Fae; she'd be as icily perfect as an orchid trapped in an icicle, and just as useless, with only the potential of danger or ruin in her future.

No, she didn't see herself living in Winter's Edge.

"We will be delighted to take you home with us when this ceremony is over," Merelith pronounced as she came gliding over the cobblestones of the square.

"Why, hello to you, too, Auntie Merelith," Rio purred. "How nice of you to wish me a happy birthday."

Merelith's eyes flared to molten silver. "Do not mistake my kindness for apathy, El'andille. It's a flaw your mother shared."

Rio touched Luke's arm when he raised flame-cloaked hands, as if to blast her aunt. "No, it's not time."

A ripple ran across the assembled Fae when the sound of stomping feet—many stomping feet marching in cadence—began on the other side of the square and then headed toward Rio. It was Chance, of course, leading a contingent of his war guards.

"Happy birthday. I see the ugly side of your family is already here, sister," he called out, and his demons pounded their chests and laughed with voices like thunder.

Rio smiled at him and waited for him to come closer.

"You told me no gifts," he said, showing her his empty hands. "I hear and obey."

Rio could imagine herself after a decade in Demon Rift; she'd be as logical-minded and vicious as her brother, afraid to trust or love or even show compassion, with only the potential for brutality or battle in her future.

No, she didn't see herself living in Demon Rift.

A solitary figure walked out of the fountain, untouched by the water, and crossed the square toward Rio. When the man arrived in front of her, he did what none of the others had.

He bowed.

"Princess, it is time," Maestro said, rising.

The Fae and the demons all fell back a step or two, but it didn't last long.

"The League of the Black Swan has no business here," Merelith cried out.

"Demon Rift agrees with the Fae," Chance yelled.

"You're not even official yet, and already you're making history," Luke said loudly enough for everyone to hear him. "You've got Demon Rift and Winter's Edge agreeing on something."

"I'm scared," Rio admitted to Luke, her lips not moving at all, in a whisper barely loud enough for him to hear. Nobody else could know. She had to present a courageous front. Hence, The Dress.

She took a deep breath and began. "Listen to my words, all of you. I want to learn about both sides of my family, but I won't be used as a tool in your politics, and I especially won't be used to incite war. For the length of one year, I'll be working for the League of the Black Swan."

Merelith and Chance both started to protest, but Rio cut them off.

"I'll visit you, and I'll study my heritage, as long as you treat me with respect and promise not to try to lock me in any dungeons or anywhere else, for 'my own good' or for any other reason," she continued.

"If we can't agree to this, then we'll all take the time to see what powers, exactly, I inherit in a few minutes."

Merelith started forward, but Luke raised his hands, and everyone in the square could see the blue flames as they rose at least ten feet into the air.

"I don't think so," he told the Fae, and then he bowed to Rio. "Happy birthday, Princess."

Clarice and Miro stepped out from behind the fountain, startling the demons nearest them. "Happy birthday, Princess."

An entire Oblong of goblins swarmed up from behind Luke's Jeep and settled themselves on the ground around Rio. "Happy birthday, Princess," their leader said.

A mountain troll carrying an enormous club sauntered

into the square and took up a position near the Fae guards. "Happy birthday, Princess," Abernathy said.

The overall effect was exactly as she and Luke had planned it, and Rio had never felt so very much the center of attention in her life. She was going to look like a complete fool if something didn't happen, and happen fast.

"No worries," Luke said, and he took her hand and then pointed to the sky with his other hand. "Something is definitely about to happen."

The starry night above them was changing; fixed points of light in the sky suddenly danced and circled each other, combining and retreating in graceful movements until the entire night sky was filled with their waltz.

A starlight waltz.

A giant band of pure silver light formed in the sky and then hurtled down toward Earth—toward the square—toward *Rio*. She had only an instant to tell herself not to panic, and then the band of light struck the ground, enclosing Rio but pushing Luke out of the circle with a loud *clap*.

When Rio could hear and see again, she was no longer alone. A woman who seemed to be made of pure starlight stood next to her, gazing wonderingly at her, and somehow Rio knew, with no room for doubt, that this was her mother.

"You are my El'andille," the woman—Berylan—said, and Rio wanted to cry or laugh or shout with joy.

"Mother? Is it really you?" Rio whispered the words. "Are you—are you really here?"

Rio's mother smiled at her, but the smile held a universe of sadness. "I can only be here as you see me, and only on the anniversary of your birth each year now that you have finally reached age twenty-five, but I have a gift for you, my beautiful, darling daughter."

Rio let her tears fall without even trying to stop them. "I don't want any gifts, Mother. I only want to spend time with you."

"And you will, my lovely, brave girl, but first I must tell you something that I've waited for twenty-five years to say."

Berylan's sadness was so obvious that Rio's chest ached for her mother, for herself—for both of them.

"Don't tell me if it makes you this sad," Rio said. She'd had enough bad news to last a lifetime.

Her mother embraced Rio with arms made of starlight, and she whispered into her ear. "I am so sorry for leaving you. I was so very ill, but I tried to fight. I tried so hard to fight so I could stay with you, my beautiful girl. Please forgive me for leaving you alone. My body wasn't strong enough to keep the promise I made to you that I would get better. Please, can you ever forgive me?"

Rio wept in her mother's arms. She wept for Berylan's pain, and for the years they'd lost and would never be able to recover. "Mother, I'll forgive you if you ask it, but there's nothing to forgive. You didn't want to leave me. I know that now."

"Never," Berylan declared, her sparkling silver eyes flashing.

"Can you stay and talk to me? I have so many questions," Rio said, not too proud to plead if it would have any effect on how long her mother could remain.

"Sadly, not this time, but I have a gift for you that will allow me to visit you for longer and longer periods each time, if you are willing and able to accept it."

"Anything," Rio said instantly.

Berylan pulled her daughter close and shared a secret, and then she called to the starlight that had infused her entire being, and it answered her call.

"Now it is time for you to conquer starlight," she said, and it was the last thing Rio heard before the river of silver fire poured into her, obliterating thought and reason.

Her consciousness expanded, and suddenly she could see the plots and plans of the two branches of her family, almost as if she were plucking them directly out of Merelith's and Chance's minds. Such amazing, twisty plans they had for her, and they didn't even know her. It made her laugh, and it made her angry, and then she felt the starlight take her, and she realized both Chance and Merelith were awestruck at the sight.

"Starlight is very powerful, and nobody now living in either family can wield it," her mother told her. "With this magic, you will be safer from their plots and hatreds."

"I want to go with you, back to the stars," she told her mother, who laughed and beckoned.

Rio danced forward, ready to take the leap into the skies, only dimly aware of Luke hurling himself against the starlit prism, but then suddenly Kit was in the circle, too, and the fox kept blocking Rio's path to her mother.

"I want to go with my mother. Don't you understand, Kit? I never again want to be that little three-year-old, cold and alone and sobbing for her mommy," Rio cried out, shoving at the fox, who was suddenly the size of a small pony.

But you are not alone. Have you not seen?

Kit's voice in Rio's mind brought a clarifying calm, and Rio could see and think again. She realized Luke had battered himself bloody from trying to break through the starlight circle to get to her, and looking beyond him, she saw and remembered that all of Fountain Square was filled with her friends.

"I'm not alone," Rio said, and her mother nodded.

"You are not alone, and I am so proud of you. It is not your time, my beautiful daughter. Come back next year, and we will share so much," Berylan said, but then she began to float up into the sky, returning to the stars that sheltered her. "Remember me."

Rio fell to the ground, sobbing, as her mother disappeared into the sky. "How could I ever forget you?"

The circle of light vanished, and Luke ran in and scooped her into his arms, holding her so tightly she couldn't breathe.

"Lungs," she croaked out, and he loosened his hold just enough for her to catch her breath.

"They kept you from me, and now I'm going to kill them all," he snarled, and then he lowered her gently until she was standing on her feet, pushed her behind him, and started to call fire to his command.

This time, though, the flames weren't blue. The fire circling his hands and arms burned a hot orange-red, and Luke's eyes burned with the same fire. Rio flinched back, but then she remembered that this was *Luke*. He would never, ever hurt her.

"Mine," he snarled.

The curse. It had to be the curse.

"He's gone over," somebody yelled.

It must have been Maestro, because suddenly he was there between them, slashing at Luke with a silver blade. When the blade connected with Luke's skin, he howled, and the air filled with the sizzle of burning flesh. Luke swung out with one foot and kicked Maestro in the head, sending the man flying across the square.

"Kill him," Maestro yelled, tossing the silver blade to Chance.

Rio's brother looked down at the blade in his hand and then at his sister.

"Don't even think about it, or I will end you," Rio said, letting her body fill with starlight again.

Chance dropped the blade and deliberately stepped on it with his heavy boot, snapping blade from hilt. "I'm on your side, Rio. Remember that in the future."

With that, Rio's brother the demon prince waved a hand, and he and his entire contingent of war guards turned and marched away.

Rio turned to Merelith, who shrugged. "I see my sister is as flighty as ever."

Rio was still wondering if the Fae had intended the pun when Merelith and her guards vanished.

Luke, deprived of his targets, whirled around and saw the goblins, who'd huddled together, probably to get out of the line of fire.

"No," Rio shouted. "They're my friends."

Rio wanted to slap some sense into him, but *El'andille* remembered that the only way to conquer a curse was with its opposite. In this case, darkness could only be defeated by love.

Rio grabbed Luke's head and pulled it down to hers, and then she kissed him with every ounce of love and caring and hope she'd ever felt for him and for their future together.

"I believe in you," she said, over and over between kisses, until finally, when she looked into his eyes again for the twentieth time or so, they glowed a beautiful deep blue instead of flame red, and Luke looked utterly bewildered.

"I believe in you, too, but why are we making out in the middle of Fountain Square?"

Some little time later, they sat on the bench facing the fountain, watching a beautiful—and very much alive—black swan float serenely in the water of the Black Swan Fountain near its marble namesake. Rio handed Luke the bottle of whiskey that Clarice had left them, and he took a long drink.

"Don't ever do that to me again," he commanded once more, and she almost laughed.

"Don't ever again get sucked into a starlight circle with my mother, who is apparently some kind of celestial being, and learn that I can conquer starlight?"

Luke looked closely at her, and then his eyes widened. "Rio, your eyes—they've gone completely silver. There's not even any pupil or white left."

"I can still see perfectly well. Apparently it's a big damn deal to conquer starlight," Rio said, and then she started giggling.

Luke grinned. "Your eyes just went back to normal. The silver is pretty, but I'd miss the amber."

Rio blinked. "Have we had too much to drink, or did that swan just turn into a naked woman?"

Luke turned to look, but Rio covered his eyes with her hand.

The swan who'd turned into a woman glared at them. "If you would give a person a little privacy to get dressed, it might be nice. Or is all that starlight affecting your brain?"

Rio started laughing, pretty sure that both starlight and whiskey were affecting her brain, but she tossed the swan-woman a salute and pulled Luke to his feet. "Time to walk home, handsome. There's no way either of us is in shape to drive."

Rio made an important discovery during the course of that trip: It takes a very long time to walk anywhere in Bordertown when you're stopping to kiss someone every five feet. She found that she didn't mind it at all.

CHAPTER 30

Luke shoved open the back door to his house and half-carried, half-dragged Rio in with him.

"We're bad," she said drunkenly, and then she started to giggle.

He tripped on something and realized that the lights in his house were all blazing, which was unexpected in the middle of the night when he'd been out, but he had nothing left. No reserves with which to protect them; his magic was fried and he was damn near fried himself.

A bottle of water sailed through the air at him, and he reflexively held up a hand to catch it, and then Alice was suddenly there and helping him carry Rio inside.

"I managed to get out of the Hawaii trip, but not until I was in Seattle. I'm sorry I didn't make it back in time, love. What happened?"

"It's a long story." He got Rio to the couch and then stopped moving long enough to drain the bottle of water. "I'll tell you after I get some sleep."

"Sleep would be great," Rio said, yawning in midsentence. "I conquered starlight tonight, Alice."

"That's lovely, dear. I'll make you pancakes in the morning." Alice patted Rio's arm, but then she shook her head at Luke. "You're in love, aren't you?"

He stroked Rio's hair—*Princess El'andille's* hair—and nodded. "Pretty much out of my mind with it. She's the princess, and I'm the frog."

Luke turned his head and scanned the room, remembering the thing he'd tripped over. "What is all that wood doing in my dining room, Alice? Are you planning to go stake some vampires or something?"

She strode over to a pile of cardboard and held a piece up, and he was shocked to see that the cardboard square was mostly covered with his picture, with some writing surrounding it. Realization dawned, and he looked around for something to blow up. Since wood and paper covered most of his house, targets were plentiful.

"Alice, I'm going to *kill* you."

Something in his voice must have alerted Rio to possible danger, because she sat straight up on the couch, already pulling starlight into her eyes, but then she fell back against Luke and started laughing.

"Luke, why is Anne Hathaway holding a *Luke Oliver for Sheriff* sign?"

Luke sighed and gave up, and then he pulled Rio into his lap and kissed the breath out of her. Alice had discreetly vanished down the hall, with Kit following her, by the time they came up for air, and Rio started laughing.

"Happy birthday to me. It's going to be a crazy damn year."

Turn the page for a preview of Alyssa Day's
League of the Black Swan novella

THE CURSE OF THE BLACK SWAN

Appearing in the *Enthralled* anthology,
coming in July 2013 from Berkley Sensation

THE CURSE OF THE BLACK SWAN

A thousand years ago, a beautiful young peasant woman was bathing in a stream, singing a song of gratitude for the golden sunshine and the magnificent day. However, unlike many who play in the daylight, the girl also sang her thanks to the moon, which rested in diurnal slumber and yet heard the lilting melody of the girl's voice and was pleased.

But others with darker purpose heard the girl's wondrous song, too. The ruler of the land, a cold, hard man who beat his hounds, his children, and his wife with equal fervor, followed the melody to the stream and found the girl, innocent and glorious in her nudity, and he determined to attack her with his rapacious lusts.

The girl pleaded with the barbarian king, which availed her nothing. So then she ran, and she fought, as her father the woodsman had taught her, and she managed to keep the king at bay until the sun dipped below twilight's horizon, when her strength finally gave out. The king, enraged by her defiance, stabbed her through the heart and left her to die. As the girl bled to death on the bank of the silvery stream, the night wind whispered in her ear that the moon, who had appreciated the gift of the girl's song, had taken pity on her.

"I will save you from this king, but you must agree never to leave me, and to become a black swan and sing to me every third night for the rest of your life, and swear that your daughters and their daughters will continue to fulfill this promise."

The girl, who had lost all hope as her blood pooled near her body and then slipped into the moonlit stream, parted her lips, barely able to speak. "And if I agree, will this gift—this curse—never end?"

The moon reigned alone over the dark night, and thus had her own measure of cruelty, but she knew well that mortals needed the promise of hope to survive, and so she offered this edited version of the truth in return:

"You and each generation's eldest daughter will be released from your vow when you meet your one true love."

The girl's tears flowed as her blood had done mere moments before when she agreed, and the moon caused a beautiful fountain to appear on that very spot. In the center of the fountain, a perfect black marble statue of the beautiful young woman, one hand held out to a swan, now stood as eternal monument to the vow.

From that day until this one, a black swan swims in the fountain and sings her songs of loss and longing, every third night, while the moon smiles her icy smile. This woman who is also a swan plots and plans for how to avoid falling in love, for her ancestors had learned and passed down the bitter truth of the moon's deadly promise.

And, somewhere, a man exists who one day will become the true love to a magical swan.

Just before she kills him.

CHAPTER 1

BORDERTOWN, A PLACE WHERE THE FAE,
DEMON, AND HUMAN WORLDS INTERSECT,
HIDDEN IN THE HEART OF NEW YORK

Sean O'Malley ran into the burning building, dodging and weaving around the rest of his colleagues who were running and limping out of the inferno before it exploded or completely collapsed, either of which was due to happen at any minute.

"O'Malley, get your ass back here," his boss, the new Bordertown fire chief, shouted.

Sean ignored him, just as he'd ignored the previous fire chief. He'd heard something in that building. Maybe it was only a cat. No matter how much it tore him up inside when he found evidence that a helpless animal had lost its life in a fire, he knew the rules: Firefighters didn't risk their lives for pets. Not that he gave a rat's ass for rules right then, and he'd certainly bent a few to save pets in the past. They all had.

But it hadn't sounded like a cat. It had sounded like a baby.

Zach, the closest thing to a friend Sean had on the crew, planted himself in front of Sean, blocking his path to the door.

"Not this time," Zach shouted.

They had to be loud to be heard over the roar of the flames that were greedily consuming the old building. Too much rotten wood, too little upkeep—it would be easy to blame that, if this hadn't been the fourth building in as many nights hit in exactly the same way. They had a serial arsonist on their hands.

"I heard a baby. Get out of my way, or I'll go through you."

Sean didn't have time to delay. Zach was just over six feet tall, and he was all lean muscle, but Sean was bigger still, by a couple of inches and probably forty pounds. Not to mention his extra abilities.

Marcus moved out of Sean's way, fast. None of them understood how Sean could hear things that nobody else could, but they knew it was true. Enhanced hearing was one of his superpowers, they liked to joke. Just as they all knew that he could withstand temperatures that would have fried most of them alive.

They didn't joke about that one.

They knew he was different, but they didn't know *how* different. Sean didn't tell *anybody* he was half fire demon. Life was easier that way.

He burst into the conflagration, head down and running for the spot where the sound had originated. Second floor, to the left. He barely paused at the staircase, but the view was enough to make a sane man flinch. A roaring wall of orange-red flame screamed toward him, and the heat knocked him back a couple of steps. His skin felt the heat even under his suit, and he found out his protective gear wasn't rated anywhere near high enough when the fabric started to melt off his body.

Whatever accelerant the bastard had used wasn't purely chemical; no way would a normal fire be burning that hot. Magic was involved here. In fact, it would take black magic to push a fire to these levels. Sean could feel his eyes flaring as his pupils contracted and he knew that anybody watching him would see his irises turn deep blood orange in color and start to glow.

Sean analyzed the situation for options, but the stairs were the only way up; no matter that the stairwell was a tunnel of flame and probably going to explode any minute. He took them four at a time, barely clearing the last one before the explosion hit and the stairs collapsed into a burning mass of tinder. He glanced back at the fiery pit at the bottom and grimaced, and a falling chunk of ceiling smashed down on his helmet, nearly knocking him on his ass.

He stood there, head ringing and skull vibrating, and realized that one of these days he was going to kill himself trying to act like a big damn hero.

But it wasn't going to be today.

The sound came again, and he still wasn't sure. Wounded animals could sound a lot like babies. It could go either way. But he'd come this far, and he'd be damned if he'd leave anybody behind. He took the first door across the hall to the left of the stairwell, unerringly finding the source of the sound. The front room of the apartment was only beginning to burn, and he had a moment to hope that the bedrooms were in good shape before he hit the door running. Two seconds later, about a hundred pounds of shaggy black fur smashed into his chest.

Sean barely stayed on his feet. There had been a lot of power behind that furry projectile. The beast hit the floor and immediately clamped its powerful jaws around Sean's ankle and pulled, hard. The pink collar on the dog's neck proclaimed that the creature was named Petunia.

"Okay, Petunia, hang on," Sean said, using his most soothing voice, but the dog's whining increased in both pitch and volume, and she pulled even harder, trying to move Sean over to the corner of the room.

The corner. There was a crib, or bassinet, or whatever the hell people called the small, lace-draped, wooden cradle tucked against the corner of the room. The crying sound came again, and now he could tell it was coming from the crib.

"I got her, buddy," Sean told Petunia. She seemed to understand, since she let go of Sean's ankle immediately and stood there, panting and making deep coughing noises. Smoke inhalation could damage dogs' lungs, too, and Sean made a mental note to have the animal looked at when they got out of there. A crash sounded in the apartment's front room, and he amended the thought.

If they got out of there.

The baby turned startled, reddened eyes up to Sean in the instant before he swept her into his arms, and then she waved one pink-pajamaed arm at him and gurgled.

"We're out of here, princess," he told her, and then he picked up the room's only chair, a wooden rocking chair, and hurled it at the window while shielding the infant.

The glass shattered outward, as planned, and Sean headed for the window. A jump from the second story was an easy one for him to make, especially carrying only a tiny baby instead of a large, screaming adult, which he'd had to do before, so he had this one in the bag.

No sweat.

And then the dog barked, reminding him that Petunia was not going to make it out alive on her own. Sean looked down at the dog's hopeful face and slowly wagging tail. Petunia had stayed in that room to protect her precious charge, and she'd even pulled a Lassie on Sean's leg to get him to find the baby.

Screw the rules. There was no way in hell he was going to leave that dog to burn to death.

"You're going to have to trust me, girl," he said, crouching down in front of the dog, but keeping an ear out for the shift in sound that would tell him that the entire apartment was about to collapse. It was close.

Too close.

The dog's big eyes looked worried, but she lifted one paw as if to shake, and Sean took that for a yes. He lifted her into the arm that wasn't full of baby, took a running leap for the window, and leapt out into the blissfully cool darkness of the autumn night.

Minutes later, he'd reunited the baby with her mother, who'd been missing after she'd run down to the building's laundry room while her child was napping. The exploding water heater had shaken debris loose from the walls and ceiling of the basement, and a big chunk of something had hit the woman and knocked her out. She was one of the people Zach had rescued, and by the time they roused her to consciousness, the EMTs were administering oxygen to her baby right next to her, so she never had even a moment's fear that her child was dead. Petunia, also wearing an oxygen mask and getting checked out, tried to wrap her furry body around her entire small family all at once.

Sean, as always, made sure to disappear before the thank-yous started and the media showed up. Bordertown's lead crime reporter, Jax Archer, was a disgraced Fae lordling who just happened to be a living, breathing lie detector, so Sean preferred to stay out of his way.

"Where the hell do you think you're going?" the fire chief shouted at him, crossing behind the hoses toward Sean while everyone else, exhausted but on the alert, watched the powerful streams of water battle the magically created fire.

"Avoiding reporters," Sean said bluntly, too tired and worried to care about playing nice with the new boss, who was turning out to be quite an asshole.

One of the reporters Sean could actually tolerate picked that moment to round the corner behind the truck. Spotting Sean, she headed straight for them.

"Pierce Holland, *Bordertown Gazette*," she said unnecessarily, thrusting her microphone in Sean's face. "Do we know what caused tonight's fire? Also, I heard you brought out a baby and a dog after everybody else evacuated, O'Malley. Care to comment?"

"I don't think you've met the new chief, have you, Pierce? He was the one who convinced me to go back in for that baby," Sean said, lying through his teeth. He pounded his boss on the back, only a little too hard. "Excellent instincts, this guy. Going to make a great chief."

The chief's eyes widened, but before either of them could say another word, Sean smiled at them and ducked behind the truck. By the time his overactive hearing picked up the beginning of the chief's response to the reporter, Sean was a block away and moving fast, stripping off his gear as he walked.

Another couple of blocks, and he made it to Black Swan Fountain Square, his favorite place for relaxation and quiet contemplation in the middle of the night. There wasn't much room in the rest of his life for peace *or* quiet. The family business, O'Malley's Pub, was always full of loud talk, laughter, music, and merriment.

It was enough to piss a man off.

Especially when he was sick with worry about his mother's unexplained "little tests," which had left her drained, weak, and nauseous for more than three weeks now. She'd refused to talk about it that afternoon, so Sean had been having a bad damn day even *before* his fire station had gotten the call that the arsonist had struck again.

He stared blindly at the black marble sculpture of the beautiful young woman and the swan in the center of the fountain, so tired that he didn't really notice the actual live swan floating serenely in the water until the second time it came around. When he did notice it, he blinked, and then a flurry of movement in the water boiled up into a cloud of sparkling mist that he hadn't been expecting, Bordertown or no.

So he figured he could be excused for rubbing his smoke-wearied eyes when the iridescent shimmer dissipated and the bird flapping its wings in the swan fountain turned into a naked woman.

A *beautiful* naked woman.

Maybe that hit he'd taken to the head had been harder than he'd thought and he was hallucinating. He didn't have long to believe that one, since the hallucination started talking to him.

"Really? Are you just going to sit there and stare at me?"

"Well, I was here before you turned naked, ah, turned human, I mean you didn't—"

"Right. Chivalry. Dead. Insert appropriate cliché." She pushed her long masses of dark curls out of her face and stalked over to him, not the least bit embarrassed that she was incredibly and gloriously naked. When she crouched down next to him, his breath got stuck in his lungs in a way that had *nothing* to do with fire but *everything* to do with heat.

She glanced up at him while reaching under the bench with one hand, and some of what he was feeling must have shown on his face, because she grinned.

"Relax, hot stuff. I'm just getting my clothes."

CAN'T GET ENOUGH
ALYSSA DAY?

**Download these Penguin Special
novellas from The Warriors of Poseidon series!**

▬ WILD HEARTS IN ATLANTIS ▬

Atlantean warrior Bastien is sent to make an alliance
with the panther shapeshifters in the Florida Everglades,
but he wants something more intimate than a political
allliance with the female shifter he's obsessed with. First,
though, he must contend with the nest of vampires who
also want the shapeshifters' allegiance.

▬ SHIFTER'S LADY ▬

Having never ventured beyond Atlantis for four
centuries, Marie, First Maiden of the Nereids, is finally
leaving for the world of the Above to see her brother and
meet the beautiful shifter he married. For Marie, an even
bigger surprise awaits—one prowling in her sister-in-
law's panther pack. No man has ever touched her quite
as exquisitely as Ethan, Alpha male of the panthers. But
being drawn into his sensual world is as irresistible as it
is dangerous when a violent turf war places both of them
in inescapable danger.

**alyssaday.com
facebook.com/ProjectParanormalBooks
penguin.com**

M1191AS0912